No One Would
Do What
The Lamberts
Have Done

Also by Sophie Hannah

A Game for All the Family
Haven't They Grown
Did You See Melody?
The Understudy
The Orphan Choir
The Visitors Book: and Other Ghost Stories
Something Untoward
The Fantastic Book of Everybody's Secrets

Hercule Poirot Mysteries
The Monogram Murders
Closed Casket
The Mystery of Three Quarters
The Killings at Kingfisher Hill
Hercule Poirot's Silent Night

Culver Valley Books
Little Face
Hurting Distance
The Point of Rescue
The Other Half Lives
A Room Swept White
Lasting Damage
Kind of Cruel
The Carrier
The Telling Error
The Narrow Bed
The Couple at the Table

Non fiction
The Double Best Method
How to Hold a Grudge: From Resentment to Contentment – The Power of Grudges to Transform Your Life
Happiness, a Mystery: And 66 Attempts to Solve It

No One Would Do What The Lamberts Have Done

Sophie
Hannah

First published in the UK in 2025 by Bedford Square Publishers
London, UK

bedfordsquarepublishers.co.uk
@bedfordsq.publishers

© Sophie Hannah, 2025

The right of Sophie Hannah to be identified as the author of this work has been asserted in accordance with the Copyright, Designs and Patents Act 1988. All rights reserved. No part of this book may be reproduced, stored in or introduced into a retrieval system, or transmitted, in any form or by any means (electronic, mechanical, photocopying, recording or otherwise) without the written permission of the publishers.

Any person who does any unauthorised act in relation to this publication may be liable to criminal prosecution and civil claims for damages.
A CIP catalogue record for this book is available from the British Library.
This is a work of fiction. Names, characters, places, and incidents either are the product of the author's imagination or are used fictitiously, and any resemblance to actual persons, living or dead, businesses, companies, events or locales is entirely coincidental.

The manufacturer's authorised representative in the EU for product safety is Easy Access System Europe, Mustamäe tee 50, 0621 Tallinn, Estonia
gpsr.requests@easproject.com

ISBN
978-1-83501-157-7 (Hardback)
978-1-83501-158-4 (Trade Paperback)
978-1-83501-159-1 (eBook)

2 4 6 8 10 9 7 5 3 1

Printed in Great Britain by CPI Group (UK) Ltd, Croydon CR0 4YY

For Carolyn and Jamie, my dream publishers for 20 years and counting, with lots of love

and for my beloved Chunk Plunkett

Last but not least, for Chunk's furry brother Brewstie – my favourite person in Level 2, and forever my Star Word.

Part 1

Monday 16 September 2024

Connor

PC Connor Chantree was afraid he'd already ruined everything and was about to be sent abruptly on his way. He should have explained to Large first, and only then handed over the bundle of papers. He'd done his best to uncrush them, straighten them out, smooth away creases and brush off what dirt he could. Then he'd arranged them into a rectangular shape, which had taken far longer than he'd expected it to. He'd added two red elastic bands, top and bottom.

The result was unimpressive. It sat in the middle of Large's desk and seemed to drink in the baffled stares of both men; and yes, Connor checked with himself, those battered pages *did* look thirsty in a way those not in the room would have called impossible.

Somehow, increasing the tidiness of the bundle's presentation had achieved the opposite of what Connor had wanted. The document (was that the right name for a few hundred pages? Should he think of it as something else? A book?) looked nothing like the sort of pristine, sharp-cornered contender he'd hoped to create.

Contender? Words were appearing in Connor's head that he was sure hadn't been there before he'd read the... thing. Ideas too. Like this one: the spruced-up, rectangularised heap looked as if it was trying to mock convention – as if it had scuffed itself and kicked itself about a bit in an act of deliberate defiance. Even to Connor, its curator – *curator?* – it seemed to be saying, 'And your point is?', whereas the mess of maimed and defeated pages he'd seen on first opening the box had screamed a different message at him: 'Pay attention! Help! Put me together!'

There was a strong chance, of course, that he was imagining some of this. He wished he'd brought in the soggy box, exactly as he'd received it and without reading any of the contents, and simply handed it over. 'Above my pay grade,' he could have said as he'd passed the problem on to Large.

Who was he kidding? He couldn't have done that; the possibility hadn't occurred to him because it had never existed. He'd felt duty-bound to drop everything and read the thing from start to finish before doing anything else. The physical package had been left for him, marked for his attention, and with it had come a powerful sense of duty that couldn't be shirked.

'What's this, Chantree?' Large said. 'Why is the name Lambert back on my desk?'

No One Would Do What The Lamberts Have Done

'Sir, I think you need to read it,' said Connor. 'Fairly urgently.'

Large picked it up and removed the elastic band at the top. He spent nearly five minutes reading small sections from randomly chosen pages. 'So,' he said eventually, in the voice of one forced to consume many disadvantageous and depressing realities all at once. 'You've written a novel about the Lambert family and their recent travails. I'll admit it: I'd prefer to live in a world where that hadn't happened. And in second place – my runner-up choice – would be not knowing it had happened and never finding out.'

Connor didn't think he ought to know what the word 'travails' meant. It alarmed him that he did. 'Sir, I didn't write it—'

'Then who did?'

'—and I'm not sure it's a novel.'

'It looks like a novel.' Large kept his eyes fixed on the bundle, in the careful way a king might watch someone he suspected of being a treasonous imposter about to stage a coup. 'It has a title – one that's probably too long to fit on a cover. Just in case you were thinking of publishing it, which would have all sorts of legal...' Large broke off, but not before Connor had frightened himself even more by finishing the sentence in his head with the word 'ramifications', another one he didn't think he ought to know.

'But you say you didn't write it.' Large frowned. 'Then what is it? Where did it come from?'

'Sir, you need to read it yourself. I can't—'

'And I'm not going to do that.' Large smiled conspiratorially, as if they had both known all along they would end up here and could now unite in celebration. 'Tell me what you hope I'd think or do if I read it. That will move us further forward without undue suffering accruing to me.'

Connor had read the thing twice and still had no idea what he thought ought to happen next. He had even less of a clue what Large's response might be. He couldn't say that, though. It was too vague, and likely to get him waved out of Large's office.

He said, 'You'd wonder, like I'm wondering, whether the coroner maybe got it wrong. Whether perhaps there's reason to suspect—'

'I see. That'll do, Chantree. Thank you.' Large let the manuscript fall from his hands. It landed on his desk with a thud. 'Take it away, please, whatever and whoever's it is. You know as well as I do: the autopsy ruled out any deliberate action. Suicide, murder – both possibilities were eliminated, happily for all concerned. Let's not seek out further trouble, shall we?'

'But then what killed her?' said Connor. 'Healthy young people don't just die for no reason. Look, I'm not saying it wasn't a natural death. We know it was. And there's nothing in those pages to support a murder charge, if that's what you're worried about. CPS won't touch it. But given that the autopsy found no trace of—'

No One Would Do What The Lamberts Have Done

'Chantree.'

This, Connor recognised, was the point beyond which no more of his unsolicited words would be allowed to pass. 'Sir?'

'The Lamberts have been through enough. Don't you think?'

'Definitely.' He'd heard the unspoken bit at the end too – *partly thanks to you, you stupid, gullible git* – whether Large had silent-said it or not. Connor had been silent-saying it to himself every day, at least ten times a day, since the truth had come out.

That was assuming the truth was what they all now believed it to be. And if it wasn't, how could it possibly be down to him, Connor, to correct the mistake? The extent to which he felt chosen was impossible to ignore. Yet, who in their right mind would choose him? He was very much an 'I do my best' kind of person, but not at all an 'I'm determined never to give up until I get the result I want' sort. The difference between the two approaches, and which camp he fell into, was made clear to him soon after he'd got married 16 months ago. He was the most useless variant of the 'I do my best' type – the sort that tended to have a wistful 'Oh well!' attached to it.

Whoever had left the box for him had picked the wrong person. They'd have done better to target his wife, Flo. Nothing fazed her. She'd have strolled into Large's office with far less trepidation than Connor had felt as he'd hovered on the threshold, not caring that she didn't work in the same building or profession.

'I trust you won't be offended if I point out that the Gaveys suffered too,' said Large.

The Lamberts and the Gaveys. Connor had been transfixed and now felt haunted – no, that wasn't an exaggeration – by the way the two families had been presented as a sort of entwined pair, predestined to be enemies to the death; that was what the voice in the pages implied over and over again.

Whose voice was it, for God's sake?

If only Large would read the manuscript…

'Yes, sir,' Connor said. 'All things considered, there's been an incredible amount of suffering on both sides. Lamberts and Gaveys.'

'We agree, then. No need for any more. Good.' Large sounded jollier. 'Is there anything else you'd like to say before you leave and take this malodorous clump with you?'

Connor had sprayed the pages with his wife's strongest perfume – '1996', it was called – but for some reason the scent hadn't stuck and the original pong had reasserted itself: a blend of earth and meat, as if the bundle of paper had been buried in the ground alongside a dead body, then dug up a few weeks later.

'Yes, sir.'

'Pardon?' said Large.

'There is something else I'd like to say.' He had to try. If he didn't take inspired action now, he never would. He found it alarming whenever Flo started to rant about her willingness to die on hills, but he knew he wouldn't be able to rest easy until he'd seen the view from the one he was about to ascend. (Last week, he'd have said 'climb'.)

'Is it about the Lamberts?' asked Large. 'The very finished-and-concluded matter of the Lamberts, about which no more needs to be said, ever?'

'No, sir.'

'What's it about?'

'My sister's tattoo,' said Connor.

'Are you being serious, Chantree?'

'Yes, sir. You see…' Was he going to take the plunge? Was he a dickhead?

Yes. Probably. 'My mum begged her not to do it, but there's no telling our Danielle. She'll always do what she wants, and enjoys it even more if it pisses you off. So she got inked up, right, and it's… well, I don't mind tatts, but it's pretty bad. Covers the whole of her left thigh, and, sir, that's not a small area.' Connor made sure not to look at Large's enormous stomach as he said this. 'And Mum thinks everyone who gets a tattoo's going to be unemployed forever or end up dead or in prison, which is obviously daft, but she's right about our Danielle's tattoo. It looks awful.'

'Chantree—'

'Sir, let me finish.'

'Are you trying to trick me into wondering whether a natural death was a murder, via an analogy involving a bad tattoo? My money's on yes.'

'It's meant to be an animal skull, but it looks like a motorbike that's been tortured to death, Mum says. I've never seen her so distraught. Couldn't stop crying for days. Absolutely gutted, she was. It's hard to explain if you don't know her—'

'Don't try,' Large advised. 'Just get on with it, if you must.'

These weren't ideal storytelling conditions, Connor thought. Ideally, his tale would unfold in a more relaxed way, and without his audience already having seen through his aim in telling it.

'Mum thought she only had two choices,' he said, 'and she hated them both: either change her mind and be fine with the tattoo – try and convince herself it wasn't the disaster she thought it was so that she and our Danielle could still see each other and have a good relationship – or else stop seeing her own daughter, like, distance herself, maybe just see her for Christmas and birthdays, that kind of thing. Sounds extreme, I know, but, sir, you don't know how much Mum hates tattoos.'

'I'm starting to get an idea,' said Large.

'And our Danielle wore nothing but shorts that were, like, up here, to show it off. Mum was convinced she had to make this awful choice: her only daughter or her… integrity, I suppose you'd call it.'

'No need for the "only",' said Large.

'Pardon, sir?'

'Her daughter or her integrity: that's the choice. It doesn't matter how many daughters she's got. She could have fourteen.'

'No, she's only got one,' said Connor. 'It's just me and our Danielle.'

Large shook his head. 'Doesn't matter. The "only" acts as a distraction. We don't need to wonder if the dilemma would be less painful if she had some daughters to spare. It wouldn't be.' He eyed the stained manuscript. Leaning forward, he tapped his fingers on the title page, then looked up at Connor expectantly. 'Well? Go on. What did she choose?'

'Neither of the options she hated, thanks to my wife, Flo, who explained to her about the boxes and saved the day.'

Large sighed. 'What boxes?'

'It's a thought experiment,' Connor told him. 'You imagine you have two boxes, right? Both big, both empty. And neither one ever has to have any contact with the other. They can just sit side by side, quite separately, being none of each other's business. That's what Flo told Mum. She said, "There's no need to change your opinion about Danielle's tattoo, or tattoos in general. In Box Number One, you put your acceptance of all the pain and anger you're feeling, and all the crying and raging and pillow-thumping you need to do about it. You'll always hate that Danielle's vandalised her body, you'll never be okay with it – and you just, like, fully accept that. You don't judge yourself for it or try to change your thoughts or feelings about it, just stick them all in Box One. Then, in Box Two, you put all your feelings and wishes and hopes for Danielle and your relationship with her. In Box Two, you want only the best for her, and trust her to make her own decisions and to know what's right for her. You accept all her choices and love her no matter what. In Box Two, you're just there for her." That's what Flo said, and it saved Mum's sanity and the relationship. She and our Danielle are closer than ever, because both boxes were full of acceptance. And acceptance and acceptance can't ever be at war, you see, sir. Nothing can ever be at war with itself. It's like Flo says: accepting that we don't like or want something doesn't mean we have to push anything away – either our true feelings or the thing we dislike.'

'I see. Is your wife some sort of counsellor?' Large asked.

'No. She's got her own catering company, though. Sir, speaking of boxes, this' – Connor put his hand on the manuscript – 'arrived in a box with my name on it. A big, damp cardboard box that disintegrated when I opened it. The pages had been stuffed in, no particular order – some scrunched, some folded, some flat. It took me ages to arrange them so they made sense. I think if you read it the way I've put it together, you'll have as many questions as I've got. Think of it like this: we've got Box One over here,' Connor drew a square shape in the air with his fingers, 'where we know it was natural causes because a coroner said so—'

'That's the only box I'm interested in,' said Large.

'— but there's also Box Two, the one I found sitting between my car and our garage door a few days ago, with this... book, thing, inside it, but all jumbled up. And in that box what happened was—'

'Inside or outside?' Large interrupted.

'Huh?'

'Your garage.'

'Outside,' said Connor. 'There's no room for the car inside the garage. It's still full of unopened boxes from when we moved.'

'Always unpack straight away, Chantree, or you'll never get the job finished.'

'Yes, sir. Sir, in Box Two, there's a murder.'

'I don't like Box Two.'

'A description of one, anyway,' Connor pressed on. 'It's one that'll be impossible to prove because nothing physical happened. So, we still get to keep our Box One, because there's no evidence—'

'What do you mean, "nothing physical"?' asked Large.

'Please consider reading the... thing, sir. If whoever wrote it is telling the truth... Though I don't think they can be...' Connor felt obliged to interrupt himself with this caveat.

'If it's a pack of lies, I don't need to read it,' said Large.

'But I don't think it's that either. It feels very... true.' It was the only way Connor could think to describe it. 'Sir, I'll be honest: I've got absolutely no idea what it is, who wrote it or who left it for me. And it contains the most unflattering portrait of me – looks and personality – that

anyone will ever write, I hope, but it's still important that you know what's in it, and nothing I can tell you about it could convey the full... effect. You need to see it for yourself. Just... please forget the horrible description of me as soon as you've read it, if you wouldn't mind. And don't share it with anyone if you can help it. Not even as a joke.'
I'm feeling bad enough about myself as it is, Connor considered adding, just in case appearing as pitiable as possible might help the cause.

No need. Large was reaching for the smelly bundle of paper, removing the second of the elastic bands.

No One Would Do What The Lamberts Have Done

by me

1

Mum didn't think I was on her side. Not at the start, and not for a long time.

That doesn't mean she thought I wasn't. It just means she didn't know I was, or how passionately I was, and so it didn't occur to her to think it. I don't blame her for that. I could easily have made it clear – maybe I should have, since trying to protect her from the truth was pointless and she ended up finding out anyway – but I chose not to. Also, it's just the way most people are: they don't think or believe a thing unless they already know it, which is a shame. Actually, it's one of the biggest, most possibility-limiting shames humanity has to contend with, but that's hardly Mum's fault.

If she'd known from the beginning that I was on her side, and especially if she'd known what I'd be able to achieve once I put my mind to it, she could have spared herself a lot of suffering. She'd have been so much happier on The Day of the Policeman, for a start.

That wasn't the start, though. That was the middle, and on that day, 17 June 2024 at 4.45pm, I was also unaware of… yes, I'm going to call it what it is, or was: my own brilliant potential. In fact, I could just as easily call 17 June The Day of the Potential, because there was so much of the stuff swirling around – for greatness and for harm, both equally strong at that point and all mixed up together, billowing through our house, gushing down the street, covering the village green so that you couldn't see it anymore. (I mean, not really, since none of those things were observable events, but also: yes, really).

This is what happened in the conventional sense of the word 'happened' – the bell rang. Mum opened the door, and there he was – the policeman. I heard a male voice followed by Mum's, but didn't pay much attention. I was in my room, letting Champ win a series of tug of war games with the knitted carrot toy. Even after he'd lolloped off downstairs to see who our visitor was, I didn't start to listen deliberately. I was a bit irritated that Champ had ditched me, and said something sarcastic like, 'Right, great. Let's *race* to the door. This is Swaffham Tilney, after all, so it's bound to be someone *thrilling*.'

Then I heard Mum sounding worried and restrained, not at all her usual welcoming self. And I noticed she wasn't inviting the policeman in, which was odd because she normally tried to pull everyone into our house and give them treats and what she called 'the full tour', as if we lived in Buckingham Palace and not a converted hayloft that used to be a dilapidated outbuilding belonging to The Farmer (who's actually the only person in Swaffham Tilney whose name I don't know; he must have one, but everyone calls him The Farmer).

The policeman eventually tried to invite himself into the house, saying it might be easier to speak inside. Mum said no, it wouldn't be, not for her. I couldn't see her – I was on the upstairs landing by now, hovering at the window above the front door – but I could see the policeman standing on the pavement, shifting from foot to foot, looking as if he wasn't enjoying himself, or perhaps he needed to go to the toilet. He was young, with a long, oblong head that reminded me of the brush from the dustpan and brush set in our utility room cupboard – rectangular and bristly. He had a way of speaking that made it sound as if he was leaning heavily on each word.

Then I heard him say horrible things that I knew were lies, one after another. Quickly, I ran through a truncated version of the meditation I learned with Mum in Abbots Langley, hoping it would have an instant calming effect:

Praise Ricky, Thank Ricky, Ricky loves me.

Praise Ricky, Thank Ricky, Ricky loves me.

I knew that wasn't how inner peace meditation ought to be done, but what about when an unforeseeable emergency happens and you need instant tranquility or else your heart will explode? That was how I felt. If you have to be calm first in order for a calming mantra to work, that's a problem.

It didn't work. And then Champ started to bark and I thought I might be sick, except there was nothing in me to throw up. He's normally quiet when people come to the house – usually the only thing that sets him off is when he hears dogs barking on television – but he could sense Mum was terrified, so he got scared too. I didn't blame him. What made it extra chilling was that Mum's never frightened or sad. She's always cheerful. Only a week or so before The Day of the Policeman, I heard her tell Champ that, after listening to the latest episode of one of her two favourite podcasts, she'd finally realised her purpose in life at the age of 53. 'Shall I tell you what it is, Champy?' she said. 'It's Enjollification, with a capital E. Do you know what that means? You don't, do you? No, you don't. You're a gorgeous boy, aren't you? Yes, you are!'

While she hugged him and stroked the fuzzy hair under his chin, I worked out what 'Enjollification' had to mean, and felt pleased with myself when Mum confirmed it: 'It means making people feel as jolly as possible, including me. I invented the word today, but it's always been my purpose, and do you know what, Champy? It's so useful and… enlightening to know that about myself.' By the time she'd finished explaining, I'd downgraded my achievement in guessing correctly – the meaning would have been obvious to anyone, probably – though not to our policeman visitor, who didn't sound clever or perceptive. He sounded like a 'This is just the way it has to be' person. (Anyone intelligent knows that nothing is ever just the way anything has to be.)

Mum had decided, understandably, that the policeman didn't deserve to be Enjollified. I glared down at the top of his head, beaming all my viciousness at the points I decided were his most vulnerable: those tiny pink patches between the light brown bristles that sprouted from his skull. I remember hoping I'd carry on feeling as savagely vengeful as I felt at that moment. Believe me, it's a less horrible emotion to grapple with than pure terror. The current of vindictiveness running through me was proof that I had power, even though I could have done so much more in the moment. I could have sent the policeman running from our home, screaming, never to return, but I was neither quick-thinking nor brave enough on 17 June.

Anyway, then he said it, as I'd known he would from the second I'd started to concentrate on what was going on. He said the dreaded name – Gavey – and the inevitability of it felt like a double layer of something stifling wrapping around me, inescapable, as indoors as it was outdoors, as stitched into the earth of every flowerbed and plant pot in Swaffham Tilney as it was blown into every cloud in the sky and dissolving into every drop of the water in the lode by the path where Mum and Dad walk Champ – and spreading from there to all the other lodes in the surrounding fenland. As I eavesdropped from the landing, trying to take in every word the policeman was saying, trying not to panic, I felt that sticky inevitability coating the walls and carpet and ceiling around me as well as every inch of what Dad likes to call 'our special little corner of ancient England'.

The Gaveys.

Of course this disruption to an until-now-happy day in the life of the Lambert family turned out to have the Gaveys behind it.

2

Monday 17 June 2024

Sally

Once the policeman has said what he came to say and is ready to leave her alone, at least for the time being, Sally Lambert begins to close her front door. She does it as gradually and quietly as she can, wanting to be able to watch through the gap as he walks away. She has to check he's really going; can't wait for her outside not to have him in it anymore. She stares after him – Connor something; she's already forgotten his surname – as he walks to his car, gets in it and drives to the corner, past The Barn and The Farmhouse.

Now he's slowing to a stop; now he's indicating. Sally waits, still looking, until his silver Audi turns onto the main road, which isn't anyone sensible's idea of a main road but is called that by all the residents of Bussow Court, apart from Sally. She used to say it too, but stopped after Vinie Skinner told her Deryn and Jimmy Dickinson, owners of

The Granary and the first to move into Bussow Court, had created and launched the nickname deliberately in order to produce a feeling of inferiority in those Swaffham Tilney residents who lived on that road rather than off it. Sally believes this story is highly likely to be true. Vinie has it in for Deryn Dickinson for sure, but it wouldn't have occurred to her to make that up.

Finally, the policeman is gone. Sally pulls her front door wide open, then slams it shut as hard as she can. She falls to the floor with a loud wail, forgetting, in her distress, that Champ, her Welsh Terrier, might be alarmed, and so might her daughter, Rhiannon, who is upstairs and must have heard. Actually, Ree is more likely to be embarrassed than worried; she's 17 and finding much of what Sally does embarrassing these days – which means Sally ought to stop making strange, howling noises, but she can't. For the first time in her adult life, she can't control what her body is doing (slouching in a heap by the front door, her back hunched against it), or the sounds she's making.

It's only when Champ starts to lick her face that she realises she's crying. Shuddering, too, as if she's just climbed out of icy water and has nothing warm to wrap herself in. Champ clambers into her lap in order to be able to lick more effectively.

Sally puts her arms round him and buries her face in his wiry coat, which feels soft sometimes and hard sometimes. Today it feels soft. 'It'll be okay, Champy,' she tries to say, but only gets half of it out. *Shall we sing your day song?* she thinks of saying next, but doesn't even manage one word of that. His day song would be impossible anyway, she realises, because of the last line. She has sung it hundreds of times without understanding that it's a sad, desperate song, not a celebratory one. Now, whatever happens next, she'll never be able to sing it again.

Wait – she knows what she'll do; she'll turn Champ's other song, his night song, into a day and night song. One song is more than enough for a three-year-old Welshie, so why does Sally feel so sorry for him? That's easy – because of the policeman, the lies, the danger – and it's also not the right question. Why is Sally feeling sorry for herself, when she should be thinking only of Champ? Why is she thinking about a milky-pink-coloured bottle of gardenia body lotion that she had when she was 13? She's fine now, she's a grown-up, she's so over that stupid incident. It wasn't even anything in the first place, and she hasn't thought about it for 40 years.

At least it makes sense that Furbert, her first beloved Welsh Terrier, should come into her mind now, but she doesn't need to feel sorry for him, not anymore. He is safe, content and well looked after in Dog Heaven, from which exalted vantage point he can clearly see that Sally's love for him is just as much a part of her daily life as it was while he was alive. You don't stop loving someone once they're gone.

And you don't start either, thinks Sally, and suddenly she can smell that gardenia lotion and is wailing louder than when she started, though Champ's fuzzy hair is muffling it, thank God. Ree must have her headphones on, or else there's no way she wouldn't have heard.

Or else she can hear everything and doesn't care. *Likely.*

No, that's not fair, Sally corrects herself. She wouldn't have thought something so disloyal if her sister and the Facebook business hadn't come up in conversation yesterday and Ree hadn't taken the opportunity to mention that she'd always been able to see it from Auntie Vicky's point of view as well as Sally's.

Champ shakes his head vigorously, so Sally has to move hers. He looks at her searchingly, as if to say, 'What's going on? Why are you thinking about all these bad things from the past and imagining everyone's against you? Remember, I'm here! I'm on your side, all the way and all the time.'

Yes. Right. Good point. Champ adores Sally. He sleeps draped across her legs or curled up next to her head every night, much to her husband Mark's disgruntlement. And Champ needs Sally's help; he's the only person she ought to be thinking about right now. Champ's personhood – and before it, Furbert's – is, has been, endlessly debated in the Lambert household. Sally acknowledges that, from a strictly factual point of view, Champ is a dog and not a human, but she allows herself to include him in the category of 'people' when she says things like 'Champ's the only person who hasn't eaten yet', because it would make no sense to say 'Champ's the only dog…' when the rest of the Lamberts (those present in bodily form in Swaffham Tilney, at least;

No One Would Do What The Lamberts Have Done

those who need to eat because they're not permanently-nourished souls in a canine paradise) aren't dogs.

It's good that Ree hasn't come downstairs, thinks Sally. It means she hasn't been caught in her unravelling. She might still get away with it. She has time to get herself together, though not much. Mark's gone to pick Tobes up from school after his exam and they could be back any second, but if she locks the front door and doesn't open it until her face looks normal again, and if Ree keeps those headphones on, then maybe no one needs to find out that Sally collapsed in a heap and began to disintegrate. Champ won't tell anyone. (Obviously she doesn't mind him knowing; he'd never mock her for it or use it against her.)

She'll have to tell Mark, Ree and Tobes about the policeman, but that's okay. The only part she needs them not to know, because she wants to forget it quickly herself, is that Sally Lambert is capable of falling apart.

3

Champ's day song. Champ's night song. Auntie Vicky and the Facebook business.

You might not need to know about the first or the last of those – we'll see – but you definitely need to know about the middle one, and it would feel strange to tell you about that without mentioning the day song, because we Lamberts for a long time viewed them very much as a pair.

So, Champ has a day song and a night song. His day song was adapted – by Mum, who else? – from the song 'You Are My Sunshine'. Mum doesn't know how to write tunes, so she takes famous songs, changes the words and then calls them 'her' songs, as if she's written them.

As I made my slow and full-of-dread way downstairs on The Day of the Policeman, I heard Mum whisper to Champy that she was sorry she was too upset to sing him his day song. The last line was the problem, she explained, and she didn't want to start and then not be able to finish. Nor did she feel together enough to come up with a new last line.

As I heard her say those words, I made a vow to myself: 'When this battle of ours against the Gaveys and Cambridgeshire Police is won – which it will be, by me, with or without help – Mum will once again be able to sing Champy's day song to him all the way to the end, without crying. That will be my measure of victory. When she can do that again, that's when I'll know everything's okay.'

I was naive to imagine that singing the song happily would be possible for Mum ever again, even after the most resounding triumph over our enemies. We cannot always forget miseries and traumas of the past, unfortunately.

Here's how Champ's day song goes:

You are my Champy,
my only Champy.
You make me happy
when skies are grey.
You'll never know, Champ,
how much I love you.
Please don't take my Champy away.

The thing is, if you've lived for nearly nine years with the mild anxiety that someone might report your first, occasionally bitey (though never with malicious intent), dog to the relevant authorities, leading to him being taken away and possibly worse, and then it actually happens to your second – a policeman comes to the door and threatens him, using lies and ominous hints as weapons – then you're unlikely ever again to be able to sing the words 'Please don't take my Champy away' without bursting into tears. So far, Mum hasn't managed it.

I used to be jealous of Champ's sunshine song. For a while, I had a bit of an obsession with picking holes in it. I'd tell myself that it didn't make sense and that the lyrics were stupid, that they only worked if the song was being sung about a person who could remove themselves from a relationship with the singer if they wanted to. Champ was never going to take himself away from Mum. Dogs never want to do that, if their owners love them – apart from briefly, maybe to the other side of the room or to the garden. But they always come back. And even if the song is being sung about a person, the lyrics are confusing. One minute the 'You' character is being told they *are* something, then the next minute they're being begged not to take away that same something, as if it's a different object. Yes, the meaning is clear, but it's still clumsy.

I'll admit, it's also true that I'd never have thought to pick holes in a harmless song if I hadn't been jealous – which I'm absolutely not anymore, I'm pleased to report. My envy was extinguished in about two seconds flat when I remembered Mum's and my trip to Abbots Langley to learn how to meditate, and that Mum chose my name as

No One Would Do What The Lamberts Have Done

her Star Word – just mine, not as one of many, or alongside the rest of the family's. I chose Ricky and she chose me. (I don't love Ricky more than Mum, Dad or Tobes, by the way. I do almost worship him, however.)

Champ's night song was supposed to be his bedtime song, but he's never accepted that he has a bedtime. Even when he's tired, he'll sit in the lounge with Mum and Dad and try to watch TV until he gets bored and starts chewing a rug tassel, or the leg of a chair, or a corner of a cushion. Eventually he falls asleep, stretched out and belly up, and stays like that until Mum and Dad go to bed. He'll then follow them upstairs and do his best to sleep balanced across Mum for the rest of the night. That's why Mum started calling what was originally his bedtime song his 'night song' instead, because it would have taken her too long to say 'Taking Champ Out For A Wee In The Middle Of The Night Song'.

This is Champ's night song, and when you see the lyrics you'll wonder, if you're sane and sensible, how on earth it managed to cause so much controversy. You need to sing it to the tune of 'Land of Hope and Glory' by Arthur Christopher Benson and Edward Elgar:

> Land of cute and furry -
> Champy, you're the best.
> You're barky, not purry!
> You pass every test!
> Louder still and louder

Does thy snoring get.
God who made thee cuddly
Make thee cuddlier yet!
God who made thee cuddly
Make thee cuddlier yet!

I've noticed that I said something inaccurate and I have to correct it, because Lamberts aren't liars: Champ's night song didn't 'cause' any controversy. Every single bit of the trouble was created not by the song but by evil people. Nothing went into Mum's version of it apart from her love for Champy. It wasn't about England. It wasn't about a country. It was about a dog, and anyone who couldn't see that was and is a fool who cares about absolute nonsense more than they care about saving the life of an innocent Welsh Terrier.

I seem to have got myself riled up, so I'm going to save the story of Auntie Vicky and the Facebook business for another time. I wouldn't enjoy telling it in my present mood.

4

Monday 17 June 2024

Sally

Sally is still in a heap with her back pressed against the front door when she hears Mark's car drive past their house a few minutes later. Or maybe it's an hour later; she has no idea how much time has passed. Champ is draped across her legs, asleep on his side, front and back paws stretched out as if he's trying to mimic three sides of a trapezium. Sally has stopped crying, which she supposes is something. What she hasn't done is go to the lounge where her phone is, call anyone, summon help of any kind, look up any useful information.

She will need to move so that Mark and Toby can get inside the house, she thinks. That can be the start of her doing something, of taking decisive action. That will be soon enough. There's a good chance it's been less than fifteen minutes since PC Connor Chantree left, and it takes days if not weeks or months for a situation like this to go from just started to too late. Sally knows she'll get a handle on it. Mark and Toby's return is just the catalyst she needs.

And it was definitely them she heard, cruising past the front door on their way to the far end of the development where the twelve parking spaces are separated from one another by neatly planted rows of shrubs: six spots for Bussow Court residents' cars and six for visitors. Unlike Mark, Sally is no expert on different sorts of engines and the noises they make, but she was nevertheless able to identify her husband's car from the sound of muffled pounding that accompanied its passing: a song (if you can call it that, which Sally doesn't think she credibly can) that belongs to a genre her children call 'drill'. There could be no clearer signal of the proximity of Toby Lambert, Sally and Mark's 16-year-old son, than the whooshing-past-the-front-door of a throbbing racket of the sort Sally just heard. Drill is Toby's latest obsession, and of course he wants to listen to as many of his favourite tracks as possible on the way back from his Music GCSE exam, which was this afternoon.

Sally is thankful that she couldn't hear any of the lyrics and hopes none of the neighbours did either. Ree, eighteen months older than Tobes and certain her own current tastes are more sophisticated (love songs aimed at God, written and performed by members of the controversial Hillsong Church, though Ree insists she's an atheist), has been known to shout-sing a brilliant mockery of a typical Toby number: 'Co-caine-up-my-nose/Gonna-give-it-to-my-hoes/Cos-that's-just-the-way-it-goes'.

No One Would Do What The Lamberts Have Done

No one from Bussow Court has yet complained about Toby's 'music' ('Shouldn't two years of GCSE-level study have taught him what music is and isn't?' Mark has grumbled more than once) and Sally has fretted for a while that it's surely only a matter of time. At home there's a strict headphones-only rule – all the Lamberts agree that they don't want to be noise-polluted by the others – but Sally knows Toby always wins The Battle of When To Switch It Off whenever it's just him and Mark in the car, and today he'll have won it decisively, as it's a GCSE day.

Sally can imagine exactly how it went: Mark will have pressed the off switch as he turned right into Swaffham Tilney off the B1102, and Tobes will have turned it back on again, saying, 'Can't I listen while we drive through the village? Pleeeeease? Come on, Dad, I've just done an exam.' Reluctantly, Mark will have agreed. Then he'll have reached out again – a hopeful arm, spurred on by desperate ears – as they approached the turning for Bussow Court. Toby, ready with his next move, will have blocked Mark's hand before it touched the on-off button. 'What difference will, like, ten more seconds make?' he'll have said plaintively.

All right. Can you at least turn it right down, though?

No, Dad, you fun-sponge. Music like this needs to be loud. The windows are shut, aren't they? Relax your trim.

And later Mark will say to Sally, 'I didn't want to crash the car while arm-wrestling with him, and I didn't have the energy to argue,' and then rant for a full twenty minutes about the inconsiderateness of teenagers, having somehow found the requisite energy for that, and oblivious to whether Sally might in fact rather listen to one of Toby's awful drill tracks than this rant-liloquy she's heard Mark perform several dozen times before.

Except it isn't going to happen like that this time. Nothing that's part of the Lamberts' ordinary routine will fit into the rest of this unbearable day. The pattern is about to be disrupted by what Sally will say the second she has someone to say it to, and soon – really, startlingly soon, she'll hear Mark and Toby's footsteps any second now – no one will be able to think about anything but the nightmare that came knocking at the door of The Hayloft today, the one that is gone for now but will keep coming back, keep knocking. The one that might get gradually worse and worse until...

No. That cannot be allowed to happen. Can't be considered, let alone tolerated, as a possibility. *I will kill absolutely everyone if I have to*, Sally thinks, *and very happily go to prison for the rest of my life. It will be worth it. I'll take the two longest, fattest-bladed knives from the wooden block next to the kettle and plunge, twist and gouge them into the chests of anyone who comes to the door and...*

A crazy idea cauterises her murderous fantasy: she could leave the house now – take Champ and just go. Why give anybody, close family member or policeman, the chance to turn up and say anything at all? There's still time to escape. Look how long it's taking Mark and Tobes to get here. Does this prove Mark's point? Sally wonders. Like

No One Would Do What The Lamberts Have Done

the Gaveys (who bought The Stables six weeks after the Lamberts bought The Hayloft) and like Deryn and Jimmy Dickinson from The Granary, Mark believes that The Farmer positioned the parking spaces for Bussow Court unacceptably far away from the houses. Sally has always been in the other camp, the 'how can any sane human believe that between twenty and forty footsteps is too far?' camp, along with Vinie and Graham Skinner from The Barn and Conrad Kennedy from The Byre.

No, she can't escape. She'd bump into Mark and Toby. Her car is parked in The Hayloft's visitor space. But what if she were to leave on foot? 'Just taking Champ out for a quick walk before I start on dinner,' she can say if Mark's outside the front door when she opens it.

And then she could go...

Where, without her car? She could ring a taxi if she took her phone, but to whose house or office would she ask to be taken? Who can help her? And why is she fantasising about escaping from her entire family instead of looking forward to the help and comfort they might give her?

Sally doesn't need a degree in psychology to know the answer to that last one. She offers a silent hat-tip to her late father, who died fortreen years ago. *Thanks, Dad. Great work.*

She hears a key in the lock and shuffles to one side, trying to disturb Champ as little as possible. He opens an eye but is asleep again by the time Mark and Tobes have come in and shut the door behind them.

'Why are you sitting in the hall?' Mark looks down at

Sally and chuckles. 'Have our chairs and sofas been repossessed? Bailiffs been?'

She shakes her head.

'Sal?' Mark sounds worried. 'Has something happened?'

'Mum, are you okay?' asks Toby.

Another shake. No. She is not okay. Then she tries to smile and says, 'I will be.' *Don't wait, though. Like: eat, have a shower. Watch some telly. It might take me a while.* This would be a good joke if only she could make the words come out.

'You don't look okay,' says Mark.

But does she look strong? That's more important. Unhappy but strong, shocked but unbeatable – either of those could work. She is a mother of four, so she has no choice. She has to be strong, for Tobes, Ree, Champ, and…

Arguably, no deceased Welsh Terrier needs his former owner to be strong for his sake, but Sally can't bear, ever, to think of Ree, Tobes and Champ without also thinking of Furbert. And she wasn't just his owner, she was – is – his adoring mother, just as she is to the other three. Furthermore, she isn't at all willing to think of herself as someone who now has one child fewer than she once had, so, yes, absolutely, she has to be strong for Furbs's sake too.

Sally only remembers that she heard footsteps thudding down the stairs a moment ago when Ree is bending down in front of her, angry-faced. She's removed all her make-up since Sally last saw her. 'Aren't you going to tell them?' she says.

No One Would Do What The Lamberts Have Done

Does this mean Ree knows? Did she hear the conversation between Sally and the policeman, and is she here to bring everyone up to speed? If so, maybe Sally won't need to speak for a few more minutes, by which time speaking will hopefully feel easier.

'We've been ratted out to the feds,' Ree says. 'Except we haven't done anything. It's that fucking lying Gavey bitch. I swear to God, she ought to just die.'

Yes, thinks Sally. *That would be helpful.*

5

I said before that Lamberts aren't liars. It's true. Gaveys are liars and enemies, and Lamberts are truthful and good. Which means I need to be as honest as I can, as soon as I can: there's something I'm not telling you. It's about me. I'm not saying anything that isn't true, but I'm leaving out something that is – a big, important detail. I'm allowing, creating, significant omissions.

Would anything I'm leaving out make you think much less of me if you knew it? Almost certainly. I'll tell you eventually, but I need you to like and trust me more, and hate and fear the Gaveys more, before I do. If I approached it in any other way, you might drop this book in disgust, and I need you to keep reading.

(Oh, my God – am I writing a book? I hope that's a quick and easy thing to do, because going through the nightmare our family's just been through in real life, real

No One Would Do What The Lamberts Have Done

time, was long and gruelling, and I'm nowhere near fully recovered, so I'm only really looking for quick, easy experiences for the foreseeable future.)

Why do I need other people to know the truth? Partly because I can't bear the thought of being the only one, but that's not all it is. The main thing is: this is my next assigned task. Just as I was sure from the start that dealing with the problem our family faced was mainly my job, I'm sure now that sharing my first-person, first-hand account with the world is my next mission, assigned to me by a force more powerful than myself.

No one will ever understand exactly what happened unless I tell them, because I'm the one who made it happen.

Also, and of equal importance: why does no one ever question why we need to know about 11 September, 2001, or why the Second World War started? Old people like Mum and Dad are always going on about the importance of knowing all that stuff (how often has Dad gone off on one of his 'The trouble is, young people these days don't get taught proper history, so they can't see the dangers' rants?), but what almost no one realises is that history is the-Lamberts-versus-the-Gaveys as much as it's the Brexit Referendum or Henry VIII's six wives. None of those things is a more or less significant element of the battle between good and evil than any of the others.

That's why people need to hear this story – and I also happen to believe there's a moral duty to spread the word whenever you hear of good winning and evil losing. That's

Enjollification in action. As Mum said once, after she'd identified her purpose in life thanks to that podcast, 'Only Enjollification can bring salvation to the nation.' She was being silly, but she was right.

So, yes, I am currently withholding a few important facts, and I have a powerful and good reason for doing so. I'm meant to tell the story of The Lamberts and The Gaveys in exactly this way, just as the Gaveys were always meant to come for us. Mum would hate this idea and try to persuade me out of believing it, but it's true. She's not the only one with a purpose. The Gaveys arrived in our lives for a reason: so that we could do what was required of us and become who we were always destined to be – and, what's more, I was certain of this from the moment Mum and I first saw Lesley Gavey outside our old house, before I'd ever heard the name 'Gavey'. I knew instantly that the appearance of this crying woman in our street somehow represented the start of the battle that would be the making of me. (Well… to be strictly accurate, I kind of both knew it and didn't know at the same time. I definitely sensed it on some level, though.)

I can't remember at what point I began to appreciate that our names sounded too good together for it to be a coincidence: 'The Lamberts and the Gaveys'. Doesn't it sound like a pairing that's bound to have a war of substance behind it? I think it's up there with 'The Hatfields and the McCoys', 'The Montagues and the Capulets', 'The Starks and the Lannisters'. (Also 'The Farmer and the

Cowman' from the musical *Oklahoma!*, though they're not families.)

There's a reason why these enemy name pairings work so well when you say them together, though for ages I couldn't work out what it was. It's partly the balance of syllables and sounds, but it's not only that. The main thing, I think, is that with each pair, you can't tell simply from hearing the names which side is good and which evil, so the intrigue factor is massive. 'Both sound as if they could be lovely,' you might think, and you can't wait to find out what went wrong between these normal-sounding people. You tell yourself that maybe their feud is the result of a misunderstanding.

It's important that you don't misunderstand the wickedness of the Gaveys. Might they have done less harm in different circumstances? Of course. Appalling life experiences might lead any of us to do terrible things with great regret, but they don't make a person innately evil. Trust me when I say the Gaveys had to be crushed, and don't quibble when you find out the full truth later on. I promise you, no immunity or favours are ever granted to quibblers once evil has taken hold of a village or a country or a world.

Repeat after me:

Alastair Gavey, CEO of a telecommunications consultancy that has words in its name like 'Core', 'Network' and 'Refresh' (trust me, they don't make any more sense in their correct order), 58 years old. Address: The Stables,

Bussow Court, Swaffham Tilney, Cambridgeshire, CB25 0TS. *Evil.*

Lesley Gavey, self-proclaimed (unconvincingly: see several previous failed career attempts) podcast producer/sponger-off her husband. 54 years old. Address: as above. *Evil.*

Tess Gavey, A-level student at Bottisham Village College. 17 years old. Address: as above. *Evil.* By far the worst of all the Gaveys. (In my opinion only, I should say. Mum would strenuously disagree.)

6

Monday 17 June 2024

Sally

Mark's face is a mixture of impatience and confusion. 'Who?' he says. 'Which bitch?'

At first he assumed 'the Gavey bitch' must be the mother, not the teenage daughter. Yet it was Ree who said it, and Sally is the one who thinks Lesley Gavey is a crazy bitch; it's Sally who theorises, speculates and invents scary scenarios around Lesley as if it's her favourite hobby. Whereas Ree hasn't ever said much about Lesley, and has said plenty about what a justifiably unpopular loser Tess Gavey is. Tess is in Ree's class at sixth-form college; they have two A-levels in common, English Language and Literature (combined) and Sociology.

So Ree knows everything, thinks Sally; she heard what PC Chantree said. In which case, why the hell didn't she come downstairs straight away, to check Sally was okay? *Maybe because Ree's not okay herself.*

Has silent crying been happening on both floors of The Hayloft? Yes. Ree's eyes are watery and red. She's as imaginative as Sally is, perhaps more so: she too will have brought all the worst-case scenarios to vivid life in her mind.

Perhaps she hoped to stay and weep in her room for a while longer, but Sally scuppered that plan by maintaining her uninformative silence in the face of the quite reasonable questions that have been aimed at her.

'Ratted out for what?' says Tobes.

'Nothing! He didn't do it!' Ree wails. 'Right, Mum? I don't get it: why didn't you tell the cop he didn't do it? I mean... *did* he do it?' She bursts into tears, which she tries to scare away with a string of obscenities. 'Please tell me he didn't.'

'Of course he didn't,' says Sally. Thank God Champ is completely, indisputably innocent. That's something good she can hold on to. Gratitude is so important, even at a time like this.

'Then why the *fuck* didn't you say that to the policeman?' demands Ree.

'Who didn't do what?' Mark asks. 'Could everyone please calm down?'

'Everyone *is* calm apart from me, and no, I can't,' says Ree. 'That bitch Tess Gavey is trying to get Champ killed. Lying about him so he'll be taken away and put down.'

'What the *fuck*?' says Tobes.

'Can everyone stop swearing, please? Champ?' Mark

asks Sally. 'Champ is the one who's been accused? Not Toby?'

''Bout time someone shared the load of unjust accusations,' Tobes mutters.

'Don't joke about it,' Ree snaps at him. 'Champ's life is literally under threat.'

'No, it's not.' Tobes looks at Sally. 'It's not, is it, Mum?'

Every cell in her body begs to be allowed to say, 'No, of course it's not', to bring a smile of relief to her son's face, but she doesn't know, and she doesn't want to dish out false hope. And what little she does know is all bad.

Champ, meanwhile, looks perfectly serene in this, the worst of all moments. He's still asleep, stretched across Sally's lap. Maybe, on some higher plane of consciousness that only dogs can reach, Champ knows all will be well in the end. Even the swearing and shouting didn't disturb him.

But this isn't a fairytale, and the world is chock-full of people who say, in a regretful tone, 'Once a dog's bitten someone, you have to put it down, just to be on the safe side' as if they care, and are sad for the dogs in question, when they quite plainly don't and aren't. Sally has nodded countless times as people have said this to her, while privately thinking, 'That's simply not true of Furbert.' Or, after he died: 'That wasn't true of Furbert. If you'd known and loved him, you'd understand. Not all bitey dogs are the same or equally dangerous.'

Champ isn't a bitey dog, though. Not even a lovely-but anxious one, who would occasionally nip you but never without mitigating circumstances. Just not at all. Champ has never, and would never, harm anyone in any way.

Sally tries to recall what happened with Pepper, her mother's chiropodist's daughter's flat-coated retriever. That was a terrible story, that ended – this is the only part Sally remembers for certain – with Pepper being issued with the dog equivalent of an anti-social behaviour order, and she hadn't even done anything wrong. Pepper's experience, like what was happening to Champ now, was an example of a nasty person causing trouble for a lovely, innocent pup.

Ree has started to tell Mark and Toby about the policeman and what he said, so Sally has to hear all those disgusting words again. She gets through it by pretending she's made of super-shiny steel that nothing can permeate. It will be over soon: the telling, if not the ordeal. There's not that much information that needs to be relayed, only the few facts that are known: Tess Gavey is claiming that Champ bit her. As bites go, it's a bad one. Deep and serious. Likely to leave a big scar. That's why the Gaveys felt they had to go to the police, especially because they knew that the Lamberts' first Welsh Terrier, Furbert, was also a biter.

When did this happen? Mark wants to know.

'It didn't,' says Sally.

No One Would Do What The Lamberts Have Done

'Yesterday is what the Gaveys are saying, the lying douchebags,' Ree says. 'Four-fifteen yesterday. Mum, where was Champ then?'

'Out with me.'

'Where?'

'On a walk. By the lode.'

'You're sure that's where he was at exactly four-fifteen? It couldn't have been earlier, or later?' Ree puts her face right in front of Sally's, like an interrogator determined to break her down.

Sally nods. She's sure. What she doesn't know is if anyone noticed her and Champ on their afternoon walk. There were a couple of people walking their dogs along the path on the other side of the lode, but no one on Sally's side and no one she recognised from the village, no one she knew. People came from Newmarket, Cambridge, Burwell, Reach, the other Swaffhams, and everywhere, to walk along Swaffham Tilney's lode path. How would the police be able to find the right ones, the witnesses who saw Sally and Champ there at the relevant time?

Then it dawns on Sally: they won't even try, of course. Wasn't she always hearing that the police were under-staffed and under-resourced and really up against it, like all the other essential services in the country? It was another of Mark's rant-liloquy subjects ('I went to Cambridge the other day, right? Two youngsters walked past me smoking joints. I nearly got high just passing them on the street.

Sickening! Nothing's illegal these days, it seems. Smoke cannabis in broad daylight in the middle of the city, burgle a house, vandalise a lamp post – no one's going to arrest you, not in this pathetic excuse for a country that we're turning into. We basically don't have law enforcement in England anymore. The police aren't more than a fancy dress party at this point.')

'Then why didn't you tell PC Ugly-Boy?' Ree asks Sally. 'Why didn't you say Champ couldn't have bitten Tess Gavey at four-fifteen because he was with you? Imagine a jury hearing that you didn't even say that, and only mentioned it later – like, suspiciously later!'

'Ree, don't yell at Mum,' says Mark.

'I... I was in shock. I didn't think of it then.' And PC Chantree hadn't asked. He'd arrived at the front door of The Hayloft in the manner of Someone Who Knew, and told Sally what Champ had been doing at four-fifteen yesterday: biting Tess Gavey's arm. 'I found it hard to say anything at all,' Sally remembers dimly, as if it happened years ago.

'Yeah, I could tell,' says Ree. 'I get that you were freaked out, but what if you missed a chance we'll never get back?'

Sally considers mentioning Pepper the flat-coated retriever, who, according to Sally's mother, is only alive today because her parents (human parents/owners/ however they thought of themselves; all Sally knows is that she is her dogs' mum and nothing else) cooperated with the police and didn't make a single argument in

No One Would Do What The Lamberts Have Done

Pepper's defence. If they'd challenged anything the accuser was alleging, Pepper could well have ended up being put down.

If it came down to Sally's word against Tess Gavey's, who would the authorities believe?

'You not sticking up for him doesn't make Champ look very innocent, does it?' Ree's voice shakes. 'What if he gets taken away from us and put to sleep because you didn't mention that he's got an alibi?'

'I'll mention it. I'll... I will. I'll get in touch and tell them,' Sally mumbles. *While we're what-iffing, what if I'm tired of accepting you lashing out at me angrily whenever you're feeling miserable? What if I decide to stop cooking you breakfast and dinner every day and giving you a generous allowance so that you can buy make-up and clothes? What if I work out what's the most upsetting thing I could say to you next time you're in bits, and then say it?*

Ree falls to the floor, sobbing, and Sally feels awful. She has never before allowed such an eruption of cruel thoughts about her daughter. Somehow, it reached Ree through the ether and made her feel worse. And it's true, Sally didn't defend Champ when she easily could have. It's not that she thinks Ree's wrong; she just can't understand why you'd ever allow yourself to say the most hurtful thing possible to someone you loved. Now, if the worst happens, Sally will always have Ree's words in her head...

But the worst won't happen. She'll do anything to stop it, whatever she has to. Ree would too, she thinks. In spite of her merciless outburst, Ree is Sally's most likely ally if it turns out that something extreme needs to be done; Sally knows this beyond the slightest doubt.

'Dog bites don't go to jury trials,' Toby says. 'Do they, Dad?'

'Of course they don't,' says Mark. 'Can both of you girls stop acting like some kind of execution order's been issued? Look at me and Tobes – we're not losing our minds, are we? I'm sure we can sort this out. It might just take a bit of communication, a bit of to-ing and fro-ing with the official channels, but the fact is, if Champ didn't do it and you were out walking him at the time—'

'You don't know anything,' Sally talks over him. 'You have no idea what could happen. Dogs that bite people get put down all the time. All it would take is for the police to believe Tess and not me. And they'll use Furbert against us, his history.'

'Sal, there's no "history".' Mark makes air quotes with his fingers. 'You're talking about Furbs like he was… Harold Shipman, or Myra Hindley or something. He nipped a few people's hands once or twice – that's it. As far as I can remember, he only drew blood once. And none of the people he nipped ever made an issue of it. The main problem was in your mind: your constant paranoia that one day something worse would happen.'

And now it has. Yes, Champ is a different dog, an entirely soft and non-bitey one, but she was nevertheless right about something bad happening.

'The Gaveys know about Furbert's... tendency,' she says. 'Lesley will make sure the police know all about it too.'

'So what if she does?' says Mark. 'There's no such thing in British law as canine guilt by... belonging to the same family association.'

Is he being deliberately obtuse? Isn't it obvious what Sally means? The police will wonder if the same woman, or family, who failed to stop one dog from biting people might also have failed to control their second dog in exactly the same way. That will strike them as quite likely, no doubt.

Sally has to stand up now, even if it means waking Champ; she has to get out of the house. 'No, you stay here, Champy,' she says as he springs upright too, with a big yawn and a stretch, and automatically follows her as she goes over to the shoe rack.

Sally bends and strokes both sides of his head at the same time. 'You wait here for a bit with Daddy and Ree and Tobes. Okay? I'll be back soon.'

'Back? Where are you going?' Mark asks.

'Out,' says Sally. 'I need to think.' She opens the front door and sees an imaginary semi-circle of armed police, guns all pointed in her direction, in the unpopulated space between her house and The Barn opposite.

7

Really, if she wanted to be accurate, Mum should have said that she needed to think some more, because she'd already packed in some fast and detailed thinking while listening to Dad explain that everything would probably be okay. That was a bad move on his part, assuming he wanted to gain any control over the situation, which he definitely did. You can always tell the difference between when he's happy for Mum to be the boss (most of the time) and when he decides he needs to be manly and take charge, and it was clear from his voice at a certain point that he'd gone into Taking Charge mode.

By trying to be reassuring, he made Mum suspicious. His role in our family is to warn us about terrible things that will probably never happen and explain why everything is more terrible than we think it is, and then Mum steps in to Enjollify the crowd and tell him he's being daft. Like, whenever Tobes talks about how he wants to go travelling in Thailand for his gap year, Dad's always straight in his face with stories about people who had drugs planted on them to take through the airport and are now rotting in Thai jails, as if this is bound to happen to Tobes too.

So when Dad started to say, in a slightly bored, impatient voice, that everything would be fine in relation to Champ and Tess Gavey's accusation against him, what Mum heard him say was, 'No one needs to worry about this, because I'm not. I love Champ, as dogs go, but I'm never going to let myself get hysterical over a dog. Nothing dog-related could ever ruin my life.'

When she heard all those things Dad hadn't said or thought (he genuinely believed everything would be sort-out-able) she decided he wasn't on her and Champ's side, and especially wouldn't be, even more than he wasn't already, if things got really bad. Not properly. Not in the way she would need and want him to be. Remember, Mum had already chosen the knives she would use to gouge out the innards of the local constabulary. She had a feeling Dad wouldn't be on board for that level of fight-back.

As soon as she had affixed that 'Not properly on my side' label to Dad, she started to think and plan, furiously and unilaterally. I wish she'd known then that she could rely on me no matter which way things went. Maybe I should have spoken up because, like Mum, I knew I'd have no qualms about killing in order to save Champ's life.

(That's not what happened and not what I did, in case you were thinking you'd guessed.)

The point is, Mum and I have a lot in common. She is very much a sides person, as am I – far more than Dad or Tobes. Or Champ, who is a side pup, singular. He's so sweet, he believes there's only one side and we're all on each other's. Champ loves everybody. Mum, in contrast, loves very few people: Dad, her children ('furry and non-furry', as she always says), Granny, Auntie Vicky and her two closest friends from school, Tash and Oonagh, each one of whom she only sees about twice a year. That's it. Although Mum's never thought of this and probably wouldn't like to know it about herself, that's why she finds it so easy to form love-bonds – one-sided, obviously – with inanimate objects: houses, usually. The way she turned our move from Shoe Cottage to The Hayloft into a weird kind of tragic love-triangle drama would have seemed utterly bizarre to anyone who wasn't used to her peculiar ways.

I feel guilty sometimes, almost like a spy, when I suddenly remember with a rush of 'Oh yeah!' that Mum has no clue how well I know her. So often I hear her talking to Champ when she doesn't think I'm listening or even in the house. She tells him everything; he's the only member of the family whose judgement she doesn't fear. When we first put Shoe Cottage up for sale (or Shukes, as we called it, because Mum once said that the way to show a house you loved it was by giving it a nickname), the way she talked about it to Champ when she thought no one was eavesdropping was insane. She patiently explained to him why we needed to move house, even though it was 'heartbreaking':

'The thing is, Champy, I know you love our house, and the garden – it's the only home you've ever known. Well, since the farm in Llandysul, but you might not remember that now. Shukes has been home to you since you were ten weeks old. And it's not even that the garden's too small for you or not nice or interesting enough – I think you love our garden, and I think you'll miss it. All those lovely smells! We'll all miss our lovely Shukes, but we have to be brave and leave it, even though it's our perfect house, really... but it's only the house and garden that are perfect, you see. Their position and situation really isn't. You're still so little, Champ, and... well, I hope you're going to live till you're at least...'

Mum fell silent for a few seconds, and I knew what she was thinking: what age should she wish for that was the perfect mix of realistic and as optimistic as possible? 'Eighteen!' she said eventually. 'I've heard of smaller dogs like you living until sixteen, definitely, and I reckon you can beat their record, Champy. Which means sixteen more years of you wanting to roam around the garden freely, going out and coming in whenever you want, as is your absolute right... and the problem with this house's garden is that it's at the front.' Mum sighed. 'Otherwise, it's perfect. Well, most people wouldn't think so – almost everyone would say it's way too small, but it's ideal for us. We don't want or need a huge garden, and we've made this one beautiful over the years... but we can't leave you unattended in it even for a minute, can we? No, we can't. We can't, my lovely boy. Anyone could open the front gate, or climb over the wall and steal you. It's terrible and it shouldn't happen, but it does: horrible people steal dogs sometimes. So we have to move house! We've been putting it off and putting it off because we love Shukes so much, and kidding ourselves that maybe it's okay... but it's just not, and that's all there is to it! We can't watch you whenever you're in the garden for the next however many years, and we don't want to restrict your garden time either, like we have to now. Don't we? Yes, we do. We do! And we had to with Furbles too, didn't we? Poor Furbles! His garden time always had to be cut short, and now yours does and... it's not ideal, is it? No! No, it's not ideal, my baby. Oh, my babiest of boys! My boy-est of babies!'

It sometimes takes Mum longer to get to the point when she's talking to Champ because she lapses into singsong mode.

'Here's the thing, Champy.' She leaned in closer to him and lowered her voice to an excited whisper. 'I've worked something out and it's a real game-changer.'

I was standing behind Mum at this point. I saw Champ's ear twitch. Was he suitably intrigued? He definitely loves listening to her voice and doesn't seem to care what she says.

'We only don't want to move because we haven't yet found our even-better-than-this-house house,' she went on.

'Do you see what I mean? This might be a bit of a complicated concept for you, but maybe not.'

Maybe not? Seriously? I had to roll my eyes and my head simultaneously when I heard that.

'At the moment we're all feeling sad because we're seeing it as a choice between Shukes, which we love, and a future, unknown house which we can't love or even like yet because we don't know who or where he is.'

So, this feels like the right moment to explain that Mum is quite a bit weirder than you might so far have gathered. In her lexicon (thank you, English Language and Literature A-level syllabus, which I looked at for just long enough to know that I had no desire to read the rest), houses are always 'him', and so are cars. They're not just objects to be called 'it'. Houses, like dogs, are at the same level of emotional significance as humans in Mum's world, and every bit as eligible for meaningful, loving relationships of a family kind. Also, it's impossible for them to let you down in a hurtful way, as people sometimes do.

I kept listening as Mum explained to Champ that, once we'd found our new house, fallen madly in love with it and knew deep in our bones that it was destined to be a member of our family, then we'd all feel much less sad about leaving Shukes. Which, by the way, was called Cowslip Cottage when Mum and Dad bought it. Mum liked the name, but wanted to choose one herself for what she thought then would be her 'forever home'. And, since she and Dad had viewed it as part of an open day, when, according to her, the place was so full of the taken-off shoes of potential buyers that it looked ridiculous – 'Like the cottage of the shoemaker in *The Elves and the Shoemaker*' – she'd suggested the name 'Shoe Cottage'.

Dad wasn't against this suggestion, though he thought it unlikely that Mum would get away with changing the name of a three-hundred-year-old cottage in Swaffham Tilney without incurring some wrath from certain quarters. Mum said she didn't care, and in the end she was lucky: saved by Corinne Sullivan, who was rumoured to be the village's wealthiest resident. Corinne did two things that grabbed everyone's attention at around the same time as Mum and Dad bought Shukes: first, she mentioned and defended her philanthropy policy to the wrong people, and then she let weeds grow high against her garden wall and made no effort to remove them. (As if that wasn't enough on the notoriety-creating front, Corinne later contributed to a third happening – the book-club debacle – that really stole the show and meant that suddenly neighbours who had previously been friendly to one another were pretending not to see each other on the street and in the village pub in order to avoid contentious clashes.)

Anyway, it was thanks to Corinne hogging all the village disapproval that Mum knew she was in the clear with regard to Shukes's name; I heard her saying so to Champ, and also that she'd have been ready to stand firm if she'd had to, because Shoe Cottage was definitely the name he was meant to have, once he became a Lambert.

No One Would Do What The Lamberts Have Done

One night, soon after Mum and Dad had exchanged contracts on our new house, The Hayloft, I heard Mum say to Champ: 'I'll never say I'm sorry we bought Shukes, because I've loved him so, so much and I always will. But, honestly? If I'd known Grandad was going to die only two months after we moved here, I'd have thought, "No, wait. Don't buy a house with only a front garden and no enclosed back garden, however much you love it – because now you can get a dog, and this kind of garden arrangement isn't safe for a dog."'

By 'Grandad', Mum meant her own dad – Champ's non-furry grandad. Correctly or not, Mum believed having a dog was impossible while he was alive. My view on that is: it would very much have depended on that dog's temperament and trainability.

'And then I'd never have fallen in love with Shukes because we wouldn't have gone to view him,' Mum went on while Champ licked his front paw. 'We'd have prioritised dog-suitability over everything else. Poor Furbert – he never got to have his ideal garden the way you will, Champy.'

I thought to myself, *Oh, for Ricky's sake!* (I mostly say 'Ricky' instead of 'God' now. It started to feel right after I'd been doing 'Praise Ricky, Thank Ricky' every day for a few months.) *For Ricky's sake, Mum,* I fumed silently, *why don't you question some of your wildly incorrect underlying assumptions once in a while?*

Here's what I know: there is nothing unsuitable-for-dogs about Shukes. His garden is stunning, with the added interest that comes from being able to watch people walking past, and coming in and out of their houses. You wouldn't believe some of the conversations and fights I've overheard in that front garden over the years. What if dogs actually prefer the excitement of some human drama to a boringly serene, enclosed back garden where you hear no neighbourly gossip at all? Mum ought to have realised she was being silly, because she'd had not one but two dogs since she'd lived at Shukes, neither of whom had suffered a single unfortunate consequence or unpleasant moment as a result of not always being able to be outside exactly whenever they wanted to be. Spending some time inside the house is fine sometimes too. A mixture of out and in is perfect for any and every dog.

Which means there was no problem that needed solving when Mum decided Shukes had to go on the market. I waited for someone to point this out to her, but no one did. It was insane; we all accepted without question that the home we loved, was, in Mum's words, 'obviously not ideal from a doggy point of view.' No one said, 'You're overreacting because Furbert died – but that's silly because he didn't die as a result of getting stolen from our garden, did he? Or of a broken heart, because one day he fancied going outside and was told he couldn't. He died, specifically, because a litter-dropper ('ground vandals', Mum calls them) dropped a peach stone on the pavement outside the church instead of putting it in a bin, and Furbert ate it, and it pierced his intestine and gave him sepsis.'

No One Would Do What The Lamberts Have Done

No one said any of that, or pointed out that there was no good reason to move house. And yes, I could have, but I chose not to. I'm glad now that I didn't, because, as it turned out, there was a very good reason why Shukes had to be put up for sale. There was the reason of the Gaveys. Whatever you want to call the force that steers all our lives, it knew that Lesley Gavey was about to decide that she wanted to move to Swaffham Tilney, and it knew what we – or rather Mum and Dad, as the home-owners – needed to do in order to help that move along, so that the war between the Lamberts and the Gaveys could begin.

8

Monday 17 June 2024

Sally

Sally turns left out of Bussow Court and starts to walk quickly – with aerobic intentions, anyone who sees her will think – towards the centre of the village. She is shivering from the chill inside her, even though it's warm and sunny. She's brought nothing but her phone and is giving herself half an hour to accomplish this first step: Phase One, or the beginning of Phase One.

Thirty minutes will have to be enough. With Champ under threat, she's not prepared to leave him alone for long – and by alone, she means with Mark, Ree and Tobes. He needs her, his mum, by his side in case the danger escalates quickly. Which it might; Sally would put no heinous act past the Gaveys.

Leaving Champ behind at The Hayloft after he'd made it clear he wanted to go with her was one of the hardest things Sally has ever done. No choice, though. They need help urgently and he would have slowed her down, wanting to sniff every tuft of greenery they passed.

Where do you go for help of the sort Sally needs? She has no idea. Her best friends, Oonagh and Tash, live too far away, in Devon and Yorkshire. And both Sally's mother and her sister Vicky would urge her to sit tight and let the police get to the bottom of it instead of doing anything rash. Both tend to trust that anyone in a position of power has best interests at heart beyond their own – like Sally's dad when he was alive, for instance.

In any case, Mum and Vicky aren't much nearer than Oonagh and Tash. Sally needs a helper who's here in Swaffham Tilney, no more than a thirty second sprint away – it's impossible to think beyond that timeframe and that distance – and who will advise her to trust no one. There's a paradox in there somewhere, and Sally wonders if she's the first to think of it: when the only person you'd consider trusting is someone who tells you not to trust anyone at all.

The best option for emergency help, she thinks as she marches along, is someone in the village whom she doesn't know particularly well – nobody the police would think to interview as a priority, or ideally at all, if Sally and Champ were to disappear.

Are they about to disappear?

Yes. That has to be the next move. For the last few minutes, Sally has been aware of a thought growing inside her, colonising ever more brain space like an opinionated, non-life-threatening (perhaps even Champ's-life-saving) tumour. It's a shock to her, because it's so off-brand – she's Sally Lambert, after all, Queen of Enjollification – but she can't ignore it.

The thought, more pessimistic than anything she'd normally allow, is: *Get out quick. Even if there's a strong chance all will be well, assume it won't be if you stay. Just get out. Go.*

What if this is what Enjollification looks like when you're presented with a terrible life circumstance that you can neither control nor wish out of existence? There's a chance that Sally's just doing what she always does: everything in her power to guarantee a happy ending and a happy right-now.

Yes, that's it. That's true. There's nothing jolly about allowing even the tiniest possibility of this situation going the wrong way. What Sally needs is a plan to get her and Champ out – beyond the reach of Swaffham Tilney and its warped notion of justice, to a safe hideaway where he can't be found and... seized. (Even thinking the word makes her shudder.)

No need to involve the rest of the family, though Sally will of course make sure they get an explanation once she's safely beyond the reach of any argument against her plan that any of them might want to put to her.

She passes the pond and the bus stop, the beginning of an idea starting to form in her mind...

Wait.

No One Would Do What The Lamberts Have Done

She comes to a standstill outside the village's only pub, The Rebel of the Reeds. How could she forget about money? She needs quite a lot of it, quickly, before she can do anything.

She pulls her phone out of the pocket of her joggers and rings her mother.

'Hello, darling. How are you? Hold on. Just hang on a minute, Sally.' As always, it sounds as if Julia is in a television studio, surrounded by at least fifteen demagogues, all bellowing their contradictory opinions at her. As usual, too, she sounds perfectly happy to be there – as if she'd gladly have lapped up many more hours of uninterrupted hectoring if only her phone hadn't rung. Sally hears, in quick succession, 'Keir Starmer', 'morally incoherent', 'foregone conclusion'.

Not for the first time, it strikes her as verging on implausible that her mother chooses to live on a noisy main road in a noisy, crowded city, in one enormous room at the top of a very tall building with no outside space apart from a tiny balcony. As if determined to stretch Sally's credulity still further, Julia voluntarily fills her home with the sound of noisy, crowded podcasts from the moment she wakes up each morning until she falls asleep at night.

Sally grew up in that same city – London. There's no reason to avoid naming it in her mind, she thinks, as if her rejection might cause others to gang up on it – and from as far back as she can remember, she has loved and yearned for its opposite: the clean, grass-scented air you get only in the countryside; short, fat, bumpy buildings instead of tall ones made of brick. Throughout Sally's childhood, her parents took her and Vicky nearly every summer to stay with family friends near Glyndyfrdwy in North Wales, in a long, white-painted stone cottage that nestled in a little dip between a hill, some dense woods and a farm.

The house, Hafan Ddiogel, had a beautiful, rocky garden that wrapped all the way around it, full of interesting flowers, succulents, vegetables and herbs. There were about ten different levels, each operating as a separate area; maintaining and tending to it all must have required significant acrobatic talent, since each individual area of the garden was as far from being flat as was the whole ensemble. It was impossible to sit or lie down without risking tumbling off some precarious ledge or other if you made one wrong move, though you could stand anywhere (with one of your legs slightly bent, for optimal balance) and see the most spectacular views right across the valley.

Whenever Sally thinks about Dog Heaven, where her beloved Furbert now lives, that Welsh-valley view with its soaring gold and green planes is what she pictures. Her love for Hafan Ddiogel and, by extension, Wales was directly responsible for the additions to the Lambert family of, first, Furbert and then Champ. How could Sally consider any breed of dog except a Welsh Terrier? She couldn't. She didn't. Rhiannon – Ree's unabbreviated name – was Welsh too.

No One Would Do What The Lamberts Have Done

At one time Sally would have said that she'd love to live in the Welsh countryside if she could, but Mark's job is in Cambridge, and Swaffham Tilney, half an hour's drive from his company's head office in good traffic, was, out of all the commutable villages, the one that most reminded Sally of the perfect rural atmosphere she'd fallen in love with as a child, though the two landscapes were very different in some ways. But if anything, she found Swaffham Tilney to be even more idyllic, and wouldn't dream of leaving – or, rather, she wouldn't have, if Champ had not been falsely accused of biting that horrible little teenage bitch of a liar, Tess Gavey.

There's a sense of deeply embedded calm and quiet running beneath everything in Swaffham Tilney. Mark likes to quip that it makes Reach, the next most peaceful village in Cambridgeshire, feel like midtown Manhattan – somewhere he's never been. Sally, who also hasn't, agrees with him whenever he says it. Their home village is surely one of the world's most unspoiled pockets of stillness and silence, in a way that feels almost sacred, like a special blessing bestowed upon no other place.

All silences, of course, are challenged when you add Sally's mother to the mix, either in physical form or telephonically. Sally holds her iPhone away from her ear as Julia yells, 'Alexa! Please turn off my podcast. Alexa! Turn. Off. The Podcast!', but the background clamour of urgently expostulating pundits shows no sign of letting up. Unlike the Alexas belonging to everyone else Sally knows (the

Lamberts do not have one), Julia's seems to ignore her instructions most of the time, and so Sally gets to hear someone berating someone else for being on the wrong side of history – something she's heard both Mark and her mum say on different occasions, about very different things.

Is it just something everyone says these days? What about right now, the present moment? Surely that matters more than history. By Sally's reckoning, the worst thing of all is to be on the wrong side of right here, right now (as Tess Gavey is) so why, all of a sudden, is it everyone's favourite hobby to imagine lots of strangers agreeing with them in hundreds or thousands of years time, after they're long dead? *Pathetic.* As pathetic as pretending to be popular by saying 'I've got a massive gang of really cool imaginary friends.'

'Alexa! Turn off *Politics in the Mix!*' Julia shrieks.

Eventually the noise stops, and Sally allows herself to bask for a fraction of a second in the silence of her village, mercifully restored. Then she says, 'I can't talk now, Mum, so please don't ask me lots of questions. There's an emergency. I need you to do exactly what I say.'

'Sally, what's wrong? Are Rhiannon and Toby all right?'

'Ree, Tobes and Champ are fine,' Sally can't resist saying, though Julia didn't ask about Champ, and Sally has given up hoping that one day her mother will come to love her furry and non-furry grandchildren equally. 'We're all fine. But I need money, urgently, so listen—'

'Why? What's going on?'

No One Would Do What The Lamberts Have Done

'Can't go into it at the moment. Here's what I need you to do immediately: ring Pascale and tell her to get my thirty-seven grand out of whatever fund of yours it's in, and transfer it to your normal account. Then transfer me ten grand from there, or from anywhere that's instantly accessible – but not to my and Mark's joint account. This is very important, Mum. The ten grand needs to go to my just-me account, the one you pay birthday and Christmas present money into. Got it?'

'Sally, you're not leaving Mark, are you?' Julia sounds horrified.

'No. Definitely not.' Sally doesn't want to involve their joint bank account because she's giving Mark no say in what's about to happen, so why should he part-fund it? That wouldn't be right. 'So, just to check you're clear,' she says, '*Not* the same account you pay Ree and Tobes's school fees into. Right?'

'I'm not mentally incompetent,' Julia huffs. 'There's no need to speak to me as if I'm five years old. I've been paying money into both your accounts regularly for many years. I know the difference between them. But—'

'Okay, so transfer me ten grand, like, *right now* – because the Pascale money will take at least a week to liberate, I'm guessing.' Whereas Sally knows from experience that money from her mother's normal accounts lands almost instantaneously. 'Then get my thirty-seven grand out from your investment whatnots with Pascale, pay yourself back the ten grand you've already given me and then transfer me the remaining twenty-seven – also to my personal account, not my and Mark's joint. Okay? Are those instructions clear? Can you do all that?'

'I can, but I'm extremely worried now, Sally, and I'd like to know—'

'Well, you can't,' Sally cuts her off. 'You can know very soon but not now. Will you please just do it?' Inside her head, Sally is screaming: *Don't you know what 'emergency' means? You have no right to say anything but, 'Yes of course.' That thirty-seven grand is my fucking money, not yours. All of it, and I earned every penny. This is life and death for me, potentially, and it will cost you nothing, absolutely nothing. Not even ten pence.*

'All right,' says Julia. She doesn't sound happy about it.

'Thank you. Thanks, Mum. You're the best.'

Sally marches around the rectangular perimeter of the village green, phone clutched in her hand, refreshing her online banking app every five seconds while simultaneously trying to calculate the odds of encountering a member of the Gavey family. Highly unlikely: they only ever drive through the village, never walk, and never at this time of day. Also, this part of the village, the main part, contains Shoe Cottage, the Lamberts' former home and also the house Lesley Gavey will never forgive for letting her down. She once told Sally, 'I can't look at the place. Have to turn away if I drive past it.' She actually said that, about Sally's beloved former home. *Despicable woman.*

And then, as if by magic, there is suddenly £10,049.50

in Sally's just-her bank account where only a few seconds ago there had been £49.50. *Good old Mum.* Now Sally can go to Avril Mattingley's house, make her proposal and pray that Avril says yes – because Avril, Sally decided while waiting for the money to come through, is going to be her helper.

Unless Corinne Sullivan would be a better bet? Would this situation fit her peculiar definition of philanthropy?

No. Philanthropy is always financial, isn't it? And Sally doesn't need money anymore. She's got enough to fund the first part of her and Champ's escape. Besides, Corinne is too complicated and too notorious, though admittedly only within Swaffham Tilney. People have thoughts about Corinne, and voice them often, whereas there is something nicely under the radar about Avril. According to one of Sally's two favourite self-help podcasts (in which all speakers have lilting, blissed-out voices) intuition is wisdom we don't know we possess. If that's true, it means Avril is the one. Hers is the house – once the village's bakery, and still called The Old Bakery – to which Sally's intuition is pulling her. It feels meant to be.

Sally continues to believe in the rightness of her choice until she knocks on the front door and Avril opens it with tears pouring down her face.

9

I should explain about Mum's thirty-seven grand, and also about why she chose Avril for the role of village-based helper – an ill-advised and apparently irrational choice, though it makes sense once you understand. First, though, I need to work out if avoiding an encounter with the Gaveys, as Mum successfully did on the village green that day, is something readers of this account will also wish to do. In other words – and although I can't imagine why any self-respecting, sentient person would feel this way – perhaps you would like to meet Alastair (dad), Lesley (mum) and Tess (rancid, monstrous daughter) Gavey? Hear what they sound like, in their own words? Maybe it's not fair for only the Lamberts to have a voice in this... whatever I'm writing.

Shudders forever

No. Bad Idea. I know this because I've made myself feel

sick simply by contemplating it. To include any kind of Gavey contribution would be as intolerable as it is impossible. This is *my* book, I'm a Lambert and I wouldn't pollute my own creation with even one short Gavey-written sentence. Anyone who wants to experience the Gaveys via their own voices can look online and find heaps: Alastair's LinkedIn screeds about how he optimised this, revolutionised that and revitalised the other; Lesley's fraudulent 'doting mother with perfect daughter' Facebook posts (yeah, you're never going to fool your immediate neighbours, who are sick of being woken in the middle of the night by the sound of the two of you screaming that you wish each other would 'die in a fire'); Tess's horrifying Instagram grid – endless close-ups of her face, the face of an amoral, heartless monster.

But... And...

There is something I can do to balance things out a bit, and I will. I think it's a good compromise, because we do need some objectivity; that's only fair. Anyone who reads this deserves to hear at least a little about the Gaveys from someone who doesn't loathe them with a seething, pulsating hatred. So I'm going to include – now, before we go any further – the words and accounts of three people who aren't Lamberts. What follows is those witnesses' own, unaltered words, and comes from the interviews they gave to detectives during the wrapping-up of things later on. (If Cambridgeshire Police knew I had access to any of this stuff, their brains would probably explode out of their skulls and land in Suffolk. Oh, wait, I forgot: not all of them have brains. Maybe, like five between all of them, and PC Connor Chantree was only allocated half a cell, and even that probably got confiscated long before he turned up on our doorstep.)

It's fine: you don't need to know what's coming in order to 'meet' the Gaveys in these three people's descriptions of them. All the statement-givers you're about to hear from are people who live in Swaffham Tilney. I've deliberately chosen three of the very loveliest residents, also for the sake of balance. Since I'm determined to devote extra page space to some of the worst people ever to walk the earth, let's bring in as much goodness as possible at the same time, to cancel out the otherwise potentially noxious effects.

Statement 1: This is from Judith Whiteley, landlady of The Rebel of the Reeds. She arranges an Easter egg-hunt for the children of Swaffham Tilney every year, and dresses up as the Easter Bunny for it! You'd want her to be your grandma if possible.

> It was just the one conversation I overheard, between Lesley and Tess, and I found it more disturbing than anything else I've ever seen or heard in this village, and I've lived here for thirty-seven years. I honestly had to stop myself from going over and... it sounds silly to talk about intervening, because it genuinely wasn't a fight or anything like that. It didn't sound like one, anyway. They were speaking in such a normal

tone of voice to each other. It was like they thought they were having an ordinary, everyday chat over dinner. And at various points, they both laughed. Never at the same time, though. I mean, they took turns to laugh.

It was a Monday night, early evening, and they were practically the only people in the pub. There was no music on for some reason – there's almost always something playing – and I was able to hear every word they said while they ate their meal. And they must've known I could hear them, which made it even odder that they didn't stop. On the contrary, they went on and on. Eventually I decided they obviously wanted me to hear, or didn't care enough to stop me from hearing.

When they first came in, they were talking about something that had happened at Tess's college, I think. She'd been in some kind of trouble and she was grandstanding about how she hadn't backed down. Properly full of herself, she was; she'd really showed that teacher. And at first Lesley seemed to approve of her swagger. There were about ten minutes, maybe a bit longer, where they were ripping into the poor teacher together. Not my idea of fun, but they were obviously enjoying themselves and in agreement about the rights and wrongs of it all. Then I was in the kitchen for a bit. When I brought their meals out, I could tell that the subject had moved on. Lesley was saying to Tess, 'But you're not kind like her, and you hate animals, and they mostly seem to feel that way about you too.' I thought, 'What's this, now? She can't be telling Tess that animals hate her.' But she was! She said, 'Remember when we went to Nanna's and her cat wouldn't stay in the room with you? Every time you walked into a room, she walked out.' And then she laughed. As if she found it amusing that she was saying it to her own daughter. She said, 'And you've never been popular, not in any of your schools, so I doubt you will be, ever. It would have happened by now if it was going to happen. You've never really had friends, have you, Tess.'

The way she said her name like that… it was horrible – but she just said it in this matter of fact, almost lighthearted way. I fully expected Tess to burst into tears and run out of the pub. That's what I'd have done if my mum had said anything like that to me when I was seventeen, or at any age, to be honest with you.

Anyway, it soon became clear what it was all about: Lesley had found out that Tess had been talking to a boy online in some kind of chat place that she'd used the name 'Elphie' to join - and you know who Elphie is, don't you? No? Oh, well, she's the heroine from *Wicked!*, the musical. From what Lesley said, it was clear she thought Tess idolised Elphie, and that's why she'd chosen to call herself that. I don't know whether that's true or not, but I do know Lesley spent about twenty minutes telling Tess all the ways she was a more worthless and less appealing human than Elphie from *Wicked!*. She said, 'Elphie's got a strong sense of honour and moral integrity, and there's nothing honourable or ethical about you, Tess.' Then she listed a few unethical things Tess had done, one of which was trying to nick another girl's boyfriend, another was spray-painting the Gledhills' gate.

And then it was Tess's turn. Cool as a cucumber, she said, 'Like mother like daughter, I guess. Where was your integrity and honour the other day, when you were telling Kellie all about how you'd have loved to have another baby after me? That whole sob story about how you tried for years and it never worked, and poor you, all those babies you lost…' I swear to you, Detective Inspector, Tess was sniggering as she said all this… and I couldn't believe my eyes, but Lesley was smiling as she listened to it. That was when I thought to myself, 'Maybe I should go over there and try to step in somehow.' I probably should've done, but I didn't, coward that I am, so on it went. 'You didn't lose the last one, though, did you?' Tess said. 'You got rid of that one by choice. Why not be honest about it, hey, Mother? Why didn't you tell Kellie that you got rid of it because it was making you fat and bloated and you thought Dad didn't fancy you anymore and was going to leave you if you got even bigger. The dumbest thing of all was that you actually believed he might fancy you again if you ended the pregnancy, but he didn't, did he? He still shagged around after you had the abortion, so it was all for nothing. And it wasn't fair on me – not that you cared about what I wanted. I'd have a brother or sister now, if you hadn't killed it.'

'Yes, and I'd have a more lovable child than you, wouldn't I?' Lesley smirked like she'd made some kind of cheeky joke. 'And I'd have loved it more – making you even less popular than you already are.' On and on it went, as if it was just cheerful chitchat, with each of them taking turns to giggle after they landed a blow. I debated if it would be reasonable to ask them to leave, and decided it wouldn't be. They were the only ones in, and if they didn't mind it... but I did. I really minded. But then it stopped as suddenly as it had started. One moment Tess was calling Lesley a liar for passing off a termination as a tragic baby-loss she couldn't have prevented, of which she was the victim, and the next it was all plans for the following weekend, and please could Lesley buy Tess the bracelet she'd seen on Etsy that she really loved, the one with the moonstone and the leather bit?

No One Would Do What The Lamberts Have Done

I couldn't wait for them to leave, and actually started hyperventilating as soon as they did. It was like being trapped in hell, then suddenly set free. Look, I'm not saying any of this means Lesley's capable of... well, you know. I don't actually think she could've done this. Could she? I mean, I suppose she could have? Someone did, didn't they? One thing I do know: if I had to choose between Lesley and Alastair, as the guilty party, I'd say her. Definitely.

★★★

Statement 2: This is Ed Debden, one of the church wardens and also a religious-icon painter and teacher of how to paint religious icons. He's the sweetest man, and everyone's loved him ever since he painted an icon of The Farmer and gave it to him as a 70th birthday present. The Farmer asked if it wasn't blasphemous, to which Ed replied, 'You'd be surprised. Our Lord is nowhere near as petty and unreasonable as so many people seem to think he is.' I love him for saying that.

Yeah, I used to play squash with Alastair Gavey when he first moved to Swaffham Tilney. I'll admit: I liked him. He was good fun, always up for a chat and a few pints. One thing I didn't enjoy, though, was the way he talked to waiters and bar staff. He couldn't seem to help himself, and he did it every single time without fail. I'd order my pint quickly and then close my eyes and pray that he'd just for once say something reasonable like, 'A pint of Kingfisher, please', but it never happened. Every time, he would lob these cheesy questions at the waiter, different ones each time. It was like he had an endless supply of the damn things. So the waiter would say, 'Right, sir, what can I get you?' and Alastair would put on this frankly embarrassing wise-looking expression, as if he was imitating an elderly owl in a tree, and say, 'Tell me this: what do you think might be possible for you, in your life, that you haven't contemplated yet?' To which the confused and bewildered reply would always be something like 'Er, dunno.' But Alastair would keep on: 'How do you think you'd be able to tell if you were moving closer to your authentic self or further away from it?' He'd turn into this kind of, I don't know, guru-harasser every time someone handed him a menu, basically. But since that was the only thing he ever did or said in my presence that was less than ideal, I carried on playing squash with him – and I think he was genuinely motivated by the idea that he could help these people, to be fair, so I'd just kind of look at my phone whenever it happened, or excuse myself to nip to the loo when I sensed he was about to pelt some poor lad or lass with more of his unsolicited personal growth nuggets.

We remained friends until the day he confided in me that he'd made a pitch to a woman he worked with that the two of them should abandon their respective families and run off together. She turned him down – he was honest enough to admit she'd been horrified by his suggestion, didn't fancy him at all and didn't know where he'd got the idea from that something amazing was brewing between them. I admired his honesty and decided that, though I disapproved, I also didn't want to be the sort of friend who ditched a pal for making a mistake. And then he said, 'I don't know what I saw in the stupid C-word anyway, to be honest. It must've been some kind of fever dream because when I looked at her in the cold light of day, I could see that she's actually pig-ugly. I'm not exaggerating: she looks like a pig, as in, her face is the face of an especially snouty pig.'

I wish I could tell you that the unpleasantness stopped there, but I'm afraid it didn't. He went on for the next half hour, saying things that were more obscenely misogynistic than you can possibly imagine. I'm not exaggerating. He said many things that I'm unwilling to repeat and wish I'd never heard. I thought to myself later that day, not only did he say those things, he also thought it was okay to say them to me. It didn't occur to him that I might not want to play squash with him anymore, having heard all that. Which I definitely didn't, though it took me a few more weeks to extricate myself from our arrangement. I had to invent a sprained ankle.

Does this mean I think Alastair did it? I don't know. Yes, I think he could've done, but that's very different from saying that I think he did, if you see what I mean. I sat opposite his wife once, at an ordeal of a quiz night at The Rebel of the Reeds, and I'd say that she also could have done it and seems as likely a candidate as him.

★★★

Statement 3: This one's from Kellie Dholakia, a primary school teacher and the fiancée of Conrad Kennedy, who lives at The Byre. Kellie's fun, bubbly and so sweet. I sometimes see her opening The Byre's front door and bending over to shake some tissue paper near the doorstep before going back in – that's her escorting individual insects out of the house and into the outdoors, when most people would probably squish them and flush them down the loo.

Yes, Lesley and I were good friends, I thought – until we weren't. It was the most bizarre thing. She broke off our friendship, not me. She had a birthday party at The Stables soon after she and her family moved there, and invited mainly people from her old life, saying she hadn't yet made many friends in Swaffham Tilney. I think she must have been paranoid that the party wasn't going well – I mean, it was a bit quiet, and I felt sorry for her, so I thought I'd try and get a more fun, chatty vibe going, by talking to another woman who was there... and before I knew what had hit me, Lesley was swearing at us both, me and this woman Abigail, and ordering us to 'Fuck off out of my house'. I had no idea what I'd done wrong, and Abigail seemed equally clueless. I left, obviously, but I went round the next day and asked Lesley what on earth I'd done to upset her so much. She was all tight-lipped and avoiding eye contact, but she told me: my mistake had been to approach Abigail – 'my friend, not yours, Kellie!' – and start chatting to her. Apparently, that was unforgivable and I was a friend-poacher. I was so shocked. All I'd done was talk to another guest at a party. Isn't that what party guests are meant to do? Lesley eventually saw that I really hadn't meant to upset her, so she invited me in and I thought she was going to apologise and say maybe she overreacted... I mean, there was no maybe about it. She did overreact. Conrad was incandescent with rage when he heard what had happened. But I thought, if she apologised... But she didn't. She started to tell me, almost as if she was describing a special gift she had, that she feels envy very strongly. Most people don't suffer from it as badly as she does, she said, and it's been something she's had to try to cope with all her life. She said, 'Kellie, if I invite you to my party and I see you walking over and talking to someone you don't even know, one of my friends, instead of coming and talking to me, when it's my birthday… that's always going to hurt me. Always. I probably shouldn't have let my feelings show in the way that I did, but if we're going to be friends, I'm going to need you to be more sensitive in future. And actually, I'm never going to apologise for feeling how I feel, because emotions are never wrong. Envy's a natural response, we all feel it. I just feel it more deeply.'

The part that really threw me was the 'instead of coming and talking to me' bit. I made the mistake of reminding her that, before the party started, I'd spent two hours helping her prepare the food and set everything up and we'd been chatting non-stop that entire time. 'So?' she snapped in my face. 'That wasn't the party, was it? That wasn't you talking to me at my birthday party.' Conrad was so upset at the thought of me carrying on my friendship with her that… well, that was it, pretty much. And she later told Michelle Hyde that I cut her out of my life because I'm shallow and can't stand it when people honestly express emotions.

No One Would Do What The Lamberts Have Done

Having said all that, I'm positive Lesley didn't do this. Why? Because look what happened to her. She suffered as much as anyone else, and her whole ethos, I eventually realised, was 'Everyone has to suffer apart from Lesley Gavey, who has to reign supreme.' No, she didn't do it. No one will ever convince me she did.

10

Like Tess Gavey, Mum would have been told no, she couldn't have a dog, if she'd asked for one as a child. She never asked, and nor did she get one as an adult – not until her father died. Grandad, from what I've gathered, had a strange, secret power: he was able to make all those close to him forbid themselves from doing things they wanted to do, if they knew or even suspected he would prefer them not to do those things. Mum once told me it was as if he'd found a way to insert a little secret police force into your brain, so that he could control you from inside your own system: *No, he won't like that at all. Better not do it. Better not ask for it. Better not suggest it.*

Grandad, according to Mum, would not have been at all happy either to be visited by a dog, ever, or to visit a house that contained a dog. Dogs, he firmly believed, required far too much attention, created inconvenience and anxiety, and you never knew when they might wreck everything, since it was impossible to ensure they would always obey the rules of civilised social behaviour. I once heard Mum say to Tobes, 'That was actually a scarily accurate description of Grandad himself, not of any dog I've ever known.'

The first thought that crossed Mum's mind when she heard from Granny that Grandad had died was, *Now I can get a dog.* Immediately afterwards she burst into tears – not because she'd just lost her father, but because she was furious with herself. She should have learned how to stop 'forbidding herself' in accordance with Grandad's wishes long before he died. If she could only have turned back the clock and gone back to when she was 17 or 18, knowing what she knew now...

She wouldn't, in fact, have chosen to travel back in time in this way, even if it were possible. No one who has endured any sort of living-in-fear situation ever wishes they could go through it all again. Much better to tell Champ what her perfect response would have been, as the two of them walked around Shukes's front garden: 'I'd have said, calmly, "It's reasonable for you to feel upset and angry sometimes, Dad. Everyone does, and your reactions are your business. But I'm afraid, from now on, I'm not going to sit here while you bellow and rage at me for as long as you feel like it. Let me know when you're ready to talk politely, respectfully and without hostility, and we can discuss it then. And please understand that if you use verbal aggression or ever raise your voice to me again, I'm going to walk away. To protect myself from you – the way *you* failed to, from the second I was born until the moment you died."'

There was no point waiting for Champ to point out that if Mum had been saying all that to Grandad, it would have made no sense to mention his death because he wouldn't have died yet. Champ has many brilliant qualities but spotting discrepancies of that sort isn't one of them.

When Grandad died, he left Mum and Auntie Vicky £17,000 each (he was always extremely generous with his money, which was a) lovely of him and b) not a bad tactic if you're planning to continue to treat your loved ones appallingly in other ways and want to incentivise them not to tell you to fuck all the way off and never come back), and he left Granny (aka Julia, whom you met in the chapter before last) everything else, which was a substantial amount – nearly half a million pounds. Grandad's financial advisor, Pascale, arranged a meeting with Granny and asked her if she'd be interested in investing some of this money she was now in charge of, so that it could grow into even more. Pascale insisted that this was nearly always what happened when people invested in stocks and shares and bonds via her company.

'Why not?' Granny said. 'I've got more than enough to live on, and no mortgage. I can afford to gamble a bit. How exciting!' Pascale was astonished by this response. Granny couldn't understand why.

No One Would Do What The Lamberts Have Done

She soon found out. 'Your husband would never let me do anything with the money if there was even the slightest risk attached,' Pascale told her. 'I explained to him eight years ago, when we first met: he could quadruple his... your joint wealth, if only he had a slightly higher tolerance for risk—'

Mum says Granny laughed at that point. Risk was something Grandad had cut out of his life as far as he'd been able to. He would have felt far more comfortable having – definitely, guaranteed – only a hundred pounds for ever than putting that hundred pounds somewhere where it might either turn into a million pounds or shrink to only fifty pounds within a few years.

'The most chilling part isn't the maybe-millions Granny missed out on thanks to Grandad's stupid choices,' Mum once said to me. 'It's that Grandad *never asked her what she thought*, or wanted to do – and then when she found out after his death that Pascale had urged him to pursue the path that was highly likely to be more profitable and he'd said no, *she didn't mind.* When she told me and Auntie Vicky, she was all "Ha ha, can you imagine Grandad taking a risk?" Like, there was no element of "Can you believe what he did?" She didn't feel even the tiniest bit... oooh, I don't know, robbed by a coercive-controller?'

Yes, this was said to me by Sally Lambert, my mother – the same person who also, on 17 June 2024, made a plan to run away with the family dog without consulting her husband or children.

Granny invested, with Pascale's help, not only most of the money Grandad left her but also ten grand each of Mum and Auntie Vicky's inheritances. Ever since, she's kept a close eye on how their 'chunks', as she calls them, are performing in the markets. Once a month, when she gets a statement from Pascale, Granny sends a homemade one of her own to Mum and Auntie Vicky. Whenever the total amount has decreased, the subject heading reads, 'Your chunk has shrunk!'

Overall, happily, there has been growth rather than shrinkage, which is how Mum knew that thirty-seven grand's worth of the stocks and shares that officially belonged to Granny were in fact hers. And when she got impatient and thought to herself, '*I earned every penny*', she obviously didn't mean she'd worked for that money, because she hadn't. What she meant was that she'd earned it by making the effort, for decades, to keep quiet about most of what she was really thinking and feeling, for the sake of keeping peace in the family.

That effort had needed to be maintained after Grandad's death too: once he was gone and the fear part of her life was over (or so we thought – until Tess Gavey and her lies came along), Mum could have turned round and said to Granny that it would have been nice, just once, to hear the words 'Stop bullying our daughter, you emotional toddler'. If she had said that though, Granny might not have felt inclined to put Mum's ten grand in with hers as part of a bigger investment – and Pascale was no longer taking on clients who had less than fifty grand to invest. Therefore, Mum believed, it was her tactful silence about certain aspects of her childhood that had netted her the thirty-seven grand she could now use to fund Champ's escape and, if necessary, his new undercover life (about which more later).

Mum's always saying she doesn't blame Granny, who was just as scared of Grandad as she was, and she doesn't even blame Grandad himself. 'You can't, in all fairness, blame a toddler for being a toddler even when he's in his late sixties,' she says.

What I've never said in response, but have often thought, is, 'Yes, but you do *blame*, though, don't you? You've got lots of blame inside you which needs to go somewhere, and it does. You blame, for instance, the smell of gardenia – which has never, at any point, done anything to hurt you. All gardenia has ever done is happen to be an irrelevant detail associated with one of the many savage bollockings you got as a teenager.'

When Mum and Dad bought Shukes and were redesigning the garden, Mum said, 'No gardenia. I can't bear the smell,' and wouldn't explain when Dad asked her why. She's never told any family member about the gardenia body lotion incident apart from me. That means a lot to me, and it's why I'm anti-gardenia too, even though I don't know what it looks or smells like. It's always been important to me to be on Mum's side the way she is unwaveringly on mine. I should have spoken up loudly and stuck up for both her and Champ on The Day of the Policeman, but I was scared in exactly the way Mum and Granny – and maybe Auntie Vicky too, though she would never say so – were scared of Grandad.

I wish I could ask Mum (I could, but the world might never be the same again if I did, so I can't) if her belief that Granny was 'always on my side, not Grandad's, deep down' is based solely on wishful thinking or on something more substantial. Does she have any proof? Or is this the same faulty intuition at work that made her believe Avril Mattingley would instantly sign up to be on her side and help her save Champ?

To be fair to Mum, sides are complicated in our village. Everyone who knows Swaffham Tilney, if asked, would agree that it's a village with two sides. The trouble is, they'd all mean different things when they said it. There are the two sides of the village green, with low, detached, thatched-roofed cottages on one side and terraced pantile-roofed ones on the other, but then there are also the two different ends of the village: one that contains the green, the large majority of the houses, the pub, the church, the village hall and the bus stop, and the other, which is where you'll find Bussow Farm, fields owned by The Farmer and a handful of enormous detached mansions with so many screening trees around them that a visitor to the village might conclude all the most prosperous residents of Swaffham Tilney are involved in shady activities which they don't want anyone to witness.

No One Would Do What The Lamberts Have Done

This is where Bussow Court has recently been added, to the posh-pads-and-Farmer side, and with these six new homes came more potential for the creation of sides. There are already four – four! – pairs observable in Bussow Court:

1) The houses on the left and the houses on the right, as you drive in. This is definitely a case of 'and' rather than 'versus', since in no way are The Barn, The Farmhouse and The Byre in any kind of joint opposition to The Granary, The Hayloft and The Stables. There's the occasional rumbling about a north-facing/south-facing distinction, but so far nothing that's escalated.

2) The people who believe that the car parking spaces for Bussow Court residents are too far away from the houses versus (and never was the word 'versus' more warranted than here) those who say, often and with escalating exasperation, 'The parking spaces are just over there! God, what's wrong with you? You've got legs, haven't you?'

3) Converted agricultural outbuildings that have belonged to Bussow Farm for centuries versus new-builds that didn't exist in any shape or form before 2022. It's a very subtle 'versus', this one: double-edged remarks, rock-solid-plausible-deniability-plated, that either hint at how much more character old buildings have or

celebrate how much cosier and better insulated new-builds are, how much less likely to contain the ghosts of machine-mutilated farmhands from days of yore.

And last but not least, the best-known and most viral exemplar of two sides in Swaffham Tilney, the one that's made our village the most notorious in the country...

4) The Lamberts versus the Gaveys.

Someone should probably make a spreadsheet, so that we can easily cross-reference where each village resident stands on all of these issues, and all the others too – all the ones that aren't Bussow Court specific, like the matter of the weeds growing up Corinne Sullivan's front wall. Unfortunately, no such spreadsheet exists, so Mum had no way of knowing that Avril Mattingley had more than once described Corinne's weeds as 'a giant "Fuck you" aimed at all of us, us peasants who don't deserve her consideration'. This couldn't be further from Mum's position, which is that nobody's front wall is anybody else's business, and Corinne's weeds look quite pretty anyway, and what if the difference between weeds and flowers is quite arbitrary?

In her desperation on 17 June, all Mum thought or remembered about Avril was that she had been the only person to see through the distortions surrounding the big book-club row (yep – another example of sides being taken in Swaffham Tilney).

Except Avril hadn't seen through anything. Mum just heard her say some words and decided, in order to feel less isolated in her own unusual perspective, to make them mean what she wanted them to mean, which, basically, was 'I agree unreservedly with Sally Lambert'.

No, Avril Mattingley was far from being her dream collaborator, as Mum was about to discover.

11

Monday 17 June 2024

Sally

Before either woman says anything, Sally starts to worry that Avril is not the right person after all. As a general rule, one's perfect helper is not already crying about something else – something you don't have time to wonder about, relating to their own life – when you most need them to focus on you and your problem.

Avril is in her late thirties with light brown, centre-parted hair that lies flat against her head as if pasted to it. The tops of her ears sometimes poke through. Sally has got into the habit of looking out for this and feeling ever so slightly disappointed when no pink ear-tip is visible, as is the case today. For the first time, Sally is getting to see the inside of Avril's house, which has dark stripy wallpaper on both sides of its tunnel-like hall – white and either navy or black, Sally can't tell. Bad choice for such a narrow space, she thinks, and way too many framed photographs on both sides.

No One Would Do What The Lamberts Have Done

Beyond the hall, in whatever room is at the far end of it, a child starts to wail. Sally can't remember how old Avril's youngest is.

'This isn't a great time, as you can probably tell,' Avril says. 'Can it wait?'

'Not really,' says Sally. 'I need help and I don't have time to... I need help *fast*.' As she says it, she knows that not a single person would agree that this is an every-second-counts crisis. They're all wrong. Given what the Gaveys have already done, there's no telling what they might do next. Sally has to get herself and Champ out of The Hayloft and far away from Swaffham Tilney, and it can't wait.

'*You* need help?' Avril looks and sounds affronted. 'I mean... no offence, but have you seen the state of me? I swear to God...' She looks over her shoulder as the wailing turns into a gargling scream.

Sally hears a man's voice repeating a mantra: 'Nothing happened. Nothing happened.' She guesses that the shrieking child is correct in thinking that something did, in fact, happen. 'Avril, can you come and give me a hand,' her husband shouts. Nick: that's his name.

'Do you sometimes wish you'd never had kids?' Avril says. 'And by "sometimes", I mean all the time?'

Sally doesn't, ever. Her children, furry and non-furry, are the best part of her life. She often used to wish Mary Poppins was real and would drift down from the sky to help with childcare, but only because she knew that would have been as much fun for Ree and Tobes as it would have been a relief for her.

'Avril, please... I know it's a lot to ask, but can you let Nick deal with whatever it is and help me?' she says. 'It'll cost you nothing: just a few minutes of your time. I wouldn't ask if I were any less desperate, but it's a life-or-death emergency.'

This has a visible perking-up effect. Now Avril's interested.

'The Gaveys are trying to kill Champ,' Sally tells her.

'Champ? Oh, right. Your dog.' There's no mistaking the downgrading that just took place in Avril's mind. The change in her expression said it all: instant de-prioritisation.

Then it gets worse.

'I'm sure that's not true,' Avril says. Does it make sense to say that a voice sounds as if it's rolling its eyes in frustrated impatience? If so, that's how her voice sounds.

'Look, Sally, hard as this might be to hear, not everyone's like you.'

'Meaning?'

'You're really going to make me say it?' Avril sighs.

'What choice do I have, when I've no clue what you're on about? Conversations don't work unless the people having them understand each other.'

Way too harsh. Shit. That was snapping, not chatting. It wasn't neighbourly, let alone friendly.

Strangely, it seems to have a softening effect on Avril. 'Look,' she says in a kinder tone. 'Not everyone loves dogs.

Not everyone wants a smelly, slightly muddy animal with bad breath slobbering all over them—'

'But that doesn't mean they want them dead?' Sally interrupts her. 'Is that what you're about to tell me? Great, I agree. The problem is, the Gaveys *do* want Champ to be killed. Or... or did you mean it's okay if the Gaveys think Champ's a smelly, muddy dog and are trying to kill him for that reason?'

Now Avril's face rolls its eyes, as well as her voice. 'You're being ridiculous,' she says.

'I really hope so,' says Sally. 'I'd be so thrilled to be wrong and have nothing to fear. Anyway, look, I'm sorry to bother you. This was a mistake.'

She turns and walks away, heads for the swings at the farthest end of the green. And the seesaw! And the roundabout! In her head, Sally greets these pieces of playground equipment she normally ignores as if they were her friends, tiny in the distance, waving to her as if to say, 'Come over here and hang out with us. You'll have a much better time.'

It's good that Avril Mattingley has revealed her true nature; now Sally won't waste any more time thinking about her. Yes, it's a set back, but Sally, unlike most people she knows, is good at changing her mind, good at responding to danger signals – which, frankly, Avril might as well have blasted into the vast, low-hanging East-Anglian sky from a massive cannon: regrets the existence of her children, doesn't understand that dogs are people too, happy to declare herself sure about something that demonstrably isn't the case without asking any questions first, horrendous taste in wallpaper…

Halfway to the swings, Sally hears footsteps behind her. She slows her pace, but doesn't turn. The padding gets louder. Sally doesn't fear it might be a Gavey; there's no doubt in her mind that it's Avril. Which is fine. She will say more unpleasant, inaccurate things, but Sally won't argue with her. In her mind, Avril Mattingley barely exists anymore. Sally doesn't need her, or anyone. She'll go home, get Champ and set off. She's got a new plan and thinks it will work.

'Your dog is very cute, right…' The breeze propels Avril's voice toward her.

Sally turns. If by any chance this is the beginning of an apology…

'… but he's just a dog! He's just a sodding pooch, Sally. He's not the second coming. A few weeks ago when I bumped into you both outside the church, he jumped up and licked my hand and nearly pulled a button off my shirt, and you were all like, "Aww, look, he likes you!" And my hand *stank* afterwards. Like, all the way home it reeked of dog breath.'

Sally tries not to laugh as she remembers what Ree once said: that Swaffham Tilney people are entirely oblivious of their 'distance privilege' – that was what she called it. 'All the way home', in this instance, meant less than a minute's walk. Sally could have hopped on one leg from the church to Avril's house without any problem at all.

'So, look, I'm sorry if I'm not at my most tactful,' Avril goes on. 'I've just had the shittiest day. Everything that could have gone wrong has. I was stressed even before I started cooking shepherd's pie for tea, and then Nick made this massive production of offering to help, as if he ought to win the Nobel Peace Prize or something. I told him to leave a tiny bit of water in the pot with the potatoes, to help make them a bit softer for when I mashed them, but instead he left about a third of the water in, mashed them himself – no milk, no butter, no seasoning – and then just slopped them out all over the meat mixture. Ruined the whole thing. Now I'm going to have to start from scratch, and there's nothing in the house. So, yes, I apologise for getting a bit impatient with your imaginary problem. I'm sure *something's* happened, and I'm not asking for the details, but come on.' Avril shakes her head. 'Turning up and saying the Gaveys are trying to kill Champ?'

'... would be unacceptable if it weren't the truth,' says Sally, as if they're playing a fun game in which her challenge is to complete Avril's sentences. 'Bye, Avril. Order a takeaway.'

Nick, destroyer of shepherd's pies, was made redundant two months earlier, so perhaps the Mattingleys can't afford takeaways at the moment. Nor do most of the restaurants that claim to deliver to Swaffham Tilney actually agree to do so when asked. 'Sorry, love, we're up to our ears in orders, and we've got three people off sick. It'd take us too long to come out your way.' Sally knows all this; that's why her comment was the perfect missile to fire at Avril. And her own address is even more unappealing to delivery drivers, being further from the B1102, and the Lamberts also can't afford takeaways apart from for birthdays and special occasions, so she doesn't feel bad. And she remembers someone from the village telling her Nick Mattingley got a full year's salary as a redundancy pay-off, and his job had been highly-paid and the best kind of London-ish job too, the sort that never seemed to require him actually to go to London.

'Go fuck yourself, Sally,' says Avril. 'Really, just get lost.'

'I am,' Sally tells her, and heads off again with a wave.

Where was she going? That's right: the swings.

No. Home. She remembers her new plan. She must get Champ before she does anything else, get him safely out of the village. But, wait, there's Corinne Sullivan standing between the swings and the roundabout. Sally didn't see her at first; the sun was in her eyes and she only saw what was ahead of her once she stepped into the shade cast by the church's tower onto the village green, then suddenly everything was fully visible again.

Why does Corinne look like she's waiting for Sally?

No. Don't risk it. Stick to the new plan.

Corinne doesn't appear to be busy or afflicted by shepherd's pie trauma. She looks… available. To help, maybe.

What if she's the perfect person? *Dangerous Corinne. Ferocious Corinne.* Is that true, though? Sally only thinks of her in this way because of her role in the book-club row, and maybe also the weeds, a little bit. Perhaps being ferocious sometimes is okay – necessary, even.

Oh no. Help. Now Corinne is walking towards her. Sally has no way of knowing if Corinne is also a 'just a dog' person. Even if she wouldn't come out and say it, especially not as dismissively as Avril had, might it be her underlying belief that dogs aren't every bit as important and valuable as humans? If she met Lorna from Sally's work, who's on her fourth round of IVF, might Corinne nod and think nothing of it if Lorna were to say, 'It's just so disgustingly insensitive to suggest to someone who's having trouble conceiving that they should settle for getting a dog instead'?

To be fair, Sally made sympathetic noises when Lorna said that very thing to her once, after being lobbied by her sister-in-law to get a pug and embrace being its 'hoomum' (Sally hated that word; 'mother' or 'mum' was the correct term, there was no need to qualify it). Later, Sally berated herself for not being brave enough to be the enormous and game-changing help to Lorna that she might have been. The truth was – and if Sally could change minds in this world about one thing and one thing only, this would be it – being the parent of a dog is exactly the same and every bit as meaningful and amazing as being a parent of humans. Sally can't bear to think that millions of infertile women don't know this and are missing out as a result. There's no need to adopt, traipse around orphanages, hire surrogates, pay egg-donors…

How mad all of that seems to Sally, who knows the truth: once you've got a dog, you've got a child. You really have – in every possible, wonderful way. You've got a canine child who feels absolutely like your flesh and blood even though he or she belongs to a different species.

Before the Lamberts got Furbert, Sally wouldn't have believed this was possible, so she suspects Lorna from work is unlikely to be persuadable. It would be widely regarded as a shocking and cruel thing to tell someone in Lorna's situation, which is why Sally didn't. She told her child-free-by-choice sister Vicky, though, in a WhatsApp message. Vicky's response was to send three of Sally's own sentences back to her inside double quote marks, followed by two laughing emojis. Presumably she'd picked what was, in her opinion, the most risible part of Sally's original message. Instead of sending back an indignant 'You often express opinions that I disagree with, yet I have never – not once – responded to you in such a rude, sneery way,' Sally pretended she didn't understand Vicky's mockery. 'I don't understand what that means,' she replied. Vicky messaged back: 'Having a dog is definitely *not* the same as having a baby,' as if no arguments or evidence needed to be provided to support that position.

You just need to be willing and able to withstand the pain of losing them, thinks Sally, and the way to do that is to understand that you never really will. Not their soul. That always stays with you – still part of your life, even when they've gone up to Dog Heaven. Vicky would probably have sent four laughing emojis in response to that. Sally ought to have known that Vicky couldn't be made to care about dogs – that much was clear from the Facebook business, which Sally has decided never to think about again. *No, I'm not thinking about it now, I'm thinking about my not-thinking-about-it policy; it's different.*

No One Would Do What The Lamberts Have Done

Corinne is getting closer, and Sally's eyes fill with tears as she contemplates all the people who don't and wouldn't care about poor Champy's predicament, imagining that Corinne will very likely turn out to be one of them. She remembers the time her mum, thinking that all she was doing was praising Champ's calm and friendly temperament, said, 'It's so nice to be able to come to your house and not get chewed to bits every time I stand up to go to the loo.' What she meant was that it was 'so nice' that Furbert wasn't there anymore. After getting attacked by another dog on a walk in Cambridge city centre when he was six months old, poor old Furbs had remained anxious about any sudden movements for the rest of his life, bless him, and couldn't always control his defensive impulses (this was how Sally thought of it. Other people described it differently, using the words, 'bite', 'bitey', 'bit' and 'bitten', words which Sally made sure to avoid, just as she'd avoided her sister Vicky for nearly three months after she'd said, 'You want to be careful, Sal. One day, Furbert will go for someone who won't just be polite and say "Oh, it's fine, think nothing of it." One day he might get reported to the police.' Sally had realised, at that moment, that there was a very fine line between a helpful warning and a threat designed to terrify.)

She complained bitterly to Mark after her mum made that 'It's so nice…' comment: 'I should have said, "Yeah, and it's fantastic being able to come to your place without getting emotionally blackmailed by a power-crazed narcissist, now that Dad's dead."'

Mark's eyes widened. 'That would have been terrible, Sal. Your mum would have been devastated. Never, ever say it, or anything like it.'

Sally didn't, and doesn't intend to. Nevertheless, she was left with the impression on that occasion, as on so many others – really, the world has been bombarding her with it for as long as she can remember – that everyone else's feelings are supposed to matter far more than Sally Lambert's. Immediately, another incident sprang to mind: her hen weekend, and the toddler who was in the swimming pool during the no-children time one day. His parents gazed at him joyfully as he yelped and whacked the surface of the water with his hands over and over, as if this should have delighted all present. 'I might say something,' Sally whispered to her six hens, all of whom looked instantly wary. Oonagh said, 'Oh, come on, Sal. Don't be that person.'

And she never has been. Evidently, she isn't allowed to be. Except maybe that needs to change now, given the threat to Champ's life. Maybe, to save him, she will have to become That Person – the one who expects fair treatment and appropriate consideration for herself and her family, and who objects when she doesn't get it.

'Sally?' Corinne puts a hand on her shoulder. 'Are you okay? What's wrong?'

'I need help.' Sally bursts into tears.

'It's okay,' Corinne says. 'I'll help you.'

12

Up until that point, Mum's experience of Corinne Sullivan had been limited. Corinne had almost made a hermit of herself in Swaffham Tilney since the determined duo of Michelle Hyde (22, The Green) and Jemima Taggart (Meadowsweet, The Drove) had waged a campaign to turn village opinion against her. They claimed she was a fake with no conscience (personal or social) and no integrity, who flat-out lied about being a philanthropist.

Mum had no idea if these accusations had any substance behind them, though she knew from Googling that Corinne was a successful businesswoman, who had founded, grown and then sold three companies so far, and did indeed describe herself as a philanthropist, passionate about helping those less materially fortunate than herself.

Mum had watched an interview on YouTube in which Corinne had given the impression of being, not a liar, but almost alarmingly honest: she'd talked quite openly about the reason she'd divorced her husband: 'I could say something that you'd find less reprehensible,' she said, 'but the truth is, I left Ronan because he was insufficiently entrepreneurial. If that sounds crazy to you, ask yourself: could you stay married to an abattoir-worker if you were a principled vegan? Or to a hangman, if you were passionately opposed to the death penalty? I bet you couldn't.'

Mum couldn't bear, and didn't trust, either Michelle Hyde or Jemima Taggart, but she strongly suspected neither of them had the imagination to come up with the precise story they told (eagerly, to anyone who would listen) about how and why Corinne's 'philanthropy' was the opposite of what it claimed to be. Surely both were incapable of inventing a lie with such a strong flavour of surely-she-can't-be-serious-but-actually-oh-wow-she-is – the very same flavour, Mum thought, as Corinne's reason for leaving her husband. It all seemed to fit.

As she followed Corinne to her house on 17 June, Mum decided she didn't care what else Corinne was, apart from willing to help, now. She'd said 'I'll help you', without qualification. There was no 'within reason' or 'as long as...' or 'if I'm able to spare the time', just an unconditional offer of help, no questions asked. Corinne was rich too, which was an Enjollifying thought. Not that Mum's plan, as she'd envisaged it up to that point, was beyond her own budget. She didn't need any of Corinne's money, but she was aware that rich people often had all kinds of power to make otherwise out-of-reach things happen. If Corinne was willing to use some of hers to help save Champ's life, then Mum was ready to love her and pledge allegiance to her forever. She was so grateful, she wished she could start up the book-club row again just so that she could take Corinne's side in the most outspoken and vehement way.

Why hadn't she at the time? She'd agreed with Corinne's point of view more than the opposing one, but there was something unnervingly 'To the death!' about the way Corinne had approached the whole matter, as if what was at stake was the survival of the whole world, not which direction a village reading group with twenty members should take in the future. And when one considered that only eight of the twenty attended all the meetings and read all the books...

Mum liked to tell the Book-Club War story to people who weren't from our village, who never believed it until she'd said at least five times, 'I swear, that's what happened. I'm not exaggerating. If anything, I'm toning it down so as not to shock you.' Part of the reason she liked to tell new people was to convince herself that it had really happened. Her mind seemed determined to keep doubting it, though she'd been there at every meeting, seen and heard it all first-hand. Yet somehow the world felt as if it made more sense when one believed, or at least considered the possibility (which wasn't one) that it couldn't have happened.

Sadly, too much damage was done – everyone agreed

about that – and, as a result, Swaffham Tilney's Book Club voted itself out of existence. For a few months afterwards, there were whispers about starting a new one, but they were generally shut down with a hushed 'It's too soon.' And for at least a year after the Book-Club War ended, everyone made sure not to utter the name 'Agatha Christie' while in Swaffham Tilney, not even to ask if anyone had caught the wonderful Peter Ustinov *Death on the Nile* on BBC2 last Saturday afternoon.

You see, the book club was specifically Agatha Christie themed. It hadn't always been, but one day someone said, 'Don't ask me to choose what we're reading next! I'd just pick an Agatha Christie every time.' Someone else chimed in, 'Oh, me too.'

Deryn Dickinson, whom everyone regarded as the group's leader even though there was no leader, said, 'There's no need to sound so self-deprecating about it, ladies. I think Agatha Christie is a significantly underrated writer. Everyone says her plots are good, but she's so much better and deeper than that. Her work has layers.'

Corinne had agreed. 'Christie was a genius on every level,' she said. 'Most people are too thick to see it. They think she just wrote disposable mysteries because that's what they've heard other people say they think.' She'd straightened up in her chair at that point – looked around the village hall and clasped her hands together. 'Why don't we do something to change that?'

By the end of that evening, the Swaffham Tilney Book

No One Would Do What The Lamberts Have Done

Club had become the Agatha Christie Book Club (ACBC for short). Corinne took over the arranging of refreshments from Beth Trevarrow (whose approach was unpopular anyway – on one occasion, the only tea available had been a fancy banana-flavoured kind called 'Monkey Chops') and the book chosen for the next meeting was an ingenious standalone Christie mystery called *Towards Zero* which both Deryn and Corinne declared was 'Top Five material'.

Things went brilliantly for several months, until Maureen Gledhill suggested *The Rose and the Yew Tree*, one of the few novels Christie published under the name 'Mary Westmacott', for the club's next read. 'Don't be silly, Maureen,' said Deryn Dickinson. 'The Westmacott novels aren't mysteries. They're romances, I think. That's why she published them under a different name. She knew Agatha Christie fans wouldn't be interested in them.'

'Wrong. She just didn't want anyone to know they were hers,' said Corinne, and in the history of the Agatha Christie Book Club War, that moment – Corinne correcting Deryn Dickinson – is generally agreed to be the equivalent of the First World War's shooting of Archduke Franz Ferdinand in Sarajevo.

'You know what? We should do *The Rose and the Yew Tree* next,' Corinne went on. 'It's in no way a romance, and there's as much suspense in it as in any crime novel. Actually, I've always thought it kind of *is* a crime novel, though in a very hidden and subtle way – but the reader has to work that out for themselves. Great suggestion, Maureen.'

Maureen Gledhill beamed. Deryn Dickinson felt victimised and ganged-up-on. 'No,' she said. 'This is an Agatha Christie Book Club. We agreed, remember? We only read Agatha Christie books.'

Corinne laughed, then stopped when she saw Deryn meant it.

(Was I there? No. Then how do I know all this? Sure, I've heard Mum talk about it, but how do I know the level of Maureen Gledhill's excitement? Mum didn't. She could have guessed, but I'm not guessing. *I know*. Remember I told you before that there's something I'm withholding? Well, it's that – the thing I'm keeping secret is also the explanation of how I know everything I'm telling you is true. Also, I want to put it on record here that I'm not enjoying keeping certain things to myself for now. In fact, I hate it, partly because it means I can't communicate straightforwardly, which is a faff, but mainly because it feels like a betrayal of someone who means the world to me. There's someone I love more than anything and I can't mention their name. I have to sort of write this as if they don't exist and it's killing me. I wish I could be entirely open about everything, but I have a powerful reason for not doing so – one you'll hopefully understand in due course.)

Mum agreed with Maureen Gledhill and Corinne, but she didn't speak up even before it got heated, mainly because Corinne was doing such an excellent job of putting forward the pro-Westmacott case, which was as follows: those novels were of course Agatha Christie books because they were written by none other than Agatha Christie. And the ACBC rule was 'Agatha Christie books only'. That was it: the full extent of the agreed restrictions, the club's entire constitution. No one had ever said anything about 'Crime-genre books only'.

Deryn disagreed. 'A book published under a different name, in a completely different genre, isn't what anyone means when they say "an Agatha Christie novel",' she said, her bottom lip trembling. 'And that's not just my opinion, it was Agatha's too. She was the one who deliberately published her Westmacott books under a pseudonym. Why? Because she very evidently wanted them *not included* in Agatha Christie's *oeuvre*.'

'Deryn, that's crazy,' Corinne said patiently. 'The most recent editions of the Westmacotts are published with "Agatha Christie" in massive letters on their covers. And since those are the editions we'd read if we read them—'

'Well, that's not what Agatha ever wanted!' Deryn insisted. 'That's what her publishers have decided to do after her death. Without her permission!'

'I mean, if you want to take it to that level…' Corinne sighed, finding it implausible that she was wasting her precious time on such nonsense. 'The publishers couldn't have done anything without her family's permission, presumably. If she'd wanted to, Christie could have left a will depriving her family of all future control over her work, but she didn't – which means she chose, of her own free will, to let them make all the decisions about her *oeuvre* after her death. Therefore, the Mary Westmacotts being added to the official Christie canon is very much, albeit indirectly, a Christie-approved move.'

After two hours of wrangling, there was a vote. Corinne, Mum and Vinie Skinner voted in favour of defining the Mary Westmacott novels as Agatha Christie books for the purposes of the book club. Deryn Dickinson, Jemima Taggart and Beth Trevarrow voted against. Two other members abstained: Ruth Sturgiss and, surprisingly, Maureen Gledhill, who was terrified, by the time they got round to voting, that she'd caused serious trouble and would never be forgiven. She kept saying that she could 'absolutely see Deryn's point, of course I can'.

A hung jury was announced, after which views and votes were solicited from the twelve members who never came to meetings (a proper number of jurors this time, so hopes were high). The opinions offered in this round included: 'I don't want to get involved', 'I'm not taking sides' and 'Blimey! Book groups are supposed to be fun, aren't they?' This last one also had a more earnest, brow-furrowed twin: 'There's just no need for all this unpleasantness and conflict. Why is everybody so intent on keeping it going? Why can't the fighting just stop?' Then there was the apathetic 'What does it matter either way?' contingent, and a couple of women (the book club was all female) who said completely different things depending on whom they were talking to.

Mum had been impressed by Avril Mattingley's response when news of it finally reached her: 'They're all the same,' Avril had apparently said one day to Michelle Hyde. 'Deryn, Corinne, all of them. There's not the slightest bit of difference between them, and they can't see it.'

Thanks to Michelle's efforts, this cryptic statement was soon the talk of Swaffham Tilney (because who did Avril think she was? She had no more special insight than anyone else.) A few weeks later, and unknown to Mum (it's impossible to overstate the extent to which, if she'd known, she'd have gone elsewhere for help on 17 June), Avril clarified what she'd meant by those mysterious words, in a bid to stop people shooting disdainful looks at her across the seesaw on the village green. She told The Farmer she'd only meant that all involved in the book club dispute were equally selfish in failing to realise that some people were beleaguered by small children, and husbands who never helped with the drudgery, and those people, like Avril herself for example, didn't have time to be pestered about stupid reading-group rows.

Mum, in her ignorance, continued to believe Avril had been trying to say something far more profound. I heard her explaining it to Champ one day, assuming that in doing so she was only supporting Avril; meanwhile, Avril thought no such thing. Mum took Champ's enthusiastic support for granted too, of course, which is understandable given the way he is when she's talking like that. He finds nothing more entertaining than hearing her speak heatedly and specifically to him, in her special, sing-song doggy voice. He senses he's being included in something important, even if the details pass him by, and can't get enough of Mum's wild hand gestures. For him, it's like the equivalent of watching a great Broadway show. In his puppyhood, it was practically the only thing that could persuade him to sit still and forget about the possibility of chewing diaries, leather phone cases or chargers for a minute or two.

What Mum guessed (incorrectly) that Avril Mattingley had meant was this: there were not, in fact, two sides to the Agatha Christie Book Club War. Everyone involved thought there were, but they were wrong. The truth was that they all agreed with each other, but didn't realise it.

They all agreed that the question of whether or not the Mary Westmacott books were Agatha Christie novels had a right answer and a wrong one, and that these existed in the realm of objective fact, unalterable by human opinion. Whereas, as far as Mum could see, there was no fixed truth and no obligation to define anything in any particular way. Humans can change the way they label things whenever the mood takes them – by group consensus or as individuals. Both Deryn Dickinson and Corinne Sullivan would have agreed that there were two separate collections of novels under discussion, even if they would have described them differently: Group number one was either 'proper Agatha Christie books' or 'Agatha's crime-genre novels', depending on your point of view, and the Mary Westmacotts were either 'the Westmacotts' (from one side) or 'Agatha's Mary books' (from the other).

In Mum's opinion, the unanimous agreement that there were two distinct groups of novels, and about which ones belonged in which group, could and should have been held up as a happy starting point. 'We agree about so much!' might have been a good opening line for a fruitful discussion.

Couldn't they all see this would be a far more promising opening gambit, likely to yield a better result for all involved? Nope. It was the 'all involved' part, in particular, that gained no traction, because everyone sought a happy ending only for their own gang and chose to view even the tiniest sliver of compromise as a betrayal of deeply held principles.

'The sad truth, Champy, is that the Agatha Christie Book Club could so easily have been saved,' I overheard Mum tell my furry little brother one day. 'And here's what no one in Swaffham Tilney will ever admit: both sides were equally responsible for the wrecking of it – yes, they were! They were, my darling boy. Each side insisted upon its own much closer relationship to God-given truth, while demonising the other side as enemies of objective reality. Once that approach infected the discussion, things went rapidly downhill.'

I saw Mum's point, though one could quibble about the 'downhill' part, since there's no flatter village in England than Swaffham Tilney. But she was right that the Agatha Christie Book Club War soon escalated on every possible front.

She first suspected the situation was getting out of hand when the what-do-we-want-to-call-everything? argument moved from books to club members. Predictably, the 'Pro-Marys' objected to their opponents calling themselves 'The Agatha Purists' claiming this was what they were too; were they suggesting that *Wuthering Heights* by Emily Brontë should be added to the reading list? No, they blooming well weren't. The Agatha Purists objected equally to their antagonists giving themselves the name 'The Pro-Marys', implying as it did that the Agatha Purists were anti the Westmacott novels – and no, they flipping well weren't. They simply believed – as had Agatha herself, they insisted, as her two separate author names proved – that Christie and Westmacott must be treated, and thought of, as two distinct authorly identities.

Deryn Dickinson and her supporters (which by this stage included a rabid Maureen Gledhill) tried to get Corinne Sullivan expelled from the book group. Vinie Skinner, a retired barrister, defended her. Mum voted in favour of Corinne then too, but felt bad for doing no more than raise her hand at the relevant moment – though surely there was nothing useful anyone could have added to Vinie's ever so polite and elegant but nonetheless blistering speech, which had included the phrase 'In the absence of any criminal or morally depraved activity'.

No One Would Do What The Lamberts Have Done

The row spread to the whole village, even to those who never read anything more than The Rebel of the Reeds's 'Lite Bites' menu. It spread to the Swaffham Tilney husbands, some of whom, without adequate forethought or preparation, launched themselves into the fray in support of their wives, only to slink off soon afterwards, having discovered that no amount of reading fat historical tomes about the Battle of the Somme could have prepared them for the indignities of this particular conflict.

For several months the strange phenomenon of sideways jogging was observed in Swaffham Tilney, regularly if not daily: a village resident would set out on his or her morning run, see a Pro-Mary or an Agatha Purist approaching (sometimes even a suspected-to-be-partisan relative of a minor player was enough to set it off), and then jog lightly (so as not to appear rude) but determinedly in an unexpected direction – on one occasion, into a field and almost under the enormous wheels of The Farmer's tractor.

What Mum couldn't know, as she followed Corinne up her winding drive to the mulberry-coloured front door of Ismys House (a huge village mystery was where the name of Corinne's house had come from and what, if anything, it meant) was how her own role in the book club drama had been perceived. Corinne would, of course, remember that Mum voted in her favour whenever voting took place, but did she think Mum had done enough? Maybe she did, and that was the only reason that unconditional 'I'll help you' had been issued. There was no doubting or disputing what Corinne had said – so why did Mum feel so afraid if being helped was all that was about to happen to her? Why did she fear that an attack was imminent?

If only Corinne could have heard the stern talking-to Mum gave Dad when she realised he'd been allowing Champ to wee against the weeds growing up Corinne's front wall...

Mum stopped the thought in its tracks. 'If onlys' were pointless, she knew, because here she was inside Corinne's home, feeling as if she'd stepped through a portal to a new reality that she'd never be able to come back from. There was something so different about Corinne, nothing like anyone else Mum had ever met...

She ordered herself to stop feeling scared, stop imagining that Corinne was about to turn on her. It made no sense to fear your angel of rescue, which Mum wanted to believe Corinne was. The irresistibility of her allure – the power you imagined you might acquire simply by being in her presence and having her full attention fall on you – was a significant part of what made her seem daunting.

Corinne clapped her hands together and turned to face Mum with a severe expression on her face. 'Right!' she said, and Mum thought, 'My life will never be the same again,' feeling absolutely certain it was true and having no idea whether it would be a good thing or a bad thing.

13

Monday 17 June 2024

Sally

'When are you coming back?' Mark's puzzled voice sounds a jarring note in Sally's ear. 'We're all starving.'

'Is Champ all right? Has anything happened? Anyone been round, or—?'

'Champ's fine. He's just had his dinner. Unlike me and the kids. Where are you?'

'Has anyone tried to make contact in any way? Police people or the Gaveys or… anyone?'

'No, Sal.' Mark sighs.

'Thank God.'

From the sofa on the other side of her lounge, Corinne does a double-thumbs-up gesture, though her expression remains grave. She wasn't best pleased when Sally said she had to ring Mark first, before she could explain anything, but Sally insisted she needed to check Champ was okay; it was important at this early stage to have as accurate a grip as possible on how fast or slowly this horror was unfolding.

'When are you coming back?' Marks says again.

'I don't know. I can't really talk now. I'm at Corinne's. She's offered to help us.' It would have been truer to say she'd already helped. Sally has no doubt she's in the best and right place. Everything Corinne has done since the two of them arrived at Ismys House has been helpful: she's made Sally a cup of some sort of smoky tea, which can't be a coincidence. Corinne must have remembered from the Agatha Christie Book Club days that Sally's favourite was Lapsang Souchong, black. This isn't Lapsang, but it's definitely smoky and its beneficial effect, after a few sips, is considerable. Corinne has also provided an iPhone charger and rigged up an extension lead so that Sally can sit in the most comfortable and comforting chair in this vast room, in which no plug socket is anywhere near an item of furniture, and talk to Mark on the phone for as long as she needs to.

'Great!' Mark says. 'If Corinne fancies coming round and whipping up a Spaghetti Puttanesca, I'm fine with that.' His attempt at a joke makes Sally feel so much worse. What the hell does he think he's doing, mentioning the name of the meal Old Sally, pre-nightmare-Sally, said this morning that she planned to cook tonight, as if that still applies or matters?

If Corinne wasn't listening, Sally would probably scream at him, 'Do you really think you're still getting a Puttanesca tonight? Made by me? Are you mad?' She doesn't want to scream, because it's not Mark's fault. He isn't upsetting her deliberately; he just doesn't get it yet, but he will.

'I need to go,' Sally tells him. *Need and want.* Mark is the last person she wants to think about at the moment. It would take too much precious energy to drum it into him that, as far as she's concerned, it doesn't matter if all the Lamberts eat nothing but cold baked beans out of tins for months on end as long as the Gaveys don't succeed in having Champ murdered. 'I'll be back in about half an hour, probably,' she says.

'Okay.' Mark sounds satisfied. 'And you'll make dinner then?'

Why do women have husbands by choice? Sally wonders. Surely it was a false economy, when you considered not only money but also time, effort and emotional energy expended. 'No,' she says. 'If you and the kids are hungry, there's plenty in the fridge you can eat.'

'Sal, for God's sake—'

'Mark, I'm not a—'

'Wait. Listen. I know I'm capable of feeding me and the kids if that's what you were going to say, and I will. But I'm worried about you. You're acting like there's a huge emergency, and… well, there isn't. Nothing's happened yet apart from one visit from the police, and if they aren't already clear on the fact that Champ can't possibly have—'

'I've got to go, Mark. Keep the front door locked. Don't let anyone in and don't answer your phone.'

'Sal, for crying out loud—'

'Bye.' Sally ends the call.

'What was he saying there at the end?' Corinne asks. '"Don't trust Corinne, everyone knows she's a ruthless monster?"' She grins. 'It's okay, you can tell me. I enjoy collecting slanderous comments about myself.'

'Not at all.' Sally is surprised. 'He was trying to persuade me everything's fine and life can go on as normal. He didn't say anything about you.'

'And everything isn't fine – correct?'

Sally nods.

'Tell me,' says Corinne. So Sally does. As her words echo around the immaculate wooden-floored, white-walled room, she decides there's a strong chance that if she's being taken seriously in such a beautiful, important looking setting – and she is; Corinne is rapt as Sally explains what's happened today as well as the whole sense-defying back-story – then her predicament must be noble and important, because… look at the richly-coloured oil paintings on the walls, and the elaborately carved legs of most of the chairs, and the navy-grey-painted wooden shutters at every window. This is the kind of lounge you might have if you were the chairman of the board of directors for a world-famous art gallery.

'Oka… ay,' Corinne says thoughtfully when Sally finally falls silent. 'The first and most important thing to say is that we're absolutely going to make sure no one kills Champ. We simply won't allow that to happen, so you can stop worrying. *Really,*' she underlines, when Sally doesn't look convinced. 'All we need to do is start immediately. Tonight – because you're right, time is of the essence. Don't worry. I have an idea.'

Sally wishes she felt reassured, but somehow Corinne's positivity and certainty feel too extreme. How can she have a plan already? Sally has only just finished telling the story.

'We need to go to your house and get Champ now,' Corinne says. 'Let's do that, and we can talk on the way.'

'On the way where?' This is happening too fast. What if Sally can't trust this woman? Is there something innately suspicious about Corinne's eagerness to drop everything and spring into action to help a stranger?

'I don't understand why you're still sitting there,' Corinne's on her feet, car keys in hand even though her house is no more than two minutes' walk from The Hayloft.

That's right – because she's planning to take me and Champ somewhere. And I'm expected to follow and comply without knowing the eventual destination.

It didn't feel okay, didn't feel safe.

'We have a huge advantage if we act quickly,' says Corinne. 'No one will be expecting you and Champ to go anywhere tonight. Do you know why? Because people in your situation never do what we're about to do. Or rarely – the kind of rarely that everyone's happy to call never. Most people, however much they love their dogs, would sit around feeling helpless and hoping for the best. And most people *don't* love their dogs quite enough to ditch their entire lives and go on the run when there's a good chance it might not even prove necessary. Whereas you *do* love Champ that much. You decided you'd do anything to save him, soon as you heard what that cop had to say.'

Sally nods.

'I understand that,' says Corinne. 'I'd be the same. You don't sit around crossing your fingers and waiting to see how things work out, not when it really matters. Not when the people in charge of the things are *other people*.' She says this with distaste. 'I'd go on the run to save my children's lives, and for you, Champ is your kid – just like… whatever your other kids are called.'

'Rhiannon, Toby and Furbert,' says Sally. 'Furbert died but his spirit is very much still…' Sally stops there, wanting to avoid getting into a wrangle for which she lacks the proper theological vocabulary. How, she wonders, can Corinne be a woman living in Swaffham Tilney and not know the names of everyone's children? The men generally don't – Mark knows the names of the oldest children in most households, but not subsequent ones. He says things like 'I just think of all three as Evie, even the boys' – but all the women do. Except, apparently, this one, whose grown-up children, Sally knows, are called Rory, Niall and Bryony.

Go on the run. Is that what Sally is about to do, with Champ? She's been thinking of it as getting him safely out of the village, that's all. Being on the run sounds as if it might be a huge and complex undertaking, potentially lasting for months, but maybe it's just two different ways of saying the same thing. Corinne seems to think so: she thought she was just repeating Sally's stated intention back to her when she said 'go on the run'.

She puts her hand on Sally's arm. 'Listen. Normal working hours are over for the day, which means the cops won't be doing anything else until tomorrow at the earliest. I promise you, they're not all sitting around now saying to each other, "I wonder if the Lamberts and Champ are a flight risk." This is a dog-bite, not a—'

'No, it isn't! Champ didn't—'

'An alleged dog-bite, I mean. Sorry.' Corinne holds up her hands. 'I only meant, there's no string of sadistic murders involved, no loudly ticking rucksack in a packed concert hall. We can be reasonably sure the authorities won't be back on the case until tomorrow at the earliest – which means we have a significant time advantage, and we need to use it – because what if PC Whatnot comes back tomorrow morning and says he's got a warrant to take Champ away?'

'You're right. You're right.' Still, Sally can't risk standing up. Panic swirls in her stomach and she very much doesn't want to throw up all over Corinne's immaculate lounge floor. And… what if this is a cruel trick? What if, secretly, Corinne is Lesley Gavey's best friend? She's ruthless enough to lie if she has to, Sally doesn't doubt that, and she knows Lesley has tried to persuade more than one person that Sally is nasty and unstable.

'How do I know I can trust you?' she whispers. Then, 'I'm sorry. I'm so sorry. You're being so kind and understanding...' And that's it: this is the problem, Sally realises. Corinne took no convincing that Champ was innocent, or that he might be killed unless urgent action is taken – lawfully executed, like innocent Timothy Evans of 10 Rillington Place. Surely a sound, truth-seeking person would think, 'But what if Champ did it?' Sally would resent Corinne forever if she thought or said that, but she would probably trust her more.

'Okay, look, I'm going to lay it all out for you,' Corinne says. 'Let's pull out all those freaky rumours and have a good look at them. You'll have heard that I pretend to be a philanthropist when I'm not really. The people spreading that rumour aren't lying – they think it's true. I disagree. Here's the deal: the sole recipients of my philanthropy are my three kids and their spouses-slash-partners. I give away hundreds of thousands a year, but never, or only very occasionally, to anyone other than those six people. I've bought them homes, cars, holiday homes, stays in private maternity hospitals, several holidays a year at the world's best resorts. The likes of Michelle Hyde don't think that counts as philanthropy.'

Corinne smiles. 'That's fine. She's allowed to have her opinion, and so am I. I call it charitable giving to those less fortunate than myself, which is the original Greek definition of philanthropy. The word means "love of humanity". I love the humans I grew, and their significant others, most of all. I don't see anything wrong with that. Find me a dictionary definition of philanthropy that specifically excludes loved ones as recipients. You won't be able to; no such thing exists.'

Sally can't take it all in. It's as if the words are bouncing off her and disappearing before she can grasp them.

'From a legal point of view, my children are independent adults,' Corinne goes on. 'And... as adults in their own right, are they underprivileged and at a disadvantage compared with most people? Hell, yeah – and then some! Let me explain why the adult offspring of the super-rich are most likely, out of everyone, to end up with very little.'

Sally would rather do this another time. Or not at all. She doesn't care.

'They grow up with money, they have everything they want,' says Corinne. 'Never suffer or go without, never need to strive in order to stand a chance of having a good life. Plus, chances are their parents are so busy with whatever wealth-creating activity they're engaged in, they have no time or energy to spend on their children at all, let alone to push them to achieve. Those kids miss out on all the existential dread and desperation poor people get as motivators to spur them on. Not only that – they're also deprived of the other main pressure that creates successful people: the "I never achieved my full potential so now you have to or else I'll feel worthless" approach to parenting that's fuelled so much brilliant scientific innovation. I mean, come on! How many genius scientists do you know who bitch about their pushy parents from their architect-designed mansions in the leafy Buckinghamshire countryside?'

'None,' says Sally.

Corinne frowns, as if this can't be the right answer. 'My point is: rich high-achievers don't need their kids to perform well in order to feel successful. We're like, "Please, no one else in this household try and achieve anything massive apart from me, because I honestly don't think I could take the stress of caring about two careers."'

Sally stands up. 'I'm ready,' she says. 'Let's go.'

But there is no escaping the rest of Corinne's lecture, which continues in her Range Rover on the way to The Hayloft to pick up Champ, even though Sally would much rather hear more details of her plan for getting far away from Swaffham Tilney and beyond the reach and remit of Cambridgeshire Police. She would feel better if she knew where she and Champ were going to be spending the night.

'How many stories do you hear about people who started with nothing and became billionaires? Oh, shut up, we'll be there in less than a minute!' Corinne snaps at her car as it makes its 'You've forgotten to put on your seatbelt' noise for the second time. 'Endless stories, right? The Have-Nots who strove hard and became Haves? Think of Oprah! She had to learn how to hustle, big time. Well, my kids never did. They never had to do anything in order to be whisked off to exotic destinations or have a swimming pool in their back garden – and that's not their fault, it's mine. So. Reparations.' Corinne chuckles. 'I love that. I'm going to start calling it reparations as well as philanthropy. Please make sure to mention that to Michelle Hyde and Jemima Taggart next time you're chatting to them.'

'I don't really ever—'

'If I didn't continue to donate generously to my children now, they might end up living in mouldy bedsits,' says Corinne. 'The leeches who steal all our money and call it "progressive" no longer care about whether most young people can buy decent houses or start families – have you noticed?'

This is getting cryptic and intense. No one has ever stolen money from Sally, as far as she's aware. Perhaps Corinne has had to contend with fraudulent business associates in the past – but if she has, Sally can't see why those white collar criminals ought to care about how hard life is for the young. Everyone should care about such things, obviously, Sally corrects herself, but anyone going through life expecting decency from crooked business cheats is going to be disappointed.

'So, am I going to carry on calling it philanthropy, the way I take care of my kids?' Corinne says. 'Yes, I bloody well am, because it's a fuck-tonne of money I give away every year, when I'm under no obligation to do so. I could be selfish and keep it all, but I *don't*. Because I'm *nice*, Sally.'

Did she say that last bit in a threatening way, or was she just being emphatic? Sally wonders.

'I'm kind, caring and sharing – that's my definition of me. No one else needs to subscribe to it. I learned a valuable lesson from all that Agatha Christie Book Club aggro: never try to coerce anyone into sharing your definition of anything. Behave in accordance with your own definitions and let everyone else get on with being wrong. Like with Champ now: we know he's innocent, right?'

'Yes,' Sally says, in a big, sudden blast of appreciation that Corinne, who cannot know any such thing, is proceeding as if she does.

'We know, because the cop told you exactly when Tess got bitten outside her house, that Champ was walking on the lode path at the time. You were with him. You know he's not guilty. So, we're not going to debate that unarguable fact with anyone. We're not going to waste our time on any... legal or judicial process in which the opposite perspective – that he's guilty – is even *heard*.'

'Right. Exactly.' Sally has decided she trusts her new friend and saviour completely. She is happy to pledge eternal allegiance to her.

'So let's see, what other crap might you have heard about me?' Corinne mutters. 'How about me divorcing my husband because he wasn't an entrepreneur? That's true – I say it myself sometimes, because it gets people's attention – and it's also bollocks. If he'd been happy teaching history at Newmarket's most dysfunctional school, fine. I'd have been thrilled for him. But he was miserable. Kept saying how much he'd love to start his own business as a personal trainer or nutritionist or something like that, but he was convinced it was the riskiest thing in the world.

No One Would Do What The Lamberts Have Done

Even though he was married to me, so, you know... the money was never going to run out. But he was scared to become, in his own mind, *someone who didn't have a job*, so he kept choosing misery and stagnation. *That's* why I left him. Someone who thinks like that drags you down after a while; it's a weird, creeping defeatism that infects everything if you let it. I still love and like Ronan, we're still good friends, but I realised I didn't want that kind of negativity in my home. Though he knows I'd still back any company or venture he ever wanted to start – that hasn't changed. I like to remind him of it constantly, not because I'm mean, but because I like to show people, every chance I get, that there's a different and better way to think.'

Sally notices she is already thinking more defiantly and... yes, victoriously (though she hasn't won anything yet) thanks to Corinne; whirling desperation is hardening into determination.

Corinne takes the turn-off for Bussow Court. 'That just leaves the weeds,' she says, and Sally realises she's talking about village rumours that paint her in an unflattering light. 'Yes, I deliberately don't do anything about the weeds growing against my wall – not because I don't care how my property looks from the outside. Actually, I hate the way those weeds make my house look all scruffy and neglected. I *hate* mess. Beauty and order are two of my core values.'

Ought Sally to have core values too? She's never thought about it. *Champ. Ree, Tobes, Furbert.* They're her core values. *Love.*

'Do you know what I hate even more than ugly weeds?' says Corinne. 'People who make snide remarks, when you've been so busy for weeks that your head's nearly falling off, about how you're letting down your neighbours and the whole community when all you've done is miss one tiny weed while you were pulling out the rest. And do you know what I love? Annoying all the right people. So we are where we are. Where can I... ? I'm just going to park here.'

It feels like an emergency stop, immediately outside The Hayloft's front door. Corinne turns to Sally with a grin. 'You should be pleased. It's thanks to those weeds that I offered to help you today when I saw you staggering around the green like the sole survivor of an apocalypse.'

'How do you mean?' Sally asks.

'Last summer. You've probably forgotten, but you yelled at Mark not to let Champ wee against my wall. Just because everyone else took their dogs there to do their business as a deliberate spiteful gesture, you said—'

'I remember,' Sally tells her. 'How on earth did you hear that?'

'I wasn't in the house. I was outside, hiding behind my big hedge, sorting out a flowerbed.'

'Oh. Well, I'm glad you heard. It's nice to think something good happened on that awful day.'

'Why awful?' asks Corinne. Then, eyes widening, 'Ohhh. Last summer. Right. Was that the day—'

'Yes,' says Sally. 'The first time I saw Lesley Gavey.'

14

Mum thought, and still thinks, that she saw the woman first, but I was there too and I'd already spotted her. She was staring at our house, crying hard, and not only that – she was crying in a particular way. When I first noticed her I was struck by the unusualness of that way, but couldn't have explained what was so odd about it to anyone. It has taken me this long to work out the best way to describe it:

The woman (Lesley Gavey, though none of us knew that when she first appeared outside our lounge window) was crying not as if she was at the beginning of something, or even in the middle. She was weeping *at our house* in a way that suggested she was close to the end of a long-running, gruelling drama involving her and it ('him', Mum would have insisted: Shukes was a 'him'), and that this – her being here now, sobbing convulsively on the village green – was perhaps the opening of the penultimate scene of that drama, one in which things could still very much go one way or the other.

'That's weird,' Mum muttered.

'What?' Tobes asked from the corner of the sofa, both hands and his entire mind on his phone.

'There's a woman standing in the middle of the green, staring at our house and crying,' Mum told him.

It was three o'clock in the afternoon. The woman had been there for about two minutes by the time Mum said anything about her. She was lurching forward and back every so often and giving an impression of extreme instability (anyone who can stagger and reel like that on something as flat as Swaffham Tilney's village green must have a dangerous amount of wobbliness inside them).

We all looked. The crying was constant and added the only wet element to a dry and sunny day. The woman gulped and heaved, opening and closing her mouth, and not making any attempt to stop the flow. It looked to me like deliberate, committed sobbing, as if coming here and doing this was her chosen project for today.

'Mum, what have you done?' Tobes asked in a tone of affected weariness. 'You must have done something to piss her off, because... jeez.' I think he was scared and didn't want to admit it. I know I was. I didn't want someone like this, someone capable of doing this, anywhere near me.

It was definitely Shukes she was focused on – the house itself, not anything inside. If she'd wanted to see the contents, living and inanimate, she'd have needed to come much closer. She seemed, while weeping, to be examining every single bit of Shukes in turn: his roof, his front door, the upstairs, the downstairs. Mum walked over and stood right in the window, but The Weeper gave no indication of having seen her, or of caring that Mum was watching her act like a freak in public.

'Mum, what's going on?' Tobes asked.

'I don't know. Shh,' Mum whispered, as if the woman outside could have heard us, which she couldn't. She was standing too far away.

Her hair was glossy, dark brown, shoulder-length – also coarse-looking and a little straw-like, despite not being straw-coloured. Her dark blue eyes were too big for her narrow nose, and her small, neat mouth was almost cartoonishly mouth-shaped, with a pronounced 'M' for a top lip: a Capital M Mouth. She was wearing a short-sleeved, fitted, knee-length dress – red with a pattern of white flowers – as if she'd escaped from a cocktail party at which something devastating had happened. Black ankle boots with pointy toes, gold hoop earrings with small pearls hanging from them, navy handbag over her shoulder. She was absurdly overdressed for the outdoor pursuit of crying in a Fenland village.

'Looks like she might be about to march up to our front door, so... before that happens, do you want to fill me in?' said Tobes. 'Am I going to have to stop her from, like, stabbing you to death?'

'I don't think she'll come any closer,' Mum told him.

'But who is she?'

'I've no idea.'

'Well, what does she want?' Tobes persisted.

Mum shook her head. 'I don't know any more than you, darling. Sorry. It's very odd. Maybe she'll… Hmm.'

I thought, but didn't say, that none of us should try to find out any more than the nothing we knew. I sensed that the best thing by far would be for the woman to go away and never come back, without us finding out anything about her. I didn't want her in my head any more than I wanted her in our village or house. There was something chilling about the way she was endlessly looking, endlessly weeping.

'I'd quite like to get dressed if I'm going to have to physically defend you,' Tobes said. He was still in pyjama-bottoms and bare-chested, with last Christmas's joke present on his feet: enormous rabbit slippers. One was missing an ear thanks to Champ, who had chewed it off towards the end of his puppy phase.

Mum took the bait. 'Defend me? I don't need defending. I haven't done anything.'

'Are you sure?' said Tobes. 'What if she's, like, Dad's other woman, come round to make a scene?' He narrowed his eyes in mock suspicion. 'Or maybe you're the one who's been playing away. Is she the furious wife of your—?'

'Don't be ridiculous, Toby.' Mum pulled a face of exaggerated impatience.

'I'm just saying: you don't know her, I don't know her… maybe Dad does.'

No One Would Do What The Lamberts Have Done

'He doesn't. Dad doesn't *know* people. He's too lazy. And too busy with work.'

'Fair.' Tobes nods. 'Shall I go and ask her what she wants? Tell her to stop staring at Shukes?'

'No,' said Mum. 'We don't own the village green, and we've got no right to tell her what to do with her... eyes. Plus, she's distraught. If I went out and said anything to her, I'd have to ask her if she's okay, be sympathetic—'

'Er, *what*? No you wouldn't.' Tobes sounded as if he'd never heard anything so outrageous in his life. 'Just say, "Get away from my house, you nutter."'

'Don't be horrible.' Mum flinched. 'Could she be the mother of someone from school, or one of your friends? Is anyone... upset with you at the moment?'

'Good try, Mother,' Tobes grinned. 'Nice attempt at buck-passing. I promise you, she's nothing to do with me. So... that just leaves... you!'

Mum got huffy then. 'I don't know why you're talking as if I've got some kind of guilty secret, Toby. The worst thing I've done in my entire life is once take some treats out of the treat barrel at the vet's without permission, one day when Champ seemed really hungry. There was no one behind the counter. I felt bad afterwards and next time I went in I told them I'd done it. The vet said it was fine.'

'I'm joking, Mum.' Tobes patted her on the back. 'Relax your trim. Also, that's so *not* the worst thing you've ever done, but... look, I'm no saint myself, so—'

'What do you mean? What else have I done?'

'Ooh, let's see. Bitched about Granny, Oonagh, Auntie Vicky—'

'Not true.' Mum was shaking her head. 'Close friends and relatives sometimes behave badly and upset you. When that happens, I sometimes talk to Dad about it, or you, or Ree. Everyone does that. It's allowed.'

Toby laughed. 'Everyone does it, yeah, and the "it" that everyone does is called bitching about people behind their backs. Mum, I'm messing with you. It's just bantz.'

Throughout this conversation, Mum's eyes and Toby's both kept drifting to the window. At no point did either of them forget the presence of the sobbing woman.

'If she stays too much longer, this turns into harassment,' said Tobes. 'We can ring the police.'

'No! Don't.'

'Where's Dad? He'll deal with this, if you won't let me do it.'

'What if she knows we're about to put Shukes up for sale?' said Mum. 'What if that's why she's here? I know it doesn't exactly make sense and there's no "For Sale" board outside yet, but—'

'How could she know?' Tobes asked.

'She might have spoken to someone at the estate agent's and they've told her.'

'What, and she's interested? Would you act like this in front of a house you might want to buy?' Tobes made a dismissive noise. 'Wait, look, here's Dad, with Champ.

This'll be crease. Watch his face when he spots her. Bet he gets off the green to avoid her.'

I moved closer to the window and saw Dad and Champ in the distance, up by the playground area, still too far away for Dad to have spotted The Weeper. I watched as he stopped a little behind Champ, who was busy sniffing the bushy weeds covering Corinne Sullivan's front wall. Champ is a very thorough sniffer and likes to approach any flower, plant or tree from all angles with his 'genius nose', as Mum calls it, before lifting a furry haunch.

'Don't let him go there, Mark!' Mum was already on her way out of the room. Seconds later, Tobes and I saw her sprinting across the green and heard her shout (because she didn't bother to close the front door), 'Don't let him pee on Corinne's wall! Pull him away!'

Too late. Champ was already relieving himself in the prohibited area. I understood why Mum was so dead set on stopping him, but she needn't have worried. Corinne is far too sensible to think that Mark and Champ Lambert could or would ever be part of the official campaign against her. Yes, there were residents of Swaffham Tilney who – egged on by Michelle Hyde's husband Richard, the campaign leader – made a point of training their dogs to relieve themselves against Corinne's front wall, but everyone knew Mark Lambert was a good sort and not like that.

What worried me far more than Champ's bathroom break was our open front door. I watched the crying woman carefully to check she hadn't started gliding eerily towards us without moving her legs.

She hadn't. Instead, Mum's bursting out of Shukes and shouting at Dad seemed to jolt the lachrymose lurker into a different frame of mind. She stopped crying, wiped her face, turned and started to walk at a brisk pace in the opposite direction, towards The Old Post Office and The Rebel of the Reeds.

Around two minutes later, I saw a blue BMW I didn't know drive too fast past the green on the other side of the road. It whizzed by too quickly for me to get a look at the driver, but I was sure it was the sobbing stalker, leaving Swaffham Tilney. Tobes had muttered, 'Bye, nutjob,' when she'd first started to walk away, and returned to the sofa.

Then Dad, Mum and Champ came inside and closed the front door. Dad was in placating mode, saying, 'Fair enough, Sal. You've made your point,' to which Mum replied, 'And if only me doing that ever resulted in you remembering for more than thirty seconds and, like, making sure it never happens again!'

'Let me make it up to you, my darling wife,' Dad said earnestly, putting his arms round Mum. 'Why don't I go over and ring Richard Hyde's doorbell right now, and, when he opens the door, just piss all over him?'

'Stop! Urgh. You're so disgusting.' He'd made her laugh, though.

Champ, curled up in his beige Sound Sleep Donut bed next to Mum's favourite leather armchair, didn't quite bark but made his rumbling-engine noise that means, 'I can wake up properly if it turns out we've got a problem, but I'd rather not.'

The Lamberts didn't have a problem, not anymore – or so they thought. The woman had gone, and we all assumed she'd never come back.

15

Monday 17 June 2024
Sally

The distance is helping. In Sally's mind, the Lambert family is officially nowhere near Swaffham Tilney anymore. It's 10 o'clock and protectively dark. The second most horrible day ever (the first was when Furbert died) has given way to a more hope-filled evening, and Sally is grateful beyond words to be spending it in Corinne's Range Rover, on the M6, having just passed Stafford – *all six of us, safe together,* Sally thinks, for she never fails to include the spirit of Furbert in her tally of Lamberts, though his whereabouts at any given moment is a more complex question, she concedes. On one level, he is obviously being driven by Corinne to her 'favourite holiday home' in Troutbeck in the Lake District along with the rest of the family. Even so, before setting off from The Hayloft Sally made sure to leave the door of his crate in the lounge open, and plump up the blankets and cushions inside it, in case he wants to nip in and out for a few long naps every day. That's what he did while he was alive.

Sally feels certain that it's possible for spirit-dogs to be in two places at once. Why shouldn't it be? What's the point of being a free-roaming soul if you still have to be stuck in one place?

It was only once Furbert had died that Sally realised how much that crate had been his special den, just his and no one else's. She saw what happened when Champ joined the family: he approached Furbert's crate over and over but never went in. Instead, he'd curl up contentedly just beyond it, with maybe one paw across its metal threshold. One day Sally realised what this meant: Champ, being a dog and therefore more attuned as well as more spiritually pure, sensed that the crate was already occupied by the spirit of Furbs.

Sally immediately told all the human Lamberts that the door to the crate had to be kept wide open at all times. Mark stupidly asked why a dog's soul couldn't travel through stainless steel mesh. That wasn't the point, said Sally; it was all about the important symbolic gesture of making Furbert feel welcome and showing him that they all understood he was as present as he'd ever been. Mark shook his head and raised his eyebrows, but didn't close the crate door again after that.

Champ's equivalent of Furbert's crate – his special den – is his beige Sound Sleep Donut bed, in which Sally hopes he is now fast asleep in the boot of Corinne's Range Rover.

It fills her with glee to think that they are leaving the Gaveys and PC Connor Chantree further behind with every minute that passes.

Corinne turns off the music she's been listening to for the last hour and says, 'Anyone want me to stop at the next services?'

Nobody does. 'Let's just get there,' says Mark abruptly, as if there's anything any of them can do to shorten the distance between (Sally reads the sign they're about to pass) Yarnfield, whatever that is, and Lake Windermere. It's making Mark nervous, she suspects, to be in a car that isn't his, driven by someone else. He'd made more of a fuss about leaving his car at home than either Ree or Tobes had about coming without their iPhones.

Corinne turns the music back on again: a deep-voiced man singing that he wishes he had a dime for every bad time, but bad times always seem to keep the change. All the way from Swaffham Tilney it's been songs about crops that won't grow, or can't be saved, or turn into dustbowls, and tractors that need to be sold to ward off hardship – that one, Corinne told Sally, is her favourite song in the world. It strikes Sally as the wrong way round that Corinne, who always wears shapely black dresses and at least three thin, delicate strings of gold around her neck, even when she's also got wellies and a raincoat on, listens to this cowboy-and-tractor stuff when the only thing Sally's ever heard blaring out of The Farmer's open windows is Lionel Richie or Michael Jackson.

No One Would Do What The Lamberts Have Done

Sally imagines what Ree and Tobes must be thinking about Corinne's choice of music, and silently beams praise in their direction for keeping their scathing opinions to themselves. She still can't believe the whole family has come with her. She didn't want them to at first – was sure they would make everything harder and worse, hated the thought of inconveniencing anyone – but now she feels comforted to have them all with her.

She'd been impressed when Mark had said to Corinne, 'Of course I'm coming too. I'm not letting you take my wife and my dog and just vanish into the night.'

'Great,' Corinne had seemed pleased in a distant sort of way, as if everything about Mark was beside the point. 'Pack a bag, then.'

'For how long? I can't be away from work for more than one day – maybe two,' he said.

'No one's forcing you to miss work, Mark,' Sally told him. 'You can stay here. I'm not asking anyone to do anything.'

'I'm definitely coming,' said Ree. 'I'm not letting Champy out of my sight for as long as the Gaveys are out to get him.'

Sally couldn't have put it better herself. 'What about your job?' she asked Ree, who clicked her fingers in an exaggerated, sarcastic 'Oh, damn and blast!' kind of way.

'What a shame. My poor job. I'll have to miss loads of days, without giving any notice. A mobile cafe with a slowly flattening tyre that no one ever fixes might fire me. Never mind!'

Ree's current job is her third casual position so far. Her attitude to interviews and employment reminds Sally very much of her own at a similar age. There's nothing Ree loves more than being told she was the best candidate by far and aced the interview. Conversely, nothing makes her more furious than being expected to do whatever job it is once she's got it. Sally is practised at nodding empathetically in the face of a barrage, from her daughter, of 'How the hell should I know how to make a "Vanilla Velvet VIP"? What even is that? No, please *don't* show me how – do I look like I care? Just everyone do the right thing and agree to have PG Tips with semi-skimmed milk, for fuck's sake. And I mean... can we all please stop pretending the Cupwardly Mobile Van in Swaffham Tilney is, like, a Starbucks in Chicago? Like, Bianca messaged the whole Cupwardly group with some bullshit about bringing our best selves to work and our A-game, whatever that is, and I was like, "How about you bring me some more interesting work that isn't just making drinks for bored people who are as desperate to turn tea into a social life as they are thirsty? Maybe then you'll get to meet my best self." No, Mum, of course I didn't actually *say* that. I'm not an idiot.'

'I'm definitely coming with you and Champ,' Toby had said nervously to Sally, as if worried she might try to stop him. 'We should all be with him in his hour of need.'

True, Sally thought. And Tobes had done his last GCSE exam, so if he wanted to join the escape party, why would she stop him? Mark didn't object, which meant it must be fine – though it alarms Sally, remembering her thought process, that she made her husband the yardstick for good parenting when she's the one with the important overview, the one making sure Champ gets to safety. If it had been left up to Mark, they'd be at home now, watching TV, just as findable-by-their-enemies as they had been before they knew they were in danger.

'So is the hot-tub cinema room in the actual house?' Toby asks Corinne. She described her favourite spare home to them when they first set off, in an attempt to convince Mark she wasn't about to lock them up in a primitive shack. She'd sensed, correctly, that he didn't entirely trust anything north of Nottingham.

'No, it's in a converted old piggery at the bottom of the field,' she tells Tobes. 'You'll love it, I promise.'

'I love it already,' he says.

'Same,' says Ree.

And so here they are, the Lamberts, off to the Lake District together. The kids have already argued, compromised and decided on the movie they'll watch when they get there: a horror film called *Speak No Evil*. Sally knows Mark, Ree and Tobes are all thinking this will be nothing more than a fun, impromptu family trip – maybe three or four nights away at most – until Sally sorts out the Tess Gavey problem and gets Champ acquitted of all charges, in the way she always sorts out everything. Tobes and his friends have even given her a nickname based on this tendency: Lester, after a character from the video game *Grand Theft*

Auto. When you get into trouble in that game and need help, you call Lester. Tobes belongs to a gang of eight best friends, five boys and three girls, and Sally is known by all of them to be the most helpful parent – the only one who will solve the group's problems without ever saying anything inconvenient like 'But why did you think it was okay to use a fake ID in the first place?' or 'But why didn't you avoid any possibility of projectile vomiting all over important paperwork by not drinking quite so much?'

I can do this, she thinks. *I am Lester. With Corinne's help and with hundreds of miles between me and Lesley Gavey, I can save the day, the week, the year, the life.* Mark, Ree and Tobes might get bored and want to go home if the mission to save Champ becomes too gruelling or takes too long, but that's okay. It's nice to have the comfort of their company for now, and if they decide they need to leave suddenly, that can be arranged. And both Sally and Corinne made it clear before they set off from The Hayloft: if Mark, Ree and Toby were along for the ride and whatever came after it, they had to be either helpful or neutral – definitely not a hindrance. They had to let Corinne and Sally be in charge. (Ree rolled her eyes and said, 'That's totally aimed at you, Dad. Mum knows me and Tobes won't spoon the whole operation. She only included us because she doesn't want you to feel picked on.')

Mark's resistance to anyone but him being in charge is hilarious. That's what Sally calls it, anyway; it's more tactful than saying 'infuriating'. Not infrequently, at home, she calls out, 'Mark!' and gets the self-satisfied reply, 'No. Not Mark.' The first time this happened, she was confused. She ran downstairs to confront him face to face – for it was undoubtedly he who had replied – and said, 'But you *are* Mark.'

'I know.' He grinned. 'But I also don't want to do whatever boring chore you're about to assign me. That's what "Not Mark" means: "Assign the task that's in your mind right now to someone who is… not Mark!" This was soon officially enshrined in family folklore as 'one of Dad's greatest hits', which made him do it more often.

'Imagine Mum saying that when we called her name,' Ree once said. '"No, not Sal." "No, not Mum." It'd just never happen, would it?'

Of course it wouldn't. You can't do that when you're Lester, thinks Sally, not if you want your loved ones to be properly looked after and your life to run smoothly.

'So, about our phones…' Tobes says tentatively.

Corinne turns off the music. 'Yes, young man?'

'You're going to bring us the burners tomorrow, you said. What time?'

Sally winces at how cheeky it sounds. Though Corinne did promise, as Ree and Tobes reluctantly went upstairs to lay down their iPhones in bedside-table drawers. She made the offer and seemed to mean it.

'I've got someone lined up to sort it out first thing tomorrow,' she says. 'Don't worry. In less than twenty-four hours, you'll be logged back into all your TikToks and Snapchats, and the phones won't be traceable to you.'

'Twenty-four *hours*?' says Ree. 'My friends'll think I've died.'

'No, 'cause you've told them,' Tobes reminds her. Before leaving home, they both notified their key people that they were about to be without internet access for a while.

'Yeah, but they won't think I meant a whole *day*.' Ree sounds slightly awestruck as she contemplates the endlessness of her social deprivation. *An entire rotation of the earth around the sun, can you imagine?*

'Long,' agrees Toby in a sombre tone.

How many minutes, or hours, before Tess Gavey hears that both Ree and Toby Lambert have gone and are temporarily unreachable? Sally wonders. Young people seem to know everything about each other's every movement these days.

Mark says, 'The leaving of the phones was ridiculous. And getting burner phones, like we're drug dealers or something. As if anyone's going to try and trace—'

'You promised not to grumble,' Sally cuts him off. It had been a strict condition of his coming too. 'As I've explained,' she goes on in a formal tone. 'It's not that I think Cambridgeshire Police are going to be putting together a squad of their finest detectives to trace our phones anytime soon. But I'll sleep better if I know they'd fail if, by some remote chance, they decided to try. I also wouldn't put anything past Lesley Gavey. She could hire detectives to find us, she could—'

'That's ridiculous,' Mark murmurs.

'Dad, you're breaking your promise,' Ree tells him.

'All right, I'll shut up.' He doesn't sound happy about it. 'But, look, at some stage I need to be allowed to ask the questions that—'

'What work do you do, Mark?' Corinne asks cheerfully. 'You're some kind of accountant, right?'

'Regional sales manager for Croft and Bower,' he says after a long pause. He wants her to know that he's noticed the deliberate hijacking of his unfinished sentence.

'Who do what?'

'We sell roofing materials. Fascias, soffitts, guttering, stuff like that.'

'Right,' says Corinne. 'And Sally, you're a… something at Quy Mill Hotel, aren't you?'

'I work for the events team. Just part time, though. Three days a week.'

'Do you like it?'

'I like my colleagues more than the work.' Sally agrees with Ree about jobs: who on earth would do paid work if they could afford not to? 'Most of all, I love the drive there and back.'

'I wish I could tell you she's joking,' says Ree.

'That's my favourite bit,' says Sally. 'What's wrong with that? I start at eleven and finish at three, and the traffic's almost nonexistent between Swaffham Tilney and Stow-cum-Quy at those times. I love driving on the almost empty road. It's like a kind of ribbon rollercoaster, between tall hedges and grass verges on either side. And then—'

'I think you've made your point, Mum.' Ree sighs. 'Also, the road's flat. Rollercoasters are the opposite of flat.'

'Yeah, but when you whizz along really fast... which I know I shouldn't, but I sometimes do. It's just so beautiful. All the fields: green, brown, yellow. When the sun's shining, there's no more stunning landscape—'

'—than a boring brown field with absolutely no distinguishing features, next to a B-road,' Ree deadpans. 'Right. Course there isn't.'

'But it's the big skies that really make it magical,' says Sally. 'They're peaceful and exhilarating at the same time. Feels like you're in an art installation or something. I get such a kick out of just being in that landscape, even in a car. I keep the windows open – in winter too. The air feels fresher when the sky's bigger. Have you ever noticed that?'

'Mum's literally the only person on the planet who works in order to commute rather than the other way round,' Toby tells Corinne.

'Well, and we need the money,' Sally says.

'Can I ask you something else?' says Corinne. 'Sorry if it's upsetting, but... how did your first dog die? He's become a bit of a legend in the village, you know.'

'Furbert?' Sally is surprised. Most people who don't have pets aren't especially interested in other people's. 'He ate a peach stone that pierced his lower intestine. They operated on him and got it out, but the wound had become infected. Sepsis. That's what killed him.'

'So it wasn't Parvo, then?' Corinne says in a peculiar

tone of voice. 'He didn't die of Parvo because you hadn't given him his vaccines? Is Parvo even a real thing?'

'Yeah, it's real, but it's not what killed Furbert,' says Sally. 'He was tested for it and the result came back negative. What killed him was some selfish, oblivious git who dropped a peach stone.'

Sally doesn't want to hear the answer but knows she's going to ask anyway. 'Where did you get the Parvo story from?' The worst, stupidest thing she has ever done is tell the whole miserable tale to Lesley Gavey, of all people – and, as if that wasn't bad enough, she'd then gone on to blab about the stress of Furbert occasionally nipping at people. Would Lesley have had the idea of framing Champ for a bite he didn't commit (it must have been her idea, not Tess's) if Sally had kept her mouth shut on the topic of Furbert? Now, clearly, Lesley had told Corinne a false version of the story of his death – a version that portrays Sally as a negligent, uncaring mother.

'I heard it from Vinie Skinner, who got it from Lesley Gavey,' says Corinne. 'I didn't believe it, though. It's obvious how much you love your dogs. There's no way you'd neglect their health stuff.'

'I did,' Sally blurts out. 'I ignored the reminder from the vet about Furbert's annual vaccine – for more than two weeks. I should have rung straight away and made him an appointment for his booster jabs, but he'd always been so strong and healthy. I was totally going to sort it out, as soon as I had a spare minute.'

'Sal, do we really have to—?' Mark starts to say.

'I just kept putting it off, though. There never seemed to be enough hours in any day, or any week,' Sally speeds up, wanting to get it all out before anyone can stop her. 'And then when Furbs suddenly got ill and the vet said the symptoms sounded like Parvo and asked if he was vaccinated, I was sure they were right, and ready to hate myself forever. What could be more important than making sure he was protected? What the hell was wrong with me, thinking it could wait?'

'But it wasn't Parvo,' Mark inserts the line into the conversation as if he's had it prepared and waiting in the wings for some time. 'The test came back negative and it turned out to be a peach stone. So it wasn't Sally's fault.'

She waits for him to deliver his next few lines: *It was no one's fault. Just one of those things. No one can stop a dog from sometimes eating something dodgy, no matter how hard they try.*

If Sally ever gets her hands on the person who dropped that peach stone… She and Mark agree that it's more likely to have been a visitor to Swaffham Tilney than a resident. Almost no one who lives in the village is the litter-dropping sort; even the children wouldn't dare, for fear of being seen by an adult who might use what they'd witnessed to blacken the reputations of the child in question's parents.

Mark had forbidden Sally from going house to house, asking all the neighbours if they'd had any guests recently who might have taken a piece of fruit outside.

No One Would Do What The Lamberts Have Done

Corinne turns her music back on without making any further comment about Furbert or his death, and soon Mark, Ree and Tobes are asleep. Sally closes her eyes but can't seem to drift off; it feels as if her eyelids are clutching each other.

No one speaks again until they pull up outside what looks like a gigantic doll's house: a wide, looming Georgian mansion with a huge door at its centre and five enormous windows in a row on either side of it. Three storeys at least – and there are probably rooms in the attic too. 'Don't tell me this is your house,' Sally says to Corinne. 'It's, like, three times the size of your main one.'

'Main what? Oh – no, I don't have a main home. I'm very clear on that. They're all equal. Of equal importance to me. In fact, the one in Swaffham Tilney...' Mischief has crept into Corinne's voice. 'Want to know why I called it Ismys House?'

She pronounces it 'Is-mice'. Sally's been saying it wrong, calling it Is-Miss. It's probably a family name, a mother or grandmother's maiden name, she guesses.

'I'm sure you can keep a secret,' says Corinne. 'Actually, it isn't a secret now that Ronan and I are divorced. Tell whoever you like! "Ismys" is an abbreviation.'

'Of what?'

'I wanted to call it This Is My Smallest House – because it is! That would have been hilarious. Ronan wouldn't let me, though, so we compromised. "Ismys" is the middle section of "This Is My Smallest".'

'So is this one your biggest?' Sally nods at the mansion up ahead. 'I assumed we were going to a tiny, white-painted stone cottage.'

'My place in Devon has about the same square footage, I think,' says Corinne. 'Anyway, here we are.' She claps her hands together and yells, suddenly, 'Wake up, Lamberts! Let's get you inside.'

Champ makes a sort of yodelling noise from the boot: an extended yawn that might be a 'Hey, don't forget I'm here too,' or perhaps a tired, doggy version of 'Yay!'

'We're here, Champy,' Sally calls out to him over the groans and stretches of her waking husband and children, opening her door at the same time. 'We've made it. Safe at last,' she whispers to herself, just in case saying it into the silence of the night can help to make it true.

16

The second time Mum encountered Lesley Gavey was just over a month after the first sighting. Shukes was on the market by then and Mum had put herself in charge of showing him off to prospective buyers, determined only to sell him to someone who would love him 'as much as we do and always will.'

(I'm assuming you've noticed that The Hayloft, our new house, was not given a nickname by Mum. At no point did The Hayloft get 'himmed'.)

On 19 September 2023, Shukes's bell rang and Mum opened the door to the woman who had wept all over our village green a few weeks earlier. Mum recognised her instantly, and a shiver rippled through her whole body – not only because of their previous encounter, but also because Mum had been expecting a Mr Henry Christensen at that exact time, 10 o'clock. 'I'm here instead of him,'

Lesley Gavey told her, vigorously nodding and smiling in a way designed to work like radiation applied to a tumour on any questions that might have been sprouting in Mum's mind.

I was there too that day, overheard the exchange and willed Mum to pry further, but she didn't. Unacceptable! I was desperate to know: was the sobbing woman Mrs Christensen, representing them as a couple? Was that what she was implying, or did her ambiguous statement hint at something more sinister? Had she, perhaps, forcibly removed Mr Christensen from the scene in order to steal his viewing appointment? Chopped him up into little bits which she'd then tipped into the pond by Swaffham Tilney's war memorial?

Astonishingly, the answer to this question turned out to be 'not exactly, but kind of.'

Lesley Gavey, though she'd stopped short of killing him, had indeed stolen Mr Christensen's appointment. She wouldn't have called it a theft, but that's what it was: the entitled, posh-accented version of one, as Mum soon discovered. While boiling a kettle to make Lesley's tea ('Oh, thank you. But if possible a tall mug, not a cup, please. I can't bear cups, not for anything.') and with two closed doors between them, Mum rang Peter, the estate agent, whispering, 'Pick up, pick up,' half expecting her visitor to burst into the room and catch her. Just because Mum had left her sitting on the sofa in the lounge, that didn't mean the weeping woman would stay put; anyone who could lurk and sob and stare could also prowl without permission. Despite today's composed and smiley demeanour, no part of Mum believed she was dealing with a normal person. How, for instance, was it possible to find drinking from a cup unbearable, unless one was of unsound mind?

I was extremely wary of our visitor too. So was Champ. Since Lesley Gavey had arrived, he'd been following Mum everywhere she went. He sat by her feet now, alert, and seemed to be watching the kitchen door. Normally, in this room, his full attention would be focused on the pantry, where his goat chews and roe deer bones lived. As Mum clutched her phone to her ear and prayed for Peter to answer, a wild-feeling, free-wheeling part of her pictured herself marching, drinkless, back to the lounge and saying, 'I'm sorry but you can't have a mug of tea or a tour of the house. You need to leave. Immediately. And don't come back.'

But then Peter answered and Mum forgot about doing or saying any of that. 'That's right,' he confirmed. 'Mr Christensen booked the ten o'clock slot originally, but don't worry. I've put him in for three o'clock this afternoon.'

Lesley Gavey wasn't his wife, then. 'I don't understand,' Mum whispered. 'Did he need to rearrange for some reason?'

'He was quite happy to rearrange, yes,' said Peter.

That didn't satisfy Mum any more than it would have satisfied me. 'Did you ask him if he'd be willing to rearrange, or did he suggest it?' she said, feeling silly and guilty for wasting Peter's time with such a trivial-sounding question. She heard Dad's voice in her mind: 'Come on, Sal. What does it matter? Do you have to analyse every tiny detail?' Yet her question felt necessary; nothing about her present predicament seemed trivial.

'I asked him,' said Peter. He hesitated, then said, 'I suppose I should tell you… It appears that Mrs Gavey is quite determined to buy your house, Mrs Lambert, so please don't accept an offer from her without talking to me first. I've got a strong hunch that she'd pay quite a bit more than the asking price.'

'What makes you say that?' Mum asked.

'Where do I start?' Peter chuckled. 'She rang at nine o'clock this morning, said she was very near Swaffham Tilney and please could she view as soon as possible? I told her no – fully booked, all morning. Offered her an afternoon slot. Nope, had to be morning, she said – and then suddenly even morning wasn't good enough, when I suggested eleven thirty. Ten o'clock, she wanted. Almost insisted. Said, "I've seen the house from the outside, studied the details, and I know I want it. I'm a cash buyer, and unless I find a cupboard full of radioactive nuclear waste under the stairs, Shoe Cottage is going to be my forever home." She didn't let up until I thought of giving her Mr Christensen's appointment. I've met Henry a few times, though, so I knew he wouldn't mind. He's a proper gentleman. And between you and me, he never offers on anything. Keeps saying he hasn't yet found anything that makes his heart sing. I told him, most people are happy if there's off-street parking, never mind a singing heart.'

When Mum told Dad all of this later that evening, it started an argument between them. 'So she was keen on the house,' said Dad. 'Great. What's the problem?'

'*Was*,' said Mum. 'She definitely isn't any more, thank the Lord above. Nothing could give me greater joy than knowing Lesley Gavey's going to forget all about Shukes and us. Not that I'd have agreed to sell him to her under any circumstances, but I'm still relieved she's lost all interest in buying him. I'd hate to find out what it feels like to go through life as someone who's prevented that woman from getting something, anything, she wants.' Mum shuddered.

'You're talking about her as if she's Satan,' said Dad.

'I reckon she's… Satan-adjacent,' Mum told him. 'When Peter gave her the ten o'clock slot, he told her he'd ring me to let me know, and she ordered him not to. Said she'd tell me herself – but she didn't have my number, and she knew she didn't. Obviously she didn't want to risk Peter consulting me and me saying, "No, actually, I'd rather we didn't rearrange Mr Christensen", so she thought she'd just turn up and present me with a *fait accompli*.'

'I doubt it,' Dad said, even though doubting what Mum knows for sure is the habit that most often gets him into trouble. 'Why would she think you'd care whether it was her or—' He broke off with a dismissive wave of his hand. 'And so what, even if you're right? She was super-keen on Shukes, or thought she was, so she got a bit ruthless. Hardly a crime, is it? And now's she's been put off by the lack of back garden, so we'll never have to see her again. End of.'

'Yes. End of, thankfully,' Mum agreed. 'I'm just saying… You weren't there, Mark. Trust me, okay? She's not right in the head. Having her in the house was chilling. I wanted to fumigate the lounge once she'd gone.'

'Did she smell?' asked Dad.

'Not physically. But spiritually, at a soul level, she reeked. And Champ didn't like her at all.'

'You mean the way he doesn't like war movies or westerns or *Master and Commander* but just happens to love *Grey's Anatomy* and *The Good Wife* and whatever you want to watch?' Dad teased.

'She acted like I'd betrayed her or something,' said Mum. 'As if our house had deliberately, callously tricked her. She said, "When you see a nice, generous-sized front garden, all well-tended and nicely planted, you assume there's an even better garden at the back, don't you? Better *and quite a bit bigger*." Mark, she made me feel like I was the Bernie Madoff of house-selling. I don't know why it didn't occur to me to say, "No, actually, I wouldn't assume that and if you did, you're a fool." A front garden of any size or in any condition tells you nothing about the likely back garden situation. I mean, does it?'

'No,' said Dad.

'If anything, you'd see a front garden like ours that's

clearly been made the most of and think, "There's probably no back garden, or else why would they have made such a song and dance about this small patch at the front?"'

'Small patch?' Finally, Dad had found something to be alarmed by, and Mum was furious that it was her words and not Lesley Gavey's behaviour. 'I've never made a song and dance, as you put it, about our garden,' he huffed. 'I keep it nice, that's all. Look after my roses. Is there something wrong with that? The cheek of it! It's not even that small. Medium-sized, I'd say.'

Mum took a deep breath. 'You know I love our garden, Mark.' She thought, but did not add: *You know – or you would if you listened to me properly – that I can't stand the thought of leaving it or Shukes behind, and the only reason I'm willing to do both is because Champ needs more freedom than Furbs ever had, to go outside whenever he wants to without one of us always having to supervise.*

'I get it, Sal.' Dad yawned. 'This Lesley Gavey woman acted a bit sharp-elbowed with the estate agent to get a viewing arranged, then decided she was a "no" because she wants a back garden. Fair enough. Is that it? I mean… did anything else happen?'

'*Yes,*' Mum sort of wailed. 'A *lot*. I'm trying to tell you what happened, so stop… sounding like we're winding up the conversation.'

'All right, calm down.' Dad had the sense to swallow his next yawn. 'Tell me, then.'

And Mum started to do just that, though privately she

was full of doubts. Was it really 'a lot'? Would Dad agree? Did it amount to any more than the easily condensable 'She's a nutter, and good riddance to her'? Why did it feel so important to Mum to go over the details, as if everything had to be logged for future reference? She didn't want any of it to matter. She wanted never to have to think about Lesley Gavey again.

'Well, for a start, I found out why she was standing on the green last month, crying and staring at Shukes,' she told Dad. 'So that's something at least; I got to tick that off my unsolved puzzles list. There was a high price to pay for the privilege, however.'

'What do you mean?' Dad looked worried, probably imagining Mum had given Lesley Gavey some of our money. Mum, however, was referring to the currency of unpleasant experiences.

'I only got to find out the truth because she started weeping again,' she told Dad.

17

Tuesday 18 June 2024

Sally

The next day, Sally wakes up in a beautiful bedroom more than twice the size of her own. She knows it's beautiful, having seen it last night with the lights on.

It's morning. She and Champ have survived one night since the policeman's visit. That means they can survive many more; it stands to reason. Everything is looking and feeling better now that the Lamberts are in this luxurious sanctuary. Corinne's Lake District home is decorated and furnished exactly like Ismys House: furniture with elaborately carved wooden legs, white walls, wooden floors, gorgeous blocks of colour everywhere, more deep and rich than bright, and patterns only in the textures of things. Corinne explained that principle last night in response to Sally's compliment about the gorgeousness of everything. There was also art, lots and lots of it, some very ancient looking and some obviously modern: a mix of bright, splodgy abstracts and more subtly-coloured, darker paintings of actual things. Sally was too tired last night to inspect anything closely but she remembers lumpy, authentic-looking faces, a tractor in a muddy field in front of an orange sunrise, girls in white dresses sitting near a clump of reeds by the side of a lake. There were some framed pieces of writing too, which she made a mental note to read tomorrow. *Today.*

Champ is lying on the duvet beside her, stretched out and pressing into her side. This is one of his habits, and very different from Furbert, who used to curl up at the foot of the bed, or on the squashy, fat back of a nearby chair. Champ likes to get as close and pressed up against his humans as he can when settling in for the night; his Donut bed is only his favourite place for daytime naps. At bedtime, only the big bed with Mum and Dad will do.

'Soz, Champy, gotta get up. Me, not you,' Sally clarifies. She walks over to open the curtains, eager to see the room again now that she'll be able to focus properly on everything in it. She has slept deeply and feels refreshed, though there was one slightly disturbing dream: that she was on the run from the police (well, that was true – but in the dream there was an official manhunt, and she was its target, not Champ). Sally was proud to be an outlaw in the dream – one who spat in the face of the law and hated all representatives thereof.

'I do hate them,' she told herself doubtfully. It was certainly true that she scorned the teenager she had once been who'd idolised Cagney and Lacey. Covid and the lockdowns had changed her feelings about the police, probably forever. Ree and Tobes had been yelled at by a local uniformed dickhead in Cambridge for sitting on a bench side by side. 'Do you two live in the same house?' the cop had demanded.

'Yes, actually,' Ree told him, probably with some attitude – his own fault, given his rude, unfriendly tone – and he accused her of lying. He ordered her and Tobes to put more physical distance between them immediately if they didn't want to be taken to the nearest police station and have their parents summoned.

'Oh, please, *please*, ring my mum and make my day,' Ree said.

'Yeah, let's get Lester involved,' Tobes agreed. 'Good idea.'

Sally feels the same pride she felt when Ree first told her the story in April 2020. *My kids know I'll defend them, no matter what. Champ knows. Furbert, wherever he is, knows too.*

Especially against any bastard who called himself police while perpetrating more injustice than most criminals. Another one had stopped Sally for looking at her phone while in stationary traffic last November. Well, in fact, he *hadn't* stopped her, which was the whole point – she'd pointed it out to him, too. She was in traffic that wasn't moving – hadn't for nearly twenty minutes – and had her car in the 'Park' setting; she was going nowhere and a danger to nobody. PC Dickhead had been thrilled to tell her that didn't matter, that it was still against the law to have her phone in her hand. It had taken him half an hour to take all her details and give her a stern lecture, and then guess what? Nothing happened. Six months later Sally still hadn't heard from anyone official about it, and Mark said that meant she'd got away with it. The so-called justice system couldn't now do anything; her crime (as if! I mean, really...) was past its sell-by date and she was off the hook.

Mark and the kids had thought the whole episode was hilarious, especially the part where PC Dickhead had asked Sally if she was 'wanted for anything'. 'Yes!' she'd told him, exasperated. 'I'm on my way to meet a friend in town, and I'm running late. And then after that my mum's coming to stay. I'm wanted and needed by lots of people!' Quickly, efficiently, she'd then reeled off every good quality she could think of that she possessed, before concluding: 'That's why people want me in their lives! And you're wasting my time with this nonsense!'

It turned out the policeman had meant something different: was she wanted for any other offences? When he put her driver's licence number into his silly little machine, would he find out that there was a warrant out for her arrest?

The curtains won't open, which is annoying. Sally can't wait to see all the objects in the room she, Mark and Champ have slept in. What might they tell her about Corinne Sullivan, her family's mysterious guardian angel?

No One Would Do What The Lamberts Have Done

Sally can't work out if there's a mystery to be solved in relation to Corinne. Maybe she's just kind and helpful. Perhaps that's her only motivation for helping, and she will ask for nothing in return. But Mark thinks she's greedy and selfish; he whispered as much to Sally in bed last night. She told him to shush, then he did the same to her when she started to sing Champ's night song.

Sally is convinced Mark misunderstood the joke Corinne made soon after they got here. She told them they could stay as long as they liked, then laughed and added, 'Or, I suppose I should say: you're welcome to stay until Keir Starmer takes over from Rishi Sunak as Thief in Chief and decides to requisition all my properties for fun communist shindigs.'

Sally is proud of the successful resistance she put up, at 2 o'clock, in the face of Mark's determination to explain why Corinne having made this joke must mean she's a terrible person. Sally told him he was wrong and that she just wanted to sleep. She'd already spent far too much of the last month saying, 'Hmm' and 'Really?' while Mark ranted about the awfulness of those very same two men: Sunak and Starmer. Yet now Corinne insults them, and he's dead against her?

Sally has no desire to understand. She believes politics is nothing more than a distracting pantomime. Is there any way of knowing which of the various candidates for Prime Minister would be keenest to help Champy escape the so-called justice system, at great cost to himself and his party? Sally doesn't think so, and so she won't bother voting in the election on 4 July. It's unlikely she'll be back in Cambridgeshire before then anyway.

Which means, since it's only 18 June now...

Will Sally lose her job if she doesn't turn up for a week or two? Or more? Mark won't, she guesses. And didn't Corinne say last night that Sally shouldn't worry about money, that all would be made good on that front? What had she meant by that?

Nothing Sally tries persuades the bedroom curtains to open. Then she remembers she's not supposed to do it in the normal way. There are buttons that look like light switches but aren't. Corinne showed her last night. As she presses the one that looks most promising, a jhoom-ing sound starts up and the curtains begin to slide open as if they have all the time in the world.

The room floods with sunlight. Champ sits up on the bed, looking startled. 'Wow,' Sally says, staring out. 'Look at this, Champly Pamps.' There's a row of stone urns topped with huge lavender bushes and, beyond these, six large square lawns set out in front of the house, separated by corridors of reddish-orange gravel. Off to the right there's a long, high hedge and past that Sally can see a large swimming pool with white-cushioned outdoor sofas and chairs around it, and a tennis court. 'Shall we live here forever?' she says. Champ, who trotted over when Sally called him – seriously, he must be the most obedient dog in the world, which is extremely unusual for a Welshie or any kind of terrier – stands on his hind paws next to her, front paws on the windowsill. 'Impressive, or what? Maybe being on the run is going to be fun.' Sally starts to sing, 'Being on the run, Is gonna be fun, Being on the run, Is going to be fun,' then stops when the door swings open with a loud creak.

Sally expects to see Mark, but it's Corinne, carrying a large yellow pottery mug. 'Earl Grey in the morning, Lapsang Souchong at night, right? That's the intel from your son. Hope he's right, 'cause this is Earl Grey. Morning, Champ!' Corinne strokes the top of his head.

Sally takes the tea and thanks her, then looks at the wall-mounted clock that's been ticking insistently all through the night. It has an antique appearance – the top is a kind of wooden balcony arrangement with a rearing horse on it, front legs pointing upward. If it's telling the correct time, then this is the latest Sally has woken up since having children: twenty to eleven.

'Tobes has surfaced this early?' Sally is surprised.

'No, he'll be asleep by now,' Corinne says. 'Ree too. I caught them at eight, on their way in from the piggery.' She grins and says approvingly, 'They'd had an all-night movie and hot tub marathon. Dripping all over the floor in their cozzies, they were.'

'Oh, God, I'm so sorry,' says Sally. Then her brain catches up and she asks, 'What cozzies?'

'Their swimming costumes.' Corinne narrows her eyes, perhaps wondering if Sally's mental faculties are in proper working order. 'The ones they packed because I told them there was a hot tub and a pool here.'

'Right. Sorry.'

'I take it you forgot yours. Don't worry, I've got plenty of spares. Listen, Sally...' Corinne's expression turns serious. 'There's something you need to see. Full disclosure: it's going to upset you.'

Sally's heart plunges to the pit of her stomach.

'It looks horrible, but it doesn't change anything, so there's no new bad news or anything,' says Corinne. 'I'm going to tell you what it is before I show you the picture, so that you're prepared. Tess Gavey has posted a photograph of the... bite on her arm. On her Instagram account. It looks awful. But the good news is, she hasn't named Champ or accused him or anything. For now, all she's done is post a photo with the comment "hashtag bitten."'

'How...' That's the most Sally can manage.

'How do I know?' Corinne fills in the blanks. 'I looked, that's how. And I found it. It's a private account, as I expected it to be, so I requested to follow from the coolest of my fake-name accounts, and I was in within the minute – that's no exaggeration – no questions asked. I'm also monitoring Lesley Gavey on Facebook, where the silly woman's dumb enough to have a public account. There's been nothing from her yet about a dog biting her daughter.'

Sally is trying very hard not to dissolve into tears. She should have made Corinne leave her phone in Swaffham

Tilney too, she thinks. Not that she had or has the power to decree any such thing, but it's horrifying to feel so ambushed. It's as if the Gaveys are here with them in this beautiful house in the Lake District, doing and saying terrible Gavey-ish things – contaminating the safe haven, teleported in by technology.

'He didn't do it, Corinne.'

'I know he didn't. Sally, I'm not an idiot. If you think I'm feeling sorry for Tess Gavey just because she's shown the world her munched up arm flesh—'

'However bad her injury looks, that doesn't mean Champ did it.' Sally's insides have turned to liquid. 'He'd never bite anyone. Never! He's so sweet and affectionate, just a big bundle of love.'

'Sally, you don't need to convince me.'

Munched up arm flesh... Oh, God.

'If Tess is so badly hurt, the police will be determined to make Champ pay.' Sally starts to cry. 'I assumed the bite was just... like, a little nick, maybe a pinprick or two of blood. That's the worst Furbert ever did. I've got four or five scars from him and they're all *tiny*. I never needed more than one little plaster.'

'Sally, it's going to be fine.' Corinne pulls her into a hug. 'I feel like a shit for upsetting you, but... I thought you'd want to be aware of what the Gaveys are doing, that's all. Maybe I should have kept quiet and just kept an eye on it myself.'

'No.' Mark's voice comes from the doorway. 'Whatever

they're doing, online and off, the more we know the better. That photo Tess posted...' He whistles.

'How do you know about it?' Sally snaps at him.

'I showed him,' says Corinne.

'Can we all meet downstairs?' Mark says. 'I want to have a serious conversation. Everything spiralled out of control yesterday, and I went along with it, but... we've got to get a grip on things, Sal.'

Corinne glances at the clock. 'Shall we say eleven? In the morning room? First door on the right past the kitchen, between the kitchen and the back stairs.'

'I need to get dressed and... sort myself out,' says Sally. Can she do that by eleven? Will she ever be able to do anything effectively again?

She's furious with Mark, and can't manage more than a nod when he suggests he take Champ for a quick walk round the garden. Calling meetings in someone else's house, talking about getting grips on things. It turns out there's no such thing as having a grip on life; doesn't he realise?

When she's alone in the room again, Sally walks over to the unmade bed and sits on it, cross-legged and crying. Just before eleven, she manages to persuade herself to stand up. She'd better text Mark to say she'll be a bit later than eleven... but, no, she can't do that, since her phone is in Swaffham Tilney at The Hayloft and so is his.

Slowly, she walks towards the framed poem that's hanging to the left of the clock. Its title is 'My Granny'

No One Would Do What The Lamberts Have Done

and the author is apparently a Maisie Sullivan. One of Corinne's grandchildren, Sally guesses. It's short:

Granny is my favourite,
Her hair flows in golden, wavy tresses,
She always wears long, black dresses.
She drives me to ballet lessons sometimes in her car.
I really love my lovely grandmarmar.

There's a drawing beneath the words that looks like a young child's attempt to create Corinne out of multicoloured felt-tip pens.

On the other side of the clock hangs another framed poem, a longer one. 'It Matters' is the title. This one definitely isn't by a grandchild. Sally's eyes are drawn to the last stanza:

Dear friend, you deserve all good things and better.
You know how much I love you and admire you.
Obey this next instruction to the letter:
Never work for someone who can fire you.

There's a bit in italics between the title and the start of the first verse, a kind of dedication: '*For my brilliant, talented friend and mentee Corinne, who keeps getting fired by ungrateful dimwits.*'

Sally looks for an indication of who the author might be, but there are only two small initials in the bottom right-hand corner – HS – and a date: 23 February, 2008. How old would Corinne have been then? She's in her early to mid-fifties now, Sally guesses, which means she was maybe mid to late thirties in 2008.

'Sally? You ready?' Mark's voice reaches her as if from very far away. 'Sal!'

'Coming!' she calls back, feeling much better suddenly. If a world in which people fired Corinne Sullivan existed as recently as 2008 – a world that, now, cannot be conceived of – that means future unrecognisable worlds are possible too. Worlds with no munched-up arm flesh, no false accusations, no need for Champ to hide from anyone.

A world with no Gaveys, Sally thinks to herself. *Wouldn't that be wonderful?*

18

Mum told Dad what happened during the stolen viewing of Shukes (stolen from poor Mr Henry Christensen) and about Lesley Gavey weeping in front of her for a second time. She didn't tell him in her usual way, however: really giving it her all, both detail-wise and emotionally. No, she decided to play a game in which she pretended to be a robot, determined to strip her account of her own point of view and relinquishing all attempts to shape Dad's opinion.

His initial responses had not been encouraging, and Mum had a self-preserving routine for such occasions (like when all the non-furry Lamberts refused to believe her car engine kept weirdly cutting out, and told her the car was fine and it must be something she was doing wrong – until Dad drove it, it broke down, and instantly everyone accepted the engine was the problem, not Mum, and the garage was summoned to tow it away and fix it).

Mum felt strangely invigorated whenever she knew she had no one's full support. It sparked a sense of power inside her, a sort of recognition that this was what she was born and trained for, that she was moving closer to her essence. She'd felt it for the first time aged thirteen, during The Gardenia Incident: a heroic (but also quite bitchy) inner voice that was braver than her had said, 'Okay, then, you soul-crushing despot. If you really want to earn my hatred, let's fucking go. I'm going to be ready for you from now on.' Mum knew there was a big difference between Dad and her own father. She didn't think *my* Dad, Mark Lambert, was a despot, but she was sure he was a contrary git who loved to quibble wherever possible.

Tonelessly, she gave him only the facts that would have been provable in a court of law: she'd shown Lesley the front garden first, then the lounge, the den, the downstairs loo, the utility room. In each of these, Lesley had emitted a loud sigh of contentment and said things like, 'Oh, it's gorgeous!' and/or 'You couldn't have made it look more incredible' and/or 'This is *so* lovely! What an exquisite colour – is it Farrow and Ball?' (It was: Vardo. A bold choice for what used to be a small lean-to at the side of the house.)

Mum wondered how the outside of Shukes could have caused Lesley Gavey such distress on 12 August, and then the inside such joy on 19 September. 'Oh, I forgot to say,' she told Dad, 'I found out from Peter that she'd rung him in early August to ask if anything would soon be going on the market in Swaffham Tilney, anything that wasn't on

Rightmove yet. He told her about Shukes – name, address, everything. *That's* why she was there that day in August.'

'Who's Peter?'

'Our estate agent.'

'Right.' Dad nodded.

'Anyway, then I took her into the kitchen, and that was her favourite room of the whole downstairs, she said. The sight of it made her yelp with joy. She started praising my good taste, but in a mad, almost desperate way, as if I'd saved her life or something.' At this point, since Dad was properly listening now, Mum abandoned her attempt at objective narration. 'It was like… I don't know how to describe it. Like I'd set up a new religion with… with our kitchen as the main deity, and she wanted to be the first…'

'Disciple?' Dad suggested.

'Exactly. It was embarrassing. Normally I'm good at taking compliments graciously, as long as it's only one or two. But she went on and on: how clever I was not to have worktops darker than the drawers and cupboard doors—'

Dad looked indignant. 'I hope you told her I was the one who chose our counter tops.'

'I couldn't get a word in edgeways – not until later, when she was miserable. For as long as she was happy, she gushed on and on, and then Champ came in and she patted and stroked him and said he was a lovely boy whose mum had just as good taste in dogs as she did in kitchen cabinets and floor tiles. At one point she froze, and I was terrified she was having a heart attack. Then she said breathlessly,

"Are these tiles Fired Earth's Galicia? They're my favourite in the whole world!" I had no idea if they were or weren't. I forgot the name and brand as soon as I'd picked them – which I was about to tell her, until she gasped with horror, having noticed what was beyond the kitchen windows. "What's that yard?" she said.

"'It's just a little yard," I told her, feeling proud of how cosy it was looking. It was full of sunlight, I'd watered the pot plants and swept and plumped up the cushions on the chairs. To be honest, she'd been so ecstatic about everything else, I was kind of waiting for her to say, "Oh, this yard is the most heavenly thing I've ever seen and you should enter it for a landscape design competition in the Small Back Yards category."'

'No such luck?' Dad guessed.

'Er, no. The honeymoon period was well and truly over. She said, "Well, then, where's the back garden?", and her voice sounded tight – completely different, total change of demeanour. And she shooed Champ away from her suddenly, as if he was a pest. That was the worst thing she did. Poor Champy! And she'd been so friendly to him until then. Honestly, I was scared when I told her there was no back garden of the kind she was clearly expecting. Her plan at first was evidently to put a brave face on it. All she said was, "I see", though she sounded furious and sort of… refused to look at me.'

'Sal, I'm not happy about you doing these viewings,' said Dad. 'Can't the estate agent take over? I don't want you having to cope with any loon who feels like turning up.'

'This particular loon won't be back, I promise you,' Mum told him. 'I put on my brightest voice and said, "Shall I show you the upstairs?" and she did a funny thing with her head. It started as a nod but turned into a weird neck-twisty head-shake. She looked, honestly, as if a malign spirit had possessed her and was writhing inside her body.'

'I hope you booted her out,' said Dad. 'I would have.'

'I left her in the lounge while I went to make her a cup… sorry, a *mug* of tea, and when I got back there, she was all heaving sobs and streaming tears, just like the day she was outside the house in August. I didn't even have the chance to ask her what was wrong. She started laying into me—'

'This is so out of order.' Dad shook his head. He looked ready to spring out of his chair and deck someone.

Lesley Gavey had accused both Mum and Peter, the estate agent, of being con-men ('Though she immediately amended it to "con-people", for added inclusivity,' Mum told Dad.) How dared they fail to draw attention, in Shukes's sale brochure, to the lack of a back garden? ('But it's there, under the heading "Outside": "beautiful, cottage-style front garden and paved back yard." How much clearer could it be?' 'I know, Mark. Please stop shouting at me. I'm not Lesley Gavey, remember?')

She'd demanded a box of tissues. Shukes didn't have one, so Mum offered to get her a roll of loo paper instead. On her way out of the room, she half heard something that was definitely intended as a complaint sent up to the heavens — a railing against Fate's twisted cruelty — but she couldn't quite make out the words on account of all the blubbing.

She turned. 'Pardon?'

'Nothing,' Lesley Gavey said in a hard voice. 'It doesn't matter.'

On her way to fetch the toilet roll, with Champ at her side, Mum whispered, 'It matters to me, actually. I'm going to make her tell me, Champy.' What she thought she'd heard, though surely it couldn't have been, was: 'This was supposed to be my poor house.'

The stress was on the 'poor', with 'house' following after it as if it was all one word, if that was indeed what Lesley had said and Mum hadn't misheard.

Mum's mind went straight to Victorian workhouses and to Dad saying, while they were watching *Scrooged* one Christmas, that the writer Charles Dickens's father had been sent to the poorhouse at some point, or the workhouse. Or maybe it was Dickens himself who'd gone there, Mum couldn't remember.

This was supposed to be my poor house.

The last Agatha Christie novel that Swaffham Tilney's book club had discussed before it died in a blaze of entirely unnecessary acrimony was *By The Pricking of My Thumbs*. That story opens with an elderly lady asking, 'Was it your poor child?' while staring into a fireplace. Knowing that Agatha's famous sleuth Miss Marple liked to look for parallels, Mum tried to do the same, but could think of nothing that made sense. How could Lesley Gavey have believed at any point that Shukes was meant to be her Victorian-style workhouse? It was surreal and ludicrous. Mum told herself she must have heard wrong.

After handing over a brand-new loo roll, which Lesley received with a wrinkled nose and fingers that bucked and fluttered, Mum asked her what she'd said before. 'Something about a poor house, wasn't it?'

'I told you, it was nothing. Will you please drop it?' Lesley snapped.

But, no, Mum wouldn't. She told Dad: 'I refused to accept that she might leave without telling me. Our house wasn't her anything, and I wanted to know what crazy story she'd made up about it. If it's my house, then it's my business. I asked her once more, and out it all came in a big splurge: she and her family were about to become what she called "dirt poor". It was all her husband's fault – bad investments, too much letting debts get out of control – and so they were having to sell their seventeen-acre smallholding in Oxfordshire and buy somewhere for maximum six-hundred grand. After a period of feeling suicidal, she identified Swaffham Tilney and a few others – Reach, Swaffham Bulbeck, Burwell – as villages that were pretty, quiet and safe, though no civilised person would live in any of them by choice, of course—'

'She said that?' asked Dad.

Mum nodded. 'Swaffham Tilney was her favourite, she realised after a few trips to Cambridgeshire. She rang round estate agents, heard about Shukes from Peter and ordered him to send photos before he'd even finished putting the brochure together, even though Shukes was right up there at her six-hundred-grand limit, and to be honest with me, Sally, she'd hoped to find something palatable for less than five-hundred, but every single other home on the market in her price range was a disgusting hovel—'

'She really said that?'

'So it felt like Shukes or nothing,' Mum went on. 'When she stood on the village green weeping in August, that was a bad day for her.'

'Yeah, we guessed as much,' said Dad.

'She'd come with high hopes, to look at Shukes for the first time. Peter had told her viewings were still some way off, we were still at the preparations stage, but she couldn't resist coming to have a nosey from the outside. She hoped she'd see Shukes and know instantly he was the one for her: the home in which she could be blissfully happy, even though dirt poor.'

'No one who can afford a six-hundred-grand house is poor at all, in any way, shape or form,' said Dad. 'This woman needs a check-up from the neck up. I hope you told her.'

'To be fair, she realised she might have offended me, and apologised: "I'm sorry, Sally. I know you probably don't think of this house as any sort of... massive comedown. I actually envy you. I wish I could see it the way you do. I'd be so much happier."'

No One Would Do What The Lamberts Have Done

Dad was shaking his head.

'When she came in August for her outdoor recce, what set her off crying was that Shukes looked so much smaller than in the photos Peter had emailed her.'

'It's not small!' Dad protested. 'We have *five* bedrooms and three reception rooms, excluding the kitchen! We have a bedroom specially for when I'm drunk and snoring and you don't want to sleep with me, and we also have the spare room you call Furbert's room. How many people have so much space, they can reserve entire bedrooms for urns containing dead pets?'

'There's no need to yell our floorplan at me.' He was so indignant, Mum couldn't help smiling. 'Also, Furbert's room isn't a spare room. It's *his* room. And Shukes is a he, not an it.'

'Yeah, if you say so.' Dad sighed.

'It's true, Mark,' Mum said patiently. 'Furbert's soul is still with us – it's not about the urn, it's about *him*. It means a lot to him to have his own dedicated room, even though he's... you know...'

'If our house was so shockingly small, why did the Gavey woman make a viewing appointment?' Dad asked.

'She didn't think she would at first, not once she'd seen it from the outside. But then she looked again at the alternatives and reminded herself of their depressing hovel-iness, and her husband, whom she seems to detest, kept telling her she needed to compromise instead of thinking she could be Lady of the Manor forever... and *then*, she said, she noticed how stunning some of the tiny little details were in the photos of each of Shukes's rooms, and at that point she fell in love. Until…'

'No back garden,' said Dad.

'Correct. That was when she decided I'd let her down, because Shukes was supposed to be flawless apart from his too-smallness: her perfect house to be poor but happy in. She'd done her bit – compromised, forgiven him his inadequate square footage – but he hadn't even met her halfway. He'd rubbed salt into her wounds, and so had I, and so had Peter, by arranging for there to be no proper back garden, just to spite Lesley Gavey.'

'Right, well, if she comes back with an offer of double the asking price, we're not selling to her.' Dad looked fierce.

'Agreed. Don't worry, she won't be back. From her point of view, Shukes fucked around and now he's going to have to find out – to use a Ree-ism. She really was awful, Mark. Having got all that off her chest, she ordered a second mug of tea as if I was a branch of Costa, then proceeded to interrogate me: was I *truly* happy, in this cramped, confined space that I called home? Was that why I'd made every inch of it so immaculate and beautiful, to compensate? Have I ever been more materially fortunate than I am now, and if so, do I miss it? Did we somehow lose our fortune or were we born poor and deprived?'

'You've got to be exaggerating now.' Dad's eyes widened. 'Tell me you're making it up.'

'Definitely not making it up,' said Mum. 'Maybe exaggerating a *tiny* bit, but trust me, that was the gist. "And you've got a dog!" she said, properly laughing in a kind of admiring-the-bonkersness way, as if pet-parenting is an absurdly ambitious thing to attempt, given the huge financial constraints we're clearly under. Then she noticed the framed portrait of Furbs and asked if that was Champ and I told her it wasn't, it was Furbert, our first dog. And then, I don't know why, but... I started to tell her all about him. It was as if her sadness kind of... reached into me and brought out all my grief, and I thought maybe she was as sad to have to leave her home as I was sad about Furbs. Maybe her house felt like a member of the family, the way Shukes does to me. But then she soon made me hate myself for telling her anything at all, because when I happened to mention Furby's full name, she looked affronted and said, "*Furbert Herbert Lambert* – are you serious, Sally?" I told her I was and guess what the nasty witch said?'

'That it's a daft name?' Dad's face assumed a mischievous expression. 'I seem to remember someone else saying something sim—'

'She frowned and said, "It's not fair to give a dog a joke name like that, Sally. It's disrespectful, actually." That's when I told her to stick it up her vicious arse and fuck off.'

'You said that? Nice one!'

'My version of that, yes,' said Mum. 'I pretended to remember an important Zoom meeting that was starting in five minutes, and told her she had to leave.'

19

Tuesday 18 June 2024

Sally

The Lamberts' burner phones arrive at Corinne's Lake District house just before midday, brought to the door by a man who gives them to her with a discreet nod, then walks away without a single word being exchanged. Soon afterwards, something else happens without the involvement of words: Sally comes to understand that Corinne Sullivan is Ree and Toby's new favourite person. Now, at her large kitchen table (carved from just one tree previously in the garden outside, Corinne told them as they sat down), they are both staring at her wide-eyed, as if she contains magic. Hot tub cinemas, miraculous phone deliveries – not only in the middle of nowhere but before breakfast, which is imminent now that the youngsters have surfaced… No one else Ree and Tobes know could lay on all of this.

Sally worries that everything is dangerously out of control. Who is the man who brought the phones? And who are the two silent, pleasant-but-blank-faced young women cooking sausages and bacon a mere twenty or so feet away? Their agreement with Corinne, clearly, is that all three of them will pretend they aren't there, and Sally feels she has no choice but to go along with this charade, though it feels extremely odd to her.

How many people are there, she wonders, who slip in and out of Corinne's life, performing various services for her? How many more will turn up today, or tomorrow? Anyone who sees the Lamberts here will be in a position, if anything reaches the news about a Welsh Terrier and his family in flight from the law, to make a call and dob them in to the authorities, even knowing what that might mean for Champ.

At one time Sally would have imagined most people were far too decent to inform on their relatives, friends and neighbours to that useless joke that calls itself a police force despite not giving a toss about justice anymore (Mark says this all the time, so Sally is inclined to believe him, especially after she was treated like a criminal for glancing at her phone while stuck in a traffic jam). Now she believes most people would betray even their nearest and dearest in order to comply with the latest nonsensical rule.

During the Covid lockdowns, Sally's friend Oonagh got a visit from some killjoys in blue after her nextdoor neighbour called the police on her. All Oonagh had done was have her lonely, elderly mother round for lunch; no one else was affected. Sally is convinced (Mark says this often too) that the majority of people have lost all their moral marbles and get angrier about people eating cake in their offices and sitting on park benches with their brothers than they do about an excrescence of evil like the Gavey family trying to get innocent dogs killed. This isn't happening only in England, either – didn't Mark say that in Canada, the president or prime minister, whatever his name is, has started confiscating the pets of any lorry drivers who disagree with him? And isn't that same chap also encouraging all Canadians who are a bit fed up to kill themselves?

Sally has laughed at Mark in the past when he's said these crazy-sounding things, but now she's thinking he's probably right. She's never felt more suspicious of supposedly trustworthy institutions in her life. She can't help eyeing Corinne's sausage-and-egg coordinators at the far end of the kitchen and wondering exactly how willing they might prove, if the price were right, to usher groups of dispirited Canadians into rooms reserved for the opposite of Enjollification – or, more to the point, to inform on poor Champy.

The more delighted her children seem by Corinne's every utterance and deed, the more afraid Sally feels. There's a danger, surely, in assuming too much about someone who's all movies and hot tubs from the word go. What if Corinne...

No. Don't doubt the only person who's made a significant positive difference since this nightmare began. Don't do that, Sally.

No One Would Do What The Lamberts Have Done

The kitchen helpers have started to transport heaped breakfast plates across the room. Pushing Ree's phone away from him, Mark says, 'Can we please log off from Tess Gavey's wound before we eat? We've all seen it now, from all angles.' His and Sally's phones are still in their boxes; Ree and Tobes leapt on theirs as soon as Corinne handed them over, and set them up within minutes. Since they and Corinne-under-a-false-name all follow Tess Gavey on Instagram, Sally has already seen Tess's mangled, bloody, bruised forearm on three separate devices.

'*Log off?*' Toby shakes his head in disgust.

'The idea that Champ would *ever* do that to anyone,' says Ree. 'I mean... she's going to be scarred for life, right, Mum?'

'Oh, yes,' says Corinne, before thanking the blank-faced servers and telling them they won't be needed for the next hour. She turns back to Ree. 'Let that be our first consolation: Tess will be hideously disfigured for the rest of her life.'

'Corinne—' Sally starts to say.

'Oh, shut up, Mum!' says Ree cheerfully, and Sally feels churlish for disapproving of the joke that cheered her up. 'Tess is already disfigured – by her personality. She's a sociopath.'

'True,' Tobes confirms.

'You've never mentioned this before,' says Sally, pressing one tine of her fork into a baked bean. She doesn't fancy eating anything, though it smells good and is glossier and better-presented than any breakfast she's ever cooked herself.

'From the minute she turned up at college, she decided she hated me. And she let me know it at every opportunity,' says Ree. 'She'd take photos of all the girls, then crop me out of every single one. I'd get three-quarters of the way through a sentence and then she'd interrupt – like turn away and say something to someone else. Then she'd turn back to me and go, "Sorry, Ree, what were you saying?" Oh, and she'd do the stupid eye-contact thing too: look at everyone else and be ever so engrossed and attentive, and no one would notice that she'd not looked in my direction once, despite being part of the same group as me for hours sometimes.'

'That's bullying,' says Sally. 'You should have told me.'

'Why? I told her instead,' says Ree. 'I said, "I can see through every single bit of your crap" – and within hours of me saying that very publicly, Tess had no friends. Hasn't had any since, either. She sits on her own every break, every lunchtime.'

'Everyone took your side?' Corinne asks.

'Yeah, but, like, not in a heartwarming or inspiring way.'

'What do you mean?' says Sally.

'The girls took my side for one reason only, same reason Tess targeted me as her social-ostracism victim in the first place. Unfortunately, I can't say what that reason is without sounding like I love myself and think I'm the shit, so...' Ree shrugs.

'You're prettier and cleverer,' says Tobes.

'Aw, cheers, bruv.' Ree leans over to try to give him a hug, but fails because the table is too big. 'No one in my year cares about clever, but... yeah, I'm better looking and I'm more confident. Especially because, soon after moving to Swaffham Tilney, Tess's looks just... I mean, this sounds nasty, but I'm just trying to be descriptive – something *terrible* happened to her face. When she first arrived, she looked sort of okay-ish—'

'Like, maybe a seven,' says Tobes. 'No, a six. But Ree's right. Her face changed shape, it was the weirdest thing. And sometimes she stinks too. I'd say she's no higher than a four now.'

Mark shoots a horrified look at Sally – *Is this our son, rating humans out of ten based on their looks?* – but, in her present mood, Sally is willing to let it pass. Champ's safety has been threatened thanks to Tess's slanderous dishonesty, so forgive Sally for hoping the lying cow is soon further demoted to a two after her face takes on an even more suboptimal shape – maybe that of a giraffe, or a sewing machine. 'Being Lesley Gavey's daughter, with all that entails, would be enough to change the shape of anyone's face,' she mutters.

'Once Tess was crying and I felt sorry for her, so I sidled over and asked her what was wrong,' Ree says. 'She started yelling at me about how the oceans were going to die from being full of too much plastic, and I didn't even care, and only she cared. After that, I thought, "Yeah, someone else can help you out next time you're upset, weirdo."'

'Show me Lesley's Facebook page,' says Sally. 'Unless... are you sure it's not traceable to me, if I look at the internet on your phone?'

Ree groans. Tobes covers his face with his hands.

Corinne picks up her phone and is about to hand it to Sally when there's a small beep. She reads a message, frowning, then closes her eyes for a second. 'Shit.'

'What?' Panic rears up inside Sally. 'Have the police found out we're here?'

'No. Sal, relax. And eat something.' Corinne looks at her sternly. 'You ate nothing last night. Wasting away isn't going to help anything – and it's also against the ethos of Champ, who, I've noticed, does a little dance of joy every time anyone puts food out for him.'

This is true. Sally knows Champ would want her to eat. Maybe a few beans and a bit of bacon. Is it okay for Corinne to be calling her 'Sal' just because she's heard Mark do so?

'But... are you sure it's... ?' She points to the phone.

'It's nothing, really. Nothing to do with you or Champ. Just a headache for me.' Corinne mumbles something sneery, tapping away at the screen with her thumbs. 'There, take that, you arse,' she tells the absent headache-creator. 'Typically I have to deal with about fifteen a day at least – cretins sticking their oars in and messing up things that are working perfectly well.'

'Innit, though,' says Tobes. 'School,' he tells a puzzled-looking Mark. 'Teachers.'

No One Would Do What The Lamberts Have Done

Corinne finds Lesley Gavey's Facebook page, then passes her phone to Sally who is soon transfixed. Mark turns the conversation to the important plans he's wanted to discuss since he woke up, and what the next normal-life-recovering move ought to be. Soon he and Corinne hit a point of disagreement, but Sally hears none of it. She can't take her eyes off what Lesley Gavey has chosen to post on social media. And her account goes back years. *This is incredible.* But wait…

Sally's heart lurches. 'Shukes,' she says. 'She's put up a photo of Shukes. Oh, my God!'

Everyone stops talking.

'Is there any way of deleting a picture or post from someone else's Facebook?' Sally asks Toby. Rage speeds through her system like an out-of-control train, unafraid of what it might crash into.

'The best you can do is report the account,' says Ree. 'Why, what is it?'

'Tenth of August last year, she posted it – two days before she turned up crying,' says Sally. 'Guess what the caption says?'

No one seems to want to guess. Eventually Mark says, '"I like this house and might want to buy it. What does everyone think?" Something like that?'

'Except without the "might",' Sally tells him. 'And much shorter. Just three words: "My new house". And there are sixteen comments – *sixteen!* – congratulating her, telling her it's beautiful. The tenth of August, Mark. Last year. Shukes was *ours* then. He hadn't even gone on the market.'

'"He"?' says Corinne, and Ree gives her a 'Don't ask' look.

'And then she came for a viewing and didn't even want him, yet this post is still here! Why hasn't she taken it down? I know why,' Sally goes on without drawing breath. 'She's a fraud through and through. There's not an *ounce* of truthfulness in her. Are there any photos of her *actual* new house? No! The Stables and Bussow Court aren't as pretty and chocolate-box-villagey as Shukes and The Green, so she's happy for everyone to believe she lives in a house that's nothing to do with her and never was. Look at this collage of lies!'

Sally holds Corinne's phone up so everyone can see. 'Nearly all the pictures are of her, Alastair and Tess hugging each other and grinning as if they're the happiest family in the world. You'd think they do nothing but trot around the world together having fun: ice-skating, bramble picking, baking, sunbathing in a field. Not screaming, though — never screaming vitriol at each other, which is what they do almost daily in real life. Every caption is just… nauseatingly dishonest. "Love my family", "Blessed with the best", "So proud of my little squad". Ugh, I thought I couldn't loathe her more, but—'

'Tell me about the screaming,' Corinne says.

'That can wait,' says Mark. 'Deciding what we're going to do takes priority. I'll put my cards on the table: I think we should go back. Home,' he clarifies.

Sally's mouth has dropped open. 'Mark, we only left

there *yesterday*. Because it wasn't and isn't safe to be in Swaffham Tilney at the moment. Remember?'

'I gave it some thought overnight and this morning,' he says. 'Champ didn't bite Tess, and we can prove it. I mean, I know no one keeps dental records for dogs, but—'

'I'm not taking Champ back,' Sally tells him. 'No way. You can all go if you want, but Champ and I stay here.'

'For how long, Sal?' Mark sighs. 'Please hear me out, okay? I don't know exactly how it would work – I know nothing about the... dog court system, or whatever it's called – but I'm reasonably confident we can assemble solid proof that convinces everyone who matters – lawyers, the police – that Champ can't have done that to Tess. All it'd take is an imprint of his teeth marks to... No, don't interrupt me. I've uprooted my existence and come with you, almost no questions asked—'

'*Uprooted your existence?*' Ree laughs. 'Dad, I mean... Peace and love, but all you've done is come to the Lake District for a night.'

'So far, yes.' Mark glares at her. 'That's my whole point. I've got a job, Ree. Mum's got a job. We can't just go off on an exciting... Champ-rescuing adventure with no end in sight.'

Exciting? Is he insane? Sally wonders.

'Look, there's never going to be a massive manhunt for a dog that goes AWOL, is there?' he goes on. 'No one cares enough to spend precious resources on something like that. It's just not going to be a high priority for the police – which means there's not likely to be a big, dramatic showdown any time soon, after which it'll all be over. If we choose to remain unfindable, no one's going to come looking. So, what, we have to stay away from home and our jobs forever? Well, we can't – we just can't. And even if we wait it out for weeks or months, the minute we go back, it'll all start up again. The police will come knocking and try to carry on where they left off, soon as they hear from the Gaveys that the Lamberts are back in Bussow Court. So, the way I see it is – let's just go home and tackle it. I think we've got a pretty good chance—'

'Pretty good isn't enough for Sally,' Corinne tells him.

Sally doesn't want to go back to The Hayloft. Not soon, and maybe not at all. It has never felt like home in the way Shukes did and still does, though she's been happy to kid herself and hope that will change. The Hayloft doesn't have a nickname, doesn't feel like a member of the Lambert family – and that's at least fifty per cent Lesley Gavey's fault. The Gaveys moved into Bussow Court three days after the Lamberts.

If only Sally had known... but for once, the village gossip network failed to deliver. News of who had bought The Stables didn't reach Sally in time, and when she finally found out, it was too late. It was scant consolation that Lesley Gavey was even more appalled: the last thing she'd expected was to end up living so close to Sally, whom she associated only with misery and disappointment. She even told Sally as much. 'Why do you think I moved to this end of the village?' she hissed. 'To be far away from you and your stifling, tiny house!' As if that wasn't offensive enough, Lesley grabbed Sally's arm, leaned in and said, 'I'm afraid you and I are never going to be friends, Sally. I hope you understand that and can come to terms with it.'

'Can I tell you my best suggestion of a plan?' says Corinne. 'Mine doesn't rely on guesswork or the reasonableness of other people.'

'I want to hear it,' says Ree. Toby nods.

'Okay, so… a question.' Corinne pushes her plate away and folds her arms. 'Is Champ microchipped?'

Sally is all ready to answer when she happens to glance down at Corinne's phone that she's been clutching all this time. She makes a strangled noise, like a scream that's fallen into a thresher.

'What's wrong, Sal?' Mark asks.

Sally holds up the phone, her hand shaking. 'The message you just got,' she manages to say. 'It's from her. You were lying,' she snaps at Corinne. 'It *was* about Champ. It's from Lesley Gavey.'

20

The convention, in circumstances such as these, is to make you wait a little longer before revealing that, although Corinne Sullivan lied about the message she received, she did not, in fact, betray Champ or Mum. I'm not going to delay in reassuring you, though, because Corinne was with the Lamberts all the way and would never have dreamed of going over to the Gaveys' side.

You have to be loyal to your people, or else what does anything matter? Corinne knows this. I know it. That's why I feel worse and worse, the further into the story I get, about the important thing I'm not telling you, and the name I'm desperate to mention but can't. If you recall, it's the name of someone who means the world to me, someone who's cared for me when I've been ill (once I even vomited on her and she didn't mind) and loved me with all her heart from the first day we met. And I have always reciprocated every ounce and inch of that love. That's why I've decided to give you a clue, as a tribute to the special person whose name I can't yet say.

The clue is: SIBLING.

Perhaps, now I've said all that, you'll understand why the thing I abhor most about the Gaveys is not the way they've treated us Lamberts, but that they aren't even kind and loyal to other Gaveys. (Remember the screaming Corinne asked about over breakfast, before Dad changed the subject?) And there are only three of them, so it shouldn't be too hard for them to be nice to each other; it's not as if there are thousands of Gaveys stretching as far as the eye can see, which might over-extend anyone's magnanimity.

I wish I'd spoken up and said this (a point I've heard no one else make so far) on the way to the boarding kennels in Weybourne, Norfolk, later that day. It would have been the perfect opportunity, since Mum and Corinne spent most of the journey listing everything they could think of that was wrong with the Gaveys, and Lesley in particular.

Dad kept trying to interrupt. After hearing Corinne's explanation of why there was a message from the enemy on her phone, we were all satisfied that Corinne wasn't a traitor, but Dad still wanted her to explain her longer-term plan for Champ and justify her short-term one for all of us. Everyone shouted him down. Even Toby couldn't wait to hear about Lesley Gavey and the swimming pool timetable, once Corinne, in a voice laced with scandal, had trailed it as a gossip agenda item.

Mum hadn't heard the story and was keen to be filled in, so, as she drove us along the A685 through Kirkby Stephen, Corinne launched in:

The nearest swimming pool to Swaffham Tilney, nearer even than Quy Mill Hotel where Mum works, is The Field View Health Club and Spa. About two months ago, a new manager took over there and introduced a new system of swimming-timetable slots in an attempt to make sure the facilities never became unpleasantly overcrowded. Prior to this, there had been no restrictions – any club member could swim whenever they wanted to and stay as long as they pleased.

One day Lesley Gavey had arrived for a swim at 1.58pm, only to be told about the new regime and informed that, yes, she was of course allowed to swim, but that she would need to get out at 2.20pm, in order to be dressed and out of the building by 2.30pm, which was when the next timetable slot was scheduled to start.

Assuming she'd be able to get her own way, Lesley smiled and said, 'Oh, don't worry – I'm here for a nice long session today, so I'll just stay in the pool for the next slot too.'

The girl behind the desk told her that wasn't allowed. No member was allowed to stay for two consecutive slots. No, not even if the next session only had two people turn up for it, or nobody. The rules were the rules and couldn't be deviated from under any circumstances. The manager had made that very clear, though 'You're very welcome to come back for a second session later on today if you'd like to – just not the session that follows straight after this one,' the girl said, naively imagining this would be received as a glad tiding.

'Not one to be thwarted, Lesley flew into a hideous temper and started shrieking. But that's not the mind-boggling part.' Corinne chuckled. 'That's just what you'd expect, right? Wait till you hear what happened next. Around a week later, Alastair Gavey fancied a swim.'

'So they're not poor at all, then, if they can afford to be members at Field View,' said Mum. 'When they moved into Bussow Court, Lesley made a point of telling me they'd only been able to afford The Stables because they found a bit more than they'd imagined they'd have when she viewed Shukes last year – but now, having moved, that really was it, they were virtually bankrupt. A bit more!' Mum snorted. 'The Stables was on for seven-hundred and fifty grand – that's a hundred and fifty more than her original budget of six-hundred.'

'So what happened when Alastair Gavey went for his swim?' Tobes asked.

'He'd been briefed by Lesley, so he knew there was a slot starting at two thirty,' said Corinne. 'He made sure to arrive in good time, and turned up at about... Well, actually, there was no "about" about it. The Farmer was very precise: Alastair Gavey arrived at the reception desk at two twenty-seven. And guess what? Cash prize for anyone who guesses right.'

This livened Toby up no end. 'Um, erm... he was barred for having a rude wife?'

'Nope.' Corinne smiled. 'Ree? Can you beat Toby to the win?'

'They made him wait in reception for three minutes instead of letting him in early?'

'Hang on,' said Mum. 'The Farmer told you this story?'

'Mm-hmm.' Corinne smiled.

'I've heard he ignores all village gossip.'

'Most of the time, yeah. Normally his mind's on crops and combine harvesters and stuff, but he owns the Field View Health Club, so he's interested in what happens there.'

'The Farmer owns the Field View Health Club?' Mum squeaked. 'I did not know that!'

'Mark?' Corinne addresses the rear-view mirror. 'Want to try and guess what happened next?'

Dad shook his head and said nothing, to remind everyone that he was waiting to discuss more serious matters. He had the expression of a recently kidnapped person who has just realised his captors are non-violent but lethally irritating.

'Well, if they didn't make him wait, they must have let him in three minutes early,' said Toby.

'Correct!'

'I win!' My canny, non-furry brother got straight down to business: 'How much is the prize?'

'Nothing yet,' said Corinne. 'Yes, the receptionist let Alastair in early, but that's not the part you have to guess in order to win. What do you think happened after that? Ree? Any hunches?'

'Alastair Gavey swam thirty lengths,' Toby said impatiently. 'Not gonna lie, I've played more fun games than this one.'

Corinne chuckled. 'Yes, but what happened after that?' She was enjoying tormenting us all.

'Oh, my God,' said Mum. 'I think I've guessed. Did Lesley go back and kick up a stink because they let Alastair in early, after telling her the rules couldn't be—?'

'Yes!' Corinne cried out, startling us all. Dad muttered something angry-sounding under his breath. 'Yes, she did. They couldn't have it both ways, she insisted: either the timetable rules were strictly observed, and no exceptions could be made, or there was flexibility. The manager agreed. He assured her there would be no flexibility ever again. That wasn't good enough for Lesley, though: she wanted someone punished for the original flexibility. The manager agreed to that too – he gave the young man who'd let Alastair in early a formal warning. Can you believe it?' Corinne shook her head.

'I can, quite easily,' said Mum.

'The poor guy had to write Lesley a letter of apology,' Corinne went on. 'You'd have thought that would be good enough for her, but no. She demanded an apology from the girl who'd dealt with her too.'

'For what?' Mum asked. 'That girl was implementing the manager's rules, wasn't she?'

'Guess again,' said Corinne. 'What would Lesley Gavey's answer to that be?'

'Shouldn't we clarify what the cash prize is?' said Tobes. 'Or are there two? Is this a new one?'

'Lesley Gavey would say…' Mum thought hard. 'God, this is scary. Why do I feel like I know what twisted crap she'd come out with in every hypothetical situation? Did she say… that the girl who'd stopped her from swimming as long as she wanted to had lied to her by saying they never made exceptions when that wasn't true, because the man who let Alastair in *did* make exceptions?'

'Bang on.' Corinne laughed. 'The manager had lost the will to live, understandably, and caved in completely. Lesley got a second apology letter, and even that wasn't good enough for her. She discontinued her and Alastair's membership and said the Gaveys would only rejoin if both those staff members were fired and the swimming slots system was completely abandoned. So now she has nowhere to swim, which she complains about bitterly to anyone who will listen.'

'Why doesn't she join Quy Mill?' asked Toby.

'Because I work there.' Mum knew she was right about that one.

'Yup,' said Corinne. 'You won't catch Lesley Gavey giving a penny of her hard-earned money to a company that employs Sally Lambert, who once callously threw her out onto the street when she was at her lowest ebb. Though she's happy to live opposite you, which makes no sense,' Corinne concluded with a shrug.

'There's nothing happy about her,' said Toby. 'No one who's happy screams the way she does.'

No One Would Do What The Lamberts Have Done

'I didn't throw her out,' Mum protested. 'I told her I had a Zoom meeting that was about to start. There's a difference.'

'Yes, I meant to ask,' said Corinne. 'Tell me about Lesley screaming at her family, Toby.'

'It happens at least once a week,' he told her. 'It's the most insane thing you've ever heard. All I need to do is open my bedroom window and I can hear every word, and then Tess screaming back or Alastair mumbling sorry and crying in the background. I've recorded a couple of the most mental episodes. I'll... Oh, I can't. They're on my phone at home. You can only ever hear Lesley, when you play them back. She sounds like she's about to kill someone.'

'What kind of thing does she say?' Corinne asked.

'There are a few recurring topics, aren't there, Tobes?' said Dad. 'Tidiness, money—'

Toby nodded. 'Yeah, it's either, like, "I break my fucking back trying to keep this house clean and tidy and then you both fucking leave your fucking shoes here instead of where shoes are meant to go in the fucking shoe cupboard, you fucking bastards—"'

'Tobes, stop swearing,' Mum said.

'I'm not swearing, Mum, I'm acting.'

'No, you're reporting,' Corinne corrected him. 'You're being a citizen-journalist.'

'Sometimes it's "No, you can't have twenty pounds for a taxi, you spoilt, entitled sponger who knows nothing about the value of money having never earned any in her life,'" Tobes was getting into his performance. '"You're so useless, it doesn't occur to you to use your brain and build your own steam engine out of twigs to get you back home, and where are you even going when you don't have any friends and no one likes you?" That sort of thing, but with the kind of swearing Mum can't handle.'

'He's not exaggerating,' Mum told Corinne. 'I mean, maybe not the steam engine bit, but the rest is pretty much word for word. Until yesterday, I'd have said, "Poor Tess", but now that she's lied about Champ and put him in harm's way…'

Evidently Mum and I ended up drawing different conclusions about who was worse, Lesley or Tess. Our later actions bore that out.

'Do you really think Tess's bite is just make-up?' Mum asked Corinne, who, under her false Instagram name, had left a comment on Tess's post saying, "Not a real wound, you lying little turd. Clearly eye-shadow, lipstick and mascara all mixed up together."'

'Nope. The wound's real,' Corinne said. 'If you're talking about what I said on Insta? I was engaging in some fairly run-of-the-mill psychological warfare. And if the Gaveys are willing to lie in one direction, they can't object to me lying in the other. Tess must have a *bona fide* injury that she'll have needed to show the police in order to swing them into action. But… not from Champ. Nothing to do with him.'

No One Would Do What The Lamberts Have Done

'Are we done bitching?' asked Dad. 'Any chance we can talk about where we're going and why, and what the broader plan is?'

He might not have enjoyed waiting to find out, but it was lucky Mum and Corinne squashed his first attempt to shut them up. If he'd succeeded in turning the conversation to plans and practicalities any sooner, we'd all have missed a clue we had no idea we would soon need. At that point in our haphazard road trip, however, none of us knew how game-changing the story of Lesley Gavey versus the Field View Health Club and Spa would turn out to be.

21

Tuesday 18 June 2024

Sally

Corinne is back, looking triumphant. 'All right, we're sorted,' she says. The two helpers who made breakfast trail in behind her. They drift over to the table and, without making eye contact or any sound at all, start to clear away the plates as if they're auditioning for dramatic roles as servants who later turn out to be ghosts.

Sally has eaten a few bits, as much as she could manage. Everyone else has finished what was on their plate. Champ is asleep in his Donut dog bed in the corner of the room, between the tall white dresser and the wine rack, his flamboyantly bushy tail sticking out at an odd angle. His unusual tail style – more like what you'd expect to see on a squirrel – was his groomer's idea: 'It's not the standard Welshie look, but I thought it might be nice to make him look a bit different from Furbert. He's such a playful little character – I decided a more frivolous tail would suit him, and it's not as if you're planning to enter him for Crufts or anything,' the groomer said. Sally agreed, and left an extra-large tip; she is always ready to love anybody who thinks about Champ or Furbert in more than a cursory way.

'So. Today we're going to Norfolk,' Corinne announces quietly. It's definitely an announcement, though, not a just-happening-to-say. 'Start packing. Let's aim to set off in half an hour.'

'What, really? Tobes and I wanted to watch more movies in the hot tub,' says Ree.

'This isn't a holiday,' Mark tells her.

Half an hour? thinks Sally. With her children involved, that's impossible, unless Corinne has arranged for some masked gunmen to appear and chase them through the corridors. Ree will need to do at least 20 minutes of sighing before she moves, and Tobes will want to interrogate the proposal rigorously from every angle (the more mature equivalent of 'But why?') to check there are no holes in it that might enable him to head straight for a luxury jacuzzi instead, as he'd hoped to.

'Where in Norfolk?' Sally asks.

'It's a dog daycare and boarding kennels called West Acres, near Weybourne on the coast. It's a good, high-end place: soft, snuggly dog beds, real wool blankets. Owners receive regular postcards from their pets while they're away, with photos of them doing fun activities.'

'No,' says Mark. 'I'm sorry, Corinne, I know you're trying to help, but I'm not prepared to keep—'

'We're going,' Sally says flatly.

'Mum, you have to let Dad speak, even if you don't listen to him,' says Ree, for which consideration Mark thanks her.

'Champ and I are going,' says Sally. 'No one else has to come if they don't want to.' She hasn't heard the plan yet, but her trust in Corinne has been consolidated, thanks to the exchange of messages with Lesley Gavey she has just read on Corinne's phone. Corinne handed it over without delay or protest, which allowed Sally to see that what had passed between the two women was anything but friendly:

Lesley: Hi Corinne, it's Lesley Gavey here from The Stables, Bussow Court. Avril Mattingley gave me this number, so I hope it's the right one to use for you. Both she and Jemima Taggart have told me, separately, that they saw Sally Lambert in your car yesterday, and now it looks like no one's in at The Hayloft, even though Mark's and Sally's cars are both there. You should be aware that the Lamberts' dog has bitten my daughter, Tess, and there's barely anything left of her arm. I think the doctors are afraid she might lose it, though they're not saying that because they don't want to frighten us. Anyway, that dog needs to be put to sleep, obviously, and the police are on it, but I'm concerned that the Lamberts have taken it into their heads to run off somewhere to protect their animal, because that's exactly the sort of stupid, arrogant thing

No One Would Do What The Lamberts Have Done

they would do. If by any chance they're with you, Corinne, you need to get on the right side of this one and tell them to come home and face up to the damage they've caused. Are they with you? Jemima says you've got houses all over the country. I'm sure I don't need to tell you how bad it would look if the papers got hold of a story about a billionaire using her immense privilege to give shelter to criminals. Are the Lamberts with you right now, Corinne? If they are, you really do need to ring me immediately and help to sort this out. Yours, Lesley Gavey.

Corinne: Hi, Lesley. Champ Lambert didn't bite your daughter. I'm not quite a billionaire, though I'm looking forward to achieving that within the next seven to ten years. You're a liar and an unhinged psychopath. Corinne.

Sally feels awful for having doubted Corinne even for a second. 'Did you tell the people in Norfolk that I won't let Champ out of my sight?' she asks. Presumably most dogs who go to West Acres Boarding Kennels stay there without their owners – they must, if sending postcards is part of their itinerary.

'First thing I said.' Corinne beams proudly. 'You can be with Champ the whole time, sleep side by side as usual.'

'No. Absolutely not. I'm not sleeping in a kennel.' Mark has never sounded more dogmatic.

'No one's trying to make you.' Sally sighs. 'Seriously, Champ and I will be fine. I'm happy to sleep with him in a luxury kennel. How long will it be for?'

'I'm definitely up for it,' says Tobes. 'Kennel party! It'll be crease. We can get some beers in, play a few tunes—'

'No, Toby, we can't,' says Sally. 'We'd wake up all the other dogs.'

'And you're supposed to let sleeping ones lie,' Ree quips.

'We need to be as silent and invisible as possible.' Sally turns to Corinne. 'How's it going to be safe? Didn't you have to give them Champ's name and ours?'

'I told them enough but not everything. Don't worry, Sal. It's risk-free. It's my son and his wife's place.'

'Oh. Okay.' This sounds more reassuring

'And… there's safety in numbers, and crowds,' says Corinne. 'A kennels with dozens of dogs in it is a great place to hide a dog.'

Either that or it's the very worst place; Sally can't decide.

'Maybe we can have a kennel each, if they're not too busy?' Ree says hopefully. 'I'd love that if it's possible. I've shared hotel rooms with Toby in the past – he manages to destroy them beyond all salvation within, like, ten minutes of entering.'

'I'm not prepared to go along with this anymore,' says Mark.

'Be quiet,' Sally orders.

'No, I won't.' He stands up. 'We've only just got here. You said we'd be safe here, Corinne, and now you're deciding we're not? Now you're asking us to do another... what? Six- or seven-hour drive? Corinne, no one knows we're here. What, just because Lesley Gavey sent you that message? That doesn't mean she knows we're here, does it?'

'It's just about possible she could find out that I own this house,' Corinne says. 'I know Sally doesn't want to take that risk. If the police turn up with a warrant—'

'A *warrant*? You're mad. You're all mad!' Mark grabs at his hair with both hands.

'Please sit down and listen,' Corinne says calmly. 'Let's be honest: none of us knows anything about how the police handle dog-bite allegations. A warrant sounds absurd, I agree. And yet. I did a bit of Googling, and... well, some people's dogs *do* get seized by the authorities and put down, Mark. It happens.'

'And so we're going to Norfolk, because *that is not happening to Champ*,' Sally says emphatically, imagining a world in which she, Sally Lambert, has the power to take Lesley Gavey to Vets4Pets in Newmarket and request that the lovely staff there inject her with something lethal...

'Sal.' Mark is waving his hand in front of her face. 'Get it together, okay. This has to stop now. We need to go home, face the music—'

'No. West Acres in Weybourne, in Norfolk,' says Sally. 'That's where I'm going. Me and Champ.'

'And me and Tobes,' says Ree. 'So go home if you want, *Dad*, but it'll be just you.'

'And then what?' says Mark. 'What happens after Norfolk? How long does our little… excursion around the country last? How do we ever solve this if all we do is run away? When do we get to go home?'

'I don't *know*!' Sally bursts into tears.

'I've got an idea,' says Corinne.

'Oh, I just bet you have,' Mark snaps.

'Dad, you oaf, quit being rude to Corinne,' says Ree. 'She's trying to help us.'

'It's fine. Be rude to me if you want to, I don't mind.' Corinne sounds unruffled. 'Let me tell you my suggested plan. You never answered my question before: is Champ microchipped?'

'Yeah, he is,' says Sally.

'Okay. First step: we get you to West Acres, get you all settled in—'

'Just us, not you?' asks Mark. 'I don't suppose you're going to be sleeping in a kennel, are you?'

Corinne laughs. 'No way in hell am I doing that. No.'

'But we are, and it's *fine*,' Sally insists, shooting a desperate look at Mark: *Please stop resisting*. 'It'll be… an adventure.'

'Where will the nearest bathroom be?' he says. 'Or are we expected to do our business in the corner, on some straw?'

'You are *so* embarrassing,' Ree tells him.

'You'll have an ensuite bathroom with a shower and a loo,' says Corinne. 'That do you?'

'Oh, really?' Mark shakes his head. 'These kennels are so luxurious they have ensuites for humans attached to them too?'

'Here's a promise,' says Corinne. 'If you don't have an ensuite you're happy with, I'll give you a hundred grand. How about that?'

'Done!' Tobes extends his hand for Corinne to shake. 'Agreed. My bank account's happy to be the initial recipient.'

'Let Corinne tell us her plan,' Sally says quietly, wondering how Mark can summon the energy to argue about trivialities in a world that contains people who won't rest until Champ is killed.

'We get you settled in at West Acres,' Corinne starts again from the beginning. 'After a few days, once you've rested and recovered, you leave Champ at the kennels with me—'

'No,' says Sally.

'—and go back home. While you're away, I get his microchip removed. You, meanwhile, go straight to the nearest policeman you can find. You lodge a serious counter-accusation. You say Champ's missing, and you're sure the Gaveys have stolen him and harmed him. You won't be able to prove it, but a good half of the village will believe you, I reckon. The Gaveys are not well-liked in Swaffham Tilney. Then weeks pass, and Champ is never found – and then a few weeks later, your "new" dog appears. A dog-lover like Sally Lambert wouldn't ever choose to be without a dog, would she? Except this time, it's not a puppy that arrives. Instead, it's – ta-da! Surprise! – a Welsh Terrier from a rescue centre. You'll be able to prove he's not Champ, if necessary, because Champ's micro-chipped and this dog won't be – except he will, of course, be Champ. You'll have to call him Fred or Bartholomew or something, and you'll need to explain that this time you didn't want a puppy because blah blah, whatever, adopt don't shop…'

Corinne stops for breath. 'What do you think? I think it's the perfect plan. How will anyone be able to prove it's Champ under a different name? And what did you do when Furbert died? Immediately went out and found another dog who looks exactly like him, right? So… to everyone else, this'll just look like you're doing the same again.'

The Lamberts stare at Corinne – all except Champ and Furbert. Actually, Sally could swear that Furbs's spirit is by her side and as horrified as she is.

Corinne looks hopefully at them. 'Solid plan, no?'

'No. I'm not doing that.' Sally has started to shake. 'He's Champ. He will always be Champ Cuthbert Lambert and no one else. I'm not changing his name, ever. I'd rather… flee the country, start a whole new life abroad—'

'Florida? Hawaii?' says Tobes.

'I'd change *our* name, our address, our jobs, before I'd—'

'We can't change the Lambert part of our name,' Ree says. 'Furbert Herbert and Champ Cuthbert don't work without the Lambert part.'

No One Would Do What The Lamberts Have Done

All Sally knows is that she's unwilling to pretend her darling boy is someone else. The way he looks up happily when she says 'Champ!' Or 'Champy', or 'Chample-moose Pamplemousse'... He'd be devastated if he didn't hear her call him Champ anymore. The story of his name is his favourite thing in the whole world to listen to. And she won't deprive Furbs of his rightful surname either, especially not when he's already been deprived of his life.

'No,' she tells Corinne firmly.

'Okay. I understand.' Corinne puts her hand on Sally's shoulder. 'Forget I suggested it.'

'So what, then?' Toby asks. 'Do we have a Plan B?' He looks hopefully at Corinne.

'Yes. We have a brilliant Plan B. Even better than Plan A,' she says. 'I can't wait to tell you all about it on the way to Norfolk – just as soon as I've worked out what it is.'

22

In our family, names matter. If Lesley Gavey had only said less, and stopped talking sooner, when she came for her viewing of Shukes… well, let's just say, a terrible thing might not have happened. There are causes, and then there are clinchers, and the memory of Lesley's fake concern – 'It's not fair to give a dog a joke name like that, Sally. It's disrespectful, actually' – fell decisively into the clincher category. The stark fact is that, if those two sentences had never been uttered, a young man named Saul Hollingwood would have gone to work as usual on 29 June 2024 instead of doing what he did after calling in sick.

(He sounds as if he matters to our story, doesn't he? Yet this is the first and last time his name will appear in these pages.)

Mum approaches the naming of anything she cares about with great reverence. She started to cry with delight when

No One Would Do What The Lamberts Have Done

we went to pick Champ up from his first home in Llandysul and she found out that his Kennel Club name was Mehefin Afon, which is Welsh for 'June river' – a fact Mum likes to tell Champ at regular intervals.

'Shall I tell you the story of your name?' she says to him all the time. Dad and Tobes tend to groan or leave the room, but I enjoy hearing the story. 'Well,' Mum says next, settling into an armchair and pulling Champ up onto her lap, rubbing his belly or under his chin. 'First of all, you were Mehefin Afon. That means June River – what a lovely name, isn't it, baby boy? – and then you were Puppy Davies-Jones, because Hadi and Bleddyn didn't want to give you your main name, did they? No, they didn't! They didn't! Because they knew you'd soon have a new family who would want to name you. Very sensible of them!'

Mum's story, which we've all heard dozens of times, is not entirely true. I'd be willing to bet that Hadi Davies and Bleddyn Jones never once thought of Champ as 'Puppy Davies-Jones'. Davies and Jones are their respective surnames, but they're neither married nor double-barrelled, so why would they have double-barrelled their puppies' names? Never mind, though; stories need a whole chain of plot developments, and I assume Mum didn't want to leap too quickly from beginning to end, so Puppy Davies-Jones got inserted as a step along the way.

'And then for a while you were *Champ* Davies-Jones!'

(Also not really true.)

'And then *we* came along, your new family, your forever

family, and then, finally, you became Champ Cuthbert Lambert. Aaaand' – this is the key moment of suspense in the story of Champ's name – 'you still are!' Mum never skimps on the big reveal energy at the end.

'"You still are?"' Tobes said scornfully the first time he heard it. 'Is that it? That's such an anti-climax.'

But that wasn't, and isn't, the end. There follows a sort of twist that no one sees coming when they hear the story for the first time: 'And you're *also* a big Mehefalump!' Mum always adds, as a final flourish.

Here's the non-cutesy version of how Champ got named: Mum decided before she met him that his name would be Gilbert Cuthbert Lambert, to follow the family's traditional triple-Bert pattern that began with Furbert Herbert Lambert. But then Hadi mentioned, before we collected him, that she'd had to take him to the vet because there was a problem with his tail. It turned out to be a form of cradle cap, called seborrheic dermatitis when a dog has it. 'He was such a little champ, though,' Hadi told Mum proudly. 'Made them all laugh at the vet's, gave everyone a *cwtch*.' (That means cuddle in Welsh.)

'Let's just call him Champ,' Dad suggested. 'I'd feel like a dick shouting "Gilbert" in the park. Gilbert's a name for a… poet or a musician or something. Not a dog. I felt daft enough shouting "Furbert" for all those years. I should never have agreed to anything so undignified.'

'You mean "un-dog-nified",' said Ree. (So, here I am, mentioning Ree for the first time. I'm sure you noticed,

No One Would Do What The Lamberts Have Done

but just in case…)

'Undignified?' Mum said, aghast. 'Mark! Just *how* can you say that to me? Now I'm going to have to remember, forever, that you said it.'

'Why?' Dad looked baffled. 'Is someone going to test you on it one day? Can't we call this new dog something normal?'

Tobes agreed. 'We should call him Champ. That's so obviously his name.'

As soon as he'd said it, Mum saw that it was true. 'You're right,' she said. 'It's Champ, not Gilbert, that has the great story behind it.'

(Great story? I mean… Champ briefly having a patch of hard skin on his tail isn't exactly *Watership Down*, but whatever.)

Anyway, that's how Champ came to be called Champ Cuthbert Lambert. In his capacity as Mehefin Afon, his official Kennel Club name, he soon received his Five Generation Pedigree certificate that 'I just know he would want' (Mum – and so she'd ordered it at considerable expense). She greeted its arrival with paroxysms of delight and quickly spotted a name that looked very familiar: Sennybridge Welsh and Wild. 'Mark!' she screamed, and Dad came running from upstairs, thinking there was an emergency; this was no time to slow things down with a 'No. Not Mark'.

'Look at this!' Mum said. 'Sennybridge Welsh and Wild – look, he's Champ's furry grandfather, see?'

'Okay. So?' said a bewildered Dad.

'Now look at Furbs's certificate.' Mum pointed to the kitchen wall, where it hung in the best and most visible display spot in the house, directly above the kitchen table. 'Sennybridge Welsh and Wild is one of Furby's litter-brothers. He's the one who went to Aylesbury, remember – with Julie and Darren? They ran a yoga school?'

'Sal, as if I'm going to remember that,' Dad said impatiently. 'So, what does that make Champ, in relation to Furbert? His... great-nephew?'

'I mean...' Mum looked confused for a second. Then she decided. 'No. It'll confuse things if we start thinking like that. Champ is still Furbs's little brother, but... even more so, because they're actual blood relatives as well as furry Lambert brothers.'

By now, knowing my foolish, foolish Dad as you do, you can probably guess what he said next: 'Sal, they're not brothers at all, I'm afraid.' He leaned down, stroked Champ ('trying to tempt him over to your side, against me,' Mum said tearfully later) and said, 'How about that, Champy? Our last dog was your Great Uncle Furbert.'

Okay, listen. Talking about family relationships and the importance of names is making me a bit emotional. I can't do it anymore, can't keep the name of the unmentioned person I love to myself any longer, not when I'm constantly going on about all the other people I love.

Besides, I've already mentioned her name. And I'm going to state it once more now, in full this time. She's called Rhiannon Madeleine Lambert, and she's my sister.

23

Connor

Hello, Large. It's me: PC Connor Chantree. First of all, I apologise for not warning you that you would meet me inside this book I've given you to read. I thought if I told you that, I'd put you off by making it sound too complicated. But, give me a chance and I'll explain.

When I opened the damp box that contained all the pages, I knew I'd have to work out the right way to arrange them if I wanted them to make sense. I was mainly successful in my attempt, but there were quite a few pages that I couldn't get to fit anywhere, no matter how hard I tried. Everything you've read so far, I had no problem putting together. And there's more to come that was equally easy to put in the clear right order too. But there was also a lot that I couldn't get to fit anywhere, though I've done my best to make some guesses about those bits, in case that helps. Those are the sections I'm going to share with you now.

You're probably thinking, 'Why include them at all if they can't be fitted into the proper sequence of events?' I agonised over this and decided to compromise. So, I've left out the completely incoherent fragments and the ones that seem to have no relevance at all to anything as far as I can see, but I've included a few odds and ends that felt too weighty to leave out. If a murder was committed (I know you think that can't possibly have happened, and so do I with the rational bit of my brain), then we have to ask ourselves: who among all these people seems most likely to turn murderous? Do these bits I'm about to share with you give us valuable insights into several of our key players' ways of looking at life? I'd say yes – or else they in some way lay the groundwork for what happens next, once we get back to the properly-organised story, which will happen immediately after this chapter of assorted passages.

So, there are three separate headings, I guess you'd call them. As follows:

1. The Gardenia Incident
2. Resemblances
3. The poem on the bedroom wall at Corinne Sullivan's Lake District house – the one Sally Lambert read that wasn't by Corinne's granddaughter.

I'll start with the poem, as it's the shortest. It was crushed into a damp ball that I found in the corner of the box.

No One Would Do What The Lamberts Have Done

The last verse you've already seen as part of one of the 'Sally' sections.

IT MATTERS

For my brilliant friend Corinne, who keeps getting fired by dimwits. With all my love, HS xx
23 February, 2008

All of us net some wins; all suffer losses,
But something I have noticed on my journey,
A truth that I have often come across is:
It matters – whether you are an attorney,

A chiropractor, vet or idling stoner,
Whatever work you do (or don't) – it matters
If you are an employee or the owner,
Since formers are more vulnerable than latters.

The stoner might be poor. We might not find him
Among the world's top luxury afforders
But no firm's board has forcibly resigned him,
No one is giving him his marching orders,

The show he stars in is his own creation
For off-his-chops or worse, till clogs start popping.
His days are free from threat and subjugation.
Yes, true, he cannot go fat diamond shopping –

Neither can most Type As with prime positions
In other people's companies. Be wiser,
IT geeks, massage therapists, opticians.
Hear this unsackable careers adviser:

No shares, no benefits and bonus package
Could ever be an adequate incentive
For the precarity, the freedom lackage.
Go it alone instead, and be inventive.

Dear friend, you deserve all good things and better.
You know how much I love you and admire you.
Obey this next instruction to the letter:
Never work for someone who can fire you.

Large, it's obviously a stretch to say that anyone who rates that poem highly enough to frame it could also commit a murder no coroner could detect, but I don't know. There's just something about it that's a bit crazy. You can't go round telling people never to get a job again, can you? What are they supposed to live on? My wife, Flo, agrees. She's successful herself as an entrepreneur (she runs a really successful catering business) but she's the first to admit 99% of start-ups fail, and so it's unavoidable that some people have to have jobs. Some of us even like our jobs and want to keep them. Also, why did Corinne Sullivan keep getting fired? What if the 'dimwits' referred to in the italics bit sensed there was something off about her?

No One Would Do What The Lamberts Have Done

All right, this next section, not crushed into a ball but also not attached to any specific part of the story in an obvious way, is all about what's referred to throughout as The Gardenia Incident. It's a bit weird, this one, because of the way it's written. Sally must be the 'I', as you'll see, and her father the 'Dad', but unlike all the other Sally bits, this one isn't all 'Sally/she' and written in the present tense. It's written in the exact style of all the other past tense bits which aren't Sally. (I mean... unless they are, if you see what I mean, Large. Who knows who wrote any of it, really?)

Anyway, make of this what you will:

Gardenia (my heading)

It took me ages to work out that it stuck in my mind not because it was Dad's worst tantruming bout or anything like that but because it was the best proof. The Gardenia story would be the one to tell if I wanted to convince anyone that I'm right about him and Mum and Vicky are wrong. The Gardenia incident didn't begin with me defying him, rebelling, complaining, or even inconveniencing him in the slightest. I'd done nothing anyone sane would consider wrong or provocative. I was only 13, too, so still completely under his power.

We'd just got back from a three-week-long summer holiday that had turned me a deep, dark brown. I didn't know anything, then, about how to stop your skin from peeling, and soon after we got back to England, I noticed that the skin on both my calves was dry and scaly. Bits started to flake off. Oonagh told me it looked disgusting and I said, 'What am I supposed to do, though? I suppose eventually the horrid bits will fall off.' She laughed and said, 'Don't be silly. Just put on some moisturiser or body lotion. If you'd done that from the start, you could have kept your tan for longer.'

That evening I pulled out a gift set my grandma had bought me the previous Christmas that I still hadn't used, a collection of gardenia-scented toiletries: body lotion, bubble bath and a wrapped soap. I put a little bit of the body lotion on one of my legs and was astonished by the difference it made. I couldn't wait to show Oonagh the next day; the scaly lines had disappeared and that patch of my left calf looked and smelled great – shiny and healthy. My next move was obvious: cover both calves with the stuff, and my problem would be solved.

I was in the process of doing this when my bedroom door opened and my father walked in. He started to tell me something – I can't remember what – but stopped mid-sentence when he saw what I was doing. His face stiffened in disapproval, and I didn't understand why he was acting as if he'd caught me injecting heroin into my eyeballs.

'What the hell is that?' he demanded. I explained quickly – anything to make the horrible hardness in his eyes disappear. At 13, I knew what it meant: between hours and days of tightlipped, hostility-radiating silence interspersed with long bouts of berating and bellowing. I remember thinking he would definitely say something along the lines of 'Oh, right, that's fine, then' once he understood.

He didn't. Instead, he swore under his breath, shook his head in disgust and left the room, slamming the door hard. I can't remember if I immediately ran after him and started apologising or if I first spent a few minutes wondering what exactly I'd done to displease him, but I recall very clearly sitting on the sofa in his study while he sat at his desk and roared at me: 'I don't understand what's happening to you! You used to read books and care about serious things! Now you've turned into someone who wastes her time on beautifying herself! All you want to do is make yourself look like some dolly bird! You're only thirteen! Why do you need to put lotion on your legs? You're a child!'

Normally my only option in such situations was to say, 'Yes, you're right, I'm sorry,' over and over again until he calmed down, having got the poison out of his system. It was important to try and do this without crying, too, because when I cried it made him angrier. 'What are you crying for?' he would yell. 'I'm the one who should be crying!'

This time, though, I thought I had a defence worth stating more than once. I was sure dry, scaly legs that needed moisturising because they were actually sore fell into the category of a health issue rather than anything to do with vanity, but Dad brushed it aside, saying that whether on this occasion I'd been caring too much about my appearance or not didn't matter; in general and overall, I had been displaying all kinds of attitudes recently that he found disappointing. My priorities and interests were all wrong, and it was terrible that I used to be better and was now so much worse. Those weren't his exact (shouted) words, but that was the gist.

Eventually, the only way I could stop the verbal onslaught was to employ my usual defensive strategy: endlessly apologise until the rage-cloud had passed. By dinner time Dad had cheered up and Mum seemed cheery enough too, though she'd heard it all. I'm sure I was in good spirits too; it was always worth celebrating when the turmoil finally ended, and never worth commenting, in the opinion of everyone around our kitchen table, on the extended psychological-intimidation ordeal that had just taken place.

That's it for the Gardenia stuff, Large. It was a bit of an eye-opener for me. I know the coroner says no murder took place, but someone who's been bullied like that by a parent for most of her life? Someone who's been trained, and trained herself, to keep her own pain under wraps at all costs while apologising to her tormentor?

I don't know. I can see someone who's been through that suddenly just losing it and killing someone. Oh, and you'll have noticed that those Gardenia pages are in a different font. I'm wondering if maybe Sally Lambert wrote them before, at some point in the past, and whoever wrote the book (maybe Sally herself, maybe someone else) stuck that bit in so that they didn't have to explain all over again.

And now for the third and final section that I didn't want to leave out. As you'll see, it's a discussion about resemblances that takes place between the Lamberts. It clearly happens at some point while they're on the run with Champ. They're watching a movie together, which they might have done several times during that period when they were away from Swaffham Tilney. There's nothing about what follows that indicates their precise whereabouts or what stage of their escape they were at, but it doesn't really matter. And in a way this conversation has nothing to do with anything but, to be honest, Large, I'm mainly including it because I'm curious to see if reading it helps you to guess anything once you meet Sarah and Bonnie Sergeant in a later chapter, or at any point before Ree Lambert says what she's going to say (she said it ages ago, obviously, but she hasn't yet said it in the book), prompting Sally Lambert to say what *she* says in response. I'll admit: it didn't occur to me, and wouldn't have in a million years. But you're cleverer than I am.

I did a bit of research, trying to work out what the film was that they were watching, but I'm afraid I failed to identify it.

Again, as with the Gardenia pages, this bit has to be Sally but it's in the first person. Present tense this time, though, not past. Was Sally experimenting with different styles, maybe, before writing the final version of the book?

The Resemblances Conversation

'No,' says Mark.

'No,' says Ree.

For a second, I'm not sure what they're objecting to. I haven't asked them to do any homework or household chores, have I? No. We're not at home. There are no chores here; keeping Champ safe and beyond the reach of the Gaveys is our only task.

Then I remember that I asked a question only a few seconds ago, about the scientist in the movie we're watching, and I'm shocked by how deep into the tunnel of my own thoughts I retreated between asking and them answering. It's as if I have to keep going into myself and hiding every now and then before coming out and facing the family again.

'What about you, Tobes?' I say.

'No, Mum. Ssshh.' He puts his finger to his lips and frowns. 'I'm trying to watch.'

Ree also frowns at me, but with just her eyes. She learned

how to do this soon after watching a video on YouTube about avoiding wrinkle lines in middle age.

'Come on, one of you must be able to see it,' I say. 'She's the image of someone we all know and see often.'

'I know who you're thinking of,' says Tobes. 'Vinie Skinner.'

'Right!' Champ, draped over my shins, makes a 'Buh!' sound in protest. He thinks it's far too late for anyone to speak so energetically. 'Sorry, Champles,' I whisper. 'I'm glad I'm not the only one who sees the resemblance.'

'You are,' says Tobes. 'She looks nothing like Vinie, apart from they're both women with dark hair.'

I can't believe this. 'You're winding me up, right?'

'No.' He seems to mean it. 'I don't think there's a resemblance. I just knew she was who you meant, that's all.'

Ree says, 'If you want to talk about strong likenesses, how about the one between Tess Gavey's wound and Tess Gavey's soul.' She smiles. 'That's good. Let me ju-ust' – she picks up her phone – 'comment that under her latest post.'

'Ree, don't,' I say, alarmed. Would she really write that? Is she joking?

'Don't dare,' says Mark. 'We don't sink to their level. No matter what.'

'Oh, Dad!' Ree laughs. 'You wouldn't say that if you knew—' She breaks off, looks away.

'What?' I say.

'Nothing.'

'Ree, what?'

'Tess named Champ earlier today. In her Snapchat story.'

I cover my mouth with my hand. My insides feel as if they've been yanked out of me and chucked down a deep lift shaft.

'Well, she didn't actually name him,' says Ree. 'But she said he was a Welshie belonging to a neighbour, so you know… people are putting two and two together.'

'Don't tell me,' I say shakily. 'And… don't reply to her, Ree. Don't comment or… do anything. Promise me. We have to just ignore it, pretend it's not happening. Block her. Can't you block people on these social media places?'

Toby and Ree exchange a long, complicated look: deeper and more multi-layered than the usual 'God, isn't Mum old and out of touch?' I know my children well enough to know they've just had a whole conversation using only their eyes.

'What's going on?' I say. 'Mark? Do you know?'

'Nothing's going on, Sal. Kids, nothing's going on, right?'

'Right.' Ree reaches over and pats my hand. 'Everything's fine, Mum. I mean, have I responded in a critical manner to some of Tess's posts, and have many of my friends done the same? Yes, but—'

'Oh, my God,' I wail.

'*But* no one knows where we are. Me and Tobes haven't given even the slightest hint – and our phones can't be traced to us. So it's fine.'

'"Tobes and I",' says Mark.

No One Would Do What The Lamberts Have Done

'It is not fine, Rhiannon,' I say. 'You're provoking an unstable girl who's already out for blood. What's she going to do to us next?'

'Mum, you're not thinking straight,' Ree says patiently. 'Tess has been about as popular as a wet shite ever since she decided to try and bully me, but now? Everyone knows Champ didn't bite her and that she's lying—'

'How does everyone know that?' I talk over her.

'Because I've told them. And they're not having it, which is great! Tess is starting to get a taste of just how *hated* she's going to be if she sticks to her lying guns. And... I'm sorry, but it's a beautiful thing. Wanna see some of it?' Ree waves her phone in the air.

I shake my head. 'I have to pretend it isn't happening. I can't go there. Both of you, I'm begging you... please don't engage.' I hate the internet. I wish it had never been invented.

'But Mum, people are defending Champ,' says Tobes. 'It'd cheer you up.'

'No!' I don't care how many of my children's friends are telling Tess Gavey what a bitch she is. The more Champ's name is mentioned, the more danger he's in.

'Kids, leave Mum be, will you?' says Mark. 'I think she's had about as much as she can take for one day.'

'Nothing bad has actually happened to any of us.' Toby sounds bemused.

'He's got a point, Dad,' says Ree. 'I do feel like we're all kind of... trapped in an irrational, menopausal panic attack, maybe?'

'I'm *fine*,' I say. Am I making too much of this? I'm bound to be overreacting. A few teenagers bitching on the internet is neither here nor there. 'Let's just watch the movie, shall we? I want to know whether any of them survive the flight to Vegas.' In reality, I couldn't give a toss. All I want is to be no longer the focus of my family's attention. I need to adjust to this new world I'm in, the one in which Champ's guilt or innocence is being fought about online as if he's OJ Simpson or something, and I can't do that while people are watching me.

We'll laugh about this one day. That's what Mark often says, to snap me out of a fuss I'm making about nothing. Will I laugh, at some point in the future, at how horrified I was to discover Tess Gavey had typed the words 'a neighbour's Welsh Terrier' into her Snapchat box or whatever you call it, in the hope of persuading God knows how many people to hate and blame and fear Champ? *Only if I'm standing over her decomposing dead body at the time* – that's my honest answer. No one who sees my smiley face as it trots around the village knows I'm capable of thinking anything as violent as that, and I want to keep it that way. I certainly don't want my family to know.

'Anyway, you can't have it both ways, Tobes,' says Mark.
'Huh?'
'She must remind you of Vinie, or you wouldn't have guessed it was Vinie she reminded Mum of.'
'Oh, have mercy.' Ree rolls her eyes. 'Like, peace and love and I'm not being funny, but can this conversation

end now, before it starts? I'm imagining how bored I'm going to be in about five minutes' time—'

'*I* don't see any resemblance,' Tobes says through a mouthful of crisps, without taking his eyes off the screen. 'Mum might do but I don't.'

'Then how come you thought of Vinie as soon as Mum challenged you to—'

'I don't know, Dad. I could easily have said someone else.'

'But you didn't,' says Mark. 'Which proves you must see some similarity between her and Vinie. I don't, personally, so I wouldn't have been able to guess.'

'I just thought, "What might someone who was wrong think?"' says Tobes.

'Why did you land on Vinie specifically, though?'

'Mark, stop,' I say.

'Why? I want to get to the bottom of this.'

'Trust me, as someone who's there already…' Ree sighs. 'It's not a desirable destination.'

'The girls can't hack it.' Mark chuckles. 'You could have named any of the other dark-haired women in the village,' he goads Toby. 'Or even the blondes. Or The Farmer.'

'Oh, my God. I'm surrounded by insanity,' says Ree. 'Me and Champy are the only sane ones here.'

'The Farmer would be… just a ridiculous level of wrong that no one would be capable of,' Tobes answers Mark easily. 'I don't know what your problem is, Dad. Haven't you ever imagined what someone else might be thinking without thinking it yourself?'

'This is so great.' Ree rolls over onto her back. 'I hope we get several more hours of it. I just can't wait to see who wins.'

'Yeah, course,' Mark tells Tobes. 'But this is different. We're talking about resemblances. You can't imagine a resemblance someone else might spot unless you've spotted it yourself. It's impossible.'

'Well, actually, it's not, because it's literally what happened.' Toby yawns.

'Please, stop, all of you,' I say. 'You're disturbing Champ.' If they keep this up, I'm going to have to leave the room, and I don't want to. It's after midnight and I'm in my nightie. As long as I live, I'll never understand anyone who argues for fun.

'Champ's fast asleep, Sal,' says Mark.

'All right, Dad, let's put this to the test.' Tobes says. 'I'm going to find someone in this film who reminds me of someone, and then I'm going to ask you—'

'Right, that's it,' Ree snaps. 'Want to talk resemblances, Toby? Mum, let me tell you about Bonnie—'

'Noooooo, let's not do that,' Tobes cuts her off.

'Then let's not do boring me to death either, little brother.' Ree gives him a pointed look.

'Who's Bonnie?' I ask.

'No one. Forget it,' Toby says tersely. 'Forget it, Dad. You're right. I guess that scientist must have reminded me of Vinie Skinner.'

'Well, of course she did.' Mark lets out a satisfied sigh.

No One Would Do What The Lamberts Have Done

Again, I have that falling-into-a-bottomless-pit feeling. 'Ree, who's Bonnie?'

'She's the scientist, Mum, okay? In the movie. Which I'm switching off now because we're clearly not watching it anymore.'

Later, once everyone is asleep apart from me, I remember that the scientist in the movie was called Anya. Not Bonnie. And why would Toby have shut Ree down so fast if she was only talking about a character in a film?

I want to shake them both awake and demand, with all the parental authority I can muster, that they tell me whatever it is they're keeping secret. But they're asleep and I've already dragged them halfway around the country, and I'm scared of knowing the truth. If it was anything important, I'm sure they'd tell me. Bonnie is probably a girl whose heart Toby has broken or is about to break. It can wait, whatever it is.

Still, I can't sleep, so I stroke the fur on the back of Champ's neck in the dark and solve the resemblances question all on my own and in silence: clearly there are two levels of resemblance-spotting. Level 1 is where you notice it straight away or unprompted. Level 2 is where you don't, but when asked, and once you know there's a possible resemblance out there to be had, then it comes to you.

Easy.

24

Rhiannon Madeleine Lambert – Ree for short – is my sister. I haven't been able to mention her until now (or her contribution to various scenes and discussions) because I wanted you to assume I was her, and that these parts of the story were her handiwork. Perhaps you even wondered if this entire book was written by Ree. It's not inconceivable that she might have chosen to present some sections from Mum's close third person perspective. That's what it's called when it's 'she' instead of 'I' but the reader nevertheless has access to that character's innermost thoughts – though Ree would never start a sentence with 'It's not inconceivable…'

Now you know I'm not her, you can wonder all these things about me too, I suppose. Am I the sole author of this account of our war with the Gaveys, or one of two? One of several, maybe? Or perhaps someone else is writing

No One Would Do What The Lamberts Have Done

about me and it's a lie that the 'I' is me, if you see what I mean.

Did you notice I told you, in the second 'Me' section, that I went downstairs immediately after PC Connor Chantree left us alone on 17 June, while Mum was whispering to Champ that she was sorry she was too upset to sing him his sunshine-y Day Song? Then in a later chapter (a 'Sally' one) you read that Ree only came down after Dad and Tobes got back. That was probably too subtle a clue, so I gave you a more overt one: SIBLING. That will have made it click for some of you, but just in case anyone is still confused, here's another even bigger clue: GHOSTWRITER.

So. Now you should all know who I am, if I tell you that Sally and Mark Lambert are my mum and dad and Ree, Toby and Champ Lambert are my brothers and sister.

I couldn't risk revealing my true identity before, for four reasons:

a) there are prejudiced people who wouldn't want to read a book written or cowritten by the likes of me. If you're one of those people, all I can say is: read on, and don't assume you know anything at all, because you *really* don't.

b) there are unimaginative people who wouldn't believe my sort could ever write a book (remember what I said at the beginning about most people being unwilling to think that anything they don't know for a fact is true?).

c) technically, you'd have to say I'm a ghostwriter, and I know what people think about those. I've seen – online, when I've looked with Mum at those writing community forums she joined after she'd recovered from the Lambert-Gavey War – so much antagonism and derision directed at other writing collaborations involving a ghostwriter, that I was determined not to get mixed up in all of that. Especially since Mum might be viewed by some as a 'celebrity' (especially after the latest two glossy, multi-page spreads: 'At Home With Sally Lambert, Hoomum of the Furry Fugitive' and '"Gone Dog" is Back; Family Speaks Openly About Ordeal For The First Time'). It's when celebrities collaborate with ghostwriters that unghostly writers turn vicious.

My final main reason, d), also explains why, even now, I'm telling you who I am without telling you. You might have noticed I'm not loudly and proudly stating my name for the record – first name, middle name, surname – even though I love my name. Mum thinks of it as a 'tiny little poem' and I agree. Yet I'm leaving it out, as a way of trying to get round The Absurdity Impediment. I can't give you any excuse to say 'Oh, come on, that's absurd!' and dismiss my story. People who aren't me need to know the truth about me – the role I played in what happened – and I don't want to risk shattering all the trust I've built up over many chapters of mature, authoritative narration by stating my name, which, shall we say, doesn't have quite so much gravitas about it.

I feel like I need to try and explain The Absurdity Impediment, though it's something those in Level 3 might find hard to understand. It's kind of a Level 2 concept, and here it has a different name, one that wouldn't make sense in the place where you're reading these words.

The Absurdity Impediment is what's at play whenever we fail to notice a situation's moral significance on account of there being a strong element of absurdity involved. The Agatha Christie Book Club War is a perfect example: it's dangerously easy to laugh and call it ridiculous when previously friendly neighbours suddenly hate each other because they can't agree about whether every book written by Agatha Christie should qualify for the label of 'Agatha Christie book'. You might chortle and roll your eyes, and say, 'Oh, come on, you must be kidding!' and in doing so, you convince yourself there's nothing important here to notice. As a wise person once said (I can't remember who, sorry), 'There's no view from nowhere.' When you're stuck in Level 3, you assume anything that's hilariously ludicrous is as far away from serious and deserving of weighty consideration as it's possible to be.

The truth is the opposite of that. It's one of the first things we learn when we move up to Level 2: all too often,

Evil wears a cloak of absurdity in order to be underestimated until it's too late for Good to win. Why do you think most people in Swaffham Tilney – all but her tiny band of fervent supporters, the likes of Maureen Gledhill – now think of Deryn Dickinson as 'a few sandwiches short of a picnic'? And it's no coincidence that there's almost a fondness to these kinds of insults – an underlying affection that implies relative harmlessness. Yet think of what Deryn Dickinson set in motion when she could so easily have done otherwise: the heart-poisoning to extinction of the reading group she loved. It would have been both easier and more pleasant to compromise and include *just one novel* of the non-murder-mystery sort that Deryn, who only cares if there are corpses strewn across every page, didn't fancy reading. (Remember, also, that according to Corinne *The Rose and the Yew Tree* is as much a murder mystery as any of Dame Agatha's other works, albeit in a subtle way and with no clear solution at the end. Corinne likes it all the more for that reason. She cannot bear mystery books in which the right answer is handed to the reader on a platter, having not got where she is today by relying on others to problem-solve for her.)

All Evil needs to do is wear a cloak of absurdity and no one will believe it's happening. Champ's case proves that. There were at least a thousand social media posts in June 2024 from people who argued that what the Lamberts' supporters were claiming Tess Gavey had done was just absurd – too preposterous to be believed. 'What, so a

No One Would Do What The Lamberts Have Done

seventeen-year-old girl wakes up one day and lies for no reason? Pretends a dog savagely bit her, just because she wants to get that dog put to death? Even though he's never harmed her at all? I don't buy it. No one would do that. Why not, like, feed the dog some rat poison if you want to kill it? Much easier!' (*big sigh* No, it isn't. Not if you want desperately to be a victim, and it seems most people do these days.)

Strangely, those very same doubters, without stopping to ponder the inconsistency involved, were also the ones declaring authoritatively that no one would do what the Lamberts had done: go on the run as a family to save their dog, leaving behind homes, jobs, phones, friends, entire lives – 'Not for the sake of a ****ing dog, I mean, come on! I don't buy it.'

I swear, as long as I live (that's forever, by the way; the best bit of Level 2 is when you find that out), I'll never understand how even a mind in Level 3 could be so dysfunctional. All those fools who confidently bashed out their 'No-one-would-do' twaddle with angry fingers and broadcast it to the world *while knowing it wasn't true*. What they were loudly proclaiming no one would do, the Lamberts of Swaffham Tilney, Cambridgeshire, had demonstrably done. And, what's more, we couldn't have done it to any greater degree, or a single jot more comprehensively, than we had. This was a known and proven fact in Level 3 at the time, yet The Absurdity Impediment prevented so many from being able to avail themselves of the truth, just as it prevented Mum from realising that Champ could swiftly be exonerated without any more driving around the country under cover of darkness. If Mum had only contacted Auntie Vicky as soon as she found out Auntie Vicky was repeatedly sending messages saying 'Ring me!!', she could have spared herself a lot of mental suffering and saved us all a lot of time.

Why was she so determined to ignore Auntie Vicky? Well, because in her ideal world – the one she firmly believed should exist, instead of the actual reality in which she was embedded – nobody she trusted would have been engaging in non-sanctioned, illicit communications with all kinds of people, therefore nobody would have (also secretly) given Auntie Vicky the numbers of all the Lamberts' burner phones. An attempted communication that should never have been possible in the first place deserves to be ignored: that was Mum's belief. Besides, she found it all too easy to convince herself that whatever her sister wanted was bound to be *absurd* – not worthy of her attention if Auntie Vicky deemed it vital.

Why had she decided this? Because of the Facebook Business...

About a week prior to the first anniversary of the peach-stone-munching that moved me up to Level 2, Mum started working on a Facebook post about how much she loved and missed me, and also the strength of her hunch that I was totally still with her (I was: sitting next to her on the sofa in Shukes's lounge and, unbeknownst to her, helping choose all the best photos of me, me and her, all of us Lamberts together), when her phone rang.

It was Auntie Vicky, who wasted no time on small talk. 'Listen,' she said, 'I know the twenty-fourth of August is coming up, and I just wanted to check: are you planning on doing some kind of... death anniversary Facebook post?'

'Yes.' Mum winced at her sister's phrasing. 'We must be telepathic. I'm just picking some photos for it now. Don't worry, you're in one of them. Mum is too.' (By 'Mum', she meant Granny. *My* mum was busy making sure no one would feel left out of her planned commemoration of my awesome life.)

'Right,' said Auntie Vicky. 'The thing is... could you... Look, I'm sorry to ask, but could you possibly *not*?'

'Not?' said Mum. 'You mean... ?'

'Not put anything on Facebook about Furbert. Like, nothing at all? I'm sorry to ask, but... God, it's so ridiculous, but it's just Liam, you know? You and he are still friends on Facebook, aren't you?'

'Ye-es,' said Mum, confused. Liam was Auntie Vicky's ex-boyfriend. He'd lost a dog, a lovely ten-year-old English Setter called Stilton, nine months after I moved up. 'Vick, Liam will expect me to post about Furbs on the first anniversary of his death. He'd think it was weird if I didn't. If you're worrying it would be an insensitive reminder that his dog also died—'

'No, it's not that.'

'Good, because grieving dog-parents feel better when they can console each other—'

'Sal, I don't have time to—' A long sigh came from Auntie Vicky, who has at least three 'Blitz your To-Do List' planners on the go at any given time and, as a result, has almost no time to do any of the things on her endlessly duplicated lists. 'Okay, listen,' she said. 'I said nothing at the time because I didn't want to have to deal with your judgement as well as Liam's, but one of the reasons he gave for leaving me was that I didn't respond to Stilton dying like I would have to the death of a human.'

'Oh.' Mum's eyes widened.

Well, well, well, I thought but didn't say.

'I'm sorry if you felt the same about my reaction to Furbert's death, by the way.'

'I didn't,' said Mum. 'You sent a beautiful bunch of flowers. I was really grateful. So was Furbs, in spirit.'

True, I thought – but what nastiness was about to come at me down the pipeline? Something highly suboptimal, that was for sure. One thing they teach us in Level 2 is that deciding to make an issue, years later, out of something you originally kept quiet about is a sign of terrible character.

'Yes, I did,' Auntie Vicky said. 'That's right: I did send flowers.' Her voice had an unmistakeable pitch of 'So now please do as I ask' about it. 'Look, Sal, I don't want to ask you to block Liam on Facebook – I know you'd lose sleep about seeming unfriendly to a fellow... pet-grief sufferer. But here's the problem: if you do a big, emotional post about Furbert, I just *know* Liam will think, "Vicky's so much worse a human than her lovely sister. How come Sally can have so much love for a dog while Vicky's so hard-hearted?" And... I just don't want him having a chance to think that, because I'm *not* hard-hearted and I wasn't about Stilton. I tried to be supportive when he died, I really did. I just... I'm sorry, but I don't think some dog dying is as big a tragedy as the kind of suffering millions of people have to endure every day.'

Some dog... There was no mistaking the dismissiveness.

'Oh,' Mum said again. *Do NOT mention any of the boring causes that you're obsessed with, half of which are on the other side of the world and literally nothing to do with you or me,* she snapped at Vicky in her imagination. *I don't give the slightest shit about any of them compared to my adorable baby Furbs, who I lost.*

(I know it's 'whom'. We're taught grammar in Level 2. But no one thinks 'whom' inside their own head, not even the poshest person.)

'*Once*, only once, I made the mistake of saying to Liam that asking for two weeks' compassionate leave from work might be viewed by some – his boss in particular – as taking the piss, when it's just a pet that's died and not an actual family member,' Vicky went on. 'It didn't go down well, and I apologised. Look, Sal, the point is: whatever you were going to put on Facebook, Liam would take one look at it and decide you're the good sister and I'm the bad one. And he'd comment on your post, of course, and express his deepest sympathies, and then I'd have to read the conversation between the two of you in the comments, about your loss and his loss, and your pain, and his pain. I know I could choose not to read it, but I wouldn't be able to help it. And Liam would be way too tactful to say, "And your insensitive sister never understood" but he'd be thinking it every single second, I promise you, and then he'd wonder if you were right and I was wrong in other ways too.'

Mum frowned. 'Vick, I'm happily married and Liam knows that perfectly well. If you're implying—'

'I'm not saying he'd decide he *fancies* you!' Vicky muttered something under her breath. 'Oh, never mind. Do what you want. He's a knobhead anyway. Why should I care what a knobhead thinks? I don't want to be with someone who doesn't notice or care if the world's burning to the ground as long as he and his dog are okay. Maybe I'll close down my Facebook account and leave altogether. I don't have time to do it properly – not anymore.'

Vicky was sounding agitated, so Mum said, 'I won't do a Furbert anniversary post if you don't want me to.'

'You won't? Sal, you're a star!'

'It's fine. No worries at all.' Remember, Mum had been trained to believe that her upsetting others mattered far more than them upsetting her, even when they were in the wrong. 'I'll ask the kids to put something up on Instagram instead,' she told Vicky. 'The Facebook post isn't the only thing I've got planned. We're having a special commemorative dinner at—'

'Thanks *so* much, Sal. Seriously. I owe you one. Bye!'

'I guess that's that, then,' Mum said once it was just the two of us again. She stopped choosing photos, blinked away a few tears, and decided she'd use the story to entertain Dad later – since who could fail to laugh in the face of such blatant absurdity? (Do you get it yet? Absurdity Impediment klaxon!)

'Oh Furbles,' Mum breathed. 'Furbles-Burbles. Your Auntie Vicky's a bonkers loon. I mean, talk about overthinking things.'

Later, she told Dad, 'It makes zero sense. Completely irrational! As if it hasn't *already* occurred to Liam, probably hundreds of times, that I'm obviously so much more of an animal-lover than Vicky. Like, what new thought might have passed through his mind that hasn't before if I'd been allowed to do the post I wanted to do?'

'Nothing,' Dad said. 'Do it.'

'It's fine,' Mum repeated her favourite self-deserting mantra. 'Ree or Tobes can do it on Instagram. And I promised Vicky I wouldn't. I shouldn't have done that, should I, if it meant that much to me?' she said thoughtfully.

'No, you shouldn't have,' Dad agreed.

'But I mean, you've got to marvel at the sheer craziness of it.' Mum laughed. 'I only worked out later that there was a lot more to it – stuff Vicky either isn't aware of or wasn't willing to say.'

'Like what?' Dad asked.

'You're going to say this is pure invention on my part and accuse me of being as insanely overthink-y as her, but I know her so well, I know I'm right. She didn't want me posting on Facebook because she'd have felt she had to leave a comment, wouldn't she? Her dog-nephew's first anniversary…'

Dad winced, fearing Mum was about to say the words 'Rainbow Bridge', which she wasn't because she knew how he felt about that; in any case, she had no desire to trivialise my ascension to a higher realm with imagery that was both childish and inaccurate.

'If I'd posted about Furbs, Vicky would have felt obliged to comment – lots of people who are Facebook friends with us both would notice if she didn't, and think it odd. And especially, *Mum* would notice. She'd say something like, "I think it'd be nice, darling, wouldn't it? I think Sally would appreciate it if you wrote something." And Vicky wouldn't be able to stand that, having always been the good, approved-of daughter, but she'd be trapped in a double bind, because if she *did* comment, Liam would see it and think, "Oh, right, I see. Expressing your sympathies so sensitively when it's your sister's dog, but you've never left a single comment on any of my posts about Stilton." That's what's *really* going on.'

Dad had the confused expression of one who had been left behind at either the second or third permutation. If Ree or Tobes had been there, they'd have accused Mum of 'deeping it' in a way that was unwarranted.

No One Would Do What The Lamberts Have Done

I'm a better listener than Dad by far, and I thought Mum's point was inspired. The trouble was, it was also incorrect, which I'd known for some time – from as soon as I'd reached Level 2, in fact, nearly a year earlier. One of the billions of new tidbits of knowledge allocated to me in Level 2 was the real explanation for Auntie Vicky's Facebook intervention, which was this:

Vicky had told Liam many times that her sister Sally was unfairly negative about their father – who'd had his moments, sure, but was fundamentally a kind, loving, good parent that any child would be lucky to have; Sally's perspective on him was ridiculously harsh. She hadn't even been to visit his grave since he died – not once. How awful was that, after all he'd done for her, everything he'd given her?

That was what Liam had heard so far, and Vicky was confident it hadn't yet occurred to him to wonder if Sally might be as more-right-than-Vicky about dads as she was about dogs. If one day it should occur to him that there was another possibility...

Vicky found the idea unpalatable. No one must ever be allowed to wonder if her sister might have had a bad dad, in case that made it impossible for her, Vicky, to have had a good one.

It's fascinating when you reach Level 2 and get to explore all the connections and explanations you couldn't see before. Here are a few 'iffers', as we call them, that blew my mind when I first discovered them:

If Mum hadn't felt forced to wait till Grandad died before getting her first dog...

If she hadn't been too scared to say, 'Actually, Dad, I'm a grown-up now and this is *my* house, not yours. If I want to get a dog, I'll get one, and you'll just have to deal with it'...

If the innocence and innate goodness of dogs hadn't felt to Mum like the opposite of whatever dark, scary thing lay at the heart of Grandad, never properly acknowledged by anyone but Mum herself...

If the world and people in it hadn't kept socking her with the message that her desires, needs and feelings mattered so much less than what everyone else wanted...

If she'd tolerated and smiled her way through substantially, or even slightly less, unreasonable and uncaring treatment in her first 53 years, so that she was much further away from her 'Enough!' point when PC Connor Chantree turned up at her door...

If even one of the above-listed 'ifs' had applied, the Lambert-Gavey War would not have ended in the gruesome and shocking way it did.

Of course, it's only in Level 3 that what happened at the end was shocking, which ought to cheer up victims and perpetrators alike. From a Level 2 perspective, nothing went wrong. Everything worked out beautifully, as it always does in True Time (nothing in that compartment is left to chance, you'll be glad to hear) and I'm proud to have been part of the team that made it happen.

25

Tuesday 18 June 2024

Sally

It's almost completely dark by the time Sally sees the sign saying 'Norfolk.' Grateful as she is for all Corinne's help, she hasn't been relishing the prospect of spending the night (maybe several nights – who knows?) in a kennel, but now she's feeling sleepier, she's willing to concede that it might be fine. Corinne's kennels of choice are bound to be snugglier than most.

Sally has always felt safe in the dark. When she was little, her parents used to take her out to their friends' houses in the evenings, and she would sleep in a dark bedroom while the grown-ups chatted downstairs until it was time for her dad to drive them home. She can remember a tea trolley in one of the houses – she would pass it as she was carried to the front door. It was orange, which she could only have known if she'd seen it. That means what her mum likes to say to Ree and Tobes can't be true: 'Sally was brilliant as a baby. We could take her anywhere with us and we never heard a peep out of her. She just stayed sound asleep while we carted her around.'

Sally's earliest memory is of the comfortable lulling motion of the car and warm streetlights studding the night sky, receding from view as they passed. She loved looking at those lights; there was a sense of being part of something exciting that she wasn't old enough to understand – thrilling and at the same time risk-free, because her mum's arms were around her.

It's nice to remember this, pleasing to acknowledge that there was a time when being looked after by her parents had felt warm and safe. Has Corinne become her temporary parent-substitute?

When Sally wakes up, she remembers asking herself that question but not answering it. The lights must have lulled her to sleep, just as they used to when she was little. This time, though, they're coming at her from ahead, on both sides. *I'm supposed to be a grown-up now*, she says to herself.

'Okay, my turn,' says Tobes. 'Oh, Mum's awake. Feel better, Mum?'

'I'm fine.' Sally is groggy and disorientated. And, fleetingly, guilty. Is she shirking her responsibilities as a parent? Should she be letting Corinne take them off to yet another new place?

'We're playing the truth game,' says Ree. 'It's Tobes's turn. I've just had mine and I abstained. Trust me, you don't want to hear my worst truth.'

'All right, my turn,' says Tobes. 'And it doesn't have to be worst. I'm proud of mine. Mum, remember all those fights I used to get into at school, before I turned into a fine, upstanding citizen?'

'Oh, yes,' says Sally. 'Painfully clearly.'

'Oh, this is a good one,' Ree says with relish.

'Ree always wanted me to tell you, because school never did, but I thought it'd make you worry even more about whether I was going to end up in prison one day—'

'I've always been your biggest fan, bro.'

'—but it's probably safe to tell you now,' Tobes goes on. 'No one's worried about me anymore, right? I'm much more mature and haven't given in to any violent impulses for at least four years.'

'I'm not sure I want to hear this,' Mark says wearily.

'I never lost,' Toby announces with feeling. 'Not once.'

'What do you mean?' asks Sally.

'He means, he's got an unbroken record of victory,' Ree says impatiently. 'Isn't that cool?'

'It's true, Mum,' Tobes chips in. He sounds hopeful. 'I've never lost a single fight. Even when the opp was twice my size, as happened sometimes. I saw a lot of what you might call active combat for quite a few years – some, I'll admit I started; some, I got started on by someone else – and I was the clear winner, every single time.'

'That's amazing, Toby,' says Corinne. 'Well done!' A small squeal of anguish comes from Sally. Corinne adds quickly, 'And obviously it's brilliant that you're now mature enough to be able to find other, non-violent solutions to problems. But winning every fight you've ever fought? That's still an achievement.'

'I think so,' says Tobes.

'We're all proud of you, Toblerone,' Ree tells him, and for once he doesn't say *Don't call me that!*

'You know who else would have been proud of you? Furbs.' Ree sighs as she always does when she mentions his name. 'Furbs was a fighter. I'm not talking about his biting – that was just an anxiety response. I'm saying: if anyone had broken into our house and gone for any of us, Furbs would have destroyed them.'

'Champ wouldn't,' says Tobes. 'He'd mooch over sleepily and try to get his belly scratched.'

Everyone apart from Mark says, 'Awwww.' He says, 'What I still don't understand is: why aren't *we* being fighters? I don't mean going back and knocking the Gaveys' teeth out or anything—'

'That sounds like fun!' says Ree.

'I mean, we go back and we strategise, work out how to prove Champ was nowhere near Tess when she's claiming he bit her. We—'

'No.' Shutting him down whenever he says this has become part of Sally's daily routine.

'Let's not have this argument again,' says Tobes, and Sally thinks: *From schoolyard brawler to diplomat.* 'Your turn, Dad. What's your worst, most difficult truth to admit?'

'Here's one you're not going to like,' says Mark. 'If I

were back at The Hayloft now and it was still yesterday, I'd refuse to leave. I certainly wouldn't agree to leave my car behind, or my phone.'

'Oh, like we didn't all totally know that already.' Ree groans. 'What a stunning revelation. *Not*. Okay, I'll do one, but don't go mad, Mum. I made a little video on my burner phone of me singing Champ's Night Song, and... well, put it this way, I posted it online.'

'"Land of Cute and Furry"?' Sally smiles. 'I thought it was so embarrassing, I wasn't allowed to sing it in front of anyone you knew?'

'Yeah, that was before. Anyway, I posted it, and this really cool thing happened. Other people – my friends – all decided...' Ree breaks off.

Sally looks in the rearview mirror but it's dark and she can't see much. She hears Ree and Tobes mumbling to each other but she can't make out the words. 'What?' She turns round in her seat to inspect their faces. Did Toby just stop Ree from saying something? 'What's going on?'

'Just online stuff, Mum,' Tobes says with a reassuring smile. 'Some of our friends saw Ree's video and made videos of themselves singing "Land of Cute and Furry" too. You know, in support of Champ. That's good, isn't it?'

'Which friends?' asks Sally.

'I'll tell you all about it later, okay? Don't worry, Mum.' Tobes leans forward and pats her arm. 'It's all good, trust. Champ's got a solid posse behind him – that's the main thing.'

'Then let's go home and—' Mark tries again.

'Dad, for God's *sake*!' says Ree. 'We've just driven all the way to Norfolk.'

'Yes, which I knew was a big mistake before we set off.'

'Then you shouldn't have come with us, should you? You numpty.'

'Do not call me a numpty, Rhiannon. I'm your father.'

'I mean... do you have to rub it in?' she says. 'That's just sadistic.'

This is typical Mark, Sally thinks. Regretting things is a bit of a hobby for him, though he'd never admit it. No sooner has he put on a jumper or chosen a route than he starts to say plaintively, 'I should have worn my blue jumper – it's warmer' or 'Damn, I knew it was a mistake to go this way.' In the early days of their marriage, Sally used to try to investigate these little mysteries. She would say things like, 'I don't understand. If you *knew* it was a mistake, then why didn't you choose to go the other way, the way you thought was better?' Mark would get flustered and say, 'I don't know!', as if she'd presented him with the most impossible conundrum in the world.

'Right, your turn, Mum,' says Tobes. 'Tell us something about you that's true, that we don't already know.' Sally would rather get to the bottom of why he was being so suspiciously reassuring a moment ago, but she knows that to say so would lead to her being labelled a fun-sponge.

'Once I pretended to walk Champ at two in the morning,' she says.

No One Would Do What The Lamberts Have Done

'*What?*' says Ree. 'Why?'

'I mean, I didn't really pretend – I did take Champ out at two in the morning, that bit was true – but it wasn't because he needed or wanted a walk. I had to wake him up. I felt terrible for days afterwards for interrupting his sleep.'

'Then why did you?' says Mark.

'I wanted to go and see Shukes.'

'In the middle of the night?'

Sally nods. 'Henry Christensen was fast asleep, poor chap. I woke him up: kept ringing the doorbell till he came downstairs. In my defence, I was in a state and not thinking straight. I'd had a dream—'

'Sally, what the hell were you thinking?' Mark is irate.

'Relax, Dad,' says Tobes. 'Jeez. Everything's fine. Carry on, Mum.'

Ree says, 'Please don't be about to tell us you cheated on Dad with Mr Christensen, because if you are? That's a confession you should make privately first, just to Dad.'

'Of course I didn't do that,' says Sally. It baffles her the way her children occasionally suggest she might have some kind of bit on the side. Even if she ever saw a man she desperately fancied, which hadn't happened for at least ten years, she'd be happy simply to imagine his face and think about the sound of his voice. That would be far more pleasurable than actually engaging with the reality of him and discovering all the infuriating nonsense clogging up his mind and life that Sally knew she'd be unwilling to make room for.

'Then what, if not an affair?' asks Ree. 'Why else would you go round to Mr Christensen's house in the middle of the night?'

Because it's not his home. It's mine. Ours.

'I begged him to sell Shukes back to us,' Sally confesses. 'I'd had such an upsetting dream, in which I hated The Hayloft and all I wanted was to get Shukes back. It's funny, but I'm pretty sure it was soon after we found out the Gaveys were moving to Bussow Court. I don't think I realised that at the time.'

'What did Mr Christensen say?' Tobes asks.

'Not much. I didn't give him the chance. As soon as I'd asked and heard myself say it out loud, it dawned on me how late it was, that I'd woken him up and he might have had to perform open heart surgery the next day for all I knew—'

'Unlikely. He's a knee surgeon,' says Ree.

'—so I just started apologising profusely and told him to forget everything I'd said, and of course I didn't mean it.'

'This is typical of so many women,' says Corinne. 'They ask for what they want, immediately feel guilty for wanting anything at all, start apologising—'

'Oh, it's nothing to do with what sex you are,' Sally says impatiently. 'Nothing at all. It's people who, as children, had to bury their own true feelings at all costs, to appease difficult parents who only cared how *they* felt and had to be pandered to.'

No One Would Do What The Lamberts Have Done

After a short pause, Corinne says, 'True. It annoys me more when women do it, though, because I am one.'

'Do you really want to move back to Shukes, Mum?' asks Tobes.

Sally says, 'I've had my turn. It must be someone else's by now.' She doesn't expect to get away with this deflection, and is relieved when she does, then sad when the only explanation she can come up with is that no one else wants to buy Shukes back. They all like The Hayloft, and why shouldn't they? It's a lovely house, and the garden situation is perfect for Champ, totally secure. Yet Sally has always been convinced that he doesn't sniff the flowers and bushes there with the same enthusiasm that he always had for Shukes's front garden.

Even if that's true, though, she can hardly go back to Henry Christensen and say, 'Could you please ignore that I told you to ignore me, and reconsider my original hysterical request?' There's no point, if Mark, Ree and Tobes would veto another move.

'Your turn, Corinne,' says Tobes. Sally glances at the satnav as Corinne slows down and turns the car into a narrow lane. There's a scratchy, thwacky noise that accompanies them all the way down this single-track road: the sound of leaves and branches brushing both sides of the car. The satnav says they're four minutes away from the kennels.

'I tell you what,' says Corinne. 'Can I wait to reveal my truth until we get there? I promise you, you're going to love it so much.'

'No,' says Ree. 'That's cheating.'

'Can I bribe you?' Corinne asks.

'Like, with actual money?' Ree laughs. 'Nope. I'm a woman of principle.'

'I'm bribable,' Tobes says. 'Always.'

'We're here, though. Too late.' Corinne pulls into a wide courtyard and turns off her car engine as floodlights come on. 'But don't worry. You're all about to find out my truth. Here comes Jill.'

Jill, Corinne has told them in the car, is the wife of Niall, Corinne's eldest son. The two of them own and manage West Acres Boarding Kennels. Corinne bought the land for them, on which to start a business of their choice, and this is what they chose. Jill, in particular, chose it, after her beloved Boston Terrier, Yoyo, was banned from two other doggy daycare facilities for, according to Jill, no good reason at all. ('If you want an ideal environment for a human or a dog, don't expect anyone else to create it for you,' Corinne said solemnly. 'Make it yourself, or it ain't never gonna happen.')

Jill is wearing, among other things, a pyjama top with 'Beddybyes' printed on it in pink cursive letters. The smell of dogs is everywhere. It's in the air, hovering over the fields that stretch out beyond the big house and the L-shaped outbuilding that make up three sides of the courtyard. It's flat here, like at home.

Sally doesn't mind the animal smell, but she imagines Mark is revving up to complain to her about it as soon as their hosts leave them alone. It will be wonderful, she thinks, if they can stay here long enough for Champ to make some friends. In Swaffham Tilney, he sometimes goes – went, Sally corrects herself, because who knows if they will ever go back? Champ sometimes *went* for walks with Tippy, Kellie Dholakia's Clumber Spaniel. It's unlikely that he's started to miss Tippy yet, so now would be a great time for him to meet some new pals.

Jill gives Corinne a quick hug, then holds out her hand to Mark, who recovers well from his surprise. Sally smiles. He has been thinking of Sally as in charge and himself as a very minor character since they left Swaffham Tilney, and was expecting anyone new they met to shake her hand first. 'I'm Jill Harris,' says Jill. 'Wife of Corinne's son, Niall Sullivan.'

'Jill wants you all to notice that she kept her maiden name,' says Corinne with a grin.

'No, I'm just introducing myself – you know, like you do when you meet new people!' Jill says brightly, her smile hardening. 'Come on in. I'll show you to your room. I'm afraid you're all in together – one big family room, single bed in each corner – but I think you'll like it. We've just had it redecorated so everything's brand-spanking new, and there's a lovely, big ensuite with bath and shower. There's a state-of-the-art smart TV—'

'Wait, we're not sleeping in a kennel?' Ree says, wide-eyed. 'I thought we were sleeping in a kennel?'

Jill looks aghast at this suggestion. 'No. The kennels are… well, they're just for dogs.'

'Surprise!' Corinne giggles. 'That's my truth! Guys, I can't believe you thought I'd make you sleep in a fucking kennel!'

'But you said...' Mark begins.

'No, I did not. I never said anything of the sort. You all assumed it. All I said was: "We're going to West Acres Kennels, you can stay there." I thought you'd know I meant stay in the house. It never occurred to me that you'd think I was planning to put you in with the dogs. I was about to correct the misunderstanding, after Mark said, "I'm not sleeping in a kennel" and then it occurred to me that it'd be way funnier to let you believe it for a while.'

'I'm not being separated from Champ,' says Sally.

'That's fine,' says Corinne. 'Champ can sleep with you all in the big bedroom. Right, Jill?'

Jill's smile looks a little strained, Sally notices. 'Is that okay?' she asks her. 'Are you sure?'

'Positive,' says Corinne. 'I've already told Niall and Jill: I'll pay for a deep clean once you've gone. Jill doesn't normally like dogs being in the house, so she's doing us a special favour.'

'You really don't need to,' Sally tells Jill. 'If you've got a spare kennel, I'll happily sleep in there with Champ.'

'Don't be silly.' Jill backs away slightly. 'It's fine. Champ is welcome in the house.' She bends down to stroke him. 'Hello, handsome boy! Are you going to be our guest for a bit? That'll be fun!'

'Can we go and check out the room?' Tobes asks. 'I feel a movie night coming on.'

'You could watch *The Wizard of Oz*,' Jill suggests.

'Why?' says Ree. 'We're not, like, eight.'

Jill looks put out. 'I just thought… *The Wizard of Oz* is all about Dorothy wanting to save her dog from evil Elvira Gulch.'

Is that true? Sally wonders. She only remembers the music: the Tin Man singing 'Just because I'm presumin' I could be kinda human if I only had a heart.' And 'Somewhere Over the Rainbow' obviously. Does *The Wizard of Oz* have a happy ending? She wants to ask Jill but doesn't, in case she gets an answer she doesn't like. She can picture Dorothy waking up at the end and saying 'There's no place like home,' but she can't remember what happens to Toto, the endangered dog. How can she have forgotten that?

Sally realises she's standing still, not following the others in the direction of the house. She starts to walk, but something pulls her back. Corinne.

'What?' says Sally. Champ, at the end of the lead she's holding, lies down again, confused about whether he's supposed to be going or staying put.

'I want to give you something, while no one's looking. Here.' Corinne pulls a small, dark object out of her pocket and hands it to Sally. It's a credit card. Or a debit, maybe. 'You couldn't reach this card's limit if you tried, so no need to worry about that,' says Corinne. 'Pin number's three seven nine two. Don't tell anyone you've got it – Mark, I mean, mainly – and feel free to use it if and when you need to. Okay?'

'Are you serious?' The name on the card is Corinne Antonia Sullivan. 'Corinne, this isn't right. You've been extraordinarily generous, but I can't just spend—'

'You can, though. Okay, look, I wouldn't normally say this, but... guess how much money I've made since we left Swaffham Tilney, from doing *nothing*? Go on, guess. Or should I tell you? Two-hundred and eighty-three grand. My money just sits there making more money for me, all the time. It's wild! Like, seriously the most miraculous thing in the world. Well, sometimes it goes down as dramatically as it can go up – we don't love those times – but... you take my point?'

Sally holds up the card. 'Any money I spend on this, I'm paying you back. Those are the only terms I'll agree to.'

'Fine, if you insist.' Corinne shrugs.

'Anyway, I won't need to. I've got money in my account. Ten grand. Though God knows how long that'll last once I lose my job, which I'm bound to.' Sally tastes a sourness in her mouth as she says this.

'You won't lose your job,' Corinne tells her. 'I can sort it out with Quy Mill, I have no doubt.'

'But, Corinne—'

'Look, Sally, all that matters for now is saving Champ, right? Making sure the authorities don't get their hands on him. We can worry about your job later if we need to.' Corinne wrinkles her nose. 'You definitely want to carry on working there, right? You like... going there and doing

No One Would Do What The Lamberts Have Done

whatever you do? I only ask because I'm not a fan of jobs, you know. I'm really not. Bad things can happen to people with jobs.'

Sally frowns. 'Worse things happen to those without them, surely – those who want and can't get them?'

Corinne raises her eyes and makes a tearing-her-hair-out gesture with both hands. 'If even a third of those people would stop wanting jobs and want something different and better for themselves instead...' She sighs. 'What would you do if you could do anything, anything at all, and you could guarantee it would work out brilliantly?'

'Apart from making sure Champ, Ree and Tobes were safe forever, you mean?'

'Safe forever is a terrible ambition, but... okay, yeah. Apart from that.'

'My dream has always been to be a famous writer. To write books.'

'Cool!' Corinne perks up. 'What kind?'

Sally shakes her head. 'I think that's why I've never tried to do it. Any ideas I had always seemed silly. I'd tell someone and they'd go, "That sounds crap, who'd want to read that?", so I never bothered.'

Corinne tilts her head, a strange expression on her face. 'You know, don't you, that that's what unimaginative mediocrities always say when presented with a new, unique and brilliant idea?'

Is this some kind of attempt to inspire? Sally wonders.

Does Corinne have designs on her beyond the saving of Champ?

'Why are you helping me?' she blurts out. 'We don't even know each other, barely. And... why can't Mark know about the credit card? Is there something you're not telling me, Corinne? I don't want to sound paranoid, but... how do you know Champ didn't bite Tess Gavey? You've just taken my word for it. How do you know for sure that he isn't a dangerous dog?'

Corinne looks down at Champ, who is now asleep, and chuckles. 'Do me a favour, Sal. I've met syrup sponge puddings that are more threatening. I'm helping you because you didn't know me either when you decided to go out of your way to make sure Champ never weed on my front wall, when every single other person in the village either wanted him to or didn't care. Plus, you're the only person apart from me who's ever bought a house in Swaffham Tilney and immediately changed its name. I approve of and want to help people like me, and you're people like me.' She shrugs. 'So is Champ.'

Sally smiles.

'As for Mark...' says Corinne. 'Look, hopefully he'll stick with us, but he's making noises that concern me. He's getting disgruntled.'

'Oh, he'll be fine. I can manage Mark.'

'Maybe. But you might find that you and Champ need to break off at a certain point,' Corinne says. 'Lay low for a bit. Disappear – as in, not even tell Mark where you're going.'

'He's my husband, Corinne.'

'I just wanted you to have the card, in case you and I get separated,' she says. 'I like to be well prepared.'

'Mark will be fine,' Sally says again. 'He's not going to let us down.'

'I hope you're right,' says Corinne. 'And also? I've lost count of the number of men I used to think that about.'

26

Mum and Corinne were both right about Dad. He was showing distinct signs of disgruntlement. At the same time, Mum's power to manage him should never be underestimated.

'Wanna watch a movie with us, Mum?' Tobes said when Mum and Champ finally appeared in the large bedroom we'd been assigned by Jill and Niall. It was immaculately done up, with a straw-coloured fitted carpet that Jill called 'size-all', I think. I haven't met that word before but I suppose it must mean you can put it in any size of room. The wallpaper was blue with a repeating pattern of gold lines that looked like the middle of a violin, sort of, and there were four small lights with round glittery gold shades hanging from the ceiling.

There was a bed in each corner, and Jill had brought in Champ's Donut bed from our car and all his blankets – some monogrammed with his name or initials – a minute

No One Would Do What The Lamberts Have Done

ago, saying, 'Corinne said you'd want these.' She'd sounded a little disapproving. People have all kinds of judgemental beliefs about where dogs should sleep, and I'm sorry, but what is the problem, really? Let us sleep where we want. What harm will it do?

That's one of the great things about Mum – she's always wanted me and Champ to sleep in our favourite places and made sure that we can. My favourite spot when I was in Level 3 was always on the checked woollen blanket Great Granny Mabel knitted for Mum when she was a baby, on the back of the fat-backed blue squishy armchair in Mum and Dad's bedroom.

'Mum doesn't want to watch a movie,' Dad said briskly. 'Can I have a word with you, Sal? Outside?'

'But I've just come in,' said Mum.

'Yeah, Dad, she's just come in,' said Ree. 'You can say it in front of us, you know: you really think Mum should see sense and let us all go back home. Did I miss out anything important?'

'*Yes.*' The word exploded out of Dad's mouth. We all steeled ourselves. 'I can't take this anymore. I'm going back. You lot can stay if you want to, but I'm sick of it. I want to sleep in my own bedroom, without a horror film playing in the background. I want to drive myself around in my own car, and go to work and do all the things I normally do when I haven't been kidnapped by Corinne Sullivan! Yes, I care about protecting Champ, obviously I do, but... I'm sorry, I also care about *me*.'

Mum was nodding by this point, as if it was all fine and she completely understood. She'd gone into Dad-defusing mode. 'Let's let Ree and Tobes watch their film and go and talk somewhere else. Kids, look after Champy, okay?'

'Roger that,' said Ree. 'Do us all a favour: go and sort out your biggest child.'

'And I won't be spoken to like that,' Dad told her as Mum ushered him out of the room.

Once they'd gone, Ree said, 'You watch: Dad'll be happily climbing into his little corner bed in no time, fully back on message.'

Mum and Dad had found a balcony at the far end of the corridor our room was on, the perfect place to continue their discussion. 'Sal, I'm begging you,' said Dad. '*Please.* What we're doing here... it's crazy. It's been crazy from the word go. I don't want to have to go back without you—'

'Then stay.'

'—but I will if I have to.'

'I understand,' Mum said with considerably more patience than she was feeling. 'Honestly, Mark, I get it. Most people wouldn't do what we've done, what *I've* done. I'm fully aware. Take the kids and go home. Champ and I will be absolutely fine. Corinne will look after us.'

Dad's face darkened. 'It's not Corinne Sullivan's job to look after my family. It's my job.'

'Right, but... you just said you want to retire early from that job, no?' Mum feigned innocence. She can be a right old trickster when she needs to be. 'And no one in the

No One Would Do What The Lamberts Have Done

world would blame you for feeling that way.' Her phone, in her pocket, pinged.

'Who's that?' asked Dad.

Mum pulled it out and looked. 'It's Vicky. How the hell did she get my burner phone number?'

'Corinne must have given it to her,' said Dad.

'No. No way,' Mum insisted. 'Corinne doesn't have Vicky's number.'

'She could easily get it. She's probably got… operatives all over the country.'

'Oh, don't be daft, Mark!'

'Sal, there's no one else it could be except Corinne. Face facts.'

'It's a fact that Corinne would not have done that. You don't know her.'

'Neither do you!' Dad's chin jutted out alarmingly, looking as if it hoped to break free from the rest of his face.

'Look, somehow, Vicky's got my new number, okay?' Mum forced herself to stay calm. 'But that doesn't mean I have to respond or pick up. She can bloody well wait, and I'll speak to her when I'm ready. When we're back home. She probably wants to impose some new, absurd restriction on what I can and can't do.' Mum was thinking, of course, about the Facebook business; that's how the Absurdity Impediment prevented her from considering the possibility that Auntie Vicky might have something important to tell her.

'Just hear me out, okay?' said Dad. 'We are currently on

the run, with the backing of some... sinister billionaire that we barely know—'

'Corinne's not a billionaire yet,' Mum interrupted. 'She will be soon, though.'

'Well, that's terrible. Billionaires shouldn't exist, period. The fact that they do means something's gone very wrong indeed.'

Mum raised her eyebrows. 'You're saying you want Corinne dead?'

'No, of course not! I'm saying: no one should be allowed to keep that much money.'

'So, what, you approve of stealing now?' Mum was furious.

'For fuck's sake, Sal...' Dad groaned. 'I don't care about Corinne's finances. I just want to go home. It's what's best for all of us, including Champ. He didn't do it. We'll be able to prove that. You said lots of people passed you and him on the path by the lode, right? We can leave no stone unturned in trying to find some of those people. I bet we'll succeed. You can give a sworn statement saying Champ was *nowhere near* Tess Gavey's arm at the relevant time—'

'Mark,' Mum said quietly. 'You're right. I'm almost sure that's all true. I'm not disagreeing.'

'You mean...' Dad's eyes lit up. 'We can go back?'

'*I* can't. Or rather, I could, but I won't. I'm so sorry. It's the "almost" that's the problem. Like you, I'm ninety-nine per cent sure we could go home and stop the police from sending Champ off to be...' Mum couldn't bring herself to say it. 'But I'm *one hundred per cent* sure they can't kill him if they don't know where he is. And I'm not willing to take that one per cent chance. I'm not even sure they won't find him if I *don't* go back. How rock-solid discreet are Tobes and Ree, really? How confident are you that they've really not told a single one of their friends where we are? They could easily have decided there's no risk if they only tell Freddie, or Ivan, or Frankie—'

'If you think that then you don't know your children.' Dad sighed. 'They're on your side. Everyone always is, about everything, and I get to be the only bad guy, as usual.'

'No one thinks you're that,' Mum told him. 'I know you've done your best to do this my way.'

'What's the latest from Corinne about her brilliant Plan B?' asked Dad.

'She's still working on it. Told me to get some sleep and she'll have something sorted out by tomorrow morning.'

'Right, but what if…' Dad broke off. He chewed his lip, staring down at his feet. The sound of a dog barking came to them from somewhere far out in the night. 'Sal, I just want what's best for all of us. I'm honestly not sure this is it.'

'Look, Mark, the truth is, I'm not sure I can save Champ. Even if we keep running and never go back—'

'We can't *never go back*. We have to—'

'The thing is, if the police came and snatched him away now, and I'd murder them before I let them take him, obviously… but if I failed and if they did the unthinkable and executed him for a crime he didn't commit, at least I'd know that I *never chose to take that one per cent chance*, I never cooperated with the system that unfairly threatened him, that I have absolutely zero confidence in. I couldn't live with myself if I went back and anything bad happened to him. So, I'm going to put all my energies into believing that Corinne's Plan B will solve all our problems. Then we can go back to Swaffham Tilney knowing Champ will be safe.'

'How are you so sure we can trust Corinne?' said Dad.

'I just am.'

'How about we make a deal, then? We agree on a deadline. We give Corinne twenty-four hours. I'd even stretch to forty-eight. If she's sorted something we all agree to by then, fine. If not, we go home and do what normal people do: fight to prove Champ's innocence, through the proper channels.'

'Absolutely,' said Mum. 'Agreed.'

'Thank you. Thank God.' Dad was satisfied, finally. He even suggested they go back to the room and join in the watching of whatever horror movie Ree and Tobes had chosen. Mum told him she was too tired and needed to sleep, though she was afraid her guilt would keep her awake.

She had flat-out lied, of course. If Corinne's plan turned out not to be the miracle they were all hoping for, then Mum would make a new one herself. She wouldn't be going back to Swaffham Tilney in twenty-four hours, or forty-eight. Dad wasn't yet ready to face facts, but Mum had come to terms with the truth. She knew that she and Champ might never be able to go home.

Just as she was falling asleep, her phone pinged again

and she reached blindly for it in the dark, patting the floor beside her bed. Seeing that it was Auntie Vicky again, she decided she was now way too tired for whatever it was. *Not now, sorry,* she thought, and switched off her phone.

I could have read Auntie Vicky's message even though Mum hadn't opened it, but I didn't. Back then I was biased in favour of thoughts and speech. Perhaps I fell for Tobes's propaganda about anything involving the written word being 'long' (as in 'tedious, not worth bothering with'). I won't make that mistake again, believe you me. From now on, I'll be checking out all written, typed or mailed communications as soon as they land. You don't have to answer immediately or even at all if you don't want to, but for goodness' sake, get the information as soon as you can. If only I'd been as wise then as I am now, so much heartache could have been avoided.

27

Wednesday 19 June 2024

Sally

Something is rocking: gently at first, then harder. It's Sally herself; she is rocking back and forth, and she's not the one making it happen. Is she on a boat? No, she's at West Acres Boarding Kennels in Norfolk. This is wrong, then.

She opens her eyes, blinks, then screams. There's a man standing in the doorway, arms folded. Longish hair – nearly shoulder-length. He's wearing a creased, grubby white T-shirt, red and black checked pyjama bottoms and a black necklace that looks like a very skinny car tyre. The hall light is on outside the room. The person shaking Sally is Corinne, in a long navy silk nightshirt, her normally sleek blonde hair falling over her eyes.

She tries to speak but Sally can't hear her over the noise Champ is making. He leapt out of his donut bed and started to bark, presumably when intruders burst into their room.

'Who's the man?' Sally asks Corinne.

'My son Niall. Can you shut Champ up? The quieter we are, the better.'

'What the fuck's going on?' says Mark. 'Why's there a bloke in here?'

Ree and Tobes are fast asleep still. Corinne nods in their direction and says to Mark, 'Wake them up. We need to go. Now.'

'*What?* What time is it? I'm not going anywhere in the middle of the night. I'm sick of—'

'Fine, stay,' Corinne tells him. 'Sally, you and Champ need to come now. I'll explain on the way.'

In the end, they all go, Mark too, though he complains all the way. Ree and Tobes are groggy, as if anaesthetised, but they all arrive, with their possessions, at Corinne's Range Rover quicker than they'd have believed possible.

Corinne hugs her son, who hasn't uttered a word, then gets into the car and drives away. Sally sees tear streaks on Niall Sullivan's face, illuminated by moonlight, as they do a swing-turn and head out of West Acres' courtyard.

Sally looks at the clock on the dashboard: 03:45. *Bloody hell.* Adrenaline races around her body. 'Tell me,' she says.

'I'm so, so sorry.' Corinne sounds more sad than scared, and Sally can't work out if that's good or bad. 'Believe me, if there'd been a choice—'

'I'm not happy, Corinne,' Mark tells her. 'I'm in a car in my pyjamas, when I should be asleep in *my* bed, in *my* house, with *my* car outside—'

'Shut up, Dad,' says Ree. 'Corinne, what's happened? Where are we going?'

'Jill is what's happened. My darling daughter-in-law.' The sarcasm is unmistakeable. 'Niall woke me up half an hour ago to tell me she'd betrayed him – and, by extension, all of us. She's been blabbing on Facebook to her friends, told them Champ Lambert was at West Acres right now.'

'Oh, my God,' Sally whispers. It didn't occur to her to worry about Jill. Jill has a dog of her own whom she loves: Yoyo.

'Niall wants nothing to do with her after this,' Corinne says. 'That's their happy marriage over.'

'Oh, come on,' says Mark. 'I doubt it.'

'Having qualms is one thing, but telling people? That's unforgivable. Niall made it very clear how important it was to keep it to herself. She's got five-hundred-odd friends on Facebook. Suddenly they all know where Champ is. Was,' Corinne corrects herself. 'Soon we'll be safe again, don't worry, Sal. Damn! I can't believe a son of mine was dumb enough to marry that trash.'

Mark makes a noise: a dissatisfied grunt. 'This is a massive overreaction,' he says. 'Even assuming one of Jill's Facebook friends is awake at this time and alerts the police, it's not like they're going to be leaping into their cars, all blues and twos, and rushing over here, is it? This isn't an international manhunt, or even a national dog-hunt. It's not a hunt at all. No one's looking for us, as far as we know. I'm not convinced anyone official is even aware Champ isn't at home.'

'Not the point,' Sally tells him. 'Our security's been compromised. Leaving as soon as we could was our only option.' Something is niggling at the back of her mind, but she can't put her finger on what it is.

'By now Niall will have booked us rooms at the Langley Hotel in Iver, Buckinghamshire,' Corinne says. 'It's a wonderful five-star hotel and there's a whole separate building where dogs are allowed in all the bedrooms. It's right on the edge of a massive park, too – perfect for Champ-walking. Great spa, too.'

'What a stroke of luck,' Mark mutters sarcastically. 'I'm sure Champ's dying to have his nails done. How's your Plan B coming along, Corinne?'

'Really well, thanks,' she replies brightly. 'Someone's coming to talk to us about it tomorrow morning.'

'At the hotel?' Sally asks.

'Yup.'

'Who? How do they know we'll be there?'

'You should try and get some sleep while I drive,' says Corinne. 'I'll explain everything first thing tomorrow.'

'Everything's going to be fine,' Ree says decisively. 'Mum, you know how I told you Tess Gavey was a massive bully at her last school, before she made the mistake of trying to bully me? Like, she drove three girls to leave, she bullied them so hard? They literally made their families leave town to get away from her?'

'Vaguely,' says Sally. Mainly, she remembers the clench of pain in her chest when she heard how unpleasantly Tess had been treating Ree.

'Well, that knowledge is all over social media now. And I mean... *all* over. Tess is losing support by the minute.'

'You mean among your schoolmates?' Sally asks.

'Well... in general,' says Corinne ambiguously.

'Yeah, just generally.' Ree laughs.

'And... what's Tess saying? Has she said any more since the last thing you told me, about a neighbour's dog biting her?' asks Sally.

There's a pause. Why does it feel as if everyone in the car knows something Sally doesn't?

Corinne says, 'Tess is saying all kinds of untrue, horrible things because she's the same old despicable Tess Gavey she's always been. It doesn't matter, though. It's all grist to our mill. Let people see her being vile.'

Sally is aware that she should ask more questions, but she's exhausted, and soon falls asleep. When she wakes up, there's a large waterfall next to her and a huge white Palladian-style mansion building ahead that looks like a royal palace. 'Wow,' she breathes.

'Don't get too excited,' says Corinne. 'You're not staying in the main hotel. You're in the building over there, also very nice.' She opens the car door and points. 'The Brew House. That's the bit of the hotel that takes dogs. I've booked you all in under false names – you're a branch of the Sullivan family for now, okay?'

The other Lamberts all look at Mark, waiting for him to protest. He gives a small nod.

'So, you're super-unlikely to be asked Champ's name, but if you are? I'd maybe use his middle name, Cuthbert. How do you feel about that, Sal?'

'Fine,' Sally says. It's temporary, and Cuthbert is legitimately part of Champ's name.

Her phone pings. Vicky again. Another romantic crisis, no doubt. Sally becomes even more determined not to look, not until at least tomorrow, maybe longer. Just this once, she will allow her own preoccupations to be all she cares about. She's been at everyone else's beck and call for 53 years, answering every message sent by her mum, dad (while alive) and sister within seconds, even when at work, even when woken from a deep sleep. That has to change.

'You all head over to The Brew House and I'll meet you there in a second,' says Corinne. 'I'll just nip over and check us all in. There's no need for them to clap eyes on a family of four with a dog, is there? I was even thinking… well, it might not be necessary if my Plan B works as well as I think it's going to, but if not, it's worth thinking about making some alterations to how you all look.'

'Ooh, yeah!' says Ree. 'You mean like, dyeing our hair?'

'Or ballying-up?' Tobes yawns.

'What's that?' Corinne asks him.

'Balaclavas. You know, like… "Opp block bally on me."' He chants, doing a funny gesture with his arms and hands.

Sally assumes he's mimicking someone famous she's never heard of.

'Ideally not balaclavas, no.' Corinne smiles. 'That'd draw attention. But cutting and shaving hair, dyeing hair.'

'Absolutely not,' says Mark.

'We can discuss it tomorrow.' Ree sounds like a proper grown-up.

Corinne heads for the main building. As the Lamberts make their way from the big waterfall to the Clockhouse, Champ suddenly stops. Sally tries to chivvy him in the right direction, but he's fixed to the spot, staring at the ground.

'It's a frog,' says Ree. 'Champy's spotted a frog. Aww, sweet little froggie.'

'There are loads,' says Toby. 'Greetings, froggie brethren!'

'Maybe they've come from the waterfall or the park,' says Ree. 'Don't let Champ eat them, Mum.'

'I think he's trying to communicate with this one,' Sally says. 'Look at him. He's… Honestly, I think he's trying to have a meaningful interaction. Good boy, Champles. Is it a froggie? A new froggie friend?'

'Sal,' Mark says in a flat voice. 'I'd quite like to get a bit of kip. I'm knackered, after the interrupted night and the long drive.'

'Well, you can't. Not till Corinne comes back with our room keys. Mark, relax. I know it's not ideal that we're awake at God knows what time, but can you try for once, just this one time, to just… surrender and be in the moment?'

No One Would Do What The Lamberts Have Done

'I'm in it whether I like it or not,' Mark huffs. 'I don't get a choice, do I?'

Much later, trying to fall asleep in her and Mark's hotel bed with Champ snoring loudly between them, Sally remembers what it was that snagged in her mind, the thing Corinne said in the car that didn't quite sound right. She'd said that Jill, her daughter-in-law, had told all her Facebook friends 'Champ Lambert was at West Acres right now.' But none of Norfolk-based Jill's friends would know who Champ Lambert was. Yet Corinne had said it as if he were a well-known public figure.

And another strange thing too: why had Ree left it to Corinne to answer Sally's question about what Tess had been saying online? There had been that ominous pause, almost as if Ree was waiting for Corinne to take over, when surely she herself was far better-placed to comment on Tess's Instagram output.

What if...

No. That makes no sense. There's no way Ree and Corinne are colluding to keep something from her. Why would they? Sally must have imagined it. All the same, she'll ask Ree in the morning, just in case. When it comes to Champ's safety, she needs to know absolutely everything.

Finally, Sally falls asleep and dreams of Champ escaping from the police by becoming a tiny frog that lives in a waterfall.

28

Mum didn't get the chance to ask Ree anything the next morning, because Ree had a more pressing agenda of her own. When Mum woke up, Ree was in her room, sitting cross-legged at the foot of her bed. 'Awake at last, Mother. About time!'

'What's up?' said Mum. 'What time is it?'

'Quarter past eleven. You've missed breakfast, I'm afraid. Though I'm sure Corinne can, like, buy all the world's sausages and eggs and have them delivered to your mouth if you're hungry. But you haven't got time for food, so forget that. It's Sarah Sergeant Day!'

'What?' Mum sat up and rubbed her eyes. 'Where's Dad?'

'Out walking Champ, with Tobes. Corinne's on her way over from reception now, with Sarah Sergeant, because – did I mention this? – it's Sarah Sergeant Day! Yay! So rise and shine, brush your teeth—'

No One Would Do What The Lamberts Have Done

'Rhiannon, you're scaring me. Who's Sarah Sergeant? What the hell's going on?'

'Corinne'll explain everything when she and Sarah get here. Who is she? A lovely, altruistic hero of our times. That's who Sarah is, and you can't wait to meet her. Oh, and Mum? Auntie Vicky might ring or text you. Tobes gave her all of our numbers. Soz, but it's actually fine? She won't give them to anyone else.'

By the time Mum was able to mould some shocked splinters of vocabulary into a useful question, Ree was gone. The question, which went unasked, was: how did Vicky get in touch with you to ask for our numbers, given that she didn't have our numbers?

Twenty minutes later, there was a knock on the door of Mum and Dad's hotel room. Mum was washed, dressed and feeling more untethered than she could remember ever feeling in her life before.

Sarah Sergeant turned out to be an elderly woman with neat grey hair in a bob, held in place on one side by a wide flower-patterned clip. She was wearing pale-blue framed glasses, a navy pinafore dress over a white blouse with puffy sleeves, and red buckle-shoes like a child's, with grey tights, even though it was June.

'I'm on your side,' she told Mum, once Corinne had introduced her. 'Your campaign to save Champ – it's *wonderful*. Inspiring.'

'What campaign?' Mum looked at Corinne, then at Ree. 'Is something going on that I don't know about?'

'Something has been, yes.' Ree looked appropriately solemn. 'A viral internet movement, which I think I might have, in a way, started? We're a bit… famous now? Soz, Mum. I promise I'll tell you all about it once you've heard what Sarah's got to say. It's all good, though, and nothing to worry about.'

Viral. Famous. Mum couldn't really think about what any of that meant while this strange flowery, smiley woman was sitting in front of her. On her and Dad's bed, too. Dad wouldn't like that one bit if he came in and saw it, thought Mum.

'Sarah's a fellow Welshie-mum,' said Corinne.

'I'll show you my Bonnie.' With shaking hands, Sarah reached into her shoulder bag and pulled out a small photo album. She passed it to Mum. 'She's fourteen and really suffering now, poor little darling. She's blind and deaf and—'

'But she's had an incredible life,' said Corinne.

'Yes, she has.' Sarah nodded.

Mum looked at the pictures in the album. Bonnie was smaller than Champ and had a patch of white stretching from the middle of her chest up to her neck.

'Sarah took Bonnie to the vet last week, because… well, I'll let you tell Sally, Sarah.' Corinne stood back.

'To keep my Bonnie alive beyond this point wouldn't be fair to her,' Sarah explained tearfully. 'Next time she goes to the vet, which might be as soon as tomorrow or the next day, she won't be coming back.'

'I'm so sorry,' Mum said, feeling tears start in her own eyes. How awful, she thought. *Poor woman. Poor, sweet Bonnie.*

No One Would Do What The Lamberts Have Done

'I'd like to go to Cambridgeshire Police, if you'll let me, and tell them a lie,' Sarah Sergeant said. 'I'd like to say that it was Bonnie who bit Tess Gavey, not Champ. If I do that, they'll have to give up their attempt to punish Champ. And they'll never be able to prove it's not true.'

'No,' said Mum. 'Absolutely not. I mean... thank you, I know you're only trying to help but—'

'Don't say no straight away,' advised Corinne.

Ree had covered her face with her hands to smother a groan. The last thing Mum wanted was to be a dasher of everyone's hopes, but she couldn't possibly agree to what was being suggested. 'No,' she said again. 'It's not right. Why should poor Bonnie's reputation be trashed? I bet she's never bitten anyone either, just like Champ.'

'You're right,' said Sarah. 'She hasn't. But I'd like to do this for you and your family, Sally. And I'm confident Bonnie would too, if she understood the situation. I've always thought... I'm too old now probably, but if I could donate an organ from my body after my death, I'd love to—'

'It's not the same,' Mum told her. 'It's not right.' Everything inside her felt as if it was shutting down. She felt sick. She could see how much everyone needed her to agree, but she would hate herself forever if she did. *Poor Bonnie...*

No, this couldn't be the way. She'd be as bad as the Gaveys if she agreed to it. Miscarriages of justice weren't solved by falsely pinning the blame on those who were equally innocent.

'Thank you. You're very kind,' she told Sarah Sergeant. 'But I can't. Please don't... don't do anything like that. I'm sorry you've had to come all this way to...' Mum broke off as tears started to pour down her face. When she finally recovered – nearly half an hour after Sarah had left, taking her Bonnie photo album with her – Mum looked up at Corinne, who'd been waiting, and said, 'So. What's our brilliant Plan C, then?'

29

Large, it's me again, Connor Chantree. Here are a few more things that I wasn't sure whether or not to include, so I have. As follows:

1. a newspaper column
2. a few pages of dialogue between members of the Lambert family
3. info about a comedian and some vodka (this will make sense when you get there)

As per when I popped up before, I'll say the same again: these things are only of interest if there's a chance that we're looking at a murder. I'll be honest, Large: it's not that I think the coroner got it wrong. I actually think we could commission three more post-mortems and they'd all conclude the same. But deep down, and even though it makes no sense, I believe someone – maybe a Lambert, maybe a Gavey, maybe Corinne Sullivan – committed a murder so clever, they knew no autopsy would be able to prove it wasn't a natural death. And the thing is, Large, I reckon that's the point of this whole book. Whoever did it is advertising what they've done and boasting about it, but in a roundabout way. You'll see when you get to the end that we're being asked to believe in a murderer who *cannot possibly have done it*. That's the real killer's way of taunting us, I reckon. Like: 'We all know this isn't what happened, but you might as well accept this silly story as the truth because it's the only explanation you're ever going to get.'

So, anyway, here goes:

Below is a newspaper column by the *Daily Telegraph*'s Deborah Partrick. I doubt you read it at the time. I didn't. It doesn't prove anything at all, except that the opinion that the world would be a better place without Tess in it was a widely shared, and almost acceptable, one between mid-June and November last year. Anyone tempted to murder Tess, therefore, might have felt encouraged to do so. Have you heard of the Overton Window, Large? It means: what's considered by society to be the normal, acceptable range of beliefs at any given time. I'd say it was widened, in the second half of last year, to include the belief that the world would be a better place without Tess Gavey in it. Given that, it seems rather a coincidence, and certainly it defies logic, for her to have died from a supposed allergic reaction even though the post-mortem report

No One Would Do What The Lamberts Have Done

swears blind that the thing she was allergic to – fish – was nowhere in her system. Anyway, here's the newspaper column:

1) Newspaper column
Deborah Partrick, *Daily Telegraph*, 20 June 2024

Some of my older readers will remember a time, not all that long ago, when our justice system was a beacon to the world. With wistful sighs (or perhaps uncontrolled sobbing, if they're anything like me), they might recall the days when we could glory in the achievements of our top universities. That golden age, alas, is no more. Nowadays young people are made to approach every work of art through a thicket of silly trigger warnings, almost all of which double up as quite unnecessary surprise-destroying plot-spoilers (*Macbeth*: murder, suicide, infanticide, supernatural elements).

The modern university student is encouraged towards victimhood instead of resilience, fed great gulps of anti-scientific bilge from many directions and taught almost no history. The perilous ignorance that results from this approach is then duly celebrated by the misguided and the deluded, all in the name of progress. Most tragically of all, youngsters these days are neither taught nor, if we're being honest, permitted to think – not logically and certainly not for themselves. Quite the reverse; they are brainwashed into rejecting concepts that have served us well for centuries.

Failure and dishonesty on such a monumental scale have grave consequences. One of these is that I, who foolishly believed until recently, had no further flabbers left that might be gasted and no more gobs available to be smacked, find myself both flabbergasted and gobsmacked by the sheer idiocy displayed by so many in relation to the Champ Lambert affair.

I don't mind admitting to my own bias: I believe, though cannot prove, that Champ was with his 'mum' (as we're told she thinks of herself) Sally Lambert, walking along the lode path in Swaffham Tilney, Cambridgeshire, at 4.15pm on 17 June, as his family say he was. I am firmly #TeamChamp. I've done my homework – read every word available online about both the Lamberts and the Gaveys – and I know which family I believe is more likely to be lying through its teeth.

It's interesting that no one from the Champ-is-Guilty squad has come forward to defend Tess Gavey's character. Her online detractors report that she's an envious, spiteful girl. At least two octogenarian grandmothers have felt compelled to master the internet in order to contribute a Tess Gavey anecdote to the online furore, and those two accounts fit perfectly with all the others we're seeing from parents who escaped to Hampstead, Hull and several points in between in order to dodge persecution by Tess Gavey. It can't be a coincidence, surely, that the common feature shared by all the tales about Tess that have surfaced so far is a granddaughter or daughter leaving a school she previously loved in order to get as far away as possible from Tess's peculiarly vicious brand of covert cruelty.

That's who Tess Gavey is. Apparently it's who she has always been. Add to this a false accusation that might result in the lawful execution of a beloved furry family member, and I don't blame the Lamberts one bit for planning and enacting a successful getaway, having first decided to ignore the official machinery of justice in favour of their own idea of what that word means. I don't doubt for a moment that Tess's presence in my village would see me fleeing the contaminated area as soon as it was practical to do so.

But, wait – let's say I'm wrong: wrong about Tess, and wrong to believe Champ didn't bite her. (I was lucky enough to attend an excellent grammar school in the 1970s, where I learned that we might, any of us, at any time, be mistaken and that people could even disagree with us most vehemently and that wouldn't constitute a breach of our fundamental rights. We could argue the toss, and win or lose based on who had the superior set of arguments at their disposal, and there was no need for anyone to accuse anybody else of an annihilatory lack of affirmation or similar nonsense.) My point, of course, is that I positively enjoy thought experiments in which I make myself wrong, so let's do one now...

Let's say Champ Lambert is guilty, and Tess Gavey is a blameless and honest victim of his terrier teeth, as well as of endless unwarranted online character assassination. Even if we assume those circumstances apply, I'm afraid the vast majority of the pro-Tess contingent look no more sane or rational. Champ Lambert happens to be a dog, yes, but he is not – crucially – an American Bully, or anything to do with the question of whether or not American Bullies are dangerous enough to warrant the outlawing of the breed. Thematically, his story has no greater a connection with that particular debate than it does with, say, a Laurel and Hardy movie or the mutiny against Captain William Bligh on HMS Bounty in 1789. Why is it, then, that so many who are gleefully drooling at the prospect of Champ being caught and put to sleep are also active members of the campaign to make American Bullies illegal? And how are they able to be so certain that Champ did it? Note: most of these strangers who have never clapped eyes on a Lambert or a Gavey in their lives seem certain enough to assure us all that there is 'simply no doubt'. Could it be that their ability to think sensibly about the specifics of a unique situation is impeded by their deeply ingrained habit of cheering on the position in any *contretemps* that is most palpably anti-dog, no matter the specific facts of the case?

No One Would Do What The Lamberts Have Done

I'd like to believe that even if I or a loved one had recently been mauled, mutilated or maimed by mastiffs, I would nevertheless retain enough discernment to see that the Champ Lambert story isn't about dangerous dogs if Champ is innocent, as the Lamberts claim, and has never bitten anyone in his life. If that's the case – and my gut tells me it is – then this story belongs to a quite different genre. It's a parable about wrongful accusation and its horrific consequences. We ought all to be thinking not about American Bullies but about the tragic Dreyfus affair, or the grotesquely unjust chemical castration of scientific hero Alan Turing, or the hanging of poor Derek Bentley, whose special educational needs sadly cannot now be re-defined to include the need not to be murdered by the state for a crime he neither committed nor properly understood. Yet this obvious fact is ignored by hundreds of online warriors who need to pretend it's all about dangerous dogs because that's the topic they happen to be obsessed with.

And they're not the only witless wonders having their loud, sweary say on the subject of Champ's 'obvious' guilt; next we have the anti-colonialists, incensed because the Lamberts' special song about their adored pet – 'Land of Cute and Furry' – is one that takes its tune from the famous 'Land of Hope and Glory'. Depressingly, that musical national treasure is now viewed by a certain sub-section of society as a paean of praise for the exploitative cruelty of colonialism – and the very same idiocy that led our 'enemies within', as I like to call them, to form that misguided view, now drives them to extend their condemnation to include lovely Champ. I kid you not: I've seen commenters claim that of course Champ must have half-chewed off Tess Gavey's arm because what else would you expect the pet dog of conscienceless coloniser-sympathisers to do? And after Sally Lambert's 17-year-old daughter Ree told the world that her mother never reads a newspaper or watches the news, and would have no clue what the word 'colonialism' even meant, did such comments stop or increase? Take a wild guess.

All of the above, my friends, is not the bad joke it deserves to be. Instead, it's the predicament in which we find ourselves after 27 years of first a Labour government, and then a version of the Tories that's been indistinguishable from Labour, destroying this once-great country. And what delectable choices do we have on offer when we go to the ballot box on 4 July? Rishi Sunak, who wants himself and his wife to be able to hang on to their billions but doesn't care if his socialists-in-disguise cronies tax away any financial cushion you or I might have managed to secure for ourselves? No, thank you. Sir Keir Starmer, who has recently presented to the British public a manifesto more left-wing than any it has ever previously been offered?

It's enough to make anyone want to go on the run, frankly. And yes, I do think the huge groundswell of support for Champ Lambert and his family has a lot to do with the desire of so many of us to get the hell out of Broken Britain and away from those who would break it further and beyond repair. Let's face it, very few of us are able to think straight these days, though some among us are more aware of their prejudices than others. Either way, I'm glad the Lamberts have fled in an attempt to save their dog. Good luck to them in their attempt to defy the regime. I hope they end up somewhere freer and more civilised than where I find myself stuck, and I only wish they'd taken me with them.

2) These next bits are all conversations between the Lamberts. I don't know where they come from, but presumably around the time Sarah Sergeant turned up with her Bonnie plan. As with some of the free-floating bits I stuck in before, this is Sally Lambert narrating in first-person again. (Large, I'm more and more convinced Sally wrote this manuscript, and at a certain point changed her sections to third person so that it felt less like she wrote it.)

★★★

Why am I convinced that the next words out of Ree's mouth are going to horrify me?

'And?' I prompt, wishing I could turn and run in the opposite direction, but I can't. I'm hemmed in, in a small room. Well, it's not small, actually, but any room feels tiny when you're aching to escape.

'She's got a Welsh Terrier, a bitch. As in female dog, not a bitch like Tess Gavey. She's called Bonnie. She's nearly fifteen years old.'

'And fading fast, according to Sarah,' says Corinne.

'And... they're here?' I say. 'Now?'

'Yes.'

'Why?'

'To speak to you. To us.' Corinne speaks slowly and gently, as if she's tending to a delicate wound. Is that how she sees me? What she's saying – what they're all saying – makes sense on one level but, more fundamentally, clashes so profoundly with my understanding of the world that I can't extract any sort of stable meaning from it.

Something about this is so, so wrong.

'If this woman's here to see me, that means she knows I'm here, that we're here, with Champ,' I say. 'And... I'm guessing she knows why?'

'Mum, it's really nothing to worry about.' Ree puts her hand on my shoulder. 'Sarah's a hundred per cent on our side, and no one who isn't has the slightest clue where we are, I promise.'

'But what's this Sarah Sergeant woman doing here with her Welsh Terrier? Who is she? What does she want?'

'No, Bonnie isn't here,' says Corinne. 'Bonnie's too old and weak to travel.'

'I don't want to hear about dogs who aren't okay,' I say. Is this the best she can come up with, trying to make me sad about someone else who maybe about to lose their furry baby? Am I supposed to feel less alone?

'Mum,' Ree says. 'Stop panic-babbling and listen. Sarah Sergeant just wants to speak to you, okay? She wants to talk to you about an idea. You don't have to agree.'

'How does she know, though?' I look at Corinne. 'Is she one of the people you pay to do things?'

A look passes between Ree and Corinne, who gives a firm nod. Ree looks at Toby next. He nods too, though less decisively.

What the hell is going on? A fraction of a second later, Mark asks that exact question. He's clueless like me.

'All right, we're doing this.' Ree pumps her fists in the air. '*Do not* panic or overreact, okay, Mum? Everything is fine. Everything's under control. And try to remember, when you're tempted to freak out, that if all this online stuff hadn't happened, Sarah Sergeant wouldn't have been able to reach out to us and—'

'All what online stuff?' says Mark.

'Okay, so…' Ree takes a deep breath. 'You know Tess Gavey started to post about her terrible bite and how it was this awful aggressive dog that did it? And you know

I didn't just take that lying down? Right, well... I mean, it'd take too long to explain exactly what happened, but basically we went viral. I did a post with "#GoneDog #TheFurryFugitive" in it—'

'And I shared it on my story,' says Tobes.

'What story?' I feel as if I'm drowning.

'Mum, seriously, don't bother getting bogged down in all of that,' says Ree. 'Focus on the main point, which is: Champ went viral.'

'*What?*' I wail.

'No, that's a good thing,' says Tobes. 'It doesn't mean he's ill. It means he got very famous very quickly, in a way that, I'm not gonna lie, most of us only dream of and have no hope of achieving. So, props to you, Champy.'

Champ stretches out his hind legs.

'Well, and to me for coming up with those amazing hashtags for the campaign,' says Ree.

'Campaign?' I whisper, horrified by each new piece of information I hear. How could they have done this to me? *How?* My family who claim to love me and care about me, who I thought would help me to protect Champ... and Corinne, who promised to help too. Don't they get it? I want Champ to be as unknown, as non-famous, as possible; that's the only way he stays safe. Do these stupid traitors not understand what hiding means?

This isn't my fault. None of this is down to me failing to make it incredibly clear what I wanted.

'Okay, look,' says Ree. 'Mum? Stay with me, please.' She

arranges herself on the floor in front of me – cross-legged, hands clasped together, bright smile spread across her face like a net wide enough to catch any possible objections. This is how I try to look when I'm pitching to a potential client at work – *Here's why we're the very best team to host your wedding.*

'I didn't think of it as a campaign at first,' says Ree. 'I had no idea anything I posted would go viral, and even when it started to happen, I assumed it'd be a just-people-my-age-who-know-me-or-have-heard-of-me kind of viral – big enough to ensure Tess Gavey has no friends in the Cambridgeshire region for the rest of her life, but not… what it turned into.'

Another look passes between her and Tobes. The silent debate is easy to follow: *Should we tell Mum the full extent? The actual numbers? No. She doesn't need to know. It would only send her into proper hysterics.*

'I only started to think of… what we were dealing with as a potentially useful campaign once I saw how many people believed in Champ's innocence. It's *thousands*, Mum.'

Thousands. That might mean only 2,000 or as many as 50,000, and maybe even more. *Must not ask.* I can't believe this is happening, and the worst part is that, unlike the police who are after Champ, this isn't something I can run away from. Soon there might be millions of people talking about Champ on the internet and there's absolutely nothing I can do to stop them.

I feel a blast of pity for my naive former self: the one

who wondered how Vicky could have got our burner phone numbers, or got in touch with Ree and Tobes in the first place. For all I knew, hundreds of thousands of strangers might have messaged my children to ask how they could contact me.

'Now, remember,' says Ree, 'None of these people have a clue where we are or where Champ is, so security has not been compromised. All anyone knows is that we've left Swaffham Tilney and why. That doesn't put us at risk of anything. I haven't told a single person that we're here… well, until Sarah Sergeant—'

'—who could have told anybody, couldn't she?' I finish the sentence in a clipped, tight voice, too scared and angry to worry about upsetting my family for once.

'No, Sally, definitely not,' says Corinne. 'You don't need to worry about that. Sarah's solid, trust me. We wouldn't have risked—'

'Corinne devised a whole… security procedure,' Toby talks over her.

'What are people saying about me?' Mark asks. 'I don't want to be viral. I don't want to be talked about by half the world, thank you very much.'

'Don't worry, Dad, no one's interested in you,' says Ree.

'Mum, people are making videos of themselves singing Champ's Night Song.' Toby tries to sound solemn, but can't contain his joyful grin. 'And posting them on TikTok. It's *mental* what's happening.'

'The campaign's official hashtag is now #InnocentChamp,'

Ree tells me. 'I had to make a tough decision with *very* little help' – she shoots a savage look at Toby – 'and I'll be honest, I didn't—'

'Oh, sorry, who stayed up half the night to pick out all the cutest Champ photos?' Tobes protests.

Ree ignores him. After a dignified two-second silence, she goes on: 'I was *really* reluctant to let go of the Furry Fugitive and Gone Dog hashtags that did so well for us at first, but once the momentum was building and it started to feel like an unstoppable force had been unleashed, I just thought, neither of those is quite right. Like, they're misleading – or they easily could be. "Fugitive" was perfect but "Furry" wasn't.'

'Furry doesn't only mean what you think it means, Mum,' says Tobes.

'And Gone Dog was so, *so* close to perfect, except that… You've read *Gone Girl*, right, Mum?'

I nod – yes, I've read it – then repeat the gesture twice more. This is something positive, a 'Yes'-themed thing I can do with my head, that I can also hide behind.

The #InnocentChamp campaign… how can such a thing exist? And, since it does, how am I not in sole charge of it? I can't bear it. I want to scream and punch the bed until I've expelled all my rage. How could Ree do all this without me? She must never, ever find out how betrayed I feel. I don't think she'd be able to forgive me for feeling as angry with her as I do now.

I tell myself that of course she hasn't betrayed or abandoned me. She's just trying to help. I'm shocked, that's all. We're on the same side, me and Ree.

It's The Universe that's let me down, I decide. *I thought we had a deal, Universe. I thought the deal was: massive suffering in family of origin accepted without complaint or even a mention, but then my reward is: no suffering in chosen, created family. None caused by family members, anyway.*

'I just didn't want anyone thinking Gone Dog and Gone Girl might have anything in common, as characters, because they don't,' says Ree.

Corinne nods. 'That's good thinking, Ree. #InnocentChamp is perfect, and bang on point. That's the key message we need to put out: he didn't do this. It wasn't him.'

'So, now it's all coordinated,' Ree tells me. 'We've got the same hashtag across all platforms: InnocentChamp. No spaces, Capital I, Capital C.'

'Right,' I say. I don't know what's happened to my emotions, which were right here only a moment ago and are usually pretty close to the surface, even if I have to hide them most of the time. *Hashtag Gone Feelings.* For the time being, I can't seem to reach them. I would need to be convinced, in fact, that I have any. This is scarier than the anger was.

Silently, I recite to myself all the most upsetting things I can think of: *Your darling dog is not your own. The authorities can take him if they want to. Nothing is safe. The legal system can take Champ and kill him if it wants to, even though he's the sweetest soul that could ever exist.*

Nothing happens. I wonder about the possibility that I

will never have a feeling again, but even that doesn't move the emotional needle away from zero.

★★★

Large – I'm guessing this next bit is from at least a week later. It's about Champ's night song. I'm sure by now you've heard all the different versions. Here's a fascinating detail you might not know, though, and I only found it out from a piece I read where someone had done a proper analysis: in the end, there were more online posts arguing about 'Land of Cute and Furry' (which lyrics are better, the whole privilege/colonialism thing) than there were arguing about Champ having bitten Tess Gavey versus him being innocent. Can you believe that? Well, according to this guy (who admittedly might be wrong – I'm not sure how to check) it's true.

★★★

'If you ask me,' says Mark, 'the worst change is "thee" to "you" and "thy" to "your". The song's a period piece. It doesn't sound right with modern language.' From there, he launches into a rant about churches in which the proper wording of the Lord's Prayer has been abandoned in favour of easier language: '"Yours" is the kingdom? What's wrong with "Thine"?' Ten minutes on the Book of Common Prayer follow, and how there are almost no churches in Cambridgeshire that care about it anymore.

'I couldn't give a monkey's about "thee" versus "you",' I say. 'What I'm not willing to tolerate is "God who made thee bitey, make thee bitier yet." Champ *isn't* bitey. He didn't—'

A groan comes from Ree. 'Mum, how many times? You can say you won't tolerate it all you like, but people are singing it – as many who are on our side as who aren't. And they'll probably carry on. Not gonna lie, there's a whole... faction of people out there who'd love Champ even more at this point if it turned out he did bite Tess! They'd love him to get bitey so that he can defeat the bad guys.'

'But you said the "bitey/bitier" version came from Tess's supporters originally,' I say. 'I just don't understand why—'

'Mum, trust,' says Tobes. 'The official #InnocentChamp campaign has made its position very clear: it's "God who made thee cuddly, Make thee cuddlier yet". The overwhelming majority of Champ fans are still singing that version.'

'It's just a shame "bitey" rhymes with "mighty",' says Mark.

'It should be "fighty,"' Tobes yawns. 'That rhymes with "mighty", but also, you can fight for justice, can't you?'

'I reckon I could bite for justice too,' says Ree.

'It doesn't matter,' says Mark. 'What matters is that this campaign has turned out to be a brilliant thing. It changes everything. Champ's case is so high profile now, there's no way the authorities could whizz him off and put him to sleep without due process – not while people are writing about him in national newspapers. We'll be able to prove—'

'And what if the police don't accept our proof?' I cut him off. 'Tess's wound's bound to be healing by now. What if the tooth marks aren't distinct enough anymore for us to prove they're not Champ's?'

'Then we work on consolidating his alibi,' says Mark. 'We launch an initiative to find people who saw you walking him by the lode that afternoon.'

'Launch an initiative?' He's been listening to Corinne for too long. 'Mark, I don't know how to launch a bloody initiative, and neither do you.'

'Never lost a fight.' Toby holds up his hands. 'Just saying.'

'We're not going back,' I say in a steely voice I've never used before apart from silently in my head. 'And the lyrics of Champ's Night Song aren't up for negotiation. It's "God who made thee cuddly/Make thee cuddlier yet." Please, somebody who visits TikTok and Instagram regularly—'

'"Visits TikTok"?' Toby yelps.

'It'd legit be crease if it wasn't so cringe,' says Ree.

'—make it clear that Champ's mum requires all his supporters to stop changing the words,' I ignore my children's derision and carry on issuing orders. 'They're *my* words, about *my* dog. No one gets to change them without my permission. Also, Ree, I don't want Champ associated *in any way* with your new crop of best mates whose dogs have eaten toddlers and chewed people's legs off.'

Ree laughs. 'Loving your new sarcastic vibe, Mum. Suits you.'

'I know you're not being straight with me about that… new lot you've just recruited,' I tell her. 'Every time I ask you directly, you change the subject. Please get rid of them. Whatever you have to do.'

'Oh, for God's sake! Do you want to know the truth about the incredibly kind and caring friends of Champ that you're so keen to cut ties with? They're mainly people whose dogs, exactly like Champ, have been unfairly vilified for no good reason. Okay? You think being lied about by Tess Gavey's the only way a dog can be unjustly persecuted? You have *no idea* what some people have been through – lovely Darren, Sue and Dennis Cooper, Craig, the Youngs – all their dogs weren't even accused of acts of violence before being carted away. They were just unlucky enough to have a breed—'

'Hang on, who are all these people?' Mark asks me.

'We don't know any of them and we don't need to,' I say firmly. 'They're nothing to do with us.'

'Oh, so, we don't care about their dogs, no?' says Ree. 'We only care about our own?'

'I care about saving Champ. That's all. That's what this is. I'm not having my… mission diluted, or turned into anything apart from that. I won't stand for it.'

'God who made Mum fighty, make her fightier yet.' Tobes sounds impressed.

★★★

3) This next little snippet will feel like it comes out of nowhere, Large. I was pretty chuffed with myself when I worked out that it's about Dutch Barn vodka and the advertising of that same drink by the comedian Ricky Gervais. Read it, and then I'll explain what I think it means. You'll notice we're in first-person past tense for this bit, and it becomes clear after a few lines that it's the dead dog talking again – Furbert, describing a scene in which Sally Lambert is talking to Champ.

★★★

'It's genius,' Mum said. 'Because it's honest – more honest than most people are when they're trying to sell you stuff. That's what makes it funny. On the surface it doesn't seem obviously funny, it just seems blunt, almost a bit rude. The humour comes from… Hm, how do I explain a joke to a dog? Maybe you understand already. Do you? Do you, Champ-alo Soldier? Yes, you're a gorgeous boy, aren't you? You are. You *are*. Do you and your doggy friends already understand all the jokes, when you arrive on earth? Is that one of the many things we humans don't know about you? Well, anyway, just in case you don't get it, it's funny because it's true. We're not going to be any happier, basically, if we buy this vodka rather than any other brand. But Ricky will be – he'll be richer and happier, like the advert says. He's not making any false claims about the drink, he's just kind of saying, "If you like me and you also happen to want to buy vodka, I'd love it if you bought mine." That's it! And what does it tell us, Champ, when plain and simple honesty starts to seem so outrageously hilarious? It tells us that most people are committed to being hypocritical and fake. I don't even like vodka, but I went out and bought a bottle of Dutch Barn when I first saw that ad, because I *do* like authenticity. And that's why we love Ricky, Champy. He makes us laugh *and* he makes us think. And he just gets on with making the world a better place for animals, to the tune of gazillions of quids every year, while being bravely willing to *look* bad in order to *do* good. Amazing! But we mainly love him because he's a big…' (tickle) '…fan…' (chin stroke) '… of gorgeous furry boys like you! Isn't he? And Furbert – he and Furbert are very alike, you know. And we'll let him off not believing in Heaven, won't we? We will! Yes, we *will*. Because when we're all up there together and we bump into him, he'll have to admit we were right about death not being the end of everything.'

★★★

Large, Ricky Gervais is an investor in the company that makes this particular kind of vodka. The advert Sally's referring to here is a big photo of him grinning, and it says something like, 'Drinking Dutch Barn vodka makes a person richer and happier – and that person is Ricky Gervais.' I just happened to have seen that advert myself,

No One Would Do What The Lamberts Have Done

so I knew straight away. Gervais is also well known for not believing in God or an afterlife.

When I read that bit, something else fell into place too: the stuff about star words, and learning meditation in Abbots Langley. You might not remember, but Furbert says in one of his chapters that his star word is 'Ricky', and that he does a meditation that goes 'Praise Ricky, Thank Ricky' when he wants to calm down. I thought to myself, 'What if that's Ricky Gervais he's talking about?' I didn't want to assume anything, since it could have been a coincidence – Ricky isn't exactly a rare name – so I searched for 'star word, praise, thank, Ricky Gervais' and got nothing. Then I looked up places in Abbots Langley where you can learn meditation, and that led me to the explanation I was seeking. Guess what? Sally Lambert, in 2018, went on a meditation course in Abbots Langley and took her dog Furbert with her. The people who ran it remember him well. Apparently he climbed up on the kitchen table and helped himself to half a pot of the vegetarian goulash that was meant only for the human guests.

This particular kind of meditation involves what the teachers call the 'Praise attitude' and the 'Gratitude attitude'. That seems to map on very neatly to 'Praise Ricky, Thank Ricky'. Star words, also, belong to this same branch of meditation, and when you go on one of these courses, you're asked to choose a word or name that represents (for you only – it's an individual choice) the highest good in the world. Some people choose God or love or hope.

If you recall, Large, we've been told that Sally Lambert chose 'Furbert Herbert Lambert' as her star word, and that's why Furbert isn't jealous that Champ's got a Day Song and a Night Song – because he alone got the special distinction of being his mum's star word.

Why am I telling you all this? Why does it matter? I think it shows how tricksy and manipulative Sally Lambert is. And clever – the long vodka paragraph above proves that, I think. She understands humour, honesty, dishonesty, subtlety.

We all know dead dogs can't write books, Large, so the late Furbert Herbert can't have written this one. It's Sally, isn't it? Pretending to be him, and laughing right in our faces, basically. Just blatantly taking the piss, making us read all about how her dead pet worships an atheist comedian so much that he's turned him into a deity. Remember The Absurdity Impediment? Sally Lambert's using it against us, entertaining herself with some truly absurd comedy and having a good laugh at our expense. And, sure, when we read it we notice the absurdity and even appreciate its entertainment value, maybe – and we miss what lies beneath it.

That's Sally Lambert's aim, I reckon. What she wants us not to notice (or maybe she does want us to work it out, I don't know) is that everything she's written, this book or whatever it is, has only one purpose and reason for existing: to contain, in a completely unprovable way, her confession to the murder of Tess Gavey.

30

Once Sarah Sergeant had been dispatched from the 'Many Frogs Hotel', as we Lamberts now call it, back to wherever she had hailed from, the social-media-savvy members of our party (Ree, Toby and Corinne) explained to the social media dunces among us how the users of many online platforms were being mobilised to save Champ from the wicked machinations of the Gavey clan and their flunkies, aka Cambridgeshire Police. I'm sure no one needs me to name the dunces in question, but just in case: I meant Mum and Dad, not Champ, as it would have been impossible for him to have had a better grasp of TikTok, Discord or Snapchat Spotlight, however hard he'd tried.

My parents, on the other hand... much as I love them both, I can't deny that our forward progress as a family was significantly impeded by their failure to grasp the basics of online life that you'd have thought any fool would be able to get to grips with relatively quickly – especially if said fools had Facebook accounts on which they'd sporadically posted pictures of me, Ree, Tobes and Champ for more than a decade. Not Mum and Dad, though. As Corinne whispered to us Lambert offspring one night after the digital dimwits had fallen asleep: 'Two Facebook accounts do not two astute social media strategists make.'

Luckily, the younger generation of Lamberts had much more flair for the sort of thing that was required. The strategy of the whole #InnocentChamp operation was devised almost entirely by Ree, while Toby's wit, charm, sense of humour and verbal dexterity made him the perfect copy-writer and content creator, and ensured that the right message was transmitted far and wide: not only was Champ innocent and immensely lovable, but supporting him was also highly likely to make you more virtuous, popular, happy and healthy than you'd ever dreamed of being before you stumbled across this worthy cause. Joining the #InnocentChamp effort, becoming a 'Champ Champion', seemed to offer instant membership of an in-crowd that Toby's words brought to life in the imaginations of thousands, implying all kinds of far-reaching and life-enhancing perks without actually naming any. Declaring yourself to be '#TeamChamp' was a life-choice and social status upgrade available to anyone with a social media account, at no cost whatsoever.

What's not to like? as my non-furry siblings say. It was all so persuasive that even I, already a Team Champ member since day one, found myself wanting to join and feeling mildly frustrated that I couldn't because I was already 'in'.

Once they'd finally grasped what was going on and that it was real and massive, not just a silly made-up game confined to Ree's and Tobes's burner phones, Mum and Dad jumped straight from baffled and bumpkin-like to horrified/irate. It would have been nice if there had been half an hour of 'Wow, kids – this is so impressive' in between.

To be fair to them both, they did later say all the right things and apologise for having been slow to get on board. And I'm grateful to have witnessed their temporary numbskullery too, because it made me ponder some important topics at a deeper level than I otherwise might have. The conclusion I drew was this: clever people are more likely than stupid people to be harmfully stupid. The stupidity of stupid people is rarely dangerous. It seems mainly to consist of needing to have the obvious endings and meanings of pretty basic movies and TV shows explained to them. You can tell how many stupid people there are in Level 3 by how easy it is to find full explanations online of film endings that ought to require no clarification. Try Googling 'end of Cinderella explained' and you'll probably find hundreds of versions of: 'What makes the prince realise it's her is that the glass slipper fits her foot. He has already been round all the other houses and tried all the other feet and not a single one was the perfect fit until Cinderella's, therefore she must be the one who ran away from him as the clock struck midnight.' (It would not surprise me at all if you also found comments saying, 'However thoroughly the Prince thinks he's searched, it's just not plausible that he's succeeded in finding and checking the shoe size of every female in the area. Also, what if she wasn't local?')

While the stupidity of stupid people might be a tedious waste of time, it's generally not capable of doing the worst kind of harms, as long as it remains unmixed with cleverness, because there's nothing beguiling about it. (I like the word 'beguiling'. I think this is the first time I've ever used it, and I'm definitely going to use it again.) Clever people, on the other hand, dress up their stupidity so that it looks like a fascinating, unusual place that everyone should want to visit – and that's when the trouble starts.

Apropos that… I often wish my whole family wasn't so in thrall to Mum's beguiling yarn about my death, and how I was callously manslaughtered by a litter-vandal whom she will one day succeed in hunting down and punishing. She thinks it's a tragedy that I moved up when I did, even though she's in no doubt that I'm still with her, and feels my presence by her side every day (I make sure of that).

It makes no sense to miss me at the same time as knowing I'm still here… until you realise that nearly everyone Mum has ever met believes moving up to Level 2 is the saddest thing that could possibly happen. She's been groomed from an early age to believe that.

No One Would Do What The Lamberts Have Done

It's a shame that those in Level 3 can't get their 'What-To-Think's from those of us who have left it, since we see a much fuller picture. It blows my mind each time I remember that they don't know about Everyone Gets Equal. (I'm sorry, but I can't explain this one. We'd be here forever if I tried, and I'm not sure it can properly be understood in Level 3 anyway.)

As soon as I arrived at Level 2, I was shown who dropped the peach stone that moved me up. It was Tavia Foster, the ex-girlfriend of Conrad Kennedy from Bussow Court's The Byre. Tavia wouldn't normally have dreamed of dropping food remains on the street, but she was a wreck that day. She'd been in the middle of eating the peach at Conrad's house when he'd told her it was all over between them. She left in a hurry and was running through the village in great distress, and when the half-eaten peach dropped from her fingers, she didn't notice, having forgotten she was holding it.

To my mind, this is entirely understandable. I keep trying to communicate to Mum that there's no reason to hate either the stone-dropper or peaches, but I haven't managed to get through to her yet on that front. The villain-victim-rescuer model is still her favourite shape of narrative, and she's still clinging to her belief that there's a peach-dropping baddy to be tracked down and destroyed.

The truth is, I'm not the victim of a peach stone; I'm the rescuer of Champ. And I needed to be in position, exactly where I was and where I am now, when the Gaveys launched their attack. Everything that happened unfolded exactly as it was always meant to.

I keep trying, gently, to guide Mum towards the conclusion that peaches are not to be hated or feared. My first attempt to transmit the message was far too clumsy; I managed to smuggle some peaches into her shopping at the big Tesco in Milton, with the help and hands of an oblivious elderly woman who was there at the same time. Mum acted as if someone had planted rat droppings in her trolley and removed the peaches as soon as she spotted them. I wanted to yell, 'I love peaches! Peaches are delicious! Peaches are innocent!' but I didn't want to cause a shake-up of all the levels by speaking out loud.

I suppose I should clarify, since I've just said the above… Yes, proper audible speaking is something I could do if I wanted to. All family-pet-spirits could. The ramifications would be seismic if any of us did, obviously, and so none of us will – not, at least, unless and until there's a crisis to which it's judged to be an appropriate response. I'll admit, it was hard to hear, and to have to accept, that the Gaveys' persecution of Champ was not viewed as such a crisis. One day, one or more of us will have to speak and be heard, but that day is at least ten years away, if the rumours are to be trusted.

It's no wonder I was so thrilled by the emergence of the #InnocentChamp movement, in which tens of thousands of wonderful people raised their voices so decisively. The sudden and intense power of that tidal wave of support for Champ was something to behold and all the proof I'll ever need that a huge outpouring of good can overcome the most corrosive evil.

Which brings me to Sarah Sergeant and her Bonnie-sacrificing plan. Sarah meant well, but to say I was relieved when Mum vetoed her proposal is an understatement. It would have been quite wrong to tarnish, publicly, the reputation of poor, innocent Bonnie. And, really, Corinne should have guessed Mum would never agree to save one dog by slandering another. I knew there were better ways to handle our problem – or rather, I was starting to know, and to plot.

Corinne's poise and confidence were undented by what Mum, Dad, Ree and Tobes viewed as our temporary stumped-ness. 'It's fine,' she kept saying, and I could tell she believed it. 'I'm already working on an even better Plan C – so good that by the time I've finished, we're going to want to re-christen it Plan A!'

I didn't doubt her, and wondered how similar her eventual plan might be to the one I was quietly assembling in my mind.

What I didn't expect was any input from anyone else – not until a torrent of blasphemous swearing erupted from Ree. 'Mum, everyone,' she said, once she'd stopped spluttering obscenities. 'Listen. No, I mean, really listen. I've thought of something massive. I can't believe it's only just occurred to me.'

31

Wednesday 19 June 2024

Sally

'Think about Bonnie, Sarah Sergeant's Welshie,' says Ree.

'Why?' Tobes is scathing. 'That plan would never have worked anyway.'

'Shut up, will you? Mum! Remember the photos Sarah showed us? Can you picture them? Dad, can you?'

'But Bonnie looks nothing like Champ,' Toby goes on, undeterred by the attempt to silence him. 'I mean, is she even a full Welshie? Didn't look like one to me.'

'She is,' says Corinne. 'Kennel Club registered and everything.'

'Well…' Tobes shrugs. 'It still wouldn't work. Tess Gavey would say, "No, that's not the dog that bit me – that dog looks completely different." And then the police would look at Champ, and look at Bonnie, and go, "Oh, yeah – no resemblance whatsoever."'

No One Would Do What The Lamberts Have Done

'Is it a boy/girl thing, the lack of resemblance?' Mark asks Corinne, who shrugs.

'If you could all just *shut up* for a second?' Ree glares around the room. 'Right. Thank you. Mum, listen. Bonnie—'

'No,' Sally says automatically.

'For God's sake,' Ree growls. 'You think you know what I'm going to say, but you don't. I don't want Bonnie getting offed by the feds any more than you do, okay? Hear me out. When Sarah showed you the photos of Bonnie, what was the first thing you thought?'

Sally thinks back. Eventually she says, 'Sarah was talking about all Welshies looking alike, and I thought, "Not this one." I thought, "You couldn't possibly have shown me a picture of a Welsh Terrier that looks less like Champ."'

'Right.' It's the answer Ree wanted. 'Exactly. Me too.' She looks and sounds like a lawyer who knows the last words out of the witness's mouth have just won the case for her. 'I thought the same. I knew you'd have said no anyway, even if Bonnie and Champ had been identical, facially – but they barely even looked like the same species. And I'd probably have thought no more about it if we hadn't watched that movie a few days ago – the one with the scientist that either looked or didn't look like Vinie Skinner, depending on your point of view. But we *did* watch the movie, and I remembered the argument we had about resemblances, and… you know how your mind just sometimes goes off in weird directions? Well, mine does

– and I found myself wondering if Tess Gavey cared whether there was a resemblance or not, between Champ and the dog who actually bit her. Like, did she get bitten by a different Welshie and think, "Aha, now I can frame Champ Lambert"? Or was the dog who attacked her a Jack Russell or a German Shepherd? Did she think, "Who will ever be able to prove it wasn't Champ, even though it was a dog that looked nothing like him?"'

'Wait…' Sally staggers to her feet. 'Wait. Let me think.'

'Have you got it, Mum?' asks Ree. 'You look a bit possessed right now, so I'm guessing you've worked it out, just like I did.'

'Worked what out?' says Mark.

Ree turns to face him. She says, 'Let's go through the possibilities. One – a dog who looked like Champ bit Tess, and she honestly believed it was him. Two – a dog who didn't look like Champ bit Tess, and she deliberately lied and pretended it was him. Since Tess is a scumbag, I don't believe she made a genuine mistake. There aren't any other Welshies in Swaffham Tilney anyway, so I think she lied. Which means *she knows it wasn't Champ who bit her.* They probably all know it – all the Gaveys.'

'Right,' says Corinne, 'but so what? I thought we were all assuming that anyway.' She looks round the room, at each of us in turn. 'Did anyone here believe it was a genuine mistake: that Tess truly believed the dog that bit her was Champ?'

Mark and Toby are shaking their heads.

No One Would Do What The Lamberts Have Done

'Oh, my God,' Sally whispers. 'Ree – oh, this is... this is... The swimming pool story!'

'Exactly!' Ree yells.

'The Field View Health Club!' says Sally.

'Yes, Mother. Well done. You've got it. No one else has got it yet.' Ree sits back, satisfied.

Sally looks at Corinne, then at Mark. 'It's not just Champ who didn't do it,' she says. 'It's not just Champ and Bonnie who are innocent. It's *all of them.*' This matters so desperately, she can't find the right words to express it. 'All the dogs are innocent. Every single dog in the world. No dog bit Tess Gavey, Mark, *no dog at all.*'

Mark frowns. 'How do you know?'

'Think about the story Corinne told us about Field View, and Lesley trying to get people fired because she wasn't allowed to stay in the pool for a second swimming session. Even after the club had apologised, it wasn't good enough for her – heads had to roll. She's the most vindictive woman alive. There's no way on God's green earth that she wouldn't want and demand justice – by which she'd mean death and nothing less – for any dog that had really bitten Tess. However much the Gaveys hate us Lamberts, there's no way they'd pretend Champ did it if that meant the guilty dog going unpunished. No way in hell would Lesley Gavey let that happen.'

'Maybe not, but... I still don't understand,' says Mark. 'Why are you women all so excited? What are Tobes and I missing here?'

'Because if we're right, and we are, we have to be... and well done, Ree, for thinking of it – brilliant, just brilliant,' says Sally as Ree blinks away happy tears. 'If we're right, then there's only one thing it can mean. And us knowing what that is gives us power. Think, Mark!'

'I've got it,' Tobes breathes. 'Nice one, Ree. But also...' He shivers. 'This is now getting a bit like something out of a horror movie, and these people are our neighbours, so—'

'Shall we just, like, watch Dad's face until he works it out?' says Ree. 'Come on, Dad. It's worth it. Soon as it clicks for you, you'll be as excited as we are.'

'I've got our new Plan A,' says Sally, decanting a sleeping Champ from her lap to the bed as she stands up. 'I don't see how it can fail.' Seeing Corinne also rising to her feet, she says, 'No. It has to be just me. You all stay here and look after Champ. This next part works better if I do it alone.'

32

In the end, Mum agreed to let Corinne be her driver and companion for the journey, though she wouldn't budge about needing to do the confrontation part on her own. Dad tried to insist on going too, in case it all went wrong and Mum got physically attacked by either Lesley or Alastair Gavey, but Mum told him firmly that wouldn't happen and that he needed to stay at the Many Frogs Hotel to look after Ree, Toby and Champ.

'If by any chance the police come and try to take my Champy baby away, stop them,' she said to Ree when Dad was out of the room for a second. She thought of Ree as the next most ruthless Lambert after her. (The actual ruthlessness hierarchy is: me at the top, then Mum, then Ree, then Dad and Tobes joint fourth, and then Champ last.) 'Do whatever you have to do,' said Mum. 'Anything.

Have you got some kind of chemical hair product with you that you could spray in the police's eyes?'

'You really need to ask me that?' said Ree. 'Of course I have.'

'Good. Dad will think he has to cooperate and go all law-abiding citizen if someone official turns up, so you might have to overpower him or lock him in the bathroom or something—'

Dad walked back into the room at that point, with what he thought was a good idea. He tried to persuade Mum and Corinne to do the drive first thing in the morning instead – 'It's ten forty-three at night. You can't set off now!' – but Mum said she wouldn't be able to sleep in any case: the buzz inside her, from knowing what she was about to do and sensing that victory was inching closer, was too strong. 'I want to be there at six, not setting off then.'

'We'll be there long before six if we leave now,' said Corinne. 'We'll get to Swaffham Tilney before one o'clock if there are no road closures or diversions. Maybe we can get some sleep at my house, or yours, before you—'

'No,' said Mum. 'If we're there at one, then I'll wake the Gaveys up at one.'

'Sal, you can't do that.'

'Oh, I can, Mark.'

'But I mean... you're not honestly going to wake people up in the middle of the night, are you? Corinne, can you talk some sense into her?'

'No, and I'm not sure I want to,' Corinne said. Everyone

but Dad was experiencing a warm inner glow as they imagined the Gaveys being woken up at one in the morning.

As it turned out, there was some nocturnal faffing of the motorway-construction kind going on, which meant a diversion off the M25 via, of all places, Abbots Langley, where I chose Ricky as my star word all those years ago. Corinne swore and grumbled, but I was thrilled. I knew what it meant, you see. What greater clue could there have been that our mission was blessed and destined to succeed? (Praise Ricky, Thank Ricky.)

I was in the car with Mum and Corinne, of course. I was hardly going to miss the big showdown. At the same time, though, I was still at the hotel with Dad, Ree, Tobes and Champ. In Level 2, we call it 'dispersing'. You can get exhausted quite quickly if you disperse too often and I'm rarely tempted – there is almost always one place I'd much rather be at any given time – but tonight was an exception and I was determined to be with all my family simultaneously.

Nothing dramatic happened at the hotel. There was no sudden influx of uniformed authoritarians bearing handcuffs. Dad fell asleep about five minutes after Mum and Corinne set off for Swaffham Tilney, having first fumed and declared himself frantic with worry for around 75 seconds. He and Champ then snored in harmony for the rest of the night, while Ree and Toby stayed up watching horror films, declaring each one to be not as horrific as the thing we'd worked out, or thought we'd worked out, about the Gaveys.

It was 2.15am when Mum arrived at their house in

Bussow Court: The Stables. Nothing happened in response to her first ring of the doorbell, so she pressed it again. This time she heard a window opening above her head. A cold yellow light came on, slicing into the darkness. 'Who's there?' a man's voice asked, sounding thin and ghostly.

'Hello, Alastair. It's Sally Lambert. I'm here to talk to Lesley.' Mum listened to the whispering, hissing and rustling that followed, and thought it was interesting that no 'How dare you?' or 'Do you know what time it is?' was lobbed down at her from the open window. It sounded as if the Gaveys were silently panicking instead – guiltily scrabbling, having been caught red-handed sleeping in their own beds in the middle of the night.

More lights went on inside The Stables. Eventually, a full seven minutes later, the front door opened. Lesley and Alastair Gavey were both standing there with enormous white towelling robes of the crest-on-chest sort wrapped around them. Alastair had brown loafer-style slippers on and Mum could see the bottoms of maroon pyjamas; Lesley's feet were bare, toenails painted white. A line of navy-blue text ran along the edge of her right foot: a tattoo. Mum couldn't read it at first, and was preparing to ask what it said, in case it was something she needed to know about, like 'Champ Lambert must die.' Then she adjusted her position and saw it had nothing to do with Champ: 'Do it for you, not for them', whatever the hell that meant.

One after the other, Lesley and Alastair tightened the belts of their robes. Neither of them spoke.

No One Would Do What The Lamberts Have Done

Mum couldn't wait to get started, but also wanted to force them to make the first move, so she waited.

Finally Lesley said, 'What do you want?'

'Just to talk. Can I come in?'

'No.'

'Okay. I'll say what I've got to say out here, then.' Mum raised her voice. 'I'm sure lots of the neighbours are crouching beneath their bedroom windowsills, listening. It's a warm night too – lots of windows open at The Byre and The Granary, to name but two. I've got nothing to hide though, so it's fine by me.'

'All right, come in,' said Lesley quickly.

'No, don't let her in!' Alastair sounded alarmed. He moved to block the doorway.

'Just go to bed!' Lesley shrieked at him suddenly. 'Let me deal with something my way for once in your fucking life!'

It was a proper, decibellicious scream. (Yes, I invented the word 'decibellicious'. Just now, in fact.) Mum was sure Corinne must have heard it all the way over at Ismys House, especially if she was outside pulling the weeds off her front wall, which had been her plan. 'I feel as if our lives in the village are about to change beyond all recognition,' she'd told Mum. 'I'm pretty sure I want to enter this new phase with a weed-free wall.'

No more lights came on in any of the nearby houses, though Mum was sure Lesley's scream had woken everyone in Bussow Court. Tess Gavey had to be awake too, though she didn't reveal herself – and since Alastair had vanished like the memory of a hologram the moment his wife raised her voice, it was just Mum and Lesley left standing on either side of the open door of The Stables.

'You coming in, then, or what?' Lesley said ungraciously.

Taking her first step across the threshold into enemy territory made Mum feel unbalanced and jumpy, but she reassured herself of the okay-ness of everything by visualising Champ, safely far away; by now he would be lying on his back on the hotel bed, head half-hidden in the groove between Dad's pillows and Mum's, with his front paws in the air and his wet black nose poking out at a funny angle.

Once she was inside and the front door was closed, Mum waited for the offer of a cup of tea or a glass of water, but no refreshments were even alluded to. That was a shame; Mum would have enjoyed specifying which sorts of drink receptacles she found intolerable, as Lesley had when she'd viewed Shukes.

A row of abstract paintings in heavy-looking black metal frames dominated the wall opposite the stairs; crude, bright splurges – blue, green, violet, orange – as if made from the dripped blood of several different alien species who wouldn't have got on well if they'd met. The wall on the stairs side was plain, a pale lilac colour, whereas the paintings-wall was papered: pink and green checks, a sort of futuristic, metallic tartan. Someone had created this effect by choice, and my only thought on seeing it for the first time (I'd been in Tess's bedroom before but not

No One Would Do What The Lamberts Have Done

the hall) was that perhaps every family got the entrance hall it deserved.

Lesley Gavey stood in front of her wide, wooden staircase, arms folded. The message was clear: downstairs only, no access granted to the upper level. Mum was fine with that; she had no desire to see any Gavey toothbrushes. 'Champ didn't bite Tess, and you know that as well as I do,' she told Lesley. 'I'm not here to argue with you, so don't bother saying anything. We both know the truth. No dog bit Tess – no dog at all. She was bitten by a human, and that human was you.'

The expression on Lesley Gavey's face was all the confirmation Mum needed: instant terror. She made a noise that sounded like the haunted engine of a very old car struggling to change gear, and didn't bother to deny it. And I have to say, Mum pulled off the tone with aplomb. It was everything it needed to be, exactly what she and Corinne had tested and honed for hours in the car *en route* from Many Frogs to Swaffham Tilney. A bored-cum-weary-cum-bureaucratic note was the right one to strike, they'd agreed – the voice you'd use to tell someone that, unfortunately, since they hadn't filled in the form in blue ink before 23 February, as stated in the small print... blah, blah, blah.

Next came the part Mum wished could be different. She'd have preferred to tell the truth and explain to Lesley how she'd worked out that there couldn't have been a guilty, bitey dog because if such an animal existed, the Gaveys, vindictive as they are, would have gone after him or her instead of Champ. To say all that would have given Lesley a way out, since it was only a theory. The smart move, Corinne had insisted, was to pretend to have concrete knowledge. Proof.

'Maybe if you'd spent less time screaming at Tess about how useless and ungrateful she is, she wouldn't have dobbed you in, but...' Mum shrugged. 'Too late for that, eh? How do you think I know you're the biter? Tess didn't tell *too* many people the truth, but...' Mum broke off with a shrug. 'How often have we all done it? You tell just one person, thinking, "This doesn't really count as telling anyone. One person is almost no one. It's as good as telling nobody at all." Wrong. Big mistake.'

Mum shook her head slowly, in apparent regret. 'Now, since Tess doesn't have any friends because her personality is so repulsive, I guess she wasn't exactly spoilt for choice when it came to confidantes.'

Lesley sat down on her staircase's lowest step. Her lower lip had started to tremble.

'Here's the plan,' Mum said calmly. 'At the moment, only a handful of people know the truth, but the story's going to break on social media very soon – tomorrow, the next day latest, I'd guess. And trust me, Lesley, what you need to do is get ahead of it. Seriously. This is the same advice I'd give my best friend: break the story yourself, with profuse apologies from you and Tess and your whole family. Ring the police, get Tess to announce it on Instagram, Snapchat, TikTok. Say you lied because of some very distressing personal circumstance your family's been dealing with, something everyone will agree deserves heaps of sympathy... So, like, I recommend *not* choosing anything along the lines of having to get out of a luxury swimming pool a few minutes earlier than you'd ideally have liked to, because no one's going to sympathise with that. Oh, and cite mental health issues! Make up some kind of borderline-bipolar-ish-ness, and pretend you can't remember anything you did during that bleak period.' By now Mum was getting into her stride and quite enjoying herself. 'I don't actually care what else you say apart from that Champ definitely didn't bite Tess,' she told Lesley. 'That's all that matters to me. You have to take back the lie that you invented in order to try and get my dog killed. If that's okay?' she added bitterly. 'And, you know, the great thing about a mental-health-based lie is that it's kind of true at the same time. I mean, no one of sound mind would go round behaving the way you do. It's not rational or healthy to weep outside other people's houses for hours, or to bite your daughter's arm and try to pin it on an innocent Welsh Terrier. So you are, in fact, a proper nutter, even if you haven't got an official diagnosis.'

Lesley had started to cry. 'I'm so sorry, Sally. I just... I can't describe how sorry I am. It's a terrible thing we've done to you and your family. I don't know what's wrong with me. How could I do it?' she gasped, eyes wide. 'How could I bite my own daughter? I... it felt like such a good idea when I first... But I never meant to bite her so hard. All we needed was a few little tooth marks to be able to say it was Champ. I don't know what went wrong, but... somehow I ended up really wounding her. I scarred my baby for life. It wasn't supposed to be a big deal. I mean, I'd bitten her before and nothing like that had happened.'

'You'd...' Mum cleared her throat. 'You'd bitten her before?'

'Yeah, when she was a baby,' said Lesley. 'When they're tiny and their little buttocks are so pink and round and perfect, it's so tempting to bite into them, isn't it? Don't tell me you never did that, Sally, and drew blood by accident.'

'I have never, ever done that,' said Mum. 'No one does it, just like no one but you embeds their teeth in their teenage daughter's arm in the hope of... what? Ruining our lives? Why? What did we ever do to harm you?'

'Nothing. You're right,' Lesley sobbed. 'Ree's been a bitch to Tess at school, but—'

'Only after Tess bullied her for months.'

'—you and the rest of the family have done nothing to deserve it. Champ did nothing to deserve it. I'm so sorry, Sally. You have to believe me. I'm so mortified, I truly am! I wish I'd never suggested it or done it. Look, please don't tell anyone. *Please*. I'll contact the police tomorrow, say it was a different dog and that we made a mistake—'

'No. Not good enough,' said Mum. 'No lying about made-up dogs. You'll tell the police the truth: that you lied. And that Alastair and Tess lied too.'

'Alastair didn't,' Lesley whispered, with a glance over her shoulder up the stairs. 'He believes the story. Sally, you've got to help me. I think I... really need help. I'm in pieces here.'

'Why not ring and tell the police right now?' Mum suggested brightly. 'I'm sure someone will be awake in a police station somewhere. It's never too late, or early, to do the right thing. Go on, why not ring now, while I'm here?'

'I don't understand why I do half the things I do, Sally.' Lesley put her head in her hands. 'I just feel so worthless sometimes, like no one gives a shit about me, and I... I lash out, you know? At whoever's there. You and I could have been friends when we both moved to Bussow Court, couldn't we?'

'I don't think so,' said Mum.

'There's something about you, Sally,' Lesley rambled on. 'You've got this quality that you probably don't realise you have. You're so lucky and so... special, in a way. Blessed. From the day we first met, when I came to view—'

'Shut up, Mum,' came a voice from above Lesley's and Mum's heads. 'Stop talking right now.'

I pulled back a little when Tess first appeared at the top of the stairs, where I was also hovering. Silly, really, since she couldn't see me. Nor did she see me the time before – three days ago, on 17 June – when I was last at The Stables and in her bedroom...

What's that? Are you wondering why I was in Tess Gavey's bedroom? (Ha! Of course you are, because I invited you to do so.) Look, I wasn't planning to interrupt this key scene with a confession, but I'd quite like to get it over with now that I've started.

The truth is that however much Lesley Gavey likes to scream at her daughter when she's feeling powerless and petulant, which is often, she wouldn't have furiously chomped into Tess's arm in the precise, lifelong-scar-creating way it was chomped into, namely, with an unquenchable lust for the raw meat of revenge.

For weeks before The Day of the Bite, I'd felt the danger-heralding hum of what Lesley intended to do to Champ vibrating in my veins; it drew me over to The Stables, where I found Lesley excitedly telling Tess the plan and how likely it was to work. I saw and heard the two of them giggling and plotting, agreeing there was no better time to take the toothy plunge than right at that moment. I fully agreed, and, in my righteous rage, allowed myself to get carried away; I threw my full force into Lesley's mouth muscles and into that bite. The degree of wounding that followed – the agonising, gruesomely disfiguring kind – wouldn't have happened without my participation.

Immediately afterwards, while Tess lay screaming and bleeding on the floor of her room, I thought, 'Lawks a mercy!', which is something Granny sometimes says. I'd been too impulsive, and knew I'd messed up. I couldn't bear the possibility that I'd sealed Champ's fate in the worst possible way, when all I'd been trying to do was punish his enemies. What if he was about to be judged more harshly by the police, when they saw the severity of Tess's injury? In Level 2, we're constantly warned to be wary of Level 3 motivations creeping into our thinking, and I'm normally good at spotting them when they try to take hold, but I completely missed it this time.

'My mum didn't bite me,' Tess told Mum, looking down from the top of the stairs. Despite being nearly 18, she was wearing a red all-in-one babygro affair with buttons all the way down the middle. 'Your dangerous dog bit me, and he's going to have to come back here at some point and face up to what he's done. You all are.'

'Your mother's just admitted it was her and not Champ,' Mum said.

Tess rolled her eyes. 'Duh. Because she's scared of you, obviously. She'd say anything. She's probably worried you'll strangle her to death or something. Maybe it's not only the Lambert dogs that are violent psychos. Maybe the human Lamberts are too.'

Silently, I willed Mum not to succumb to the rage that must have been thumping inside her, and to stick to the strategy. It was a good one, and our best bet. She just had to keep it constantly in mind.

'Lesley?' she said. 'Anything to say?'

'Tess is… It's true what Tess just said.' Lesley was busy wiping away her tears with the towelling belt of her robe, now undone. 'I was scared. I told you what you wanted to hear.'

'See?' Tess gloats down at Mum.

'I'd imagine you get quite a lot of that, Sally,' Lesley muttered. 'You can be very intimidating, whether you realise it or not.'

'Well, I suppose we'll have to let our online audience decide who's right and who's lying, then,' said Mum. 'Luckily, they'll soon all be able to hear every word of who said what.'

I exhaled with relief when I heard this key line, flawlessly delivered. This was the plan; we were on track. Still, it was hard not to feel as if we'd had a setback. Lesley's confession followed by her repudiation of it felt like an amazing gift, withdrawn. I reminded myself, and hoped Mum was doing the same, that we hadn't in our wildest dreams expected any of the Gaveys to admit to anything. That had been a bonus, of which we had retained a significant part: the recording. That had been Corinne's idea. 'She's never going to admit it,' Mum had protested, and Corinne had sensibly said, 'It doesn't matter. Every time she opens her mouth she reveals what a baddy she is, and she'll certainly say something, probably lots of things, which we can then share far and wide. And if there's really nothing on the recording, you can always delete it later – but I can't think of any good reason not to record, just in case. It's so easy to do.'

Mum pulled her burner phone out of her bag and said, 'Shall we have a little listen? A preview?'

Please let the sound quality be top notch, I prayed. *Please, Ricky. I'll never ask you for anything again.*

Mum happened to rewind to the perfect bit – assuming it wasn't an instant intervention from Ricky that made her choose that particular point to press 'Play', which I for

No One Would Do What The Lamberts Have Done

one believe it might well have been – and we all listened to the voice of Lesley Gavey say, 'I never meant to bite Tess so hard. All we needed was a few little tooth marks to be able to say it was Champ.'

'That ought to do it,' said Mum, moving towards The Stables' front door.

'Grab her phone, Mum!' Tess yelled. 'Don't let her leave!'

'Aa-and that'll now be in the recording too,' said Mum. 'You didn't think I'd press record *again*, did you? Well, I just did, so your attempt to hide the evidence of your and your mother's dog-murdering aspirations just failed. Thanks for that.'

'How dare you?' Lesley stood up and staggered forward. Mum took a step back.

Keys, I thought. I concentrated on it so hard, I became the word: *keys, keys, keys*. A fraction of a second later Mum noticed them, hanging from the front door lock on the inside. In a quick, seamless sequence (which must have been choreographed by Ricky; I don't see how it could have happened so beautifully otherwise) she grabbed them, opened the door, stepped outside, closed the door and locked the Gaveys in – all while Lesley was screaming at her that she was a demon and a C-word.

Then Mum and I ran as fast as Mum could (I could have got there much faster whizzing over on my own, obviously) to Corinne and Ismys House.

33

Thursday 20 June 2024

Sally

By the time Sally and Corinne arrive back at Many Frogs Hotel, Lesley Gavey's confession has been played all over the world and (at the last count) 373,000 times. Ree has provided regular updates and has been extremely busy online since Sally sent her the recording from Swaffham Tilney. What Sally can't work out is whether the Gaveys, or at least the two female members of the family, would have killed her if they'd had the chance. If she hadn't thought of locking them in, if she'd stood still or not been quite so quick on her feet... what would have happened?

Her phone pings as she and Corinne are walking across the hotel lobby to the lift. *More news from Ree,* Sally thinks, and stops to see what this latest update is, though she'll be in the same room as the rest of her family in less than five minutes. That's not soon enough, though; she needs to know whatever it is right now this instant. Things are happening fast, and every ping so far has been something amazing and miraculous: rapidly rising numbers of supporters, the conversion on a mass scale of the previously unconvinced, whole extended families who have filmed themselves performing harmonised acapella choruses of Champ's Night Song.

This latest one's the best yet: Ree has forwarded a photo of a... Sally can't tell if it should be described as a tweet or a post, or which channel of the internet it hails from, but it's a short statement from Cambridgeshire Police to the effect that they're taking the recording of Lesley Gavey's confession very seriously and will be investigating as a matter of urgency. Ree's added commentary says, 'Thats the actual feds awesome work mum gaveys going prison yay ahaha'.

Is that true? Sally isn't sure. Is it a crime to bite your daughter and pretend a neighbour's dog did it? Since dogs can't commit crimes – which they can't, because they have no understanding of the law – doesn't that mean that trying to frame a dog can't be illegal either? Cambridgeshire Police might take a dim view of it and will hopefully administer a stern rebuke, but is it an imprisonable offence? Sally doesn't want Ree to be disappointed. She would love it if Lesley Gavey got sent to prison, but...

An uncomfortable thought accosts her: what if Lesley gets punished for the grievous bodily harm she committed against Tess's arm (grievous bodily arm, Sally thinks) but not for what she did, or tried to do, to Champ? That would be awful. She should be, *must* be, punished for all the things or else it won't be proper.

'So what's it going to be?' Corinne scoops a handful of wrapped sweets out of the *bonbonniere* as they wait for the lift. 'Are we going back to Swaffy T and fighting, now that we've got our proof and most of the world is behind us, or are we still running? Have you decided?' She presses a wrapped orange sweet into Sally's hand.

'Swaffy T?' Sally makes a face. 'Really?'

'Yeah, I've always called it that.'

Sally isn't in the mood to give the village an affectionate nickname. The Gaveys live there, after all. 'I've decided,' she says. 'I can't go back yet. Mark might, but I'm not. And most importantly, neither is Champ.'

'As I guessed!' Corinne laughs as they step into the lift.

'Did you? How?'

'Because you're Sally Lambert, and Sally Lambert believes that even when things look very, very good indeed, you shouldn't take even a 0.00001 per cent chance when it comes to Champ's safety.'

'Exactly.' Sally smiles. 'I'm glad you understand. I'm not sure Mark or the kids will.'

'But, Sal—'

'I know. For as long as the Gaveys live there, the village won't be safe for Champ. Unless they're all locked up for a very long time... but let's face it, that's not going to happen, and I can't be worrying every day that they might poison him or kidnap him. I know they'll stop at nothing, now.'

When the lift doors open on the fourth floor, Ree is

No One Would Do What The Lamberts Have Done

waiting there. She throws her arms round Sally's neck. Disentangling herself almost immediately, she says, 'Mum, you aren't going to believe it. Something absolutely incredible has happened!'

'What?' says Corinne. 'Let me guess: King Charles has publicly called the Gaveys twats and decreed that they be exiled from his kingdom?'

Champ, Mark and Tobes are standing behind Ree: an exuberant greeting committee. Champ rushes over to Sally and bounces up and down on his hind legs, pawing at her and licking her face as she bends down to hug him. 'Hello, baby boy,' she says. 'Hello, my darlingest one. So, how many listens are we at now, guys?'

'The numbers are huge, but that's not it,' says Tobes. 'That's not the incredible thing that's happened. It's Auntie Vicky. She's saved the day. I mean, it was already saved, but she's saved it even more.'

Sally frowns. This sounds unlikely. 'My sister Vicky?'

'The very same.' Mark is smiling. 'Apparently she's been messaging you and you've been ignoring her?'

'Yup. Didn't want to give her a chance to tell me about her latest love-life melodrama, or that Champ's just a dog.'

'Yeah, well, she was actually trying to help. She read about all the Champ stuff online and has been trying to get in touch with you ever since. When it didn't work, she texted me. Sal, she's got proof that Champ couldn't have been in Bussow Court at 4.15pm on 17 June biting Tess Gavey. So, just in case the police decide that Lesley confessing to lying on tape isn't enough, we've now got independent proof of Champ's innocence.'

'*What?*' Sally asks. She can't understand how any evidence exonerating Champ can have come from her sister, who was nowhere near Swaffham Tilney when Lesley bit Tess and Champ did not.

'Come to our room, I'll show you,' says Mark.

They all hurry along the corridor, past a polished wooden table with curved legs and two trays strewn with dirty crockery and shapeless chunks of cold food, the remnants of someone's room service.

Once inside their room, Mark jabs at his phone for a few seconds, then hands it to Sally. There's a photo on the screen of a text Sally remembers sending to Vicky, though she can't remember when. Then she sees the date: 17 June – The Day of the Bite, The Day of PC Connor Chantree coming to The Hayloft's front door to say that a complaint had been made about Champ…

That's right, Sally remembers now: she'd tried to have a WhatsApp chat with Vicky while she walked Champ by the lode that afternoon. She'd spoken most of her bits out loud and then her phone had converted them into text, because that was easier if you were holding a dog's lead with one hand.

'The time you sent Auntie Vicky that message is on it, at the bottom,' Ree says. '4.14pm, see? *One minute* before Tess claims Champ bit her outside her house in Bussow Court. Read it, Mum.'

No One Would Do What The Lamberts Have Done

'But it just stops with a dot-dot-dot after the first sentence.' Sally frowns.

'No, you have to click where it says "Read more",' says Ree impatiently. 'The clue's in the... That's right. Good.' Corinne, reading the message over Sally's shoulder, suddenly screams, 'Fuuuuuuuck!'

'What? I don't get what you're all so excited about,' says Sally, 'It's just me banging on about work and this couple who wanted us to do their wedding but—' She stops as she sees it. 'Oh, my God,' she whispers, barely able to believe what's in front of her eyes.

Her message to Vicky reads as follows: 'V, I can't stress this strongly enough: don't go to Fort Collins Colorado to stay with a man you've never met in the flesh. You don't even know if he looks like his photos no not in the water my baby oh you're a sweet baby aren't you yes, you are you are you're my lovely baby boy and that's why I don't want you to fall into the water no I don't I don't look let's say hello to the ducks instead and the fact that he says you can't stay with him in his house and he'll put you in a hotel instead? Well bloody dodgy! And why won't he chat on Zoom? He's almost definitely married.'

'I... That's me talking to Champ in there,' Sally says, excited. 'How did I... no, I know exactly how. I know why I pressed send without checking my message for mistakes like I usually do: I was too annoyed. Vicky was being so stupid and oblivious to the obvious risks—'

'None of that matters,' says Tobes. 'What matters is: we've got those Gavey fuckers bang to rights.'

Sally is too overwhelmed to speak.

'Thank God you didn't notice and delete the Champy bits before sending it,' says Ree. 'Now we've got concrete proof. You were with Champ at 4.14pm on 17 June, and since there's no water and no ducks at Bussow Court, which is at least ten minutes' walk from the lode—'

'More like twenty if you're with Champ,' Sally corrects her.

'As you kids would know if you ever walked him,' Mark adds.

'He likes to inspect every plant we pass very thoroughly,' says Sally. 'Don't you, my babiest of boys? Yes, you do, my boy-est of babies!' Champ raises his chin to make it easier for her to stroke underneath it.

'Mum, cringe,' Tobes protests.

'Thank God for Mum Cringe,' Ree says sharply. 'We can go home now, clear Champ's name and grind the Gaveys' reputations into the dust where they belong – all thanks to Mum having no clue how to use her phone properly.'

Sally can feel Corinne trying to make eye contact with her. She keeps her eyes on Champ. Corinne must be wondering why Sally isn't telling her family what she's decided, and whether she's changed her mind in the face of this new information.

It doesn't matter, Sally thinks to herself. There's going to be a happy ending either way. She's just not yet sure what form it will take.

34

Cause is often a difficult thing to determine. The cause of a person's death, for instance, can have physical and psychological components, so it's important to ask the question: how much of a contributing factor was the going-viral of the recording Mum made of Lesley and Tess Gavey fessing up to their wicked scheme? Or perhaps it was the response to the recording that tipped Tess over the edge – the multitudes who dropped their support for her and switched sides as soon as they'd heard her ordering Lesley to trap Mum at The Stables, take her phone from her and destroy the evidence.

Let me be clear: when I say 'tipped Tess over the edge', I'm not suggesting she took her own life. Trust me: I know she didn't. She wasn't the sort who would ever have done that, and she certainly couldn't have been shamed into it; she was incapable of feeling shame. The day before she died she was more vocal than ever on Instagram, Snapchat and TikTok, insisting that, whatever anyone imagined had been proven against her, she hadn't lied about anything and Champ Lambert, not her own mother, was the one who had so ferally mutilated her arm.

All the same, I can't believe there's a single person on earth whose mood wouldn't be adversely affected by the knowledge that half the world now hates them. It's the sort of development that might weaken an immune system considerably.

Needless to say, the name of Furbert Herbert Lambert was not mentioned by anybody in connection with Tess's death.

Here are some of the facts about how her life ended: it happened on 29 June 2024 at 1.10am, not even two weeks after the day of the bite. The coroner recorded an open verdict and said there was no doubt that she'd died of natural causes, but that it was nevertheless a peculiar death that raised questions to which we would probably never know the answers.

I knew the truth, but to the rest of the world, Tess's death made no sense. There was a fire, but the flames didn't reach her room before emergency services arrived. Nor did she die of smoke inhalation. She was, in fact, already dead before the blaze started and was in the process of being admitted to Level 4 as the fire engine pulled up outside The Stables.

Very soon after Tess died, Lesley and Alastair Gavey left Swaffham Tilney.

No One Would Do What The Lamberts Have Done

Before any official announcement had been made, news of her death was leaked by a pseudonymous TikTok account belonging to Corinne's son, Niall, who by that point was staying at Ismys House to keep an eye on things in the village while Corinne looked after Mum and Champ at the Many Frogs Hotel (Dad, Ree and Tobes had already gone back to Swaffham Tilney at this point).

Almost immediately after the fire – by which I mean within the hour – the main topic of online Tess-related debate changed. Champ's innocence or guilt was no longer a talking point. Insofar as he was mentioned at all, it was in passing and with the presumption that of course he didn't bite that lying dead bitch and we all knew it from the start. Astonishingly (though I shouldn't have been in the least bit surprised, knowing what I know about human shamelessness) this was said by many thousands of people who had not seemed to know it even as recently as a day earlier.

Now the central question under discussion was: did or didn't Tess Gavey deserve to die for what she'd tried to do? If she did, was it nevertheless crass to say so all over the internet? And/or was it hypocritical to express regret for her death if one had loathed her while she was alive?

Mum made a dignified statement some weeks later – not on social media or in public, but to our family and Corinne only. She gave us the answers we had all (except perhaps Dad) been eagerly awaiting. Would she still have sent Ree the recording and instructions to release it if she'd known Tess would be dead less than a fortnight later? Yes – because in Mum's opinion there was no connection between those two happenings. The policy of never speaking ill of the dead cannot fairly be applied to still-alive people who are going to die in the future, she argued, because that would rule out everybody. And that, Mum said, was the last thing she would ever say on the subject of the Gaveys; she was looking forward to never thinking about them again.

Ree and Tobes spent a lot of time on social media in the weeks following Tess's death, saying not a word about Tess or her family and focussing solely on Champ: how thrilled the Lamberts were that he'd been vindicated, how wonderful it was to be able to return to their home and give up the fugitive lifestyle. 'It wasn't difficult, though,' said Mum. 'I suppose we had the one interrupted night at the boarding kennels, but our room there was beautiful. And before that we were at Corinne's Lake District mansion, and afterwards at a five-star hotel.'

'It was incredibly difficult emotionally,' Ree told her, fingers tapping away at the keyboard of the new MacBook Air that Corinne had bought her and Tobes, on which they had already started to design Champ's website. Tobes kept announcing that it was going to 'change the world and make big bucks', while Ree patiently explained to Dad why it was vital that Champ's hundreds of thousands of fans should have a way of keeping in touch with him now that his troubles were over. On Corinne's advice, Tobes had written an email to the Sound Sleep Donut Dog Bed people to see if they might offer sponsorship in exchange

No One Would Do What The Lamberts Have Done

for Champ promoting their bed as his top favourite sleep accessory, which it genuinely was.

Back to Tess Gavey's death by natural causes, then. The medical findings were surprising. All her life, Tess had suffered from an allergy to fish, and it was a serious one. Here's a limerick I wrote about it:

If she ate just the tiniest flake
Of a haddock, a pollock, a hake
And then died in a flash,
That obtuse piece of trash
Still would never admit her mistake.

I was so proud of this poem, I considered sneaking it onto Champ's website somewhere (perhaps a hidden page, not linked to from the main menu), but I resisted the urge to tamper with my non-furry siblings' project because, unlike Tess, I have the ability to distinguish between my best and worst impulses, and to let the former carry the day. (Almost always.)

I'm delighted to report that there's a page on Champ's website that's devoted solely to me. (That's where my Tess limerick could go, if it went anywhere.) Ree, bless her heart, said very early on that there had to be a special Furbert sleep page as part of Champ's online operation, commemorating Champy's late furry brother, and Toby said he'd contact the Chuckit! balls people and ask if they wanted to be sponsors too, like the Sound Sleep Donut Bed team were.

Such a great idea! God, I love those orange Chuckit! balls. Mum and Dad left one in Shukes's garden when they moved, and Henry Christensen, the new owner, never found it. I often used to nip round there to play with it when Henry was out: I'd throw it for myself, then run after it. Sometimes I buried it deep in the earth, so that I could dig it out again. I loved doing that, especially with a treasured possession. The joy of finding it all over again!

Back to Tess Gavey's death. There's no point me being coy about it, since I've decided to tell you the truth. Here's the part that everyone thinks is a medical mystery: when her cadaver was inspected by the relevant experts, they found all the symptoms of a severe allergic reaction to fish, but none of the fish. Indeed, they were able to prove to their own satisfaction that no fish or fish-adjacent substances were present in Tess's system – nothing that even hinted in the direction of creatures aquatic, anamniotic and gill-bearing. In due course, those following the Dead Tess saga found out about this oddity and started to wonder whether perhaps the allergic reaction her body was accustomed to producing might on this occasion have been triggered by something else: specifically, by knowing that thousands of strangers all over the world were busy calling her a depraved liar and having a whale (a mammal, not a fish) of a time doing so.

It was a decent theory, I suppose. And it's well known that severe psychological distress can produce all kinds of physical symptoms. But those pushing that hypothesis – and many still are, even now – are barking beneath the

No One Would Do What The Lamberts Have Done

wrong letterbox. (How often, by comparison, do you see dogs bark up trees? Exactly.)

In fact, what killed Tess was exactly what her symptoms suggested: fish. Yes, even though none was found in her body.

Here is how her death happened: she was lying on her bed, not sure if she was awake or asleep. It was after midnight. Lesley and Alastair, her parents, had said goodnight and disappeared into their respective bedrooms more than an hour earlier. All was dark and quiet at The Stables and on Bussow Court.

Tess, lying with her duvet half on and half off her, found that she couldn't move. She thought to herself, 'This is probably one of those dreams where you're paralysed.' She was further persuaded that she must have been dreaming of the presence of a Welsh Terrier in her room. This dog looked almost exactly like Champ Lambert from The Hayloft, though he was smaller. So she must have been dreaming, right? Because *as if* she'd let a gross, smelly beast like that sit on her bed. Yuck, and also, fuck him and fuck Ree Lambert who thought she was so much better than Tess.

Then the Welshie stood up on his two hind legs, opened his mouth and started to speak in Mum's voice. (My mum, Sally Lambert – not Tess's mum.) He recited some verse, sounding female and maternal, about a fish who liked to tell stories. The lines came from the wonderful *Tiddler* by Julia Donaldson and Axel Scheffler, but Tess Gavey didn't know that because her mother had never made an effort to read her the best that children's literature had to offer.

Tess wanted to say to the Welshie in her dream, 'Stop listing different kinds of fish. It's making me feel panicky,' but she found she couldn't speak.

'Hearing the names of a few fish won't kill you,' said the Dream Welshie, this time in his own voice. 'That's not how allergies work, is it? It's all the fish inside you that you need to worry about.'

'What fish inside me?' asked Tess. 'There isn't any, you stupid, smelly, overgrown rat. I never eat fish. You don't know what you're talking about.'

'You don't need to eat fish for it to be inside you,' said the dog. 'I'm not talking about anchovies, smoked salmon, rollmop herrings—'

'Shut up!' Tess snapped.

'—tequila splitfins, diamond darters, Sakhalin sturgeons, kissing loaches—'

'SHUT UP!'

'I'm talking about your essence,' the Dream Welshie went on. 'Your "Tessence", if you like, which is selfishness. Pure selfishness – it's your entire personality. You are one hundred per cent selfish, Tess. And since "fish" is more than fifty per cent of "selfish"… well, the way I see it, that means more than half of you is fish.'

'That's ridiculous.' Tess tried to laugh, but couldn't quite manage it. Her throat was starting to tighten.

'More than half of you is fish,' the dog repeated. 'Fish

is in you, fish is most of you. If you were a private company about to float on the stock market, the overwhelming majority of shares in you would be *owned by fish*.' The Welshie saw that Tess was looking confused, so he reverted to his most effective line: 'More than half of you is fish.' He said it over and over again, aiming to create a hypnotic effect, and soon Tess couldn't breathe at all.

The funny thing was, the numbers were nonsense and I knew it. It was selfish*ness* that was Tess's entire character, not selfish, which is an adjective, not a noun. Strictly speaking, then, she was only 36.364% fish. (If she'd known that, she would still have died of the same allergic reaction. It might have taken a little longer, that's all.)

That's what caused Tess's death, anyway. Not the fire.

And now let me tell you what followed her death. There was much rejoicing in Level 2, and I was asked if I wanted to move up. I said no, because I'm happy where I am and can't imagine being happier. In Level 1 there is pure bliss and eternal life, but there are no names, no personalities, no individuation. There's no opposite of bliss, either – and how can that not mean that bliss starts to feel a bit humdrum and ordinary? Most importantly of all, there are no families in Level 1. There isn't even the concept of family there, which wouldn't work for me at all. I want to remain a Lambert for as long as there are Lamberts in Swaffham Tilney or anywhere.

Luckily, sticking at Level 2 is allowed, and I'm not the only one to have chosen it. You might remember Stilton, the pet dog of Auntie Vicky's ex-boyfriend, Liam? He's a Level 2 stalwart like me. And actually, the online controversy of Champ versus the Gaveys ended up bringing his dad and Auntie Vicky back together – and that was just one of what can only be described as a cascade of happy endings.

Henry Christensen agreed to sell Shukes back to Mum and Dad, and we Lamberts moved back into our true forever home. I found an extra orange Chuckit! ball behind one of the sofas once Mr Christensen had moved out, so I now have two: one for inside and one for outside. The other day I allowed Mum to notice that the balls frequently move around, even though no Level 3 Lamberts are moving them. When she spotted this and understood what it meant, she burst into tears, got down on her knees and hugged my crate for a long time. 'Furby,' she whispered. 'My darling Furbs. I *knew* you were still with us.' Now I open and close the door of my crate myself, to show Mum when I'm in it and when I'm not. She's waiting for the right time to tell Dad, Ree and Tobes.

So, yes, good old Mr Henry Christensen! Guess where he moved to? The Hayloft! We swapped houses, and we all prefer where we are now to where we were before. And when The Stables was repaired after the fire, Henry's son and his family bought it so that they could be close to him. Champ was invited to visit as a matter of urgency, to perform what we all knew was a sort of exorcism, though we didn't call it that; officially it was referred to as 'afternoon tea', and it was a very jolly occasion indeed, enjoyed by Lamberts, Christensens and Sullivans alike. One thorough romp through all the rooms by Champ and the house was free of noxious Gavey vibes forever.

Back at Shukes, Champ was able to spend as much time as he wanted in our lovely front garden, even when Mum and Dad weren't able to be outside too, keeping an eye on him. Mum knew I would be there to supervise at all times. 'Champ'll be fine,' she said confidently. 'Trust me. He's a Swaffham Tilney hero. Now the danger's passed, everyone in the village will look out for him and keep him safe. He's got so many guardian angels now. Not just me. Not just us.'

Champleby Fine soon became his main nickname – Champleby for short. And he really was treated as a hero in our village. The Farmer suggested a party to celebrate his victory and offered the use of one of the disused barns in his field. Everyone came to Champ's party, apart from Avril Mattingley and Michelle Hyde whom Mum certainly didn't miss. It was enough for her to know that both women couldn't have avoided hearing the booming choruses of 'Land of Cute and Furry' that filled the air, with everyone singing at the top of their lungs. (The Farmer even did a solo chorus at the end, to round it off. 'He got all the words right – every last one,' Mum whispered to Ree tearfully afterwards. 'He sang *my original version*.')

Despite the best efforts of Champ himself and Peter the estate agent to eat everything in sight, there were dozens of cupcakes left over (made by the Quy Mill Hotel's catering team), all with Champ's face on them. Deryn Dickinson offered to take them round to Michelle's and Avril's houses once the party was finished. Corinne frowned. 'Cupcakes for bitches? Say what?'

'We should let them know there's a way back into our good graces,' Deryn told her. 'I don't believe they really think Sally murdered anyone. They're just too proud to admit it.'

'And you think a cupcake will change that?' Corinne wasn't convinced, but she agreed.

Wait, what? She agreed with Deryn Dickinson?

That's right: the long Agatha-Christie-related *froideur* had finally ended. It would be too simplistic to say that Swaffham Tilney had become the Land of Cute and Furry thanks to Champ's victory, though that was how it felt. For those readers who prefer a more practical explanation: Deryn had confided to Niall Sullivan, Corinne's son, that she was none other than 'ChampLambertFan' on Facebook, Instagram and Threads – a trio of accounts that had tirelessly provided examples of Tess Gavey's awfulness and dishonesty ('Take it from one of her very near neighbours') during the campaign to save Champ: Tess had stolen a block of fudge from the Cupwardly Mobile van's fudge tray; she regularly smoked cannabis out of her window; she had got drunk on her own one night and grafitti-ed the word 'Jittleyang' across Maureen Gledhill's wooden gates.

No One Would Do What The Lamberts Have Done

Corinne had been as impressed by Deryn's efforts as Deryn was by Corinne's rescuing of the Lamberts when they'd most needed help. It wasn't too long before Deryn was admitting to having secretly read Mary Westmacott's (Agatha Christie's?) *The Rose and the Yew Tree*. 'I agree with you,' she told Corinne. 'It *is* a murder story, but almost no one will spot it, which makes it so much more sinister and dark. No punishment for the murderer, either – not even a firm acknowledgment from the book that that person *is* definitely a killer. And you have to read until the very last lines to catch a glimpse of the truth. Anyone who ducks out early deprives themselves not only of that final bit of the story, but of the *entire* story, really.'

'Yes,' Corinne agreed happily. 'Exactly. Maybe Agatha wanted to punish anyone who wasn't discerning enough to read right to the end.'

'Would any writer do that, though?' asked Deryn. It was a question neither woman attempted to answer, because it was followed immediately by what felt to both like a more pressing one: should the Agatha Christie Book Club be restarted, and should *The Rose and the Yew Tree* be the very first novel they read and discuss?

Which brings me to the last, but by no means least, of the happy endings: the Agatha Christie Book Club relaunched itself, bigger and better than before and declared all Mary Westmacott novels and their fans welcome. And though many members subsequently reported that they'd been gripped by *The Rose and the Yew Tree*, no one else spotted the hidden murder plot. Corinne and Deryn decided not to draw it to the group's attention, though they did share the secret with Mum, who immediately offered a theory of her own.

'If Agatha Christie did do what you're saying, if she planted this... hidden strand or whatever, it won't have been as a punishment for anyone. She'll have thought of it as the opposite: a treat!'

'Spot on, Mum,' I thought. (I'm Level 2, remember? Where do you think Agatha Christie hangs out these days? Precisely.) It ought to have been obvious anyway, even in Level 3: of course a writer who loves her readers would want to give them a treat and not a punishment at the end of her book. If you ask me, a novel should operate a bit like an advent calendar: you save the best and most tempting goodies until the very end, the last page – the last paragraph, if you can possibly manage it.

That's what I thought, though I didn't say it out loud.

Wednesday 25 September 2024

Large

Bill 'Large' Wendt watched his wife Lissa as she read. She was coming to the end. The pile on the coffee table was growing, and only a few sheets were left in her hands. She'd been at it all day.

Was she reading those final few pages more slowly? Had he? He didn't think so – but he'd read the last chapter more than once. It was hard not to go back, when you reached the end and realised that the writer had neglected to give you the much-needed instructions on what to make of it all. There was a strong temptation to think that if you looked again with a different mental attitude, all would be clear. Had Connor Chantree felt the same?

Or had Chantree written the document himself?

Last week Bill and Lissa had watched a new Netflix movie about a missing child whose parents had trudged through dark woods night after night for weeks, calling his name, long after the official search teams had accepted there was no trace of him to be found there. Bill felt a bit like those parents now – out searching in a forest for the solution to an impossible puzzle – though to an observer he would have looked like a middle-aged man in blue pyjamas and a purple paisley dressing gown (from Liberty in London – a thirtieth-wedding-anniversary present from Lissa) having a much quieter evening than usual in his own lounge, watching, from his favourite battered leather chair, his reading wife instead of the television.

What would Lissa make of the manuscript? Had she decided yet? Bill hoped so – she was much better at deciding than he was – and he was ready to agree with her conclusion, whatever it turned out to be. *Hurry up, Liss.*

Bill disapproved of the old adage about a watched pot never boiling. Of course it would, assuming it wasn't prematurely removed from the heat source. No other equally well-known proverb was quite so untrue. *The early bird catches the worm*: an undeniable fact; if you turn up first, you're more likely to get the goodies. Every year Bill tried to get to the best ripe blackberries growing by the riverbank before the birds or other local pickers did. First-mover advantage was a real thing, whereas the act of watching a pot did absolutely nothing to cool either fire or water, so—

'Finished!' Lissa cried out. She added the pages she'd been holding to the top of the pile on the table.

'You've boiled,' said Bill.

No One Would Do What The Lamberts Have Done

'What?'

'Never mind. Thoughts?' He pointed at the manuscript.

'Connor Chantree didn't write it, that's for sure,' said Lissa. 'And yet—'

'How sure?'

'Bill, come on!' She stretched out her legs beneath the yellow blanket she'd draped over them hours ago. Pink-painted toes appeared close to the sofa arm. 'I can't think of anyone less likely to have come up with all of that than Connor. Lovely though he is, he's too normal. There aren't many people I'd say that about, but he's one of them.'

'I suppose it could have been his wife,' said Bill. 'The chef. How well do you know her?'

'Flo Chantree? No. Not if she named her own catering business, which I expect she did. Anyone who calls their company Scrumplicious would have written a very different kind of book from the one I've just read. Trust me, Bill, it's neither of the Chantrees. My money's on the mad mum, Sally Lambert, who calls her houses "him" and believes her dogs are her children.'

'Trouble is, there's no trace of even the tiniest part of that… book document, or anything resembling it, on any of the Lamberts' devices,' Bill told her. 'Please don't ask how I know, or what resources I put into finding out, or on what false pretexts.'

Lissa looked worried. 'I thought the Large-in-Charge era was steering clear of all dodgy practices?'

'Give me a break.' Bill rubbed the stomach that had

earned him the nickname 'Large', realising he was hungry when he shouldn't be. He'd had a second helping of shepherd's pie only two hours ago. 'I've hardly been beating confessions out of people. If Connor Chantree wrote it, which I think he must have, it'll be on his home computer. He didn't do it at work.'

'He didn't do it at all, Bill.'

'But, Liss, he must have. He lied to me: said he'd found the pages all messed up in a box – dirty, out of their proper order – and all he did was tidy them up to bring and show me. Yet there are chapters written by him—'

'*Purporting* to be written by him,' Lissa amended.

'— and the pages of those chapters are just as stained and scuffed as all the others. If he'd really written those two sections, why aren't their pages pristine? And before the pages got dirty, someone numbered them continuously, and numbered the chapters continuously too: the Sally ones, the dog ones and the Connor ones. Which means whoever wrote the other chapters must have written the Connor bits too – and I still say it was him. Connor. He did it on his home computer, printed it out and then, for some reason best known to himself, kicked the living daylights out of it to make his found-in-a-box nonsense seem more credible.'

'Bill,' Liss sat up with a groan, swinging her legs round so that her feet were on the floor. She looked ready to dash over and inject him with something painful but necessary. 'How much time have you spent on this? Far too much is the answer, isn't it? Have you asked Connor if he wrote Chapters twenty-two and thirty-one?'

Bill frowned. 'No.'

'Sally Lambert might have thought it was fun to use him as a narrator in her story. She turned her bloomin' dead dog into a narrator, didn't she?'

'No. Connor would have said something,' said Bill. 'He'd have said, "Large, there are two chapters pretending I wrote them, and I didn't." He's pretty thorough in his approach to things. No way he wouldn't have mentioned it.'

'Ask him,' Liss suggested. 'Or, and this is the far better option, forget the whole thing.'

'Forget?' Was she serious? 'What if Tess Gavey was murdered?'

'She wasn't: a coroner's court has said so. Bill, come on. If you think a description of Tess having a scary dream is going to cut it in court... And I mean, the dream's as ludicrous as it's frightening, isn't it? "Most of you is fish" or whatever. Ridiculous! Someone's trying to waste your time: Sally Lambert. Don't let her.'

'I could go round Swaffham Tilney, door to door, ask at every house if anyone knows anything about a book called *No One Would Do What The Lamberts Have Done*.'

'No, you're not doing that. I'm not letting you. Bill, it's a book, not a crime. Ignore it.'

'There's no point anyway,' he said. 'Whoever they are, the culprit will never admit it.'

'Well, that's culprits for you,' said Lissa, 'But please stop suspecting poor Connor Chantree of writing it. He would never describe himself as looking like the brush from a dustpan-and-brush set, and neither would Flo describe him that way.'

'I spoke to the coroner today,' Bill told her. 'There's no getting round it: Tess Gavey didn't eat any fish or anything else just before she died. There was nothing in her system. Yet she had all the same allergic reaction symptoms as if she'd swallowed a whole bucket of mackerel. Nothing explains it. The only way it makes sense is if...' He broke off.

'Biii... ill,' Lissa said carefully, as if his name were a ticking bomb that required expert handling. 'We know the explanation for her death hinted at in the book can't be true. Don't we?'

Did he, though? He was aware that he ought to know it, just like he oughtn't to be hungry after two helpings of shepherd's pie.

'For goodness' sake, Bill. Whatever killed Tess Gavey, it wasn't a ghostly visit from the vengeful spirit of Furbert Herbert Lambert, and it wasn't anything to do with "fish" being part of "selfish". Physical allergic reactions are not caused by word play.'

'When you put it like that...' Bill smiled. 'Though they could, actually, be caused by serious psychological trauma. Remember that book I read about how to heal back pain, which said it was all caused by repressed emo—'

'Here's what I think,' said Lissa. 'Sally Lambert probably believes Tess deserved to die after what she tried to do to Champ. Would she admit it, though? Probably not, because... well, a teenage girl is dead. She had her whole life before her and now that's just gone. Snuffed out, and no discernible cause. That's a tragedy, however nasty and conniving Tess's worst behaviour was. Everyone who hears about her death is going to think, "Oh, how awful, poor girl. Poor family."'

'And... therefore what?' asked Bill. He didn't have the heart to tell his wife that 'What a tragedy' was certainly not what everyone was thinking and saying about the demise of Tess.

'Well, none of that will sit well with Sally Lambert, will it?' said Lissa. 'She might well be keen to control the narrative around Tess's death, and the story has a clear moral lesson if Furbert heroically punishes Tess and it's all part of evil being defeated by good. This version of the story is exactly the one Sally Lambert would want to put out there: her darling Furbert Herbert as an agent of justice.'

Bill wasn't convinced. 'You may be right,' he said. 'But look, whoever wrote it, why toss the pages into a box and bury it first, then dig it up?'

'Was anything printed on the cardboard box? Company name or anything? Stickers? Postage labels?'

'Nothing. Just a plain, brown cardboard box.'

Lissa hauled herself into a standing position. 'I need to go to bed, Bill. It's late.'

'I'm starving. Is there any shepherd's pie left?'

'Stacks. I'll put some out for you in the kitchen before I go up.'

A few seconds later she reappeared. 'Bill. Don't just sit there going round in circles all night, fretting about it. Your brain'll work better after a good night's sleep. And remember: there's no crime involved – nothing that meets the legal definition of a crime. You're not duty-bound to pursue this, and there's a strong chance you'll never know the truth, so save yourself the bother. Night!'

Bill thought his brain was working pretty well. He didn't feel tired. He felt easily up to the task of trying to figure out why the manuscript had been buried in a box and then, later, dug up.

Obviously dead dogs didn't write books. Bill knew that. But what if a living person, temporarily possessed by a spirit that's not his own, could maybe have... I mean, the Connor chapters contained some words that Bill was sure Connor Chantree didn't know and would never use. So what if Connor's hands did all the typing, but Furbert Herbert Lambert was the book's true author?

And then maybe... yes! It made sense: what if Sally Lambert somehow got her hands on the manuscript and read it. She might have panicked and buried it in her garden, to protect Furbert's reputation. At which point Furbert, stubborn and proud – also, crucially, spirit rather than flesh and therefore untouchable both by the law and by conventional morality – dug it up and dropped it between Connor Chantree's car and his garage, believing it deserved a wider audience.

Ridiculous! Bill scolded himself. Utterly, embarrassingly absurd. How could he be sitting here coming up with theories that involved supernatural possession? It felt almost as if he'd been possessed himself – by idiocy. He was supposed to be sensible. He was a senior police detective, well respected by his colleagues. Lissa was right. Enough of this nonsense.

He stood up and staggered a few paces before his limbs unstiffened and he was able to walk normally to the kitchen. This brought to mind a funny poem he'd read years ago and had remembered ever since:

In youth, before I knew the cares
of middle age, I never dreamt
that getting out of comfy chairs
could take me more than one attempt.

In the kitchen, he found a small peach on the table, positioned at the centre of one of his and Lissa's largest dinner plates. It looked a little like a contemporary artwork of the sort he enjoyed sneering at. He squeezed it and his thumb broke through its furry skin.

No shepherd's pie in sight.

Bill frowned. He'd told Lissa, he planned to return to his healthy eating protocol as soon as work felt more manageable. He'd meant it, too – there had been no slackening of his good intentions – so there was no need for her to drop pointed hints like this. Still, this peach needed eating now that he'd tunnelled into it with his thumb. It could be his pre-bed snack starter, he decided. He'd dig the shepherd's pie leftovers out of the freezer afterwards and heat them up. There was no defeating Bill Wendt's appetite at its most determined.

A minute or so later, he descended, with great care, the bumpy stone steps that led to the lower part of the kitchen (Lissa called it 'The Galley', a name that was too pretentious for Bill). The steps were a disaster waiting to happen, but Bill had been forbidden from doing anything to make them safer. According to Lissa they were made from imported Cornish stone, and contained fossils. Why anyone would bother bringing Cornish stone to Cambridgeshire, Bill had no idea – nor why Lissa thought it meant he ought to be willing to risk breaking bones.

On his way to dispose of the peach stone, he caught sight of something silver and shiny in his peripheral vision. He turned and saw another dinner plate from the too-big-to-fit-in-their-dishwasher set, bearing a mound of something he couldn't see, wrapped in clingfilm. It was sitting across the tops of two of the four rectangular straw basket-drawer things, in the alcove next to the bin, where Lissa kept things like sellotape, paperclips and clothes pegs.

Bill threw away the peach pit, reached for the plate and lifted the clingfilm. Shepherd's pie! Joy of joys – even more so because he'd imagined a puritanical attempt to deprive him of it.

Good old Lissa. But why had she put it there, where he could so easily not have spotted it, after saying she'd leave it in the kitchen, where the microwave was?

Bill smiled. He knew why. She wasn't normally absent minded, but her head had no doubt been too full of Lamberts-related theories and speculation to attend properly to practicalities.

Anyway: shepherd's pie!

Part 2

Wednesday 19 March 2025 London
Meredith and Josh

'I can bring you anything to drink while you wait for your friend?' the waiter asks. 'I should bring the cocktail menu, maybe?'

Meredith Miles almost flinches. It feels like such a wildly inappropriate question in the circumstances. The idea that she might have fizzy orange drinks with pink and gold paper umbrellas sticking out of them on her mind, today of all days... Though it's not the waiter's fault; he has no idea she's here to have possibly the most important conversation of her career so far. 'A large bottle of sparkling mineral water would be great, thanks.' She smiles up at him.

She has chosen her favourite restaurant in the whole of London for the occasion: Yauatcha, Broadgate Circle – so much more atmospheric, with its curved contours and wide views, than its Soho twin. Meredith would swear this somehow makes the food taste better too. And at one o'clock on a weekday it's always full of business types in suits, and noisy, which is what she wants; there's nothing worse than having an important conversation in one of those small, quiet London bistros with more waiters than there are tables, where every word you say is heard in the kitchen too.

'Actually, I'm ready to order food as well,' Meredith says. 'I can order for both of us.' When the waiter looks doubtful, she adds, 'I'm early, and my colleague is obsessively punctual. He'll be here by the time you bring the starters.'

Hurry up, Josh. She had hoped he would be early too, as early as her.

Josh Varndall is her friend as much as he's her colleague; he and Meredith have worked together for twenty-two years. In fact – and this is a strange thought for Meredith – if you wanted to be strictly accurate, you'd have to say that, currently, she and Josh are *not* colleagues for the first time in twenty-two years, though they both know they very soon will be again.

And, friend or colleague or both, Meredith has had enough Chinese meals with Josh to be certain of what he will order: sesame prawn toast followed by crispy aromatic duck. If only she felt as confident in relation to his thoughts about *Lamberts* as she did about his menu choices. They started referring to it as *Lamberts* almost immediately; its full name is too long to say every time.

For herself, Meredith orders only dim sum: wild mushroom, lobster, seafood black truffle and spicy pork Szechuan: two to come out with Josh's starter and two with his main. By the time the waiter has written down and checked everything, Josh is here, shaking off his coat as he approaches the table.

'I've just ordered for both of us,' Meredith tells him.

'Great, thanks.' He sits, takes off his glasses and wipes them on the sleeve of his shirt. 'Bit rainy out there. Which... obviously you can see, out of this massive window right next to us.' He laughs. 'Sorry. I'm a bit nervous, which is silly. Shall we get the scary part out of the way first, so we can enjoy our lunch? Are you a "No" or a "Yes"?'

This makes Meredith feel instantly better. If he thinks they're going to have an enjoyable lunch, no matter how they both vote, that means there's nothing to worry about.

'I'm a "No",' she says.

Relief lifts Josh's features. 'Me too.'

'Really? Amazing. Excellent. I was afraid you'd be a "Yes" and I'd have to talk you down.'

'Nope. I don't see how we can publish it. I don't *want* to publish it, actually.'

'Because?' Meredith asks. 'I agree, but I'm curious to hear how you got there.' She has spent hours – unnecessarily, as it turns out – worrying that they'd disagree, that there would be a difficult discussion with a winner and a loser, that this might get their new business off to a bad start. What if some resentment crept in, no matter how hard they tried to ensure it didn't? It all feels very high stakes, because the Champ Lambert story is world famous. Even now, eight months later, true crime podcasts and discussion forums about who killed the Gavey family are everywhere. Was it a murder-suicide by Lesley Gavey? Or are the commenters who insist it was a man's crime correct? Was Alastair Gavey, Lesley's husband and Tess's father, responsible? 'Only a man' – one columnist wrote – 'takes out his entire family in this particular way. It's called family-annihilation killing and it is, sadly, a genre we've become accustomed to. And it is, I'm afraid, an overwhelmingly male thing to do.'

Meredith couldn't resist replying in the comments: 'Whoever set that fire, it didn't annihilate the whole Gavey family. Tess was already dead when the fire started.' She has heard so many opinions about the Gaveys' deaths since last summer. Some she has read online or in newspapers; others she's picked up in snippets of gossip while walking Cinnamon in the park, or in the changing room after Pilates. Many have been ridiculously far-fetched, like the theory that Toby Lambert was the evil murderous genius who'd burned the Gaveys to death in their home and got away with it; it was bound to have been him, apparently, because he used to get into fights at school and be cheeky to teachers.

Meredith has been afraid of successfully persuading Josh that they shouldn't publish the book. And then, each time he realised the world was still fascinated by the unexplained deaths of the Gaveys, he might think, 'If only Meredith had been braver. If only we'd published *Lamberts*, we could

No One Would Do What The Lamberts Have Done

have made an absolute killing.' At their previous company, which they both now jokingly refer to as 'the old country', they disagreed often about whether a particular book was worth the risk, but none of those were books connected to famous murders — or murder-suicides, depending on your point of view.

The facts don't change: Tess was already dead. Either Alastair or Lesley or someone else started the fire that burned down their house. Or Alastair *and* Lesley, acting as one. So there were either two murder victims, or one, or none. Or (same point, different way of putting it) two suicides, or one, or none. Or three murders, if you believe that Tess was killed in her dream by the ghost of Furbert Lambert — which Meredith does not.

'We're a brand-new start-up, still trying to establish its reputation,' says Josh. 'Or rather we will be, once we start up. Whatever the police say, there's no way round it: *Lamberts* is a novel — or a memoir or whatever — that has quite possibly been written by a murderer who's escaped justice and seems more than a little bit chuffed and gloaty about having done so.'

'Agree,' says Meredith.

'And what is it? A novel? A memoir? Would we be putting it out as some sort of… entertainment? Because, let's face it, there's nothing to guarantee the truth of any of it. It doesn't even include the fairly pertinent fact that Lesley and Alastair died, not just Tess. Then there's the strong chance of us getting sued by the Lamberts—'

'They wouldn't sue us,' Meredith says quietly.

'I would if I were them, given what the book strongly implies. I don't know.' Josh sighs. 'At first I thought maybe we could put it out as true crime – not claiming it's the truth, but presenting it neutrally as a document that may or may not shed some light, making no claims whatsoever of it being proof of anything.'

'I thought the same.'

'But I couldn't convince myself,' Josh says. 'The fact is, its author – who won't tell us who she is, which doesn't help me to trust her – clearly believes her book has a perfect, happy ending just because Champ's no longer in danger. Whereas in reality, three people are dead. So… it just all feels wrong.'

Meredith felt happy – quite jubilant, actually – when she reached the Enjollifying ending of *Lamberts*, but she understands why Josh didn't. He has no dark side. That's one of the things she has always liked about him. Like Champ Lambert himself, Josh Varndall is an entirely benign force for good in the world.

'So we're agreed we're not taking it forward,' says Meredith. 'Good. And do we think the writer will… I mean, we're not making ourselves targets or anything, if we say no?'

'I don't think so – and that you feel the need to ask that question is another good reason to pass on the book,' Josh says. 'Imagine the strapline for our launch: "Varndall Miles – home of great books by writers who'd murder us if we didn't publish them."'

No One Would Do What The Lamberts Have Done

Meredith almost laughs, then remembers how weird it is that they're having this conversation. The waiter brings their first course, and she asks him if she can have a knife and fork; she's never managed to get the hang of chopsticks. Once he's gone, she says to Josh, 'So we're going to be Varndall Miles, then? It's official?'

He nods. 'Sorry, I thought I'd told you. I decided you were right. You usually are. Posh Vandal is gutsy and sounds like a market disruptor, yes, but as you said—'

'Just because it was a nickname you had at school, that doesn't make it a great name for a business?' Meredith grins.

'You said Posh Vandal sounds like a fashion label created by twenty-year-olds with tattoos and piercings, operating out of a disused warehouse.'

'And *you* said "she",' says Meredith. 'When you were talking about the author of *Lamberts*. You think it's a woman?'

'It's got to be Sally Lambert, surely? I think it's *all* Sally,' Josh admits after a brief pause. 'I think she killed Tess – somehow, she must have... I don't know... got some fish into her. I know, I know, the post-mortem. I can't justify my position, but...' He shrugs. 'I think it was Sally who set fire to the Gaveys' house, Sally who wrote the book. The book tells us itself: she wanted to be a famous writer. It also tells us she joined an online writing community at a certain point. The clues are there.'

'See, *I* think it's all Corinne Sullivan,' says Meredith.

'Corinne, or one of her helpers, found a way to kill Tess without it registering as an unnatural death. Corinne then arranged for the fire to be started at The Stables. Again, one of her minions will have done it, not her personally. And maybe Sally wrote some of the book, but I reckon Corinne had a hand in that too. I think she'd be able to produce something as polished as *Lamberts*, whereas I'm not sure Sally Lambert would, especially if she's never written anything before. Maybe they wrote it together.'

'Maybe they committed the three murders together,' Josh says.

'Why aren't the deaths of Lesley and Alastair Gavey mentioned?' Meredith asks him. 'The fire is, but their deaths aren't. All it says about the Gavey parents at the end is "Very soon after Tess's death, Lesley and Alastair Gavey left the village." Doesn't mention that they left in body bags. Why not?'

'Oh, that's easy,' says Josh.

'Is it?'

'Yeah, I think so. You can't put deaths in a book and not explain them. Tess's death can be explained – Furbert was responsible, and he can safely admit it, being a spirit in Level 2 and therefore un-arrestable for murder.'

'Oh, I see.' This made sense to Meredith. 'Yes, and in the writer's invented point of view for Furbert, he doesn't want to implicate the other killer, if the arsonist wasn't him. But he's mentioning the fire, right? And whoever wrote the book knows that anyone reading it will know about Lesley and Alastair dying in that fire, so... maybe Furbert's happy to leave their deaths as unsolved mysteries. Are we meant to think he's doing what Agatha Christie did in *The Rose and the Yew Tree*? Remember the bit where he tells us Corinne Sullivan "cannot bear mystery books in which the solution is handed to the reader on a platter, having not got where she is today by relying on others to problem-solve for her"? You see, I think Corinne wrote that. Not Sally.'

'It's clearly a novel written by an obsessive dog-lover, though,' says Josh. 'A devoted "dog mum" for whom having her dead pet narrate sections of a book might satisfy all kinds of emotional yearnings, help to process grief...'

'If my dog had died, writing a novel in which he narrates killing a teenage girl as if it's a great accomplishment... that wouldn't cheer me up,' Meredith says.

'True.'

'I'm not Sally Lambert, though. I wouldn't burn my neighbours to death.'

Josh laughs. 'If you were capable of doing that, it would have happened by now.'

'True.' Meredith's next-door neighbours are rancorous headcases. 'No, I'm sticking with Corinne, I'm afraid – maybe not as killer but definitely as author. Why is the "Never work for someone who can fire you" poem included in full, apart from to promote Corinne's world view, in which anyone who isn't entrepreneurial is a waste of space?'

The waiter is making his way towards them, to clear

away their starter plates. Meredith sits and waits, listening to snatches of the various conversations that are going on around her. Contracts, software, roll-out, implementation, stag do, appraisal, hangover, pickle ball, consultant, seating plan, implementation again. Everyone is, thank goodness, too busy talking to eavesdrop.

Once the waiter and the used plates are gone, Meredith says, 'Any thoughts about who Saul Hollingwood might be?'

'None whatsoever. You?'

She starts to recite from memory: '"There are causes, and then there are clinchers, and the memory of Lesley's fake concern – 'It's not fair to give a dog a joke name like that, Sally. It's disrespectful, actually' – fell decisively into the clincher category. The stark fact is that, if those two sentences had never been uttered, a young man named Saul Hollingwood would have gone to work as usual on 29 June 2024 instead of doing what he did after calling in sick. (He sounds as if he matters to our story, doesn't he? Yet this is the first and last time his name will appear in these pages.)"'

Josh looks impressed. 'I bet you know the whole book by heart, don't you?'

'I think that passage is digging into the motive for the murders. The *cause*, as in the main motive, was everything terrible the Gaveys did to the Lamberts.'

'And the fact that, even though Champ was in the clear, Sally knew Lesley Gavey was so hate-fuelled, she might try to harm him in a different way,' says Josh.

'Right. Yes, that also counts as cause. But the *clincher* was that particular memory – that Lesley had actually sat in Sally's living room and said something so insensitive about poor departed Furbert.'

'Sounds like you agree Sally Lambert's the murderer, then,' Josh points out. 'Because that would be a clincher for Sally, but not Corinne. That's Sally's memory, not Corinne's.'

'Very true,' Meredith concedes. 'And yet... I'm also keen on the theory that Saul Hollingwood is one of Corinne's many flunkies – the one who was given the arson assignment.'

'Sally and Corinne working together,' says Josh, nodding. 'Writing together, murdering together... Thinking about it, Corinne must have been involved. I doubt Sally would have been able to find out that we're about to launch a new publishing company.'

Meredith nods. 'Corinne'll have people on tap to look into everything for her. She'll have contacts who have contacts.'

'Exactly.'

'Josh, I need to tell you something. I went to Cambridgeshire last week. To Swaffham Tilney. I... spoke to people.' This is the other thing Meredith has been scared of: admitting how far she has taken her interest in the Lamberts and the Gaveys.

Josh looks alarmed – excited, maybe – but not annoyed, not worried about her sanity. 'Why didn't you tell me?'

'Mainly because I felt like a deluded, naive schoolgirl trying to have some kind of stupid adventure. I doubted I'd find out any more than we'd already got from your call to Cambridgeshire Police. But... I think I found out quite a bit. Which maybe matters less now that we know we're not publishing—'

'Tell me,' says Josh. 'Every single detail.'

'Okay, so... we already knew Bill Wendt is real. I spoke to him. Believe me, he couldn't have cared less, just wanted to get rid of me as quickly as possible. He's not a lovable shepherd's-pie-eating chubster. He's *thin*. I don't know, maybe he lost weight, which he's allowed to, but I was disappointed. I was looking forward to meeting "Large" and having a jolly chat. No such luck. He's a jobsworth and an arsehole. He told me what he'd told you and no more: Tess died roughly two hours before Lesley and Alastair did. There was no smoke in her lungs, and evidence of an allergic reaction of the kind she'd had before, to fish. The fire was started deliberately and no one beyond Lesley and Alastair Gavey had ever been considered as a possible suspect. The police were satisfied that it must have been one of the Gavey parents who did it.'

Meredith waits while their main courses are laid out on the table in front of them: more dim sum for her, with delicious steam rising from them. 'Once Wendt had washed his hands of me, I asked for PC Connor Chantree, and guess what? He's a real cop too, works for Cambridgeshire Police, but he's not the one who went round to the Lamberts on 17 June to say that Champ had been reported for biting Tess. Guess which cop he is?'

'Um... a different one?' says Josh. 'He and Large are the only two police characters in the book.'

'A third one gets a quick mention,' says Meredith. 'The one who pulled Sally Lambert over for using her mobile phone while in a traffic jam. *That* was PC Connor Chantree. Who does, it has to be said, look a little like the brush from a dustpan-and-brush set, and whose wife Flo runs a catering company called Scrumplicious.'

'You met Connor Chantree? Spoke to him?'

Meredith nods. 'It was one of the dullest experiences of my life. I had to listen to nearly ten minutes of waffle about why it was, actually, very vital to write up all incidents of people looking at their phones while in tailbacks.'

Josh smiles. 'Oh, dear.'

'Yeah. Not the most fascinating exchange I've ever had.'

'Interesting that the writer or writers of *Lamberts* didn't just use the name of the officer who came round on 17 June, though.'

'So then I went to Shoe Cottage, "Shukes", and spoke to none other than Sally Lambert herself.'

'Really? Is that...'

'A good idea?' Meredith finishes Josh's question for him. 'It turned out to be, yes. Sally, Ree and Champ Lambert were the only ones home. Champ is absolutely adorable, by the way. Even the cutest of the pictures on his website don't quite do him justice. Sally was interesting. She was super-friendly and lovely – offered me tea, homemade scones, a cuddle or a walk with Champ, whichever I preferred – but she was adamant that she wasn't willing to talk about anything connected to what she called "that horrible time". I went for a walk with her and Champ, round and round the village green, and every time I tried to sneak in a question, she instantly repeated the same thing: "I'm so sorry, and I know how frustrating it must be for everyone, but I won't be speaking about any of that again. Ever."'

'Did you ask her about *Lamberts* the book?' says Josh.

'I did, yes, after we'd said our goodbyes on her doorstep. I did that cheesy TV-show thing of turning back and going, "Oh, just one more thing…"'

'What did she say?'

'Picture of complete and total innocence! "What book? No, I haven't sent you anything." I spelled it out: asked her if she'd written a novel about Champ's… adventures, and sent it to you and me in the hope that we'd publish it. She looked sad for a second and said, "I've always wanted to write a book, but I never have. Maybe I will one day." And… I don't know. She seemed very sincere and genuine, which is probably why my money's on Corinne as the writer. Anyway, I was getting into my car to head home when Ree appeared, banging on my window – a bonus I was not expecting. She and I ended up going for a drink together at the local pub, The Rebel of the Reeds. That's real, by the way. So is Cupwardly Mobile, the van-cafe, which Ree said we couldn't go to because they'd unreasonably fired her for calling her boss a heartless cow who didn't understand that sometimes you were too busy saving your dog's life to turn up for your coffee-selling shifts. Josh, so much of what's in the book is real and accurate. And so much isn't! So much is completely made up. Ree told me which parts were real and which were invented. Oh!' Meredith changes tack. 'I told her about *Lamberts* the book, and she confirmed Sally hadn't written it. They're all still so busy with Champ's new fame, apparently – no time to think about doing much else. Ree was desperate to see *Lamberts*, though. Wants to read it as soon as possible, she said. Come to think of it… she did kind of behave throughout our chat as if us publishing the book were a given.'

'Which bits aren't true?' asks Josh.

'Well, for a start, there was never a Sarah Sergeant or a Bonnie – can you believe that? That was all made up.'

'What, really?' says Josh. 'How weird.'

'And the chronology's all messed up, from what Ree told me,' Meredith goes on. 'In the real-life version, both the strong suspicion that Lesley Gavey must have been the biter and the message from Auntie Vicky about Sally's WhatsApp message came later – whereas in the manuscript it's, like, 19 June, just two days after the Lamberts and Corinne first fled Swaffham Tilney. Oh – and there was no five-star hotel either. The Langley Hotel in Buckingham is real, but the Lamberts and Corinne never went there.

Ree was annoyed about that – she liked the sound of it. And that's another reason why I think Corinne's the author. I've looked up the Langley. It's top of the range. Corinne's bound to have stayed there and... met all those frogs. Whereas Sally? Less likely.'

'Okay, so they didn't go to the hotel...' mutters Josh. 'What about the Norfolk boarding kennels?'

'Yeah, that bit's true. Except – oh, God, how could I forget this? Niall Sullivan's wife, the surprise betrayer of Champ, is not called Jill Harris. Like, not even a little bit. Her name is Julie Sullivan. But, since she's a definite baddy in the story, my theory is that Corinne couldn't resist the opportunity to take a swipe at both Jill Biden and Kamala Harris when naming her.'

'Oh, come on! That's a stretch.' Josh is laughing.

'Maybe. Maybe not,' Meredith says. 'Can you think of any other reason for the writer to change this nasty-piece-of-work character's name to Jill Harris? I can't. Corinne's politically switched on and Sally isn't; it was Corinne who made the remark about Rishi Sunak and Keir Starmer vying for the position of "Thief in Chief".'

'Fair point,' Josh concedes.

'Anyway, the boarding kennels are real and the Lamberts went there, and to Corinne's Lake District House – and after Norfolk they went to Taunton to stay with Corinne's ex-husband, Ronan, the non-entrepreneurial one, for nearly a week. And it was while they were *there* that Vicky started trying to contact Sally about her WhatsApp, with the twee

No One Would Do What The Lamberts Have Done

Champ-talk in it. And Sally working out Lesley must have bitten Tess happened there too.'

'It's all so bizarre.' Josh stands up. 'I'm dying to hear the rest. I'll be one minute.'

'That's pretty much it,' Meredith tells him. He heads for the bathroom, and she reaches for her phone, then puts it down immediately, realising that she does have one more important thing to say: part of the reason she's certain Corinne wrote *Lamberts* is that surely Sally would have sent any book she wrote to a publisher that already existed, rather than seeking out a brand-new start-up that hadn't even leased office space yet; Corinne was the one who would want to reward entrepreneurship by doing that.

Multi-millionaires who are nearly billionaires are far more likely than ordinary working-mums from East Anglia to have people killed, also. Everything makes sense if Corinne is the killer, or the kill-commissioner, except…

There's just one thing Meredith can't come up with a plausible theory about.

Unless…

'No,' Meredith mutters to herself. 'No way.' It's such an outlandish idea, so out there… She should definitely forget all about it. No point wasting a phone call on it.

On the other hand, there's nothing foolish about ruling out a possibility – that is, in fact, the best way to proceed when you want to forget about something. Not checking will only make it stick in her mind.

She looks up the number for Cambridgeshire Police, rings it, and is given a different number to ring. After three people pass her on to other people, she is finally able to ask if Saul Hollingwood is an officer with Cambridgeshire Police, because she would very much like to speak to him if he is.

Josh, back at the table and listening avidly, says, 'This is all a bit out of left field, isn't it? Why have you decided Saul Hollingwood is a cop?'

Meredith moves her phone away from her mouth and says, 'All I know is: the name Saul Hollingwood is significant. Must be. The writer tells us it is. And I can think of no good reason why the real name of the cop who turned up at The Hayloft to accuse Champ on 17 June wouldn't be in the book, unless—'

'Can't find any Saul Hollingwood, I'm afraid,' says the voice on the other end of the call. 'You sure he's Cambridgeshire?'

'Never mind,' Meredith tells her. 'It was a long shot.'

'Hold on, let me just check once more. He might be… Hold on.'

No point, thinks Meredith, but she can hardly disappear. That would be rude. She'll have to wait for the woman who's trying to help her to return. To Josh she says, 'Imagine if Saul Hollingwood was the 17 June cop – and then, when Champ was revealed as being the victim of an attempted miscarriage of justice, he felt awful for having been part of it… And next imagine that he somehow got persuaded by Corinne, or bribed, to make up for what he'd done by starting that fire.'

'I'm imagining it all,' says Josh, 'but... you're making it up as you go along, to be fair.'

'I know.' Meredith sighs. 'There *must* be a reason why that name got changed, though.'

'Nope, sorry, love,' says the woman from Cambridgeshire Police. 'No Saul Hollingwood here.'

'Never mind. Thanks for looking.'

'Not anymore – says here he left us last November. Oh, that's funny – it looks like he went to work for Therriault, for their security team. Oops – shouldn't really have told you that. Never mind. Funny coincidence, though, because my daughter works for Therriault, in HR. It's some sort of fancy, new bio-fuel start-up company, up at Milton Science Park.'

Meredith feels as if she's just been given an electric shock.

Start-up. And we know who loves start-ups...

She manages a quick 'Thanks', then ends the call and does a search on her phone: 'Therriault Milton Science Park Companies House'

Here we go... Hurry up, the internet.

Meredith clicks on the 'People' tab and there she is: Corinne Sullivan, company director. 'Corinne paid him to do it,' she murmurs. 'Then got him a new job...'

'For you, Madam!' It's the waiter, at her side. He places a full cocktail glass on the table in front of her: long stemmed, full of orange liquid that's fizzing. 'Here is your Bellini,' he says. There's a pink and gold umbrella in it. Meredith didn't order the drink, but she knows it well. It's the one she pictured before Josh arrived, the exact drink that was in her mind: same glass, same colour, same colour umbrella. Also a type of drink she would never order even if it wasn't lunchtime on a weekday.

'I didn't order an alcoholic drink,' she says.

'You did not,' the waiter agrees. 'Consider it a gift. A delicious, peach-flavoured gift. Peaches and bubbles – what is there not to like?'

Peaches...

It's a coincidence. It must be. Coincidences are an everyday occurrence. That's what she and Josh must do when Varndall Miles opens for business: publish lots of novels, hundreds, in which huge coincidences happen and no one seems surprised or doubtful when they do. Coincidences are everywhere, and as real as the glass in Meredith's hand – because she does seem, now, to be drinking the cocktail. That's not the point, though. The point is that it's time for the publishing industry to stop acting as a form of controlled opposition to the prominent role coincidence plays in all of our lives.

Josh's voice comes to her as if from far away. 'Meredith, what's happening?'

'I can't believe we haven't talked about Alastair Gavey being innocent, and what it means,' she tells him. 'Alastair didn't know that Champ biting Tess was a lie, and that's why he had to die too. It makes sense: the Lamberts nearly lost someone innocent – Champ – thanks to the Gaveys. That's why punishing the guilty Gaveys wasn't enough. Their army had to lose an innocent too.'

'You're scaring me,' Josh says.

He's being silly. There's nothing scary about a coincidence, and that's all this is – that and her talent for having creative ideas about how to fill plot holes, because… how many intricately plotted mystery novels has she edited over the years? Loads. Her guess about Alastair was simply that: a guess. There's nothing going on here that can't be explained. Meredith is far too rational to believe she's been gifted a drink, or let into any special secrets, by the ghost of Furbert Herbert Lambert.

'Maybe we should publish the book after all,' she says. 'Shall we give ourselves a bit longer to think about it before saying no?'

Acknowledgements

So many people to thank! First of all, everyone at Bedford Square Publishers – Carolyn Mays, Jamie Hodder-Williams, Laura Fletcher, Anastasia Boama-Aboagye, Claudia Bullmore, Polly Halsey and Rebecca Weigler. You've all been so brilliant and made the experience of writing and publishing this book a total joy from start to finish. Thank you to Jamie Keenan for designing the cover, which I fell in love with the second I saw it.

Thank you to my brilliant agent Peter Straus and his team at Rogers, Coleridge and White, and huge thanks also to my wonderful new US agent Kimberly Witherspoon, who swiftly found me the most amazing new American publishers. Thank you to Anna Michels, Dominique Raccah, Shana Drehs and everyone at Sourcebooks, the chief Champ champions in America. I can't wait to work with you all on this and future books.

Thanks to my sister Jenny for believing in and endlessly discussing my 'Gone Dog' book idea and for the advice I will never forget: 'You can't have Gone Dog getting into a Twitter spat with Dan Hodges, that's too preposterous'.

No One Would Do What The Lamberts Have Done

Thank you to my husband Dan for 'Ismys House' and for insisting this is my best book by far even though he hasn't read it yet. Thanks to my mother Adele for her encouragement and unparalleled jolliness, to my daughter Phoebe for her faith and support and also for Ree Lambert's attitude to her part-time job with the Cupwardly Mobile drinks van. Thank you to my son Guy for his enthusiasm and belief in me, his regular 'appraisals/performance reviews', and for the 'Lester' nickname which I love (thanks, also, to Erik Balzani for that one). Thank you to Lewis and Hanna for the scary 'Dog ASBO' miscarriage of justice story (#TeamInkaAlways).

I'm hugely grateful to the Curry Agenda Club members, who voted unanimously for the most daring version of this novel, to Emily Winslow, whose brilliant input at an early stage (not to mention her advocacy for the more traditional approach to philanthropy) was invaluable, and to Kate Jones – both for spotting a continuity error that would have messed up the plot and for more generally helping to keep the show on the road on every possible level.

Last but not least, enormous thanks, for various different kinds of help, Enjollification and inspiration to: Faith Tilleray, Naomi Adams; David Allen; Peter Bean; Isabella Bennett (those Sound Sleep Donut beds are truly incredible!); Quy Mill Hotel and its spa, and the lovely people who work there and brought me approximately a million Diet Cokes while I finished this book; the Cambridge policeman who said, 'You're not wanted for anything, are you?' and then, after I misunderstood him, listened politely while I recited my entire day's To-Do list and held forth about what a hurry I was in; everyone who took part in my various Lamberts-related opinion polls; my Dream Authors and my lovely readers.

The poem in the final chapter of Part 1 is by Nic Aubury, my favourite living poet and author of the brilliant *Things My Children Think I'm Wrong About*.

About the Author

Author photo courtesy of Sophie Hannah

Sophie Hannah is a *Sunday Times*, *New York Times* and Amazon Kindle UK No. 1 bestselling author and her books have sold millions of copies worldwide. She writes contemporary psychological thrillers and, at the request of Agatha Christie's family and estate, the new series of Hercule Poirot novels. She lives in Cambridge with her family.

sophiehannah.com

Bedford Square Publishers

Bedford Square Publishers is an independent publisher of fiction and non-fiction, founded in 2022 in the historic streets of Bedford Square London and the sea mist shrouded green of Bedford Square Brighton.

Our goal is to discover irresistible stories and voices that illuminate our world.

We are passionate about connecting our authors to readers across the globe and our independence allows us to do this in original and nimble ways.

The team at Bedford Square Publishers has years of experience and we aim to use that knowledge and creative insight, alongside evolving technology, to reach the right readers for our books. From the ones who read a lot, to the ones who don't consider themselves readers, we aim to find those who will love our books and talk about them as much as we do.

We are hunting for vital new voices from all backgrounds – with books that take the reader to new places and transform perceptions of the world we live in.

Follow us on social media for the latest Bedford Square Publishers news.

@bedsqpublishers
facebook.com/bedfordsq.publishers/
@bedfordsq.publishers

https://bedfordsquarepublishers.co.uk/